PENGUIN B

LIE DOWN WITH LIONS

Ken Follett is one of the world's best-loved authors, selling more than 160 million copies of his thirty books. Follett's first bestseller was *Eye of the Needle*, a spy story set in the Second World War.

In 1989 *The Pillars of the Earth* was published, and has since become the author's most successful novel. It reached number one on bestseller lists around the world and was an Oprah's Book Club pick.

Its sequels, *World Without End* and *A Column of Fire*, proved equally popular, and the Kingsbridge series has sold 38 million copies worldwide.

Ken lives in Hertfordshire, England, with his wife Barbara. Between them they have five children, six grandchildren, and three Labradors.

Praise for
Lie Down with Lions

"An exciting and complex tale."   —*The Philadelphia Inquirer*

"Masterful . . . plot and counterplot, treachery, cunning, and killing . . . keep you on edge every moment."   —The Associated Press

"Combines modern warfare, international espionage, and a love story while also, in typical Follett fashion, playing out the fate of his characters amid thrilling escapes and shattering revelations."   —*Richmond Times-Dispatch*

"There is an incredible sex scene and desperate trek across ice-covered mountains . . . an exotic setting, a strong, courageous heroine, a strong, courageous hero, good guys, bad guys, and a supporting cast of thousands . . . a roaring good read."   —*The Atlanta Journal-Constitution*

"Solid suspense fiction . . . romance, adventure, exotic settings with a healthy dash of intrigue . . . When it comes to reliable entertainment, few authors deliver as consistently as Follett."   —*The Pittsburgh Press*

"Follett's great strength is his female characters—they are smart, strong, independent, and when they love a man, by golly, he knows the game is up."
                    —*People*

KEN FOLLETT

LIE DOWN WITH LIONS

PENGUIN BOOKS

PENGUIN BOOKS
An imprint of Penguin Random House LLC
375 Hudson Street
New York, New York 10014
penguin.com

Previously published in a William Morrow and Company, Inc., hardcover edition
and a Signet mass market edition
Published by New American Library, a division of Penguin Group (USA) Inc., 2003
Published in Penguin Books 2018

ISBN 9780451210463

Printed in the United States of America
19   21   23   25   26   24   22   20   18

Set in Goudy
Designed by Ginger Legato

This is a work of fiction. Names, characters, places, and incidents either are the product
of the author's imagination or are used fictitiously, and any resemblance to actual persons,
living or dead, businesses, companies, events, or locales is entirely coincidental.

To Barbara

There are several real organizations that send volunteer doctors to Afghanistan but *Médecins pour la Liberté* is fictional. All the locations described in this book are real except for the villages of Banda and Darg, which are fictional. All the characters are fictional except Masud.

Although I have tried to make the background authentic, this is a work of the imagination, and should not be treated as a source of infallible information about Afghanistan or anything else. Readers who would like to know more will find a reading list at the end of this book.

PART I

☙

1981

CHAPTER ONE

The men who wanted to kill Ahmet Yilmaz were serious people. They were exiled Turkish students living in Paris, and they had already murdered an attaché at the Turkish Embassy and fire-bombed the home of a senior executive of Turkish Airlines. They chose Yilmaz as their next target because he was a wealthy supporter of the military dictatorship and because he lived, conveniently, in Paris.

His home and office were well guarded and his Mercedes limousine was armored, but every man has a weakness, the students believed, and that weakness is usually sex. In the case of Yilmaz they were right. A couple of weeks of casual surveillance revealed that Yilmaz would leave his house, on two or three evenings each week, driving the Renault station wagon his servants used for shopping, and go to a side street in the Fifteenth District to visit a beautiful young Turkish woman who was in love with him.

The students decided to put a bomb in the Renault while Yilmaz was getting laid.

They knew where to get the explosives: from Pepe Gozzi, one of the many sons of the Corsican godfather Mémé Gozzi. Pepe was a weapons dealer. He would sell to anyone, but he preferred political customers, for—as he cheerfully admitted—"Idealists pay higher prices." He had helped the Turkish students with both their previous outrages.

There was a snag in the car-bomb plan. Usually Yilmaz would leave the girl's place alone in the Renault—but not always. Sometimes he took her out to dinner. Often she went off in the car and returned half an hour later laden with bread, fruit, cheese and wine, evidently for a cozy feast. Occasionally Yilmaz would go home in a taxi, and the girl would borrow the car for a day or two. The students were romantic, like all terrorists, and they were reluctant to risk killing a beautiful woman whose only crime was the readily pardonable one of loving a man unworthy of her.

They discussed this problem in a democratic fashion. They made all decisions by vote and acknowledged no leaders; but all the same there was one among them whose strength of personality made him dominant. His name was Rahmi Coskun, and he was a handsome, passionate young man with a bushy mustache and a certain bound-for-glory light in his eyes. It was his energy and determination which had pushed through the previous two projects despite the problems and the risks. Rahmi proposed consulting a bomb expert.

At first the others did not like this idea. Whom could they trust? they asked. Rahmi suggested Ellis Thaler. An American who called himself a poet but in fact made a living giving English lessons, he had learned about explosives as a conscript in Vietnam. Rahmi had known him for a year or so: they had both worked on a short-lived revolutionary newspaper called *Chaos*, and together they had organized a poetry reading to raise funds for the Palestine Liberation Organization. He seemed to understand Rahmi's rage at what was being done to Turkey and his hatred of the barbarians who were doing it. Some of the other students also knew Ellis slightly: he had been seen at several demonstrations, and they had assumed he was a graduate student or a young professor. Still, they were reluctant to bring in a non-Turk; but Rahmi was insistent and in the end they consented.

Ellis came up with the solution to their problem immediately. The bomb should have a radio-controlled arming device, he said. Rahmi would sit at a window opposite the girl's apartment, or in a parked car along the street, watching the Renault. In his hand he would have a small radio transmitter the size of a pack of cigarettes—the kind of thing one used to open automatic garage doors. If Yilmaz got into the car alone, as he most often did, then Rahmi would press the button on the transmitter, and a radio signal would activate a switch in the bomb, which would then be armed and would explode as soon as Yilmaz started the engine. But if it should be the girl who got into the car, Rahmi would not press the button, and she could drive away in blissful ignorance. The bomb would be quite safe until it was armed. No button, no bang, said Ellis.

Rahmi liked the idea and asked Ellis if he would collaborate with Pepe Gozzi on making the bomb.

Sure, said Ellis.

Then there was one more snag.

I've got a friend, Rahmi said, who wants to meet you both, Ellis and Pepe. To tell the truth, he *must* meet you; otherwise the whole deal is off; for this is the friend who gives us the money for explosives and cars and bribes and guns and everything.

Why does he want to meet us? Ellis and Pepe wanted to know.

He needs to be sure that the bomb will work, and he wants to feel that he can trust you, Rahmi said apologetically. All you have to do is bring the bomb to him and explain to him how it will work and shake his hand and let him look you in the eye—is that so much to ask, for the man who is making the whole thing possible?

It's all right with me, said Ellis.

Pepe hesitated. He wanted the money he would make on the deal—he always wanted money, as a pig always wants the trough—but he hated to meet new people.

Ellis reasoned with him. Listen, he said, these student groups bloom and die like mimosa in the spring, and Rahmi is sure to be blown away before long; but if you know his "friend" then you will be able to continue to do business after Rahmi is gone.

You're right, said Pepe, who was no genius but could grasp business principles if they were explained simply.

Ellis told Rahmi that Pepe had agreed, and Rahmi set up a rendezvous for the three of them on the following Sunday.

That morning Ellis woke up in Jane's bed. He came awake suddenly, feeling frightened, as if he had had a nightmare. A moment later he remembered the reason why he was so tense.

He glanced at the clock. He was early. In his mind he ran over his plan. If all went well, today would be the triumphant conclusion to more than a year of patient, careful work. And he would be able to share that triumph with Jane, if he was still alive at the end of the day.

He turned his head to look at her, moving carefully to avoid waking her. His heart leaped, as it did every time he saw her face. She lay flat on her back, with her turned-up nose pointing at the ceiling and her dark hair spread across the pillow like a bird's unfolded wing. He looked at her wide

mouth, the full lips that kissed him so often and so lusciously. Spring sunlight revealed the dense blond down on her cheeks—her beard, he called
it, when he wanted to tease her.

It was a rare delight to see her like this, in repose, her face relaxed and
expressionless. Normally she was animated—laughing, frowning, grimacing, registering surprise or skepticism or compassion. Her commonest expression was a wicked grin, like that of a mischievous small boy who has just
perpetrated a particularly fiendish practical joke. Only when she was sleeping or thinking very hard was she like this; yet this was how he loved her
most, for now, when she was unguarded and unself-conscious, her appearance hinted at the languid sensuality that burned just beneath her surface
like a slow, hot underground fire. When he saw her like this, his hands almost itched to touch her.

This had surprised him. When he had first met her, soon after he came
to Paris, she had struck him as typical of the kind of busybody always found
among the young and the radical in capital cities, chairing committees and
organizing campaigns against apartheid and for nuclear disarmament, leading protest marches about El Salvador and water pollution, raising money
for starving people in Chad, or trying to promote a talented young film-
maker. People were drawn to her by her striking good looks, captivated by
her charm, and energized by her enthusiasm. He had dated her a couple of
times, just for the pleasure of watching a pretty girl demolish a steak; and
then—he could never remember exactly how it happened—he had discovered that inside this excitable girl there lived a passionate woman, and he
had fallen in love.

His gaze wandered around her little studio flat. He noted with pleasure
the familiar personal possessions that marked the place as hers: a pretty
lamp made of a small Chinese vase; a shelf of books on economics and
world poverty; a big soft sofa you could drown in; a photograph of her father, a handsome man in a double-breasted coat, probably taken in the early
sixties; a small silver cup won by her on her pony, Dandelion, and dated
1971, ten years ago. She was thirteen, Ellis thought, and I was twenty-three;
and while she was winning pony trials in Hampshire I was in Laos, laying
antipersonnel mines along the Ho Chi Minh Trail.

When he had first seen the flat, almost a year ago, she had just moved
here from the suburbs, and it had been rather bare: a little attic room with
a kitchen in an alcove, a shower in a closet, and a toilet down the hall.
Gradually she had transformed it from a grimy garret into a cheerful nest.
She earned a good salary as an interpreter, translating French and Russian

into English, but her rent was high—the apartment was near the Boulevard St.-Michel—so she had bought carefully, saving her money for just the right mahogany table, antique bedstead and Tabriz rug. She was what Ellis's father would call a classy dame. You're going to like her, Dad, thought Ellis. You're going to be just crazy about her.

He rolled onto his side, facing her, and the movement woke her, as he had known it would. Her large blue eyes stared at the ceiling for a fraction of a second; then she looked at him, smiled, and rolled over into his arms. "Hello," she whispered, and he kissed her.

He got hard immediately. They lay together for a while, half asleep, kissing now and again; then she draped one leg across his hips and they began to make love languorously, without speaking.

When they had first become lovers, and they had started to make love morning and night and often midafternoon too, Ellis had assumed that such horniness would not last, and that after a few days, or maybe a couple of weeks, the novelty would wear off and they would revert to the statistical average of two-and-a-half times a week, or whatever it was. He had been wrong. A year later they were still screwing like honeymooners.

She rolled on top of him, letting her full weight rest on his body. Her damp skin clung to his. He wrapped his arms around her small body and hugged her as he thrust deep inside her. She sensed that his climax was coming, and she lifted her head and looked down at him, then kissed him with her mouth open while he was coming inside her. Immediately afterward she gave a soft, low-pitched moan, and he felt her come with a long, gentle, wavy Sunday-morning orgasm. She stayed on top of him, half asleep still. He stroked her hair.

After a while she stirred. "Do you know what day it is?" she mumbled.

"Sunday."

"It's your Sunday to make lunch."

"I hadn't forgotten."

"Good." There was a pause. "What are you going to give me?"

"Steak, potatoes, snow peas, goat's cheese, strawberries and Chantilly cream."

She lifted her head, laughing. "That's what you always make!"

"It is not. Last time we had French beans."

"And the time before that you had forgotten, so we ate out. How about some variety in your cooking?"

"Hey, wait a minute. The deal was, each of us would make lunch on alternate Sundays. Nobody said anything about making a *different* lunch each time."

She slumped on him again, feigning defeat.

His day's work had been at the back of his mind all along. He was going to need her unconscious help, and this was the moment to ask her. "I have to see Rahmi this morning," he began.

"All right. I'll meet you at your place later."

"There's something you could do for me, if you wouldn't mind getting there a little early."

"What?"

"Cook the lunch. No! No! Just kidding. I want you to help me with a little conspiracy."

"Go on," she said.

"Today is Rahmi's birthday, and his brother, Mustafa, is in town, but Rahmi doesn't know." If this works out, Ellis thought, I'll never lie to you again. "I want Mustafa to turn up at Rahmi's lunch party as a surprise. But I need an accomplice."

"I'm game," she said. She rolled off him and sat upright, crossing her legs. Her breasts were like apples, smooth and round and hard. The ends of her hair teased her nipples. "What do I have to do?"

"The problem is simple. I have to tell Mustafa where to go, but Rahmi hasn't yet made up his mind where he wants to eat. So I have to get the message to Mustafa at the last minute. And Rahmi will probably be beside me when I make the call."

"And the solution?"

"I'll call *you*. I'll talk nonsense. Ignore everything except the address. Call Mustafa, give him the address and tell him how to get there." All this had sounded okay when Ellis dreamed it up, but now it seemed wildly implausible.

However, Jane did not seem suspicious. "It sounds simple enough," she said.

"Good," Ellis said briskly, concealing his relief.

"And after you call, how soon will you be home?"

"Less than an hour. I want to wait and see the surprise, but I'll get out of having lunch there."

Jane looked thoughtful. "They invited you but not me."

Ellis shrugged. "I presume it's a masculine celebration." He reached for the notepad on the bedside table and wrote *Mustafa* and the phone number.

Jane got off the bed and crossed the room to the shower closet. She opened the door and turned on the tap. Her mood had changed. She was not smiling. Ellis said: "What are you mad about?"

"I'm not mad," she said. "Sometimes I dislike the way your friends treat me."

"But you know how the Turks are about girls."

"Exactly—*girls*. They don't mind respectable women, but I'm a *girl*."

Ellis sighed. "It's not like you to get needled by the prehistoric attitudes of a few chauvinists. What are you *really* trying to tell me?"

She considered for a moment, standing naked beside the shower, and she was so lovely that Ellis wanted to make love again. She said: "I suppose I'm saying that I don't like my status. I'm committed to you. Everyone knows that—I don't sleep with anyone else, don't even go out with other men—but you're not committed to me. We don't live together, I don't know where you go or what you do a lot of the time, we've never met one another's parents . . . and people know all this, so they treat me like a tart."

"I think you're exaggerating."

"You always say that." She stepped into the shower and banged the door. Ellis took his razor from the drawer where he kept his overnight kit and began to shave at the kitchen sink. They had had this argument before, at much greater length, and he knew what was at the bottom of it: Jane wanted them to live together.

He wanted it too, of course; he wanted to marry her and live with her for the rest of his life. But he had to wait until this assignment was over; and he could not tell her that, so he said such things as *I'm not ready* and *All I need is time*, and these vague evasions infuriated her. It seemed to her that a year was a long time to love a man without getting any kind of commitment from him. She was right, of course. But if all went well today he could make everything right.

He finished shaving, wrapped his razor in a towel and put it in his drawer. Jane got out of the shower and he took her place. We're not talking, he thought; this is silly.

While he was in the shower she made coffee. He dressed quickly in faded denim jeans and a black T-shirt and sat opposite her at the little mahogany table. She poured his coffee and said: "I want to have a serious talk with you."

"Okay," he said quickly, "let's do it at lunchtime."

"Why not now?"

"I don't have time."

"Is Rahmi's birthday more important than our relationship?"

"Of course not." Ellis heard irritation in his tone, and a warning voice told him. *Be gentle—you could lose her.* "But I promised, and it's important that I keep my promises; whereas it doesn't seem very important whether we have this conversation now or later."

Jane's face took on a set, stubborn look that he knew: she wore it when she had made a decision and someone tried to deflect her from her path. "It's important to *me* that we talk *now.*"

For a moment he was tempted to tell her the whole truth right away. But this was not the way he had planned it. He was short of time, his mind was on something else, and he was not prepared. It would be much better later, when they were both relaxed, and he would be able to tell her that his job in Paris was done. So he said: "I think you're being silly, and I won't be bullied. Please let's talk later. I have to go now." He stood up.

As he walked to the door she said: "Jean-Pierre has asked me to go to Afghanistan with him."

This was so completely unexpected that Ellis had to think for a moment before he could take it in. "Are you *serious?*" he said incredulously.

"I'm serious."

Ellis knew Jean-Pierre was in love with Jane. So were half a dozen other men: that kind of thing was inevitable with such a woman. None of the men were serious rivals, though; at least, he had thought not, until this moment. He began to recover his composure. He said: "Why would you want to visit a war zone with a wimp?"

"It's not a joking matter!" she said fiercely. "I'm talking about my *life.*"

He shook his head in disbelief. "You can't go to Afghanistan."

"Why not?"

"Because you love me."

"That doesn't put me at your disposal."

At least she had not said *No, I don't.* He looked at his watch. This was ridiculous: in a few hours' time he was going to tell her everything she wanted to hear. "I'm not willing to do this," he said. "We're talking about our future, and it's a discussion that can't be rushed."

"I won't wait forever," she said.

"I'm not asking you to wait forever. I'm asking you to wait a few hours." He touched her cheek. "Let's not fight about a few hours."

She stood up and kissed his mouth hard.

He said: "You won't go to Afghanistan, will you?"

"I don't know," she said levelly.

He tried a grin. "At least, not before lunch."

She smiled back and nodded. "Not before lunch."

He looked at her for a moment longer; then he went out.

The broad boulevards of the Champs-Élysées were thronged with tourists and Parisians out for a morning stroll, milling about like sheep in a fold under the warm spring sun, and all the pavement cafés were full. Ellis stood near the appointed place, carrying a backpack he had bought in a cheap luggage store. He looked like an American on a hitchhiking tour of Europe.

He wished Jane had not chosen this morning for a confrontation: she would be brooding now, and would be in a jagged mood by the time he arrived.

Well, he would just have to smooth her ruffled feathers for a while.

He put Jane out of his mind and concentrated on the task ahead of him.

There were two possibilities as to the identity of Rahmi's "friend," the one who financed the little terrorist group. The first was that he was a wealthy freedom-loving Turk who had decided, for political or personal reasons, that violence was justified against the military dictatorship and its supporters. If this was the case then Ellis would be disappointed.

The second possibility was that he was Boris.

"Boris" was a legendary figure in the circles within which Ellis moved— among the revolutionary students, the exiled Palestinians, the part-time politics lecturers, the editors of badly printed extremist newspapers, the anarchists and the Maoists and the Armenians and the militant vegetarians. He was said to be a Russian, a KGB man willing to fund any leftist act of violence in the West. Many people doubted his existence, especially those who had tried and failed to get funds out of the Russians. But Ellis had noticed, from time to time, that a group who for months had done nothing but complain that they could not afford a duplicating machine would suddenly stop talking about money and become very security-conscious; and then, a little later, there would be a kidnapping or a shooting or a bomb.

It was certain, Ellis thought, that the Russians gave money to such groups as the Turkish dissidents: they could hardly resist such a cheap and low-risk way of causing trouble. Besides, the U.S. financed kidnappers and murderers in Central America, and he could not imagine that the Soviet Union would be more scrupulous than his own country. And since in this line of work money was not kept in bank accounts or moved around by

Telex, somebody had to hand over the actual banknotes; so it followed that there had to be a Boris figure.

Ellis wanted very badly to meet him.

Rahmi walked by at exactly ten thirty, looking edgy, wearing a pink Lacoste shirt and immaculately pressed tan pants. He threw one burning glance at Ellis, then turned his head away.

Ellis followed him, staying ten or fifteen yards behind, as they had previously arranged.

At the next pavement café sat the muscular, overweight form of Pepe Gozzi, in a black silk suit as if he had been to Mass, which he probably had. He held a large briefcase in his lap. He got up and fell in more or less alongside Ellis, in such a way that a casual observer would have been unsure whether they were together or not.

Rahmi headed up the hill toward the Arc de Triomphe.

Ellis watched Pepe out of the corner of his eye. The Corsican had an animal's instinct for self-preservation: unobtrusively, he checked whether he was being followed—once when he crossed the road, and could quite naturally glance back along the boulevard while he stood waiting for the light to change, and again passing a corner shop, where he could see the people behind him reflected in the diagonal window.

Ellis liked Rahmi but not Pepe. Rahmi was sincere and high-principled, and the people he killed probably deserved to die. Pepe was completely different. He did this for money, and because he was too coarse and stupid to survive in the world of legitimate business.

Three blocks east of the Arc de Triomphe, Rahmi turned onto a side street. Ellis and Pepe followed. Rahmi led them across the road and entered the Hôtel Lancaster.

So this was the rendezvous. Ellis hoped the meeting was to take place in a bar or restaurant in the hotel: he would feel safer in a public room.

The marbled entrance hall was cool after the heat of the street. Ellis shivered. A waiter in a tuxedo looked askance at his jeans. Rahmi was getting into a tiny elevator at the far end of the L-shaped lobby. It was to be a hotel room, then. So be it. Ellis followed Rahmi into the elevator and Pepe squeezed in behind. Ellis's nerves were drawn wire-tight as they went up. They got off at the fourth floor and Rahmi led them to Room 41 and knocked.

Ellis tried to make his face calm and impassive.

The door opened slowly.

It was Boris. Ellis knew it as soon as he set eyes on the man, and he felt a thrill of triumph and at the same time a cold shiver of fear. Moscow was written all over the man, from his cheap haircut to his solidly practical shoes, and there was the unmistakable style of the KGB in his hard-eyed look of appraisal and the brutal set of his mouth. This man was not like Rahmi or Pepe; he was neither a hotheaded idealist nor a swinish mafioso. Boris was a stone-hearted professional terrorist who would not hesitate to blow the head off any or all of the three men who now stood before him.

I've been looking for you for a long time, thought Ellis.

Boris held the door half open for a moment, partly shielding his body while he studied them; then he stepped back and said in French: "Come in."

They walked into the sitting room of a suite. It was rather exquisitely decorated, and furnished with chairs, occasional tables and a cupboard which appeared to be eighteenth-century antiques. A carton of Marlboro cigarettes and a duty-free liter of brandy stood on a delicate bowlegged side table. In the far corner a half-open door led to a bedroom.

Rahmi's introductions were nervously perfunctory: "Pepe. Ellis. My friend."

Boris was a broad-shouldered man wearing a white shirt with the sleeves rolled to show meaty, hair-covered forearms. His blue serge trousers were too heavy for this weather. Over the back of a chair was slung a black-and-tan-checked jacket, which would look wrong with the blue trousers.

Ellis put his backpack on the rug and sat down.

Boris gestured at the brandy bottle. "A drink?"

Ellis did not want brandy at eleven o'clock in the morning. He said: "Yes, please—coffee."

Boris gave him a hard, hostile look, then said: "We'll all have coffee," and went to the phone. He's used to everyone being afraid of him, Ellis thought; he doesn't like it that I treat him as an equal.

Rahmi was plainly in awe of Boris, and fidgeted anxiously, fastening and unfastening the top button of his pink polo shirt while the Russian called room service.

Boris hung up the phone and addressed Pepe. "I'm glad to meet you," he said in French. "I think we can help each other."

Pepe nodded without speaking. He sat forward in the velvet chair, his powerful bulk in the black suit looking oddly vulnerable against the pretty furniture, as if *it* might break *him*. Pepe has a lot in common with Boris, thought Ellis: they're both strong, cruel men without decency or compassion. If Pepe were Russian, he would be in the KGB; and if Boris were French he'd be in the Mafia.

"Show me the bomb," said Boris.

Pepe opened his briefcase. It was packed with blocks, about a foot long and a couple of inches square, of a yellowish substance. Boris knelt on the rug beside the case and poked one of the blocks with a forefinger. The substance yielded like putty. Boris sniffed it. "I presume this is C_3," he said to Pepe.

Pepe nodded.

"Where is the mechanism?"

Rahmi said: "Ellis has it in his backpack."

Ellis said: "No, I don't."

The room went very quiet for a moment. A look of panic came over Rahmi's handsome young face. "What do you mean?" he said agitatedly. His frightened eyes switched from Ellis to Boris and back again. "You said . . . I told him you would—"

"Shut up," Boris said harshly. Rahmi fell silent. Boris looked expectantly at Ellis.

Ellis spoke with a casual indifference that he did not feel. "I was afraid this might be a trap, so I left the mechanism at home. It can be here in a few minutes. I just have to call my girl."

Boris stared at him for several seconds. Ellis returned his look as coolly as he could. Finally Boris said: "Why did you think this might be a trap?"

Ellis decided that to try to justify himself would appear defensive. It was a dumb question, anyway. He shot an arrogant look at Boris, then shrugged and said nothing.

Boris continued to look searchingly at him. Finally the Russian said: "I shall make the call."

A protest rose to Ellis's lips and he choked it back. This was a development he had not expected. He carefully maintained his I-don't-give-a-damn pose while thinking furiously. How would Jane react to the voice of a stranger? And what if she were not there? What if she had decided to break her promise? He regretted using her as a cutout. But it was too late now.

"You're a careful man," he said to Boris.

"You, too. What is your phone number?"

Ellis told him. Boris wrote the number on the message pad by the phone, then began to dial.

The others waited in silence.

Boris said: "Hello? I am calling on behalf of Ellis."

Perhaps the unknown voice would not throw her, Ellis thought: she had been expecting a somewhat wacky call anyway. *Ignore everything except the address,* he had told her.

"What?" Boris said irritably, and Ellis thought: Oh, shit, what is she saying now? "Yes, I am, but never mind that," Boris said. "Ellis wants you to bring the mechanism to Room Forty-one at the Hôtel Lancaster in the rue de Berri."

There was another pause.

Play the game, Jane, thought Ellis.

"Yes, it's a very nice hotel."

Stop kidding around! Just tell the man you'll do it—please!

"Thank you," Boris said, and he added sarcastically: "You are most kind." Then he hung up.

Ellis tried to look as if he had expected all along there would be no problem.

Boris said: "She knew I was Russian. How did she find out?"

Ellis was puzzled for a moment, then realized. "She's a linguist," he said. "She knows accents."

Pepe spoke for the first time. "While we're waiting for this cunt to arrive, let's see the money."

"All right." Boris went into the bedroom.

While he was out, Rahmi spoke to Ellis in a low hiss. "I didn't know you were going to pull that trick!"

"Of course you didn't," said Ellis in a feigned tone of boredom. "If you had known what I was going to do, it wouldn't have worked as a safeguard, would it?"

Boris came back in with a large brown envelope and handed it to Pepe. Pepe opened it and began counting one-hundred-franc notes.

Boris unwrapped the carton of Marlboros and lit a cigarette.

Ellis thought: I hope Jane doesn't *wait* before making the call to "Mustafa." I should have told her it was important to pass the message on immediately.

After a while Pepe said: "It's all there." He put the money back into the envelope, licked the flap, sealed it and put it on a side table.

The four men sat in silence for several minutes.

Boris asked Ellis: "How far away is your place?"

"Fifteen minutes on a motor scooter."

There was a knock at the door. Ellis tensed.

"She drove fast," Boris said. He opened the door. "Coffee," he said disgustedly, and returned to his seat.

Two white-jacketed waiters wheeled a trolley into the room. They straightened up and turned around, each holding in his hand a Model "D" MAB pistol, standard issue for French detectives. One of them said: "Nobody move."

Ellis felt Boris gather himself to spring. Why were there only two detectives? If Rahmi were to do something foolish, and get himself shot, it would create enough of a diversion for Pepe and Boris together to overpower the armed men—

The bedroom door flew open, and two more men in waiters' uniforms stood there, armed like their colleagues.

Boris relaxed, and a look of resignation came over his face.

Ellis realized he had been holding his breath. He let it out in a long sigh. It was all over.

A uniformed police officer walked into the room.

"A trap!" Rahmi burst out. "This *is* a trap!"

"Shut up," said Boris, and once again his harsh voice silenced Rahmi. He addressed the police officer. "I object most strongly to this outrage," he began. "Please take note that—"

The policeman punched him in the mouth with a leather-gloved fist.

Boris touched his lips, then looked at the smear of blood on his hand. His manner changed completely as he realized this was far too serious for him to bluff his way out. "Remember my face," he told the police officer in a voice as cold as the grave. "You will see it again."

"But who is the traitor?" cried Rahmi. "Who betrayed us?"

"Him," said Boris, pointing at Ellis.

"Ellis?" Rahmi said incredulously.

"The phone call," said Boris. "The address."

Rahmi stared at Ellis. He looked wounded to the quick.

Several more uniformed policemen came in. The officer pointed at Pepe. "That's Gozzi," he said. Two policemen handcuffed Pepe and led him away. The officer looked at Boris. "Who are you?"

Boris looked bored. "My name is Jan Hocht," he said. "I am a citizen of Argentina—"

"Don't bother," said the officer disgustedly. "Take him away." He turned to Rahmi. "Well?"

"I have nothing to say!" Rahmi said, managing to make it sound heroic.

The officer gave a jerk of his head and Rahmi, too, was handcuffed. He glared at Ellis until he was led out.

The prisoners were taken down in the elevator one at a time. Pepe's briefcase and the envelope full of hundred-franc notes were shrouded in polythene. A police photographer came in and set up his tripod.

The officer said to Ellis: "There is a black Citroën DS parked outside the hotel." Hesitantly he added: "Sir."

I'm back on the side of the law, Ellis thought. A pity Rahmi is so much more attractive a man than this cop.

He went down in the elevator. In the hotel lobby the manager, in black coat and striped trousers, stood with a pained expression frozen to his face as more policemen marched in.

Ellis went out into the sunshine. The black Citroën was on the other side of the street. There was a driver in the front and a passenger in the back. Ellis got into the back. The car pulled away fast.

The passenger turned to Ellis and said: "Hello, John."

Ellis smiled. The use of his real name was strange after more than a year. He said: "How are you, Bill?"

"Relieved!" said Bill. "For thirteen months we hear nothing from you but demands for money. Then we get a peremptory phone call telling us we've got twenty-four hours to arrange a local arrest squad. Imagine what we had to do to persuade the French to do that without telling them why! The squad had to be ready in the vicinity of the Champs-Élysées, but to get the exact address we had to wait for a phone call from an unknown woman asking for Mustafa. And that's all we know!"

"It was the only way," Ellis said apologetically.

"Well, it took some doing—and I now owe some big favors in this town—but we did it. So tell me whether it was worth it. Who have we got in the bag?"

"The Russian is Boris," said Ellis.

Bill's face broke into a broad grin. "I'll be a son of a bitch," he said. "You brought in Boris. No kidding."

"No kidding."

"Jesus, I better get him back from the French before they figure out who he is."

Ellis shrugged. "Nobody's going to get much information out of him anyway. He's the dedicated type. The important thing is that we've taken him out of circulation. It will take them a couple of years to break in a replacement and for the new Boris to build his contacts. Meanwhile we've really slowed their operation down."

"You just bet we have. This is sensational."

"The Corsican is Pepe Gozzi, a weapons dealer," Ellis went on. "He supplied the hardware for just about every terrorist action in France in the last couple of years, and a lot more in other countries. He's the one to interrogate. Send a French detective to talk to his father, Mémé Gozzi, in Marseilles. I predict you'll find the old man never did like the idea of the family getting involved in political crimes. Offer him a deal: immunity for Pepe if Pepe will testify against all the political people he sold stuff to—none of the ordinary criminals. Mémé will go for that, because it won't count as betrayal of friends. And if Mémé goes for it, Pepe will do it. The French can prosecute for years."

"Incredible." Bill looked dazed. "In one day you've nailed probably the two biggest instigators of terrorism in the world."

"One day?" Ellis smiled. "It took a year."

"It was worth it."

"The young guy is Rahmi Coskun," Ellis said. He was hurrying on because there was someone else to whom he wanted to tell all this. "Rahmi and his group did the Turkish Airlines firebombing a couple of months ago and killed an Embassy attaché before that. If you round up the whole group you're sure to find some forensic evidence."

"Or the French police will persuade them to confess."

"Yes. Give me a pencil and I'll write down the names and addresses."

"Save it," said Bill. "I'm going to debrief you completely back at the Embassy."

"I'm not going back to the Embassy."

"John, don't fight the program."

"I'll give you these names. Then you'll have all the really essential information, even if I get run down by a mad French cab driver this afternoon. If I survive, I'll meet you tomorrow morning and give you the detail stuff."

"Why wait?"

"I have a lunch date."

Bill rolled his eyes up. "I suppose we owe you this," he said reluctantly.

"That's what I figured."

"Who's your date?"

"Jane Lambert. Hers was one of the names you gave me when you originally briefed me."

"I remember. I told you that if you wormed your way into her affections she would introduce you to every mad leftist, Arab terrorist, Baader-Meinhof hanger-on and avant-garde poet in Paris."

"That's how it worked, except I fell in love with her."

Bill looked like a Connecticut banker being told that his son is going to marry the daughter of a black millionaire: he did not know whether to be thrilled or appalled. "Uh, what's she really like?"

"She's not crazy although she has some crazy friends. What can I tell you? She's as pretty as a picture, bright as a pin, and horny as a jackass. She's wonderful. She's the woman I've been looking for all my life."

"Well, I can see why you'd rather celebrate with her than with me. What are you going to do?"

Ellis smiled. "I'm going to open a bottle of wine, fry a couple of steaks, tell her I catch terrorists for a living and ask her to marry me."

CHAPTER TWO

J ean-Pierre leaned forward across the canteen table and fixed the brunette with a compassionate gaze. "I think I know how you feel," he said warmly. "I remember being very depressed toward the end of my first year in medical school. It seems as if you've been given more information than one brain can absorb and you just don't know how you're going to master it in time for the exams."

"That's *exactly* it," she said, nodding vigorously. She was almost in tears.

"It's a good sign," he reassured her. "It means you're on top of the course. The people who aren't worried are the ones who will flunk."

Her brown eyes were moist with gratitude. "Do you really think so?"

"I'm sure of it."

She looked adoringly at him. You'd rather eat me than your lunch, wouldn't you? he thought. She shifted slightly, and the neck of her sweater gaped open, showing the lacy trimming of her bra. Jean-Pierre was momentarily tempted. In the east wing of the hospital there was a linen closet that was never used after about nine thirty in the morning. Jean-Pierre had taken advantage of it more than once. You could lock the door from the inside and lie down on a soft pile of clean sheets. . . .

The brunette sighed and forked a piece of steak into her mouth, and as she began to chew, Jean-Pierre lost interest. He hated to watch people eat. Anyway, he had only been flexing his muscles, to prove he could still do it: he did not really want to seduce her. She was very pretty, with curly hair and warm Mediterranean coloring, and she had a lovely body, but lately Jean-Pierre had no enthusiasm for casual conquests. The only girl who could fascinate him for more than a few minutes was Jane Lambert—and she would not even kiss him.

He looked away from the brunette, and his gaze roamed restlessly around the hospital canteen. He saw no one he knew. The place was almost empty: he was having lunch early because he was working the early shift.

It was six months now since he had first seen Jane's stunningly pretty face across a crowded room at a cocktail party to launch a new book on feminist gynecology. He had suggested to her that there was no such thing as feminist medicine: there was just good medicine and bad medicine. She had replied that there was no such thing as Christian mathematics, but still it took a heretic such as Galileo to prove that the earth goes around the sun. Jean-Pierre had exclaimed: "You are right!" in his most disarming manner and they had become friends.

Yet she was resistant to his charms, if not quite impervious. She liked him, but she seemed to be committed to the American, even though Ellis was a good deal older than she. Somehow that made her even more desirable to Jean-Pierre. If only Ellis would drop out of the picture—get run over by a bus, or something . . . Lately Jane's resistance had seemed to be weakening—or was that wishful thinking?

The brunette said: "Is it true you're going to Afghanistan for two years?"

"That's right."

"Why?"

"Because I believe in freedom, I suppose. And because I didn't go through all this training just to do coronary bypasses for fat businessmen." The lies came automatically to his lips.

"But why two years? People who do this usually go for three to six months, a year at the most. Two years seems like forever."

"Does it?" Jean-Pierre gave a wry smile. "It's difficult, you see, to achieve anything of real value in a shorter period. The idea of sending doctors there for a brief visit is highly inefficient. What the rebels need is some kind of permanent medical setup, a hospital that stays in the same place and has at least some of the same staff from one year to the next. As things are, half the people don't know where to take their sick and wounded, they don't follow the doctor's orders because they never get to know him well enough to trust him, and nobody has any time for health education. And the cost of transporting the volunteers to the country and bringing them back makes their 'free' services rather expensive." Jean-Pierre put so much effort into this speech that he almost believed it himself, and he had to remind him-self of his true motive for going to Afghanistan, and of the real reason he had to stay for two years.

A voice behind him said: "Who's going to give their services free?"

He turned around to see another couple carrying trays of food: Valérie, who was an intern like him; and her boyfriend, a radiologist. They sat down with Jean-Pierre and the brunette.

The brunette answered Valérie's question. "Jean-Pierre is going to Afghanistan to work for the rebels."

"Really?" Valérie was surprised. "I heard you had been offered a mar-velous job in Houston."

"I turned it down."

She was impressed. "But why?"

"I consider it worthwhile to save the lives of freedom fighters; but a few Texan millionaires more or less won't make any difference to anything."

The radiologist was not as fascinated by Jean-Pierre as his girlfriend was. He swallowed a mouthful of potatoes and said: "No sweat. After you come back, you'll have no trouble getting that same job offer again—you'll be a hero as well as a doctor."

"Do you think so?" said Jean-Pierre coolly. He did not like the turn the conversation was taking.

"Two people from this hospital went to Afghanistan last year," the radi-ologist went on. "They both got great jobs when they came back."

Jean-Pierre gave a tolerant smile. "It's nice to know that I'll be employ-able if I survive."

"I should hope so!" said the brunette indignantly. "After such a sac-rifice!"

"What do your parents think of the idea?" wondered Valérie.

"My mother approves," said Jean-Pierre. Of course she approved: she loved a hero. Jean-Pierre could imagine what his father would say about idealistic young doctors who went to work for the Afghan rebels. *Socialism doesn't mean everyone can do what they want!* he would say, his voice hoarse and urgent, his face reddening a little. *What do you think those rebels are? They're bandits, preying on the law-abiding peasants. Feudal institutions have to be wiped out before socialism can come in.* He would hammer the table with one great fist. *To make a soufflé, you have to break eggs—to make socialism, you have to break heads!* Don't worry, Papa, I know all that. "My father is dead," Jean-Pierre said. "But he was a freedom fighter himself. He fought in the Resistance during the war."

"What did he do?" asked the skeptical radiologist, but Jean-Pierre never answered him because he had seen, coming across the canteen, Raoul Clermont, the editor of *La Révolte*, sweating in his Sunday suit. What the devil was the fat journalist doing in the hospital canteen?

"I need to have a word with you," said Raoul without preamble. He was out of breath. Jean-Pierre gestured to a chair. "Raoul—"

"It's urgent," Raoul cut in, almost as if he did not want the others to hear his name.

"Why don't you join us for lunch? Then we could talk at leisure."

"I regret I cannot."

Jean-Pierre heard a note of panic in the fat man's voice. Looking into his eyes, he saw that they were pleading with him to stop fooling around. Surprised, Jean-Pierre stood up. "Okay," he said. To cover the suddenness of it all he said playfully to the others: "Don't eat my lunch—I'll be back." He took Raoul's arm and they walked out of the canteen.

Jean-Pierre had intended to stop and talk outside the door, but Raoul kept on walking along the corridor. "Monsieur Leblond sent me," he said.

"I was beginning to think he must be behind this," said Jean-Pierre. It was a month ago that Raoul had taken him to meet Leblond, who had asked him to go to Afghanistan, ostensibly to help the rebels as many young French doctors did, but actually to spy for the Russians. Jean-Pierre had felt proud, apprehensive and most of all thrilled at the opportunity to do something really spectacular for the cause. His only fear had been that the organizations which sent doctors to Afghanistan would turn him down because he was a Communist. They had no way of knowing he was actually a Party member, and he certainly would not tell them—but they might know he was a Communist sympathizer. However, there were plenty of French Communists who were opposed to the invasion of Afghanistan. There was nevertheless a remote possibility that a cautious organization might suggest that Jean-Pierre would be happier working for some other group of freedom fighters—they also sent people to help the rebels in El Salvador, for example. In the end it had not happened: Jean-Pierre had been accepted immediately by *Médecins pour la Liberté*. He had told Raoul the good news, and Raoul had said there would be another meeting with Leblond. Perhaps this was to do with that. "But why the panic?"

"He wants to see you now."

"*Now?*" Jean-Pierre was annoyed. "I'm on duty. I have patients—"

"Surely someone else will take care of them."

"But what is the urgency? I don't leave for another two months."

"It's not about Afghanistan."

"Well, what *is* it about?"

"I don't know."

Then what has frightened you? wondered Jean-Pierre. "Have you no idea at all?"

"I know that Rahmi Coskun has been arrested."

"The Turkish student?"

"Yes."

"What for?"

"I don't know."

"And what is it to do with me? I hardly know him."

"Monsieur Leblond will explain."

Jean-Pierre threw up his hands. "I can't just walk out of here."

"What would happen if you were taken ill?" said Raoul.

"I would tell the Nursing Officer, and she would call in a replacement. But—"

"So call her." They had reached the entrance of the hospital, and there was a bank of internal phones on the wall.

This may be a test, thought Jean-Pierre, a loyalty test, to see whether I am serious enough to be given this mission. He decided to risk the wrath of the hospital authorities. He picked up the phone.

"I have been called away by a sudden family emergency," he said when he got through. "You must get in touch with Dr. Roche immediately."

"Yes, Doctor," the nurse replied calmly. "I hope you have not received sad news."

"I'll tell you later," he said hastily. "Good-bye. Oh—just a minute." He had a postoperative patient who had been hemorrhaging during the night. "How is Madame Ferier?"

"Fine. The bleeding has not recommenced."

"Good. Keep a close watch on her."

"Yes, Doctor."

Jean-Pierre hung up. "All right," he said to Raoul. "Let's go."

They walked to the car park and got into Raoul's Renault 5. The inside of the car was hot from the midday sun. Raoul drove fast through back streets. Jean-Pierre felt nervous. He did not know exactly who Leblond was, but he assumed the man was something in the KGB. Jean-Pierre found himself wondering whether he had done anything to offend that much-feared organization; and, if so, what the punishment might be.

Surely they could not have found out about Jane.

His asking her to go to Afghanistan with him was no business of theirs. There were sure to be others in the Party anyway, perhaps a nurse to help Jean-Pierre at his destination, perhaps other doctors headed for various parts of the country: why shouldn't Jane be among them? She was not a nurse, but she could take a crash course, and her great advantage was that she could speak some Farsi, the Persian language, a form of which was spoken in the area where Jean-Pierre was going.

He hoped she would go with him out of idealism and a sense of adventure. He hoped she would forget about Ellis while she was there, and would fall in love with the nearest European, who would of course be Jean-Pierre.

He had also hoped the Party would never know that he had encouraged her to go for his own reasons. There was no need for them to know, no way they would find out, normally—or so he had thought. Perhaps he had been wrong. Perhaps they were angry.

This is foolish, he told himself. I've done nothing wrong, really; and even if I had there would be no punishment. This is the real KGB, not the mythical institution that strikes fear into the hearts of subscribers to the *Reader's Digest*.

Raoul parked the car. They had stopped outside an expensive apartment building in the rue de l'Université. It was the place where Jean-Pierre had met Leblond the last time. They left the car and went inside. The lobby was gloomy. They climbed the curving staircase to the first floor and rang a bell. How much my life has changed, thought Jean-Pierre, since the last time I waited at this door!

Monsieur Leblond opened it. He was a short, slight, balding man with spectacles, and in his charcoal gray suit and silver tie he looked like a butler. He led them to the room at the back of the building where Jean-Pierre had been interviewed. The tall windows and the elaborate moldings indicated that it had once been an elegant drawing room, but now it had a nylon carpet, a cheap office desk and some molded-plastic chairs, orange in color.

"Wait here for a moment," said Leblond. His voice was quiet, clipped and as dry as dust. A slight accent suggested that his real name was not Leblond. He went out through a different door.

Jean-Pierre sat on one of the plastic chairs. Raoul remained standing. In this room, thought Jean-Pierre, that dry voice said to me *You have been a quietly loyal member of the Party since childhood. Your character and your family background suggest that you would serve the Party well in a covert role.*

I hope I haven't ruined everything because of Jane, he thought.

Leblond came back in with another man. The two of them stood in the doorway, and Leblond pointed at Jean-Pierre. The second man looked hard at Jean-Pierre, as if committing his face to memory. Jean-Pierre returned his gaze. The man was very big, with broad shoulders like those of a football player. His hair was long at the sides but thinning on top, and he had a droopy mustache. He wore a green corduroy jacket with a rip in the sleeve. After a few seconds he nodded and went out.

Leblond closed the door behind him and sat at the desk. "There has been a disaster," he said.

It's not about Jane, thought Jean-Pierre. Thank God.

Leblond said: "There is a CIA agent among your circle of friends."

"My God!" said Jean-Pierre.

"That is not the disaster," Leblond said irritably. "It is hardly surprising that there should be an American spy among your friends. No doubt there are Israeli and South African and French spies, too. What would these people have to do if they did not infiltrate groups of young political activists? And we also have one, of course."

"Who?"

"You."

"Oh!" Jean-Pierre was taken aback: he had not thought of himself as a *spy*, exactly. But what else did it mean to *serve the Party in a covert role?* "Who is the CIA agent?" he asked, intensely curious.

"Someone called Ellis Thaler."

Jean-Pierre was so shocked that he stood up. *"Ellis?"*

"You *do* know him. Good."

"Ellis is a CIA spy?"

"Sit down," Leblond said levelly. "Our problem is not who he is, but what he has done."

Jean-Pierre was thinking: If Jane finds out about this she will drop Ellis like a hot brick. Will they let me tell her? If not, will she find out some other way? Will she believe it? Will Ellis deny it?

Leblond was speaking. Jean-Pierre forced himself to concentrate on what was being said. "The disaster is that Ellis set a trap, and in it he has caught someone rather important to us."

Jean-Pierre remembered Raoul saying that Rahmi Coskun had been arrested. "Rahmi is important to us?"

"Not Rahmi."

"Who, then?"

"You don't need to know."

"Then why have you brought me here?"

"Shut up and listen," Leblond snapped, and for the first time Jean-Pierre was afraid of him. "I have never met your friend Ellis, of course. Unhappily, Raoul has not either. Therefore neither of us knows what he looks like. But you do. That is why I have brought you here. Do you also know where Ellis lives?"

"Yes. He has a room above a restaurant in the rue de l'Ancienne Comédie."

"Does the room overlook the street?"

Jean-Pierre frowned. He had been there only once: Ellis did not invite people home much. "I think it does."

"You're not sure?"

"Let me think." He had gone there late one night, with Jane and a bunch of other people, after a film show at the Sorbonne. Ellis had given them coffee. It was a small room. Jane had sat on the floor by the window. . . . "Yes. The window faces the street. Why is it important?"

"It means you can signal."

"Me? Why? To whom?"

Leblond shot a dangerous look at him.

"Sorry," said Jean-Pierre.

Leblond hesitated. When he spoke again, his voice was just a shade softer, although his expression remained blank. "You're suffering a baptism of fire. I regret having to use you in an . . . *action* . . . such as this when you have never done anything for us before. But you know Ellis, and you are here, and right now we don't have anybody else who knows him; and what we want to do will lose its impact if it is not done immediately. So. Listen carefully, for this is important. You are to go to his room. If he is there, you will go inside—think of some pretext. Go to the window, lean out and make sure you are seen by Raoul, who will be waiting in the street."

Raoul fidgeted like a dog that hears people mention its name in conversation.

Jean-Pierre asked: "And if Ellis is not there?"

"Speak to his neighbors. Try to find out where he has gone and when he will be back. If it seems he has left only for a few minutes, or even an hour or so, wait for him. When he returns, proceed as before: go inside, go to the window and make sure you are seen by Raoul. Your appearance at the window is the sign that Ellis is inside—so, whatever you do, don't go to the window if he is not there. Have you understood?"

"I know what you want me to do," said Jean-Pierre. "I don't understand the purpose of all this."

"To identify Ellis."

"And when I have identified him?"

Leblond gave the answer Jean-Pierre had hardly dared to hope for, and it thrilled him to the core: "We are going to kill him, of course."

CHAPTER THREE

J ane spread a patched white cloth on Ellis's tiny table and laid two places with an assortment of battered cutlery. She found a bottle of Fleurie in the cupboard under the sink, and opened it. She was tempted to taste it, then decided to wait for Ellis. She put out glasses, salt and pepper, mustard and paper napkins. She wondered whether to start cooking. No, it was better to leave it to him.

She did not like Ellis's room. It was bare, cramped and impersonal. She had been quite shocked when she first saw it. She had been dating this warm, relaxed, mature man, and she had expected him to live in a place that expressed his personality, an attractive, comfortable apartment containing mementos of a past rich in experience. But you would never guess that the man who lived here had been married, had fought in a war, had taken LSD, had captained his school football team. The cold white walls were decorated with a few hastily chosen posters. The china came from junk shops and the cooking pots were cheap tinware. There were no inscriptions in the paper-back volumes of poetry on the bookshelf. He kept his jeans and sweaters in a plastic suitcase under the creaky bed. Where were his old school reports, the photographs of his nephews and nieces, his treasured copy of *Heartbreak Hotel*, his souvenir penknife from Boulogne or Niagara Falls, the teak salad bowl everybody gets from their parents sooner or later? The room contained nothing really important, none of those things one keeps not for what they are but for what they represent, no part of his soul.

It was the room of a withdrawn man, a secretive man, a man who would never share his innermost thoughts with anyone. Gradually, and with terrible sadness, Jane had come to realize that Ellis was like that, like his room, cold and secretive.

It was incredible. He was such a self-confident man. He walked with his head high, as if he had never been afraid of anyone in his life. In bed he was utterly uninhibited, totally at ease with his sexuality. He would do anything and say anything, without anxiety or hesitation or shame. Jane had never known a man like this. But there had been too many times— in bed, or in restaurants, or just walking on the street—when she had been laughing with him, or listening to him talk, or watching the skin around his eyes crinkle as he thought hard, or hugging his warm body, only to find that he had suddenly turned off. In those switched-off moods he was no longer loving, no longer amusing, no longer thoughtful or considerate or gentlemanly or compassionate. He made her feel excluded, a stranger, an intruder into his private world. It was like the sun going behind a cloud.

She knew she was going to have to leave him. She loved him to distraction, but it seemed he could not love her the same way. He was thirty-three years old, and if he had not learned the art of intimacy by now, he never would.

She sat on the sofa and began to read *The Observer*, which she had bought from an international newsstand on the Boulevard Raspail on her way over. There was a report from Afghanistan on the front page. It sounded like a good place to go to forget Ellis.

The idea had appealed to her immediately. Although she loved Paris, and her job was at least varied, she wanted more: experience, adventure, and a chance to strike a blow for freedom. She was not afraid. Jean-Pierre said the doctors were considered too valuable to be sent into the combat zone. There was a risk of being hit by a stray bomb or caught in a skirmish, but it was probably no worse than the danger of being run down by a Parisian motorist. She was intensely curious about the lifestyle of the Afghan rebels. "What do they eat there?" she had asked Jean-Pierre. "What do they wear? Do they live in tents? Do they have toilets?"

"No toilets," he had replied. "No electricity. No roads. No wine. No cars. No central heating. No dentists. No postmen. No phones. No restaurants. No advertisements. No Coca-Cola. No weather forecasts, no stock market reports, no decorators, no social workers, no lipstick, no Tampax, no fashions, no dinner parties, no taxi ranks, no bus queues—"

"Stop!" she had interrupted him: he could go on like that for hours. "They must have buses and taxis."

"Not in the countryside. I'm going to a region called Five Lions Valley, a rebel stronghold in the foothills of the Himalayas. It was primitive even before the Russians bombed it."

Jane was quite sure she could live happily without plumbing or lipstick or weather forecasts. She suspected he was underestimating the danger, even outside the combat zone; but somehow that did not deter her. Her mother would have hysterics, of course. Her father, if he were still alive, would have said: "Good luck, Janey." He had understood the importance of doing something *worthwhile* with one's life. Although he had been a good doctor, he had never made any money, because wherever they lived—Nassau, Cairo, Singapore, but mostly Rhodesia—he would always treat poor people free, so they had come to him in crowds, and had driven away the fee-paying customers.

Her reverie was disturbed by a footfall on the stairs. She had not read more than a few lines of the newspaper, she realized. She cocked her head, listening. It did not sound like Ellis's step. Nevertheless, there was a tap at the door.

Jane put down her paper and opened the door. There stood Jean-Pierre. He was almost as surprised as she was.

They stared at one another in silence for a moment. Jane said: "You look guilty. Do I?"

"Yes," he said, and he grinned.

"I was just thinking about you. Come in."

He stepped inside and glanced around. "Ellis not here?"

"I'm expecting him soon. Have a seat."

Jean-Pierre lowered his long body onto the sofa. Jane thought, not for the first time, that he was probably the most beautiful man she had ever met. His face was perfectly regular in shape, with a high forehead, a strong, rather aristocratic nose, liquid brown eyes, and a sensual mouth partly hidden by a full, dark brown beard with stray flashes of auburn in the mustache. His clothes were cheap but carefully chosen, and he wore them with a nonchalant elegance that Jane herself envied.

She liked him a lot. His great fault was that he thought too well of himself; but in this he was so naïve as to be disarming, like a boastful child. She liked his idealism and his dedication to medicine. He had enormous charm. He also had a manic imagination which could sometimes be very funny: sparked by some absurdity, perhaps just a slip of the tongue, he would launch into a fanciful monologue which could go on for ten or fifteen minutes. When someone had quoted a remark made by Jean-Paul Sartre about soccer, Jean-Pierre had spontaneously given a commentary on a football match as it might have been described by an existentialist philosopher. Jane had laughed until it hurt. People said that his gaiety had its reverse side, in moods of black depression, but Jane had never seen any evidence of that.

"Have some of Ellis's wine," she said, picking up the bottle from the table.

"No, thanks."

"Are you rehearsing for life in a Muslim country?"

"Not especially." He was looking very solemn.

"What's the matter?" she asked.

"I need to have a serious talk with you," he said.

"We had it, three days ago—don't you remember?" she said flippantly. "You asked me to leave my boyfriend and go to Afghanistan with you—an offer few girls could resist."

"Be serious."

"All right. I still haven't made up my mind."

"Jane. I've discovered something terrible about Ellis."

She looked at him speculatively. What was coming? Would he invent a story, tell a lie, in order to persuade her to go with him? She thought not. "Okay, what?"

"He's not what he pretends to be," said Jean-Pierre.

He was being terribly melodramatic. "There's no need to speak in a voice like an undertaker. What do you mean?"

"He's not a penniless poet. He works for the American government."

Jane frowned. "For the American government?" Her first thought was that Jean-Pierre had got the wrong end of the stick. "He gives English lessons to some French people who work for the U.S. government—"

"I don't mean that. He spies on radical groups. He's an agent. He works for the CIA."

Jane burst out laughing. "You're absurd! Did you think you could make me leave him by telling me that?"

"It's true, Jane."

"It's not true. Ellis couldn't be a spy. Don't you think I'd know? I've been practically living with him for a year."

"But you haven't, though, have you?"

"It makes no difference. I *know* him." Even while she spoke Jane was thinking: it could explain a lot. She did not *really* know Ellis. But she knew him well enough to be sure that he was not base, mean, treacherous and just plain *evil*.

"It's all over town," Jean-Pierre was saying. "Rahmi Coskun was arrested this morning and everyone says Ellis was responsible."

"Why was Rahmi arrested?"

Jean-Pierre shrugged. "Subversion, no doubt. Anyway, Raoul Clermont is running around town trying to find Ellis and *somebody* wants revenge."

"Oh, Jean-Pierre, it's laughable," said Jane. She suddenly felt very warm. She went to the window and threw it open. As she glanced down at the street she saw Ellis's blond head ducking into the front door. "Well," she said to Jean-Pierre, "here he comes. Now you're going to have to repeat this ludicrous story in front of him." She heard Ellis's step on the stairs.

"I intend to," said Jean-Pierre. "Why do you think I am here? I came to warn him that they're after him."

Jane realized that Jean-Pierre was actually sincere: he really believed this story. Well, Ellis would soon set him straight.

The door opened and Ellis walked in.

He looked very happy, as if he were bursting with good news, and when she saw his round, smiling face with its broken nose and penetrating blue eyes, Jane's heart leaped with guilt to think she had been flirting with Jean-Pierre.

Ellis stopped in the doorway, surprised to see Jean-Pierre. His smile faded a little. "Hello, you two," he said. He closed the door behind him and locked it, as was his habit. Jane had always thought that an eccentricity, but now it occurred to her that it was what a spy would do. She pushed the thought out of her mind.

Jean-Pierre spoke first. "They're on to you, Ellis. They know. They're coming after you."

Jane looked from one to the other. Jean-Pierre was taller than Ellis, but Ellis was broad-shouldered and deep-chested. They stood looking at each other like two cats sizing each other up.

Jane put her arms around Ellis, kissed him guiltily and said: "Jean-Pierre has been told some absurd story about you being a CIA spy."

Jean-Pierre was leaning out of the window, scanning the street below. Now he turned back to face him. "Tell her, Ellis."

"Where did you get this idea?" Ellis asked him.

"It's all around town."

"And who, exactly, did *you* hear it from?" asked Ellis in a steely voice.

"Raoul Clermont."

Ellis nodded. Switching into English, he said: "Jane, would you sit down?"

"I don't want to sit down," she said irritably.

"I have something to tell you," he said.

It couldn't be true—it *couldn't*. Jane felt panic rise in her throat. "Then tell me," she said, "and stop asking me to sit down!"

Ellis glanced at Jean-Pierre. "Would you leave us?" he said in French.

Jane began to feel angry. "What are you going to tell me? Why won't you simply say that Jean-Pierre is wrong? Tell me you're not a spy, Ellis, before I go crazy!"

"It's not that simple," said Ellis.

"It is simple!" She could no longer keep the hysterical note out of her voice. "He says that you're a spy, that you work for the American government, and that you've been lying to me, continuously and shamelessly and treacherously, ever since I met you. Is that true? Is that true or not? Well?"

Ellis sighed. "I guess it's true."

Jane felt she would explode. "You bastard!" she screamed. "You fucking bastard!"

Ellis's face was set like stone. "I was going to tell you today," he said.

There was a knock at the door. They both ignored it. "You've been spying on me and all my friends!" Jane yelled. "I feel so *ashamed*."

"My work here is finished," Ellis said. "I don't need to lie to you anymore."

"You won't get the chance. I never want to see you again."

The knocking came again, and Jean-Pierre said in French: "There's someone at the door."

Ellis said: "You don't mean that—that you don't want to see me again."

"You just don't understand what you've done to me, do you?" she said.

Jean-Pierre said: "Open the damn door, for God's sake!"

Jane muttered: "Jesus *Christ*," and stepped to the door. She unlocked it and opened it. There stood a big, broad-shouldered man in a green corduroy jacket with a rip in the sleeve. Jane had never seen him before. She said: "What the hell do you want?" Then she saw that he had a gun in his hand.

The next few seconds seemed to pass very slowly.

Jane realized, in a flash, that if Jean-Pierre had been right about Ellis being a spy then probably he was also right about somebody wanting revenge, and that in the world Ellis secretly inhabited, "revenge" really could mean a knock at the door and a man with a gun.

She opened her mouth to scream.

The man hesitated for a fraction of a second. He looked surprised, as if he had not expected to see a woman. His eyes went from Jane to Jean-Pierre and back: he knew that Jean-Pierre was not his target. But he was confused because he could not see Ellis, who was hidden by the half-open door.

Instead of screaming, Jane tried to slam the door.

As she swung it toward the gunman, he saw what she was doing and stuck his foot in the way. The door hit his shoe and bounced back. But in the act of stepping forward he had spread his arms, for balance, and now his gun was pointing up into the corner of the ceiling.

He's going to kill Ellis, Jane thought. He's going to kill Ellis.

She threw herself at the gunman, beating his face with her fists, for suddenly, although she hated Ellis, she did not want him to die.

The man was distracted for only a fraction of a second. With one strong arm he hurled Jane aside. She fell heavily, landing in a sitting position, bruising the base of her spine.

She saw what happened next with terrible clarity.

The arm that had shoved her aside came back and flung the door wide. As the man swung his gun hand around, Ellis came at him with the bottle of wine raised high above his head. The gun went off as the bottle came down, and the shot coincided with the sound of glass breaking.

Jane stared, horrified, at the two men.

Then the gunman slumped, and Ellis remained standing, and she realized that the shot had missed.

Ellis bent down and snatched the gun from the man's hand.

Jane got to her feet with an effort.

"Are you all right?" Ellis asked her.

"Alive," she said.

He turned to Jean-Pierre. "How many on the street?"

Jean-Pierre glanced out of the window. "None."

Ellis looked surprised. "They must be concealed." He pocketed the gun and went to his bookcase. "Stand back," he said, and hurled it to the floor.

Behind it was a door.

Ellis opened the door.

He looked at Jane for a long moment, as if he had something to say but could not find the words. Then he stepped through the door and was gone.

After a moment Jane walked slowly over to the secret door and looked through. There was another studio flat, sparsely furnished and dreadfully dusty, as if it had not been occupied for a year. There was an open door and, beyond it, a staircase.

She turned back and looked into Ellis's room. The gunman lay on the floor, out cold in a puddle of wine. He had tried to kill Ellis, right here in this room: already it seemed unreal. It all seemed unreal: Ellis being a spy; Jean-Pierre knowing about it; Rahmi being arrested; and Ellis's escape route.

He had gone. *I never want to see you again*, she had said to him just a few seconds ago. It seemed that her wish would be granted.

She heard footsteps on the stairs.

She raised her gaze from the gunman and looked at Jean-Pierre. He, too, seemed stunned. After a moment he crossed the room to her and put his arms around her. She slumped on his shoulder and burst into tears.

PART II

1982

CHAPTER FOUR

The river came down from the ice line, cold and clear and always in a rush, and it filled the Valley with its noise as it boiled through the ravines and flashed past the wheatfields in a headlong dash for the faraway lowlands. For almost a year that sound had been constantly in Jane's ears: sometimes loud, when she went to bathe or when she took the winding cliffside paths between villages; and sometimes soft, as now, when she was high on the hillside and the Five Lions River was just a glint and a murmur in the distance. When eventually she left the Valley she would find the silence unnerving, she thought, like city dwellers on holiday in the countryside who cannot sleep because it is too quiet. Listening, she heard something else, and she realized that the new sound had made her aware of the old. Swelling over the river's chorus came the baritone of a propeller-driven aircraft.

Jane opened her eyes. It was an Antonov, the predatory, slow-moving reconnaissance plane whose incessant growl was the usual herald of faster, noisier jet aircraft on a bombing run. She sat up and looked anxiously across the Valley.

She was in her secret refuge, a broad, flat shelf halfway up a cliff. Above her, the overhang hid her from view without blocking the sun, and would dissuade anyone but a mountaineer from climbing down. Below, the approach to her refuge was steep and stony and bare of vegetation: no one could climb it without being heard and seen by Jane. There was no reason

for anyone to come here anyway. Jane had only found the place by wandering from the path and getting lost. The privacy of the place was important because she came here to take off her clothes and lie in the sun, and
the Afghans were as modest as nuns: if she were seen naked she would be
lynched.

To her right the dusty hillside fell away rapidly. Toward its foot, where
the slope began to level out near the river, was the village of Banda, fifty or
sixty houses clinging to a patch of uneven, rocky ground that no one could
farm. The houses were made of gray stones and mud bricks, and each one
had a flat roof of pressed earth laid over mats. Next to the little mosque was
a small group of wrecked houses: one of the Russian bombers had scored a
direct hit a couple of months back. Jane could see the village clearly, although it was a twenty-minute scramble away. She scanned the roofs and
walled courtyards and mud footpaths, looking for stray children, but happily
there were none—Banda was deserted under the hot blue sky.

To her left, the Valley broadened out. The small stony fields were dotted with bomb craters, and on the lower slopes of the mountainside several
of the ancient terrace walls had collapsed. The wheat was ripe, but no one
was reaping.

Beyond the fields, at the foot of the cliff wall that formed the far side of
the Valley, ran the Five Lions River: deep in places, shallow in others; now
broad, now narrow; always fast and always rocky. Jane scrutinized its length.
There were no women bathing or washing clothes, no children playing in
the shallows, no men leading horses or donkeys across the ford.

Jane contemplated throwing on her clothes and leaving her refuge to
climb farther up the mountainside to the caves. That was where the villagers were, the men sleeping after a night of working in their fields, the
women cooking and trying to stop the children wandering, the cows
penned and the goats tethered and the dogs fighting over scraps. She was
probably quite safe here, for the Russians bombed the villages, not the bare
hillsides; but there was always the chance of a stray bomb, and a cave would
protect her from everything but a direct hit.

Before she had made up her mind she heard the roar of the jets. She
squinted into the sun to look at them. Their noise filled the Valley, swamp-
ing the rush of the river, as they passed over her, heading northeast, high
but descending, one, two, three, four silver killers, the summit of mankind's
ingenuity deployed to maim illiterate farmers and knock down mud-brick
houses and return to base at seven hundred miles per hour.

In a minute they were gone. Banda was to be spared, for today. Slowly,

Jane relaxed. The jets terrified her. Banda had escaped bombing completely last summer, and the whole of the Valley got a respite during the winter; but it had started again in earnest this spring, and Banda had been hit several times, once in the center of the village. Since then Jane had hated the jets.

The courage of the villagers was amazing. Each family had made a second home up in the caves, and they climbed the hill every morning to spend the day there, returning at dusk, for there was no bombing at night. Since it was unsafe to work in the fields by day, the men did it at night—or rather the older ones did, for the young men were away most of the time, shooting at Russians down at the southern end of the Valley or farther afield. This summer the bombing was more intensive than ever in *all* the rebel areas, according to what Jean-Pierre heard from the guerrillas. If Afghans in other parts of the country were like these here in the Valley, they were able to adapt and survive: salvaging a few precious possessions from the rubble of a bombed house, tirelessly replanting a ruined vegetable garden, nursing the wounded and burying the dead, and sending ever-younger teenage boys to join the guerrilla leaders. The Russians could never defeat these people, Jane felt, unless they turned the whole country into a radioactive desert.

As to whether the rebels could ever defeat the Russians—that was another question. They were brave and irrepressible, and they controlled the countryside, but rival tribes hated one another almost as much as they hated the invaders, and their rifles were useless against jet bombers and armored helicopters.

She pushed thoughts of war out of her mind. This was the heat of the day, the siesta time, when she liked to be alone and relax. She put her hand into a goatskin bag of clarified butter and began to oil the taut skin of her enormous belly, wondering how she could possibly have been so foolish as to get pregnant in Afghanistan.

She had arrived with a two-year supply of contraceptive pills, a diaphragm, and a whole carton of spermicidal jelly; and yet, just a few weeks later, she had forgotten to restart the pills after her period and then forgotten to put in the diaphragm—several times. "How could you make such a mistake?" Jean-Pierre had yelled, and she had had no answer.

But now, lying in the sun, cheerfully pregnant with lovely swollen breasts and a permanent backache, she could see that it had been a deliberate mistake, a kind of professional foul perpetrated by her unconscious mind. She had wanted a baby, and she knew Jean-Pierre did not, so she had started one by accident.

Why did I want a baby so badly? she asked herself, and the answer came
to her out of nowhere: because I was lonely.

"Is that true?" she said aloud. It would be ironic. She had never felt
lonely in Paris, living on her own and shopping for one and talking to herself in the mirror; but when she was married, and spent every evening and
every night with her husband and worked alongside him most of every day,
then she had felt isolated, frightened and alone.

They had married in Paris just before coming here. It had seemed a natural part of the adventure, somehow: another challenge, another risk, another thrill. Everyone had said how happy and beautiful and brave and in
love they were, and it had been true.

No doubt she had expected too much. She had looked forward to ever-
growing love and intimacy with Jean-Pierre. She had thought she would
learn about his childhood sweetheart and what he was *really* frightened of
and whether it was true that men shook the drops off after peeing; and in
turn she would tell him that her father had been an alcoholic and that she
had a fantasy about being raped by a black man and that she sometimes
sucked her thumb when she was anxious. But Jean-Pierre seemed to think
their relationship after marriage should be just what it had been before. He
treated her courteously, made her laugh in his manic moods, fell helpless
into her arms when he was depressed, discussed politics and the war, made
love to her expertly once a week with his lean young body and his strong,
sensitive surgeon's hands, and behaved in every way like a boyfriend rather
than a husband. She still felt unable to talk to him about silly, embarrassing things such as whether a hat made her nose look longer and how angry
she still was about having been spanked for spilling red ink on the
drawing room rug when in fact her sister, Pauline, had done it. She wanted
to ask someone *Is this how it's supposed to be, or will it get better?* but her
friends and family were all far away and the Afghan women would have
found her expectations outrageous. She had resisted the temptation to
confront Jean-Pierre with her disappointment, partly because her complaint was so vague, and partly because she was frightened of what his answer might be.

Looking back, she could see that the idea of a baby had been creeping
up on her even earlier, when she was seeing Ellis Thaler. That year she had
flown from Paris to London for the christening of her sister, Pauline's, third
child, something she would not normally have done, for she disliked formal
family occasions. She had also started baby-sitting for a couple in her building, a hysterical antiques dealer and his aristocratic wife, and she had en-

joyed it most when the baby had cried and she had had to pick him up and comfort him.

And then, here in the Valley, where her duty was to encourage the women to space their babies for the sake of healthier children, she had found herself sharing the joy with which each new pregnancy was greeted even in the poorest and most overcrowded households. Thus loneliness and the maternal instinct had conspired against common sense.

Had there been a time—even just a fleeting instant—when she realized that her unconscious mind was trying to get her pregnant? Had she thought *I might have a baby* at the moment when Jean-Pierre penetrated her, gliding in slowly and gracefully like a ship into a dock, while she tightened her arms about his body; or in the second of hesitation, immediately before his climax, when he shut his eyes tightly and seemed to retreat from her deep into himself, a spaceship falling into the heart of the sun; or afterward, as she was drifting blissfully into sleep with his seed hot inside her? "Did I realize?" she said aloud; but thinking about making love had turned her on, and she began to caress herself luxuriously with her butter-slippery hands, forgetting the question and letting her mind fill with vague swirling images of passion.

The scream of jets jerked her back to the real world. She stared, frightened, as another four bombers streaked up the Valley and disappeared. When the noise died away she started to touch herself again, but her mood had been spoiled. She lay still in the sun and thought about her baby.

Jean-Pierre had reacted to her pregnancy just as if it had been premeditated. So furious had he been that he had wanted to perform an abortion himself, immediately. Jane had found that wish of his dreadfully macabre, and he had suddenly seemed a stranger. But hardest to bear was the feeling of having been rejected. The thought that her husband did not want her baby had made her utterly desolate. He had made matters worse by refusing to touch her. She had never been so miserable in her life. For the first time she understood why people sometimes tried to kill themselves. The withdrawal of physical contact was the worst torture of all—she genuinely wished Jean-Pierre would beat her instead, so badly did she need to be touched. When she remembered those days she still felt angry with him, even though she knew she had brought it on herself.

Then, one morning, he had put his arm around her and apologized for his behavior; and although part of her had wanted to say *Being* sorry *isn't enough, you bastard*, the rest of her was desperate for his love, and she had forgiven him immediately. He had explained that he was already afraid of losing her; and that if she were to be the mother of his son he would be absolutely terrified, for then he would lose them both. This confession had moved her to tears, and she had realized that in getting pregnant she had made the ultimate commitment to Jean-Pierre, and she made up her mind that she would make this marriage work, come what may.

He had been warmer to her after that. He had taken an interest in the growing baby, and had become anxious about Jane's health and safety, the way expectant fathers were supposed to. Their marriage would be an imperfect but happy union, Jane thought, and she envisaged an ideal future, with Jean-Pierre as the French Minister of Health in a Socialist administration, herself as a member of the European Parliament, and three brilliant children, one at the Sorbonne, one at the London School of Economics, and one at the New York High School for the Performing Arts.

In this fantasy the eldest and most brilliant child was a girl. Jane touched her tummy, pressing gently with her fingertips, feeling the shape of the baby: according to Rabia Gul, the old village midwife, it would be a girl, for it could be felt on the left side, whereas boys grew on the right side. Rabia had accordingly prescribed a diet of vegetables. For a boy she would have recommended plenty of meat. In Afghanistan the males were better fed even before they were born.

Jane's thoughts were interrupted by a loud bang. For a moment she was confused, associating the explosion with the jets which had passed overhead several minutes before on their way to bomb some other village; then she heard, quite close by, the high continuous scream of a child in pain and panicking.

She realized instantly what had happened. The Russians, using tactics they had learned from the Americans in Vietnam, had littered the countryside with antipersonnel mines. Their ostensible aim was to block guerrilla supply lines; but since the "guerrilla supply lines" were the mountain pathways used daily by old men, women, children and animals, the real purpose was straightforward terror. That scream meant a child had detonated a mine.

Jane jumped to her feet. The sound seemed to be coming from somewhere near the mullah's house, which was about half a mile outside the village on the hillside footpath. Jane could just see it, away to her left and a little lower down. She stepped into her shoes, grabbed her clothes and ran that way. The first long scream ended and became a series of short, terrified yells: it sounded to Jane as if the child had seen the damage the mine had done to its body and was screaming with fright now. Rushing through the coarse undergrowth, Jane realized that she herself was panicking, so peremptory was the summons of a child in distress. "Calm down," she said breathlessly to herself. If she were to fall badly there would be two people in trouble and no one to help; and anyway the worst thing for a frightened child was a frightened adult.

She was near now. The child would be hidden in the bushes, not on the footpath, for all the paths were cleared by the menfolk each time they were mined, but it was impossible to sweep the entire mountainside.

She stopped, listening. Her panting was so loud that she had to hold her breath. The screams were coming from a clump of camel grass and juniper bushes. She pushed through the shrubbery and glimpsed part of a bright blue coat. The child must be Mousa, the nine-year-old son of Mohammed Khan, one of the leading guerrillas. A moment later she was beside him.

He was kneeling on the dusty ground. He had evidently tried to pick up the mine, for it had blown off his hand, and now he was staring wild-eyed at the bloody stump and screaming in terror.

Jane had seen a lot of wounds in the past year, but still this one moved her to pity. "Oh, dear God," she said. "You poor child." She knelt in front of him, hugged him, and murmured soothing noises. After a minute he stopped screaming. She hoped he would begin to cry instead, but he was too shocked, and lapsed into silence. As she held him she searched for and found the pressure point in his armpit, and stopped the gush of blood.

She was going to need his help. She must make him speak. "Mousa, what was it?" she said in Dari.

He made no reply. She asked him again.

"I thought . . ." His eyes opened wide as he remembered, and his voice rose to a scream as he said: "I thought it was A BALL!"

"Hush, hush," she murmured. "Tell me what you did."

"I PICKED IT UP! I PICKED IT UP!"

She held him tight, soothing him. "And what happened?"

His voice was shaky but no longer hysterical. "It went bang," he said. He was rapidly becoming calmer.

She took his right hand and put it under his left arm. "Press where I'm pressing," she said. She guided his fingertips to the point, then withdrew her own. The blood started to flow from the wound again. "Push hard," she told him. He did as she said. The flow stopped. She kissed his forehead. It was damp and cold.

She had dropped her bundle of clothing on the ground beside Mousa. Her clothes were what the Afghan women wore: a sack-shaped dress over cotton trousers. She picked up the dress and tore the thin material into several strips, then began to make a tourniquet. Mousa watched her, wide-eyed and silent. She snapped a dry twig from a juniper bush and used it to finish the tourniquet.

Now he needed a dressing, a sedative, an antibiotic to prevent infection, and his mother to prevent trauma.

Jane pulled on her trousers and tied the drawstring. She wished she had been less hasty about tearing up her dress, for she might have preserved enough of it to cover her upper half. Now she would just have to hope she did not meet any men on the way to the caves.

And how would she get Mousa there? She did not want to try to make him walk. She could not carry him on her back, for he could not hold on. She sighed: she would just have to take him in her arms. She crouched down, put one arm around his shoulders and the other under his thighs, and picked him up, lifting with her knees rather than with her back, the way she had learned at her feminist fitness class. Cradling the child to her bosom with his back lying on the rise of her belly, she began to walk slowly up the hill. She could manage it only because he was half starved: a nine-year-old European child would have been too heavy. She soon emerged from the bushes and found the footpath. But after forty or fifty yards she became exhausted. In the last few weeks she had found herself tiring very quickly, and it infuriated her, but she had learned not to fight it. She set Mousa down and stood with him, hugging him gently, while she rested, leaning against the cliff wall that ran along one side of the mountain path. He had lapsed into a frozen silence which she found more worrying than his screams. As soon as she felt better she picked him up and started again.

She was resting near the top of the hill, fifteen minutes later, when a man appeared on the path ahead. Jane recognized him. "Oh, no," she said in English. "Of all people—Abdullah."

He was a short man of about fifty-five and he was rather tubby despite the local shortage of food. With his tan turban and billowing black trousers he wore an argyle sweater and a blue double-breasted pinstriped suit coat that looked as if it had once been worn by a London stockbroker. His luxuriant beard was dyed red: he was Banda's mullah.

Abdullah mistrusted foreigners, despised women and hated all practitioners of foreign medicine. Jane, being all three, had never had the least chance of winning his affection. To make matters worse, many people in the Valley had realized that taking Jane's antibiotics was a more effective treatment for infections than inhaling the smoke from a burning slip of paper on which Abdullah had written with saffron ink, and consequently the mullah was losing money. His reaction was to refer to Jane as "the West-ern whore," but it was difficult for him to do more, for she and Jean-Pierre were under the protection of Ahmed Shah Masud, the guerrilla leader, and even a mullah hesitated to cross swords with such a great hero.

When he saw her he stopped dead in his tracks, an expression of utter incredulity transforming his normally solemn face into a comic mask. He was the worst possible person to meet. Any of the other village men would have been embarrassed, and perhaps offended, to see her half-naked; but Abdullah would be enraged.

Jane decided to brazen it out. She said in Dari: "Peace be with you." This was the beginning of a formal exchange of greetings which could sometimes go on for several minutes. But Abdullah did not respond with the usual *And with you*. Instead he opened his mouth and began in a high-pitched shout to abuse her with a stream of imprecations which included the Dari words for *prostitute, pervert* and *seducer of children*. His face empur-pled with fury, he walked toward her and raised his stick.

This was going too far. She pointed at Mousa, who stood silent by her side, dazed by pain and weak from loss of blood. "Look!" she yelled at Ab-dullah. "Can't you see—"

But he was blinded by rage. Before she could finish what she was trying to say he brought down his stick on her head with a whack. Jane cried out with pain and anger: she was surprised at how *much* it hurt and how *furious* she was that he should do this.

He still had not noticed Mousa's wound. The mullah's staring eyes were focused on Jane's chest, and she realized in a flash that for him to see in broad daylight the naked breasts of a pregnant white Western woman was a sight so overloaded with different kinds of sexual anxiety that he was bound to blow his top. He was not planning to chastise her with a blow or two, as he might chastise his wife for disobedience. There was murder in his heart.

Suddenly Jane was very frightened—for herself, for Mousa and for her unborn child. She stumbled backward, out of range, but he stepped toward her and raised his stick again. Suddenly inspired, she leaped at him and poked her fingers into his eyes.

He roared like a wounded bull. He was not hurt so much as indignant that a woman he was beating should have the temerity to fight back. While he was blinded, Jane grabbed his beard with both hands and tugged. He stumbled forward, tripped and fell. He rolled a couple of yards downhill and came to rest in a dwarf willow bush.

Jane thought: Oh, God, what have I done?

Looking at the pompous, malevolent priest in his humiliation, Jane knew he would never forget what she had done. He might complain to the "whitebeards"—the village elders. He might go to Masud and demand that the foreign doctors be sent home. He might even try to inflame the menfolk of Banda into stoning Jane. But almost as soon as she had this thought, it struck her that, in order to make any kind of complaint, he would have to tell his story in all its ignominious details, and the villagers would ridicule him forever afterward—the Afghans were nothing if not cruel. So perhaps she would get away with it.

She turned around. She had something more important to worry about. Mousa was standing where she had set him down, silent and expressionless, too shocked to understand what had been going on. Jane took a deep breath, picked him up and walked on.

She reached the crest of the hill after a few paces, and she was able to walk faster as the ground leveled out. She crossed the stony plateau. She was tired and her back hurt but she was almost there: the caves were just below the brow of the mountain. She reached the far side of the ridge and heard children's voices as she began to descend. A moment later she saw a group of six-year-olds playing Heaven-and-Hell, a game which involved holding your toes while two other children carried you to Heaven—if you succeeded in keeping hold of your toes—or Hell, usually a rubbish dump or a latrine, if you let go. She realized that Mousa would never play that game again, and she was suddenly overwhelmed by a sense of tragedy. The children noticed her then, and as she passed them they stopped playing and stared. One of them whispered: "Mousa." Another repeated the name; then the spell was broken and they all ran ahead of Jane, shouting the news.

The daytime hideout of the villagers of Banda looked like the desert encampment of a tribe of nomads: the dusty ground, the blazing midday sun, the remains of cooking fires, the hooded women, the dirty children. Jane crossed the small square of level ground in front of the caves. The women were already converging on the largest cave, which Jane and Jean-Pierre had made their clinic. Jean-Pierre heard the commotion and came out. Gratefully, Jane handed Mousa to him, saying in French: "It was a mine. He's lost his hand. Give me your shirt."

Jean-Pierre took Mousa inside and laid him down on the rug which served as an examination table. Before attending to the child he stripped off his bleached-khaki shirt and gave it to Jane. She put it on.

She felt a little light-headed. She thought she would sit down and rest in the cool rear of the cave, but after taking a couple of steps in that direction, she changed her mind and sat down immediately. Jean-Pierre said: "Get me some swabs." She ignored him. Mousa's mother, Halima, came running into the cave and began screaming when she saw her son. I should calm her, Jane thought, so that she can comfort the child; why can't I get up? I think I'll close my eyes. Just for a minute.

By nightfall Jane knew her baby was coming.

When she came around after fainting in the cave, she had what she thought was a backache—caused, she assumed, by carrying Mousa. Jean-Pierre agreed with her diagnosis, gave her an aspirin and told her to lie still. Rabia, the midwife, came into the cave to see Mousa, and gave Jane a hard look, but at the time Jane did not understand its significance. Jean-Pierre cleaned and dressed Mousa's stump, gave him penicillin and injected him against tetanus. The child would not die of infection, as almost certainly he would have without Western medicine; but all the same Jane wondered whether his life would be worth living—survival here was hard even for the fittest, and crippled children generally died young.

Late in the afternoon Jean-Pierre prepared to leave. He was scheduled to hold a clinic tomorrow in a village several miles away, and—for some reason Jane had never quite understood—he never missed such appointments, even though he knew that no Afghan would have been surprised if he had been a day or even a week late.

By the time he kissed Jane good-bye she was beginning to wonder whether her backache might be the beginning of labor, brought on early by her ordeal with Mousa, but as she had never had a baby before, she could not tell, and it seemed unlikely. She asked Jean-Pierre. "Don't worry," he said briskly. "You've got another six weeks to wait." She asked him whether he ought perhaps to stay, just in case, but he thought it was quite unnecessary, and she began to feel foolish; so she let him go, with his medical supplies loaded on a scrawny horse, to reach his destination before dark so that he could begin work first thing in the morning.

When the sun began to set behind the western cliff wall, and the valley was brimful of shadow, Jane walked with the women and children down the mountainside to the darkening village, and the men headed for their fields, to reap their crops while the bombers slept.

The house in which Jane and Jean-Pierre lived actually belonged to the village shopkeeper, who had given up hope of making money in wartime—

there was almost nothing to sell—and had decamped, with his family, to
Pakistan. The front room, formerly the shop, had been Jean-Pierre's clinic
until the intensity of the summer bombing had driven the villagers to the
caves during the day. The house had two back rooms, one would have been
for the men and their guests, the other for women and children. Jane and
Jean-Pierre used them as bedroom and living room. At the side of the house
was a mud-walled courtyard containing the cooking fire and a small pool for
washing clothes, dishes and children. The shopkeeper had left behind some
homemade wooden furniture, and the villagers had loaned Jane several
beautiful rugs for the floors. Jane and Jean-Pierre slept on a mattress, like
the Afghans, but they had a down sleeping bag instead of blankets. Like the
Afghans, they rolled up the mattress during the day or put it on the flat roof
to air in fine weather. In the summer everyone slept on the roofs.

Walking from the cave to the house had a peculiar effect on Jane. Her
backache got much worse, and when she reached home she was ready to
collapse with pain and exhaustion. She had a desperate urge to pee, but she
was too tired to go outside to the latrine, so she used the emergency pot behind the screen in the bedroom. It was then that she noticed a small blood-
streaked stain in the crotch of her cotton trousers.

She did not have the energy to climb up the outside ladder onto the roof
to fetch the mattress, so she lay on a rug in the bedroom. The "backache"
came in waves. She put her hands on her tummy during the next wave, and
felt the bulge shift, sticking farther out as the pain increased then flattening
again as it eased. Now she was in no doubt that she was having contractions.

She was frightened. She recalled talking to her sister, Pauline, about
childbirth. After Pauline's first, Jane had visited her, taking a bottle of
champagne and a little marijuana. When they were both extremely relaxed,
Jane had asked what it was really like, and Pauline had replied: "Like shit-
ting a melon." They had giggled for what seemed like hours.

But Pauline had given birth at University College Hospital in the heart
of London, not in a mud-brick house in the Five Lions Valley.

Jane thought: What am I going to *do?*

I mustn't panic. I must wash myself with warm water and soap; find a
sharp scissors and put it in boiling water for fifteen minutes; get clean sheets
to lie on; sip liquids; and relax.

But before she could do anything, another contraction began, and this
one *really* hurt. She closed her eyes and tried to take slow, deep, regular
breaths, as Jean-Pierre had explained, but it was difficult to be so controlled
when all she wanted to do was cry out in fear and pain.

The spasm left her drained. She lay still, recovering. She realized she could not do any of the things she had listed: she could not manage on her own. As soon as she felt strong enough she would get up and go to the nearest house and ask the women to fetch the midwife.

The next contraction came sooner than she had expected, after what seemed like only a minute or two. As the tension reached its peak Jane said aloud: "Why don't they *tell* you how much it *hurts?*"

As soon as it passed its peak she forced herself to get up. The terror of giving birth all alone gave her strength. She hobbled from the bedroom into the living room. She felt a little stronger with each step. She made it out into the courtyard; then suddenly there was a gush of warm fluid between her thighs, and her trousers were instantly drenched: the waters had broken. "Oh, no," she groaned. She leaned against the doorpost. She was not sure she could walk even a few yards with her trousers falling down like this. She felt humiliated. "I must," she said; but a new contraction began, and she sank to the ground, thinking: I'm going to have to do this alone.

Next time she opened her eyes there was a man's face close to her own. He looked like an Arab sheikh: he had dark brown skin, black eyes and a black mustache, and his features were aristocratic—high cheekbones, a Roman nose, white teeth and a long jaw. It was Mohammed Khan, the father of Mousa.

"Thank God," Jane muttered thickly.

"I came to thank you for saving the life of my only son," Mohammed said in Dari. "Are you sick?"

"I'm having a baby."

"Now?" he said, startled.

"Soon. Help me into the house."

He hesitated—childbirth, like all things uniquely feminine, was considered unclean—but to his credit the hesitation was only momentary. He lifted her to her feet and supported her as she walked through the living room and into the bedroom. She lay down on the rug again. "Get help," she told him.

He frowned, unsure what to do, looking very boyish and handsome. "Where is Jean-Pierre?"

"Gone to Khawak. I need Rabia."

"Yes," he said. "I'll send my wife."

"Before you go . . ."

"Yes?"

"Please give me some water."

He looked shocked. It was unheard of for a man to serve a woman, even with a simple drink of water.

Jane added: "From the special jug." She kept handy a jug of filtered boiled water for drinking: this was the only way to avoid the numerous intestinal parasites from which almost all the local people suffered all their lives.

Mohammed decided to flout convention. "Of course," he said. He went into the next room and returned a moment later with a cup of water. Jane thanked him and sipped gratefully.

"I'll send Halima to fetch the midwife," he said.

Halima was his wife. "Thank you," said Jane. "Tell her to hurry."

Mohammed left. Jane was lucky it was he and not one of the other men. The others would have refused to touch a sick woman, but Mohammed was different. He was one of the most important guerrillas, and in practice was the local representative of the rebel leader, Masud. Mohammed was only twenty-four, but in this country that was not too young to be a guerrilla leader or to have a nine-year-old son. He had studied in Kabul, he spoke a little French, and he knew that the customs of the Valley were not the only forms of polite behavior in the world. His main responsibility was to organize the convoys to and from Pakistan with their vital supplies of arms and ammunition for the rebels. It was one such convoy that had brought Jane and Jean-Pierre to the Valley.

Waiting for the next contraction, Jane recalled that awful journey. She had thought of herself as a healthy, active and strong person, easily capable of walking all day; but she had not anticipated the shortage of food, the steep climbs, the rough stony paths and the incapacitating diarrhea. For parts of the trip they had moved only at night, for fear of Russian helicopters. They had also had to contend with hostile villagers in places: fearing that the convoy would attract a Russian attack, the locals would refuse to sell food to the guerrillas, or hide behind barred doors, or direct the convoy to a meadow or orchard a few miles away, a perfect camping spot which turned out not to exist.

Because of the Russian attacks, Mohammed changed his routes constantly. Jean-Pierre had got hold of American maps of Afghanistan in Paris, and they were better than anything the rebels had, so Mohammed often came to the house to look at them before sending off a new convoy.

In fact Mohammed came oftener than was really necessary. He also addressed Jane more than Afghan men usually did, and made eye contact with her a little too much, and stole too many glances at her body. She thought he was in love with her, or at least he had been until her pregnancy became visible.

She in turn had been drawn to him at the time when she was miserable about Jean-Pierre. Mohammed was lean and brown and strong and powerful, and for the first time in her life, Jane had been attracted to a dyed-in-the-wool male chauvinist pig.

She could have had an affair with him. He was a devout Muslim, as were all the guerrillas, but she doubted whether that would have made any difference. She believed what her father used to say: "Religious conviction may thwart a timid desire but nothing can stand against genuine lust." That particular line had enraged Mummy. No, there was as much adultery in this puritan peasant community as anywhere else, as Jane had realized listening to the riverside gossip among the women while they fetched water or bathed. Jane knew how it was managed, too. Mohammed had told her. "You can see the fish jump at dusk under the waterfall beyond the last water mill," he had said one day. "I go there some nights to catch them." At dusk the women were all cooking, and the men were sitting in the courtyard of the mosque, talking and smoking: lovers would not be discovered so far from the village, and neither Jane nor Mohammed would have been missed.

The idea of making love by a waterfall with this handsome, primitive tribesman tempted Jane; but then she had got pregnant, and Jean-Pierre had confessed how frightened he was of losing her, and she had decided to devote all her energies to making her marriage work, come what may; and so she never went to the waterfall, and after her pregnancy began to show, Mohammed did not look at her body.

Perhaps it was their latent intimacy that had emboldened Mohammed to come in and to help her, when other men would have refused and might even have turned away at the door. Or perhaps it was Mousa. Mohammed had only one son—and three daughters—and he probably now felt unbearably indebted to Jane. I made a friend and an enemy today, she thought: Mohammed and Abdullah.

The pain began again, and she realized she had enjoyed a longer-than-usual respite. Were the contractions becoming irregular? Why? Jean-Pierre had said nothing about that. But he had forgotten much of the gynecology he had studied three or four years ago.

This one was the worst so far, and it left her feeling shivery and nauseated. What had happened to the midwife? Mohammed *must* have sent his wife to fetch her—he would not forget, or change his mind. But would she obey her husband? Of course—Afghan women always did. But she might walk slowly, gossiping on the way, or even stop off at some other house to drink tea. If there was adultery in the Five Lions Valley there would be jealousy, too, and Halima was sure to know or at least guess at her husband's feelings for Jane—wives always did. She might resent being asked to rush to the aid of her rival, the exotic white-skinned educated foreigner who so fascinated her husband. Suddenly Jane felt very angry with Mohammed and with Halima, too. I've done nothing wrong, she thought. Why have they all deserted me? Why isn't my husband here?

When another contraction began, she burst into tears. It was just too much. "I can't go on," she said aloud. She was shaking uncontrollably. She wanted to die before the pain could get worse. "Mummy, help me, Mummy," she sobbed.

Suddenly there was a strong arm around her shoulders and a woman's voice in her ear, murmuring something incomprehensible but soothing in Dari. Without opening her eyes, she held on to the other woman, weeping and crying out as the contraction grew more intense; until at length it began to fade, too slowly, but with a feeling of finality, as if it might be the last, or perhaps the last bad one.

She looked up and saw the serene brown eyes and nutshell cheeks of old Rabia, the midwife.

"May God be with you, Jane Debout."

Jane felt relief like the lifting of a crushing burden. "And with you, Rabia Gul," she whispered gratefully.

"Are the pains coming fast?"

"Every minute or two."

Another woman's voice said: "The baby is coming early."

Jane turned her head and saw Zahara Gul, Rabia's daughter-in-law, a voluptuous girl of Jane's age with wavy near-black hair and a wide, laughing mouth. Of all the women in the village, Zahara was the one to whom Jane felt close. "I'm glad you're here," she said.

Rabia said: "The birth has been brought on by carrying Mousa up the hillside."

"Is that all?" said Jane.

"It is plenty."

So they don't know about the fight with Abdullah, Jane thought. He has decided to keep it to himself.

Rabia said: "Shall I make everything ready for the baby?"

"Yes, please." Goodness knows what kind of primitive gynecology I'm letting myself in for, Jane thought; but I can't do this alone—I just can't.

"Would you like Zahara to make some tea?" Rabia asked.

"Yes, please." There was nothing superstitious about that, at least.

The two women got busy. Just having them there made Jane feel better. It was nice, she thought, that Rabia had asked permission to help—a Western doctor would have walked in and taken charge as if he owned the place. Rabia washed her hands ritually, calling on the prophets to make her red-faced—which meant successful—and then washed them again, thoroughly, with soap and lots of water. Zahara brought in a jar of wild rue, and Rabia lit a handful of the small dark seeds with some charcoal. Jane recalled that evil spirits were said to be frightened off by the smell of burning rue. She consoled herself with the thought that the acrid smoke would serve to keep flies out of the room.

Rabia was a little more than a midwife. Delivering babies was her main work, but she also had herbal and magical treatments to increase the fertility of women who were having difficulty getting pregnant. She had methods of preventing conception and bringing on abortion, too, but there was much less demand for these: Afghan women generally wanted lots of children. Rabia would also be consulted about any "feminine" illness. And she was usually asked to wash the dead—a task which, like delivering babies, was considered unclean.

Jane watched her move around the room. She was probably the oldest woman in the village, being somewhere around sixty. She was short—not much more than five feet tall—and very thin, like most of the people here. Her wrinkled brown face was surrounded by white hair. She moved quietly, her bony old hands precise and efficient.

Jane's relationship with her had begun in mistrust and hostility. When Jane had asked whom Rabia called upon in case of difficult deliveries, Rabia had snapped: "May the devil be deaf, I've never had a difficult birth and I've never lost a mother or a child." But later, when village women came to Jane with minor menstrual problems or routine pregnancies, Jane would send them to Rabia instead of prescribing placebos; and this was the beginning of a working relationship. Rabia had consulted Jane about a recently delivered mother who had a vaginal infection. Jane had given Rabia a supply of penicillin and had explained how to prescribe it. Rabia's prestige had rocketed when it became known that she had been entrusted with Western medicine; and Jane had been able to tell her, without giving offense, that Rabia herself had probably caused the infection by her practice of manually lubricating the birth canal during delivery.

From then on Rabia began to turn up at the clinic once or twice a week to talk to Jane and watch her work. Jane took these opportunities to explain, rather casually, such things as why she washed her hands so often, why she put all her instruments in boiling water after using them, and why she gave lots of fluids to infants with diarrhea.

In turn, Rabia told Jane some of her secrets. Jane was interested to learn what was in the potions Rabia made, and she could guess now some of them might work: medicines to promote pregnancy contained rabbit brains or cat spleen, which might provide hormones missing from the patient's metabolism; and the mint and catnip in many preparations probably helped to clear up infections which hindered conception. Rabia also had a physic for wives to give to impotent husbands, and there was no doubt about how that worked: it contained opium.

Mistrust had given way to wary mutual respect, but Jane had not consulted Rabia about her own pregnancy. It was one thing to allow that Rabia's mixture of folklore and witchcraft might work on Afghan women, and quite another to subject herself to it. Besides, Jane had expected Jean-Pierre to deliver her baby. So, when Rabia had asked about the position of the baby, and had prescribed a vegetable diet for a girl, Jane had made it clear that this pregnancy was going to be a Western one. Rabia had looked hurt, but had accepted the ruling with dignity. And now Jean-Pierre was in Khawak and Rabia was right here, and Jane was glad to have the help of an old woman who had delivered hundreds of babies and had herself given birth to eleven.

There had been no pain for a while, but in the last few minutes, as she watched Rabia move quietly around the room, Jane had been feeling new sensations in her abdomen: a distinct feeling of pressure accompanied by a growing urge to *push*. The urge became irresistible, and as she pushed, she groaned, not because she was in pain, but just with the sheer effort of pushing.

She heard Rabia's voice, as if from a distance, saying: "It begins. This is good."

After a while the urge went away. Zahara brought a cup of green tea. Jane sat upright and sipped gratefully. It was warm and very sweet. Zahara is the same age as me, Jane thought, and she's had four children already, not counting miscarriages and stillborn babies. But she was one of those women who seemed to be full of vitality, like a healthy young lioness. She would probably have several more children. She had greeted Jane with open curiosity, when most of the women had been suspicious and hostile, in the early days; and Jane had discovered that Zahara was impatient with the sillier customs and traditions of the Valley and eager to learn what she could of foreign ideas on health, child care and nutrition. Consequently Zahara had become not just Jane's friend but the spearhead of her health education program.

Today, however, Jane was learning about Afghan methods. She watched Rabia spread a plastic sheet on the floor (What had they used in the days before there was all this waste plastic around?) and cover it with a layer of sandy earth, which Zahara brought from outside in a bucket. Rabia had laid out a few things on a cloth on the floor, and Jane was pleased to see clean cotton rags and a new razor blade still in its wrapping.

The need to push came again, and Jane closed her eyes to concentrate. It did not *hurt* exactly; it was more like being incredibly, impossibly constipated. She found it helpful to groan as she strained, and she wanted to explain to Rabia that this was not a groan of agony, but she was too busy pushing to talk.

In the next pause, Rabia knelt down and untied the drawstring of Jane's trousers, then eased them off. "Do you want to make water before I wash you?" she asked.

"Yes."

She helped Jane get up and walk behind the screen, then held her shoulders while she sat on the pot.

Zahara brought a bowl of warm water and took the pot away. Rabia washed Jane's tummy, thighs and private parts, assuming for the first time a rather brisk air as she did so. Then Jane lay down again. Rabia washed her own hands and dried them. She showed Jane a small jar of blue powder—copper sulfate, Jane guessed—and said: "This color frightens the evil spirits."

"What do you want to do?"

"Put a little on your brow."

"All right," said Jane; then she added: "Thank you."

Rabia smeared a little of the powder on Jane's forehead. I don't mind magic when it's harmless, Jane thought, but what will she do if there is a real medical problem? And just exactly how many weeks premature is this baby?

She was still worrying when the next contraction began, so she was not concentrating on riding the wave of pressure and in consequence it was very painful. I mustn't worry, she thought; I must make myself relax.

Afterward she felt exhausted and rather sleepy. She closed her eyes. She felt Rabia unbutton her shirt—the one she had borrowed from Jean-Pierre that afternoon, a hundred years ago. Rabia began to massage Jane's tummy with some kind of lubricant, probably clarified butter. She dug her fingers in. Jane opened her eyes and said: "Don't try to move the baby."

Rabia nodded, but continued to probe, one hand on the top of Jane's bulge and the other at the bottom. "The head is down," she said finally. "All is well. But the baby will come very soon. You should get up now."

Zahara and Rabia helped Jane stand and take two steps forward onto the earth-covered plastic sheet. Rabia got behind her and said: "Stand on my feet."

Jane did as she was told, although she was not sure of the logic of this. Rabia eased her into a squat, crouching behind her. So this was the local birthing position. "Sit on me," said Rabia. "I can hold you." Jane let her weight settle on the old woman's thighs. The position was surprisingly comfortable and reassuring.

Jane felt her muscles begin to tighten again. She gritted her teeth and bore down, groaning. Zahara squatted in front of her. For a while there was nothing in Jane's mind but the pressure. At last it eased, and she slumped, exhausted and half asleep, letting Rabia take her weight.

When it started again there was a new pain, a sharp burning sensation in her crotch. Zahara suddenly said: "It comes."

"Don't push now," said Rabia. "Let the baby swim out."

The pressure eased. Rabia and Zahara changed places, and now Rabia squatted between Jane's legs, watching intently. The pressure began again. Jane gritted her teeth. Rabia said: "Don't push. Be calm." Jane tried to relax. Rabia looked at her and reached up to touch her face, saying: "Don't bite down. Make your mouth loose." Jane let her jaw sag, and found that it helped her to relax.

The burning sensation came again, worse than ever, and Jane knew the baby was almost born: she could feel its head pushing through, stretching her opening impossibly wide. She cried out with the pain—and suddenly it eased, and for a moment she could feel nothing. She looked down. Rabia reached between her thighs, calling out the names of the prophets. Through a haze of tears Jane saw something round and dark in the midwife's hands.

"Don't pull," Jane said. "Don't pull the head."

"No," said Rabia.

Jane felt the pressure again. At that moment Rabia said: "A small push for the shoulder." Jane closed her eyes and squeezed gently.

A few moments later Rabia said: "Now the other shoulder."

Jane squeezed again, and then there was an enormous relief of tension, and she knew that the baby was born. She looked down and saw its tiny form cradled on Rabia's arm. Its skin was wrinkled and wet, and its head was covered with damp dark hair. The umbilical cord looked weird, a thick blue rope pulsing like a vein.

"Is it all right?" Jane asked.

Rabia did not reply. She pursed her lips and blew on the baby's squashed, immobile face.

Oh, God, it's dead, thought Jane.

"Is it all right?" she repeated.

Rabia blew again, and the baby opened its tiny mouth and cried.

Jane said: "Oh, thank God—it's alive."

Rabia picked up a clean cotton rag and wiped the baby's face.

"Is it normal?" asked Jane.

At last Rabia spoke. She looked into Jane's eyes, smiled and said: "Yes. She is normal."

She's normal, Jane thought. She. I made a little girl. A girl.

Suddenly she felt utterly drained. She could not remain upright a moment longer. "I want to lie down," she said.

Zahara helped her step back to the mattress and put cushions behind her so that she was sitting up, while Rabia held the baby, still attached to Jane by the cord. When Jane was settled, Rabia began to pat the baby dry with cotton rags.

Jane saw the cord stop pulsing, shrivel and turn white. "You can cut the cord," she said to Rabia.

"We always wait for the afterbirth," Rabia said.

"Do it now, please."

Rabia looked dubious, but complied. She took a piece of white string from her table and tied it around the cord a few inches from the baby's navel. It should have been closer, Jane thought; but it doesn't matter.

Rabia unwrapped the new razor blade. "In the name of Allah," she said, and cut the cord.

"Give her to me," said Jane.

Rabia handed the baby to her, saying: "Don't let her suckle."

Jane knew Rabia was wrong about this. "It helps the afterbirth," she said.

Rabia shrugged.

Jane put the baby's face to her breast. Her nipples were enlarged and felt deliciously sensitive, like when Jean-Pierre kissed them. As her nipple touched the baby's cheek, the child turned her head reflexively and opened her little mouth. As soon as the nipple went in, she began to suck. Jane was astonished to find that it felt sexy. For a moment she was shocked and embarrassed; then she thought: What the hell.

She sensed further movements in her abdomen. She obeyed an urge to push, and then felt the placenta come out, a slippery small birth. Rabia wrapped it carefully in a rag.

The baby stopped sucking and seemed to fall asleep.

Zahara handed Jane a cup of water. She drank it in one gulp. It tasted wonderful. She asked for more.

She was sore, exhausted and blissfully happy. She looked down at the little girl sleeping peacefully at her breast. She felt ready to sleep herself.

Rabia said: "We should wrap the little one."

Jane lifted the baby—she was as light as a doll—and handed her to the old woman. "Chantal," she said as Rabia took her. "Her name is Chantal." Then she closed her eyes.

CHAPTER FIVE

E llis Thaler took the Eastern Airlines shuttle from Washington to New York. At La Guardia Airport he got a cab to the Plaza Hotel in New York City. The cab dropped him at the Fifth Avenue entrance to the hotel. Ellis went inside. In the lobby he turned left and went to the 58th Street elevators. A man in a business suit and a woman carrying a Saks shopping bag got in with him. The man got out on the seventh floor. Ellis got out at the eighth. The woman went on up. Ellis walked along the cavernous hotel corridor, all alone, until he came to the 59th Street elevators. He went down to the ground floor and left the hotel by the 59th Street entrance.

Satisfied that no one was following him, he hailed a cab on Central Park South, went to Penn Station and took the train to Douglaston, Queens.

Some lines from Auden's "Lullaby" were repeating in his head as he rode the train:

> Time and fevers burn away
> Individual beauty from
> Thoughtful children, and the grave
> Proves the child ephemeral.

It was more than a year since he had posed as an aspiring American poet in Paris, but he had not lost the taste for verse.

He continued to check for a tail, for this was one assignation his enemies must never learn about. He got off the train at Flushing and waited on
the platform for the next train. No one waited with him.

Because of his elaborate precautions it was five o'clock when he reached
Douglaston. From the station he walked briskly for half an hour, running
over in his mind the approach he was about to make, the words he would
use, the various possible reactions he might expect.

He reached a suburban street within sight of Long Island Sound and
stopped outside a small, neat house with mock-Tudor gables and a stained-
glass window in one wall. There was a small Japanese car in the driveway.
As he walked up the path, the front door was opened by a blond girl of thirteen.

Ellis said: "Hello, Petal."

"Hi, Daddy," she replied.

He bent down to kiss her, feeling as always a glow of pride simultaneously with a stab of guilt.

He looked her up and down. Underneath her Michael Jackson T-shirt
she was wearing a bra. He was pretty sure that was new. She's turning into
a woman, he thought. I'll be damned.

"Would you like to come inside for a moment?" she said politely.

"Sure."

He followed her into the house. From behind she looked even more
womanly. He was reminded of his first girlfriend. He had been fifteen and
she had been not much older than Petal. . . . No, wait, he thought; she was
younger, she was *twelve*. And I used to put my hand up her sweater. Lord
protect my daughter from fifteen-year-old boys.

They went into a small, neat living room. "Won't you sit down?" said
Petal.

Ellis sat down.

"Can I get you something?" she asked.

"Relax," Ellis told her. "You don't have to be so polite. I'm your daddy."

She looked puzzled and uncertain, as if she had been rebuked for something she did not know to be wrong. After a moment she said: "I have to
brush my hair. Then we can go. Excuse me."

"Sure," said Ellis. She went out. He found her courtesy painful. It was a
sign that he was still a stranger. He had not yet succeeded in becoming a
normal member of her family.

He had been seeing her at least once a month for the past year, ever
since he came back from Paris. Sometimes they would spend a day together,

but more often he would just take her out to dinner, as he was going to today. To be with her for that hour, he had to make a five-hour trip with maximum security, but of course she did not know that. His aim was a modest one: without any fuss or drama he wanted to take a small but permanent place in his daughter's life.

It had meant changing the type of work he did. He had given up fieldwork. His superiors had been highly displeased: there were too few good undercover agents (and hundreds of bad ones). He, too, had been reluctant, feeling that he had a duty to use his talent. But he could not win his daughter's affection if he had to disappear every year or so to some remote corner of the world, unable to tell her where he was going or why or even for how long. And he could not risk getting himself killed just when she was learning to love him.

He missed the excitement, the danger, the thrill of the chase, and the feeling that he was doing an important job that nobody else could do quite as well. But for too long his only emotional attachments had been fleeting ones, and after he lost Jane he felt the need of at least one person whose love was permanent.

While he was waiting, Gill came into the room. Ellis stood up. His ex-wife was cool and composed in a white summer dress. He kissed her proffered cheek. "How are you?" she said.

"The same as ever. You?"

"I'm *incredibly* busy." She started to tell him, in some detail, how much she had to do, and, as always, Ellis tuned out. He was fond of her, although she bored him to death. It was odd to think he had once been married to her. But she had been the prettiest girl in the English Department, and he had been the cleverest boy, and it was 1967, when everyone was stoned and anything could happen, especially in California. They were married in white robes, at the end of their first year, and someone played the "Wedding March" on a sitar. Then Ellis flunked his exams and got thrown out of college and therefore was drafted, and instead of going to Canada or Sweden he went to the draft office, like a lamb to the slaughter, surprising the hell out of everyone except Gill, who knew by then that the marriage was not going to work and was just waiting to see how Ellis would make his escape.

He was in the hospital in Saigon with a bullet wound in his calf—the helicopter pilot's commonest injury, because his seat is armored but the floor is not—when the divorce became final. Someone dumped the notification on his bed while he was in the john, and he found it when he got back, along with another oak-leaf cluster, his twenty-fifth (they were passing out medals kind of fast in those days). *I just got divorced*, he had said, and the soldier in the next bed had replied *No shit. Want to play a little cards?*

She had not told him about the baby. He found out, a few years later, when he became a spy and tracked Gill down as an exercise, and learned that she had a child with the unmistakably late-sixties name of Petal, and a husband called Bernard who was seeing a fertility specialist. Not telling him about Petal was the only truly mean thing Gill had ever done to him, he thought, although she still maintained it had been for his own good.

He had insisted on seeing Petal from time to time, and he had stopped her calling Bernard "Daddy." But he had not sought to become part of their family life, not until last year.

"Do you want to take my car?" Gill was saying.

"If it's all right."

"Sure it is."

"Thanks." It was embarrassing having to borrow Gill's car, but the drive from Washington was too long, and Ellis did not want to rent cars frequently in this area, for then one day his enemies would find out, through the records of the rental agencies or the credit card companies, and then they would be on the way to finding out about Petal. The alternative would be to use a different identity every time he rented a car, but identities were expensive and the Agency would not provide them for a desk man. So he used Gill's Honda, or hired the local taxi.

Petal came back in, with her blond hair wafting about her shoulders. Ellis stood up. Gill said: "The keys are in the car."

Ellis said to Petal: "Jump in the car. I'll be right there." Petal went out. He said to Gill: "I'd like to invite her to Washington for a weekend."

Gill was kind but firm. "If she wants to go, she certainly can, but if she doesn't, I won't make her."

Ellis nodded. "That's fair. See you later."

He drove Petal to a Chinese restaurant in Little Neck. She liked Chinese food. She relaxed a little once she was away from the house. She thanked Ellis for sending her a poem on her birthday. "Nobody I know has ever had a poem for their birthday," she said.

He was not sure whether that was good or bad. "Better than a birthday card with a picture of a cute kitten on the front, I hope."

"Yeah." She laughed. "All my friends think you're so romantic. My English teacher asked me if you had ever had anything published."

"I've never written anything good enough," he said. "Are you still enjoying English?"

"I like it a *lot* better than math. I'm *terrible* at math."

"What do you study? Any plays?"

"No, but we have poems sometimes."

"Any you like?"

She thought for a moment. "I like the one about the daffodils."

Ellis nodded. "I do, too."

"I forgot who wrote it."

"William Wordsworth."

"Oh, right."

"Any others?"

"Not really. I'm more into music. Do you like Michael Jackson?"

"I don't know. I'm not sure I've heard his records."

"He's really cute." She giggled. "All my friends are crazy about him."

It was the second time she had mentioned *all my friends*. Right now her peer group was the most important thing in her life. "I'd like to meet some of your friends, sometime," he said.

"Oh, *Daddy*," she chided him. "You wouldn't like that—they're just *girls*."

Feeling mildly rebuffed, Ellis concentrated on his food for a while. He drank a glass of white wine with it: French habits had stayed with him.

When he finished he said: "Listen, I've been thinking. Why don't you come to Washington and stay at my place one weekend? It's only an hour on the plane, and we could have a good time."

She was quite surprised. "What's in Washington?"

"Well, we could take a tour of the White House, where the President lives. And Washington has some of the best museums in the whole world. And you've never even seen my apartment. I have a spare bedroom . . ." He trailed off. He could see she was not interested.

"Oh, Daddy, I don't know," she said. "I have so much to do on weekends—homework, and parties, and shopping, and dance lessons and everything. . . ."

Ellis hid his disappointment. "Don't worry," he said. "Maybe sometime when you're not so busy you could come."

"Yes, okay," she said, visibly relieved.

"I could fix up the spare bedroom so you could come anytime you like."

"Okay."

"What color shall I paint it?"

"I don't know."

"What's your favorite color?"

"Pink. I guess."

"Pink it is." Ellis forced a smile. "Let's go."

In the car on the way home she asked him whether he would mind if she had her ears pierced.

"I don't know," he said guardedly. "How does Mommy feel about it?"

"She said it's okay with her if it's okay with you." Was Gill thoughtfully including him in the decision or just passing the buck? "I don't think I like the idea," Ellis said. "You may be a little young to begin making holes in yourself for decoration."

"Do you think I'm too young to have a boyfriend?"

Ellis wanted to say yes. She seemed far too young. But he couldn't stop her growing up. "You're old enough to date, but not to go steady," he said. He glanced at her to catch her reaction. She looked amused. Maybe they don't talk about going steady anymore, he thought.

When they reached the house, Bernard's Ford was parked in the driveway. Ellis pulled the Honda in behind it and went in with Petal. Bernard was in the living room. A small man with very short hair, he was good-natured and utterly without imagination. Petal greeted him enthusiastically, hugging and kissing him. He seemed a little embarrassed. He shook Ellis's hand firmly, saying: "Government still ticking over okay, back in Washington?"

"Same as always," Ellis said. They thought that he worked for the State Department and that his job was to read French newspapers and magazines and prepare a daily digest for the France Desk.

"How about a beer?"

Ellis did not really want one, but he accepted just to be friendly. Bernard went into the kitchen to get it. He was credit manager for a department store in New York City. Petal seemed to like and respect him, and he was gently affectionate with her. He and Gill had no other children: that fertility specialist had done him no good.

He came back with two glasses of beer and handed one to Ellis. "Go and do your homework now," he said to Petal. "Daddy will say good-bye before he leaves."

She kissed him again and ran off. When she was out of earshot he said: "She isn't normally so affectionate. She seems to overdo it when you're around. I don't understand it."

Ellis understood it only too well, but he did not want to think about it yet. "Don't worry about it," he said. "How's business?"

"Not bad. High interest rates haven't hit us as badly as we feared they might. It seems that people are still willing to borrow money to buy things—in New York, at least." He sat down and sipped his beer.

Ellis always felt that Bernard was physically frightened of him. It showed in the way the man walked around, like a pet dog that is not really allowed indoors, careful to stay an inch or two out of kicking distance.

They talked about the economy for a few minutes, and Ellis drank his beer as fast as he could, then got up to leave. He went to the foot of the staircase and called: "Bye, Petal."

She came to the top of the stairs. "What about having my ears pierced?"

"Can I think about it?" he said.

"Sure. Bye."

Gill came down the stairs. "I'll drive you to the airport," she said.

Ellis was surprised. "Okay. Thanks."

When they were on the road Gill said: "She told me she didn't want to spend a weekend with you."

"Right."

"You're upset, aren't you?"

"Does it show?"

"To me it does. I used to be married to you." She paused. "I'm sorry, John."

"It's my fault. I didn't think it through. Before I came along, she had a mommy and a daddy and a home—all any child wants. I'm not *just* superfluous, though. By being around I threaten her happiness. I'm an intruder, a destabilizing factor. That's why she hugs Bernard in front of me. She doesn't mean to hurt me. She does it because she's afraid of losing *him*. And it's me who makes her afraid."

"She'll get over it," Gill said. "America is full of kids with two daddies."

"That's no excuse. I fucked up, and I should face it."

She surprised him again by patting his knee. "Don't be too hard on yourself," she said. "You just weren't made for this. I knew that within a month of marrying you. You don't want a house, a job, the suburbs, children. You're a little weird. That's why I fell in love with you, and that's why I let you go so readily. I loved you because you were different, crazy, original, exciting. You would do *anything*. But you're no family man."

He sat in silence, thinking about what she had said, while she drove. It was meant kindly, and for that he was warmly grateful; but was it true? He thought not. I don't want a house in the suburbs, he thought, but I'd like a home: maybe a villa in Morocco or a loft in Greenwich Village or a penthouse in Rome. I don't want a wife to be my housekeeper, cooking and cleaning and shopping and taking the minutes at the PTA; but I'd like a companion, someone to share books and movies and poetry with, someone to talk to at night. I'd even like to have kids, and raise them to know about something more than Michael Jackson.

He did not say any of this to Gill.

She stopped the car and he realized they were outside the Eastern terminal. He looked at his watch: eight fifty. If he hurried he would get on the nine o'clock shuttle. "Thanks for the ride," he said.

"What you need is a woman like you, one of your kind," Gill said.

Ellis thought of Jane. "I met one, once."

"What happened?"

"She married a handsome doctor."

"Is the doctor crazy like you?"

"I don't think so."

"Then it won't last. When did she get married?"

"About a year ago."

"Ah." Gill was probably figuring that that was when Ellis had come back into Petal's life in a big way; but she had the grace not to say so. "Take my advice," she said. "Check her out."

Ellis got out of the car. "Talk to you soon."

"Bye."

He slammed the door and she drove off.

Ellis hurried into the building. He made the flight with a minute or two to spare. As the plane took off he found a newsmagazine in the seat pocket in front of him and looked for a report from Afghanistan.

He had been following the war closely since he had heard, from Bill in Paris, that Jane had carried out her intention of going there with Jean-Pierre. The war was no longer front-page news. Often a week or two would go by with no reports about it at all. But now the winter lull was over and there was something in the press at least once a week.

This magazine had an analysis of the Russian situation in Afghanistan. Ellis began it mistrustfully, for he knew that many such articles in newsmagazines emanated from the CIA: a reporter would get an exclusive briefing on the CIA's intelligence appraisal of some situation, but in fact he would be the unconscious channel for a piece of disinformation aimed at another country's intelligence service, and the report he wrote would have no more relation to the truth than an article in *Pravda*.

However, this article seemed straight. There was a buildup of Russian troops and arms going on, it said, in preparation for a major summer offensive. This was seen by Moscow as a make-or-break summer: they *had* to crush the Resistance this year or they would be forced to reach an accommodation of some kind with the rebels. This made sense to Ellis: he would check to see what the CIA's people in Moscow were saying, but he had a feeling it would tally.

Among the crucial target areas, the article listed the Panisher Valley.

Ellis remembered Jean-Pierre talking about the Five Lions Valley. The article also mentioned Masud, the rebel leader: Ellis recalled Jean-Pierre speaking of him, too.

He looked out of the window, watching the sun set. There was no doubt, he thought with a pang of dread, that Jane was going to be in grave danger this summer.

But it was none of his business. She was married to someone else now. Anyway, there was nothing Ellis could do about it.

He looked down at his magazine, turned the page, and started reading about El Salvador. The plane roared on toward Washington. In the west the sun went down, and darkness fell.

Allen Winderman took Ellis Thaler to lunch at a seafood restaurant overlooking the Potomac River. Winderman arrived a half hour late. He was a typical Washington operator: dark gray suit, white shirt, striped tie; as smooth as a shark. As the White House was paying, Ellis ordered lobster and a glass of white wine. Winderman asked for Perrier and a salad. Everything about Winderman was too tight: his tie, his shoes, his schedule and his self-control.

Ellis was on his guard. He could not refuse such an invitation from a presidential aide, but he did not like discreet, unofficial lunches, and he did not like Allen Winderman.

Winderman got right down to business. "I want your advice," he began.

Ellis stopped him. "First of all, I need to know whether you told the Agency about our meeting." If the White House wanted to plan covert action without telling the CIA, Ellis would have nothing to do with it.

"Of course," Winderman said. "What do you know about Afghanistan?"

Ellis felt suddenly cold. Sooner or later, this is going to involve Jane, he

thought. They know about her, of course: I made no secret of it. I told Bill
in Paris I was going to ask her to marry me. I called Bill subsequently to find
out whether she really did go to Afghanistan. All that went down on my
file. Now this bastard knows about her, and he's going to use his knowledge.
"I know a little about it," he said cautiously, and then he recalled a verse of
Kipling, and recited it:

> When you're wounded an' left on Afghanistan's plains,
> An' the women come out to cut up your remains,
> Just roll to your rifle an' blow out your brains,
> An' go to your Gawd like a soldier.

Winderman looked ill at ease for the first time. "After two years of pos-
ing as a poet you must know a lot of that stuff."

"So do the Afghans," said Ellis. "They're all poets, the way all Frenchmen are gourmets and all Welshmen are singers."

"Is that so?"

"It's because they can't read or write. Poetry is a spoken art form." Winderman was getting visibly impatient: his schedule did not allow for poetry.
Ellis went on: "The Afghans are wild, ragged, fierce mountain tribesmen,
hardly out of the Middle Ages. They're said to be elaborately polite, brave
as lions and pitilessly cruel. Their country is harsh and arid and barren.
What do you know about them?"

"There's no such thing as an Afghan," Winderman said. "There are six
million Pushtuns in the south, three million Tajiks in the west, a million
Uzbaks in the north, and another dozen or so nationalities with fewer than
a million. Modern borders mean little to them: there are Tajiks in the Soviet Union and Pushtuns in Pakistan. Some of them are divided into tribes.
They're like the Red Indians, who never thought of themselves as American, but Apache or Crow or Sioux. And they would just as soon fight one
another as fight the Russians. Our problem is to get the Apache and the
Sioux to unite against the palefaces."

"I see." Ellis nodded. He was wondering: When does Jane come into all
this? He said: "So the main question is: who will be the Big Chief?"

"That's easy. The most promising of the guerrilla leaders, by far, is
Ahmed Shah Masud, in the Panisher Valley."

The Five Lions Valley. What are you up to, you slimy bastard? Ellis studied Winderman's smooth-shaven face. The man was imperturbable. Ellis
asked: "What makes Masud so special?"

"Most of the rebel leaders are content to control their tribes, collect taxes and deny the government access to their territory. Masud does more than that. He comes out of his mountain stronghold and attacks. He's within striking distance of three strategic targets: the capital city, Kabul; the Salang tunnel, on the only highway from Kabul to the Soviet Union; and Bagram, the principal military air base. He's in a position to inflict major damage, and he does. He has studied the art of guerrilla warfare. He's read Mao. He's easily the best military brain in the country. And he has finance. Emeralds are mined in his valley and sold in Pakistan: Masud takes a ten percent tax on all sales and uses the money to fund his army. He's twenty-eight years old, and charismatic—the people worship him. Finally, he's a Tajik. The largest group is the Pushtuns, and all the others hate *them*, so the leader can't be a Pushtun. Tajiks are the next biggest nation. There's a chance they might unite under a Tajik."

"And we want to facilitate this?"

"That's right. The stronger the rebels are, the more damage they do to the Russians. Furthermore, a triumph for the U.S. intelligence community would be very useful this year."

It was of no consequence to Winderman and his kind that the Afghans were fighting for their freedom against a brutal invader, Ellis thought. Morality was out of fashion in Washington: the power game was all that mattered. If Winderman had been born in Leningrad instead of Los Angeles, he would have been just as happy, just as successful and just as powerful, and he would have used just the same tactics fighting for the other side. "What do you want from me?" Ellis asked him.

"I want to pick your brain. Is there any way an undercover agent could promote an alliance between the different Afghan tribes?"

"I expect so," said Ellis. The food came, interrupting him and giving him a few moments to think. When the waiter had gone away, he said: "It should be possible, provided there is something *they* want from *us*—and I imagine that would be weapons."

"Right." Winderman started to eat, hesitantly, like a man who has an ulcer. Between small mouthfuls he said: "At the moment they buy their weapons across the border in Pakistan. All they can get there is copies of Victorian British rifles—or, if not copies, the genuine damned article, a hundred years old and still firing. They also steal Kalashnikovs from dead Russian soldiers. But they're desperate for small artillery—antiaircraft guns and hand-launched ground-to-air missiles—so they can shoot down planes and helicopters."

"Are we willing to give them these weapons?"

"Yes. Not directly—we would want to conceal our involvement by sending them through intermediaries. But that's no problem. We could use the Saudis."

"Okay." Ellis swallowed some lobster. It was good. "Let me say what I think is the first step. In each guerrilla group you need a nucleus of men who know, understand and trust Masud. That nucleus then becomes the liaison group for communications with Masud. They build their role gradually: exchange of information first, then mutual cooperation, and finally coordinated battle plans."

"Sounds good," said Winderman. "How might that be set up?"

"I'd have Masud run a training scheme in the Five Lions Valley. Each rebel group would send a few young men to fight alongside Masud for a while and learn the methods that make him so successful. They would also learn to respect him and trust him, if he is as good a leader as you say."

Winderman nodded thoughtfully. "That's the kind of proposal that might be acceptable to tribal leaders who would reject any plan that committed them to take orders from Masud."

"Is there one rival leader in particular whose cooperation is essential to any alliance?"

"Yes. In fact there are two: Jahan Kamil and Amal Azizi, both Pushtuns."

"Then I would send in an undercover agent with the objective of getting the two of them around a table with Masud. When he came back with all three signatures on a piece of paper, we would send the first load of rocket launchers. Further consignments would depend on how well the training program was going."

Winderman put down his fork and lit a cigarette. He definitely has an ulcer, Ellis thought. Winderman said: "This is exactly the kind of thing I had in mind." Ellis could see he was already figuring out how to take the credit for the idea. By tomorrow he would be saying *We cooked up a scheme over lunch* and his written report would read *Covert action specialists assessed my scheme as viable.* "What's the downside risk?"

Ellis considered. "If the Russians caught the agent, they could get considerable propaganda value out of the whole thing. At the moment they have what the White House would call 'an image problem' in Afghanistan. Their allies in the Third World don't enjoy watching them overrun a small primitive country. Their Muslim friends, in particular, tend to sympathize with the rebels. Now, the Russians' line is that the so-called rebels are just bandits, financed and armed by the CIA. They would just love to be able to prove it by catching a real live CIA spook right there in the country and putting him on trial. In terms of global politics, I imagine that could do us a lot of damage."

"What are the chances that the Russians would catch our man?"

"Slender. If they can't catch Masud, why would they be able to catch an undercover agent sent to meet Masud?"

"Good." Winderman stubbed out his cigarette. "I want you to be that agent."

Ellis was taken by surprise. He should have seen this coming, he realized, but he had been engrossed in the problem. "I don't do that stuff anymore," he said, but his voice sounded thick and he could not help thinking: I would see Jane. I would see Jane!

"I talked to your boss on the phone," Winderman said. "His opinion was that an assignment in Afghanistan might tempt you back into fieldwork."

So it was a setup. The White House wanted to achieve something dramatic in Afghanistan, so they asked the CIA to lend them an agent. The CIA wanted Ellis to work in the field again, so they told the White House to offer him this assignment, knowing or suspecting that the prospect of meeting up with Jane again was almost irresistible.

Ellis hated to be manipulated.

But he wanted to go to the Five Lions Valley.

There had been a long silence. Winderman said impatiently: "Will you do it?"

"I'll think about it," Ellis replied.

Ellis's father belched quietly, begged pardon and said: "That was good."

Ellis pushed away his dish of cherry pie and whipped cream. He was having to watch his weight for the first time in his life. "Real good, Mom, but I can't eat any more," he said apologetically.

"Nobody eats like they used to," she said. She stood up and began clearing away. "It's because they go everywhere in cars."

His father pushed back his chair. "I've got some figures to look over."

"You *still* don't have an accountant?" Ellis said.

"Nobody takes care of your money as well as you do," his father said. "You'll find that out if you ever make any." He left the room, heading for his den.

Ellis helped his mother clear away. The family had moved into this four-bedroom house in Teaneck, New Jersey, when Ellis was thirteen, but

he could remember the move as if it were yesterday. It had been anticipated literally for years. His father had built the house, on his own at
first, later using employees of his growing construction business, but always doing the work in slack periods and leaving it when business was
good. When they moved in, it was not really finished: the heating did
not work, there were no cupboards in the kitchen and nothing had been
painted. They got hot water the following day only because Mom threatened divorce otherwise. But it got finished eventually, and Ellis and his
brothers and sisters all had room to grow up in it. It was bigger than Mom
and Dad needed now, but he hoped they would keep it. It had a good feel
about it.

When they had loaded the dishwasher he said: "Mom, do you remember that suitcase I left here when I came back from Asia?"

"Sure. It's in the closet in the small bedroom."

"Thanks. I want to look through it."

"Go on, then. I'll finish up here."

Ellis climbed the stairs and went to the little bedroom at the top of the
house. It was rarely used, and around the single bed were crowded a couple
of broken chairs, an old sofa and four or five cardboard boxes containing
children's books and toys. Ellis opened the cupboard and took out a small
black plastic suitcase. He laid it on the bed, turned the combination locks
and lifted the lid. There was a musty smell: it had not been opened for a
decade. Everything was there: the medals; both the bullets they had taken
out of him; Army Field Manual FM 5-31, entitled *Booby Traps*; a picture of
Ellis standing beside a helicopter, his first Huey, grinning, looking young
and (*oh, shit*) thin; a note from Frankie Amalfi which said *To the bastard that
stole my leg*—a brave joke, for Ellis had gently untied Frankie's lace, then
tugged at his boot and pulled away his foot and half his leg, severed at the
knee by a wildly flexing rotor blade; Jimmy Jones's watch, stopped forever
at half past five—*You keep it, son*, Jimmy's father had said to Ellis through
an alcoholic haze, *'cause you were his frien', and that's more than I ever wuz*;
and the diary.

He leafed through the pages. He only had to read a few words to recall a
whole day, a week, a battle. The journal began cheerfully, with a sense of adventure, and very self-consciously; and it got progressively disenchanted,
somber, bleak, despairing and eventually suicidal. The grim phrases brought
vivid scenes to his mind: *goddam Arvins wouldn't get out of the helicopter, if
they're so keen to be rescued from Communism how come they don't fight?* and
then *Capt. Johnson always was an A. hole I guess but what a way to die, grenaded*

by one of his own men, and later *The women have rifles up their skirts and the kids have grenades in their shirts so what the fuck are we supposed to do, surrender?* The last entry read *What is wrong with this war is that we are on the wrong side. We are the bad guys. That is why kids dodge the draft; that is why the Vietnamese won't fight; that is why we kill women and children; that is why the generals lie to the politicians, and the politicians lie to the reporters, and the newspapers lie to the public.* After that, his thoughts had become too seditious to be committed to paper, his guilt too great to be expiated by mere words. It seemed to him that he would have to spend the rest of his life righting the wrongs he had done in that war. After all these years it still seemed that way. When he added up the murderers he had jailed since then, the kidnappers and the hijackers and the bombers he had arrested, they were as nothing when balanced against the tons of explosives he had dropped and the thousands of rounds of ammunition he had fired in Vietnam, Laos and Cambodia.

It was irrational, he knew. He had realized that when he came back from Paris and reflected for a while on how his job had ruined his life. He had decided to stop trying to redeem the sins of America. But this . . . this was different. Here was a chance to fight for the little guy, to fight against the lying generals and the power brokers and the blinkered journalists—a chance not just to fight, not just to pay a small contribution, but to make a real difference, to change the course of a war, to alter the fate of a country, and to strike a blow for freedom on a big scale.

And then there was Jane.

The mere possibility of seeing her again had rekindled his passion. Just a few days ago he had been able to think of her and the danger she was in, and then put the thought out of his mind and turn the page of the magazine. Now he could hardly stop thinking about her. He wondered whether her hair was long or short, was she fatter or thinner, did she feel good about what she was doing with her life, did the Afghans like her, and—most of all—did she still love Jean-Pierre? *Take my advice*, Gill had said; *check her out.* Clever Gill.

Finally he thought about Petal. I tried, he said to himself; I really tried, and I don't think I handled it too badly—I think it was a doomed project. Gill and Bernard give her all she needs. There is no room for me in her life. She's happy without me.

He closed the diary and returned it to the case. Next he took out a small, cheap jeweler's box. Inside was a small pair of gold earrings, each with a pearl in the center. The woman they had been intended for, a slant-eyed girl with small breasts who had taught him that nothing is taboo, had died—killed by a drunken soldier in a Saigon bar—before he gave them to her. He had not loved her: he had just liked her and felt grateful to her. The earrings were to have been a farewell gift.

He took a plain card and a pen from his shirt pocket. He thought for a minute, then wrote:

> *To Petal—*
> *Yes, you can have them pierced.*
> *With love from Daddy*

CHAPTER SIX

T he Five Lions River was never warm, but it seemed a little less cold now, in the balmy evening air at the end of a dusty day, when the women came down to their own exclusive stretch of the bank to bathe. Jane gritted her teeth against the chill and waded into the water with the others, lifting her dress inch by inch as it got deeper, until it was up to her waist; then she began to wash: after long practice she had mastered the peculiar Afghan skill of getting clean all over without undressing.

When she had finished she came out of the river, shivering, and stood near Zahara, who was washing her hair in a pool with much splashing and spluttering, and at the same time carrying on a boisterous conversation. Zahara dipped her head in the water one more time, then reached for her towel. She scrabbled around in a hollow in the sandy earth, but the towel was not there. "Where's my towel?" she yelled. "I put it in this hole. Who stole it?"

Jane picked up the towel from behind Zahara and said: "Here it is. You put it in the wrong hole."

"That's what the mullah's wife said!" Zahara shouted, and the others shrieked with laughter.

Jane was now accepted by the village women as one of them. The last vestiges of reserve or wariness had vanished after the birth of Chantal, which seemed to have confirmed that Jane was a woman like any other.

The talk at the riverside was surprisingly frank—perhaps because the children were left behind in the care of older sisters and grandmothers, but more probably because of Zahara. Her loud voice, her flashing eyes and her rich, throaty laughter dominated the scene. No doubt she was all the more extroverted here for having to repress her personality the rest of the day. She had a vulgar sense of humor, which Jane had not come across in any other Afghan, male or female, and Zahara's ribald remarks and double-meaning jokes often opened the way for serious discussion. Consequently Jane was sometimes able to turn the evening bathing session into an impromptu health education class. Birth control was the most popular topic, although the women of Banda were more interested in how to ensure pregnancy than how to prevent it. However, there was some sympathy for the idea, which Jane was trying to promote, that a woman was better able to feed and care for her children if they were born two years apart rather than every twelve or fifteen months. Yesterday they had talked about the menstrual cycle, and it transpired that Afghan women thought the fertile time was just before and just after the period. Jane had told them that it was from the twelfth day to the sixteenth, and they appeared to accept this, but she had a disconcerting suspicion that they thought *she* was wrong and were too polite to say so.

Today there was an air of excitement. The latest Pakistan convoy was due back. The men would bring small luxuries—a shawl, some oranges, plastic bangles—as well as the all-important guns, ammunition and explosives for the war.

Zahara's husband, Ahmed Gul, one of the sons of the midwife Rabia, was leader of the convoy, and Zahara was visibly excited at the prospect of seeing him again. When they were together they were like all Afghan couples: she silent and subservient, he casually imperious. But Jane could tell, by the way they looked at one another, that they were in love; and it was clear from the way Zahara talked that their love was highly physical. Today she was almost beside herself with desire, rubbing her hair dry with fierce, frantic energy. Jane sympathized: she had felt that ways herself sometimes. No doubt she and Zahara had become friends because each recognized a kindred spirit in the other.

Jane's skin dried almost immediately in the warm, dusty air. It was now the height of summer, and every day was long, dry and hot. The good weather would last a month or two longer, and then for the rest of the year it would be bitterly cold.

Zahara was still interested in yesterday's topic of conversation. She stopped rubbing her hair for a moment to say: "Whatever anyone says, the way to get pregnant is to Do It every day."

There was agreement from Halima, the sullen, dark-eyed wife of Mohammed Khan. "And the only way *not* to get pregnant is *never* to Do It." She had four children, but only one of them—Mousa—was a boy, and she had been disappointed to learn that Jane knew of no way to improve one's chances of having a boy.

Zahara said: "But then, what do you say to your husband when he comes home after six weeks with a convoy?"

Jane said: "Be like the mullah's wife, and put it in the wrong hole."

Zahara roared with laughter. Jane smiled. That was a birth control technique which had not been mentioned in her crash courses in Paris, but it was clear that modern methods would not arrive in the Five Lions Valley for many years yet, so traditional means would have to serve—helped, perhaps, by a little education.

The talk turned to the harvest. The Valley was a sea of golden wheat and bearded barley, but much of it would rot in the fields, for the young men were away fighting most of the time and the older ones found it slow work reaping by moonlight. Toward the end of the summer all the families would add up their sacks of flour and baskets of dried fruit, look at their chickens and goats, and count their pennies; and they would contemplate the coming shortages of eggs and meat, and hazard a guess at this winter's prices for rice and yogurt; and some of them would pack a few precious possessions and make the long trek across the mountains to set up new homes in the refugee camps of Pakistan, as the shopkeeper had, along with millions of other Afghans.

Jane feared that the Russians would make this evacuation their policy—that, unable to defeat the guerrillas, they would try to destroy the communities within which the guerrillas lived, as the Americans had in Vietnam, by carpet bombing whole areas of the countryside, so that the Five Lions Valley would become an uninhabited wasteland, and Mohammed and Zahara and Rabia would join the homeless, stateless, aimless occupants of the camps. The rebels could not begin to resist an all-out blitzkrieg, for they had virtually no antiaircraft weapons.

It was getting dark. The women began to drift back to the village. Jane walked with Zahara, half listening to the talk and thinking about Chantal. Her feelings about the baby had gone through several stages. Immediately after the birth she had felt exhilarated by relief, triumph and joy, at having produced a living, perfect baby. When the reaction set in she had felt utterly miserable. She had not known how to look after a baby, and contrary to what people said, she had no instinctive knowledge at all. She had been frightened of the baby. There had been no gush of maternal love. Instead she had suffered weird and terrifying dreams and fantasies in which the baby died—dropped in the river, or killed by a bomb, or stolen away in the night by the snow tiger. She still had not told Jean-Pierre about these thoughts in case he should think her mad.

There had been conflicts with her midwife, Rabia Gul. She said women should not breast-feed for the first three days, because what came out was not milk. Jane decided it was ludicrous to believe that nature would make women's breasts produce something that was bad for newborn babies, and she ignored the old woman's advice. Rabia also said the baby should not be washed for forty days, but Chantal was bathed every day like any other Western baby. Then Jane had caught Rabia giving Chantal butter mixed with sugar, feeding the stuff to the child on the end of her wrinkled old finger; and Jane had got cross. The next day Rabia went to attend another birth, and sent one of her many granddaughters, a thirteen-year-old called Fara, to help Jane. This was a great improvement. Fara had no preconceptions about child care and simply did as she was told. She required no pay: she worked for her food—which was better at Jane's house than at Fara's parents'—and for the privilege of learning about babies in preparation for her own marriage, which would probably take place within a year or two. Jane also thought Rabia might be grooming Fara as a future midwife, in which case the girl would gain kudos from having helped the Western nurse care for her baby.

With Rabia out of the way, Jean-Pierre had come into his own. He was gentle yet confident with Chantal, and considerate and loving with Jane. It was he who had suggested, rather firmly, that Chantal could be given boiled goat's milk when she woke in the night, and he had improvised a feeding bottle from his medical supplies so that he could be the one to get up. Of course Jane always woke when Chantal cried, and stayed awake while Jean-Pierre fed her; but this was much less tiring, and at last she got rid of that feeling of utter, despairing exhaustion which had been so depressing.

Finally, although she was still anxious and unself-confident, she had found within herself a degree of patience she had never previously possessed; and this, though it was not the deep instinctive knowledge and assurance she had been hoping for, nevertheless enabled her to confront the daily crises with equanimity. Even now, she realized, she had been away from Chantal for almost an hour without worrying.

The group of women reached the cluster of houses which formed the nucleus of the village, and one by one they disappeared behind the mud walls of their courtyards. Jane scared off a flurry of chickens and shoved aside a scrawny cow to get into her own house. Inside, she found Fara singing to Chantal in the lamplight. The baby was alert and wide-eyed, apparently fascinated by the sound of the girl's singing. It was a lullaby with simple words and a complex, Oriental-sounding tune. She's such a *pretty* baby, Jane thought, with her fat cheeks and her tiny nose and her blue, blue eyes.

She sent Fara to make tea. The girl was terribly shy and had arrived in fear and trembling to work for the foreigners; but her nervousness was easing, and her initial awe of Jane was gradually turning into something more like adoring loyalty.

A few minutes later Jean-Pierre came in. His baggy cotton trousers and shirt were grimy and bloodstained, and there was dust in his long brown hair and his dark beard. He looked tired. He had been to Khenj, a village ten miles down the Valley, to treat the survivors of a bombing raid. Jane stood on tiptoe to kiss him. "How was it?" she said in French.

"Bad." He gave her a squeeze, then went to lean over Chantal. "Hello, little one." He smiled, and Chantal gurgled.

"What happened?" Jane asked.

"It was a family whose house was some distance from the rest of the village, so they thought they were safe," Jean-Pierre shrugged. "Then some wounded guerrillas were brought in from a skirmish farther south. That's why I'm so late." He sat down on a pile of cushions. "Is there any tea?"

"It's coming," Jane said. "What kind of skirmish?"

He closed his eyes. "Usual thing. The army came in helicopters and occupied a village for reasons known only to themselves. The villagers fled. The menfolk regrouped, got reinforcements and started to harry the Russians from the hillsides. Casualties on both sides. The guerrillas finally ran out of ammunition and withdrew."

Jane nodded. She felt sorry for Jean-Pierre: it was a depressing task to tend the victims of a pointless battle. Banda had never been raided, but she lived in constant fear of it—she had a nightmare vision of herself running, running, with Chantal clutched to her, while the helicopters beat the air above and the machine-gun bullets thudded into the dusty ground at her feet.

Fara came in with hot green tea, some of the flat bread they called *nan*, and a stone jar of new butter. Jane and Jean-Pierre began to eat. The butter was a rare treat. Their evening *nan* was usually dipped in yogurt, curds or oil. At midday they normally ate rice with a meat-flavored sauce that might or might not have meat in it. Once a week they had chicken or goat. Jane, eating for two still, indulged in the luxury of an egg every day. At this time of year there was plenty of fresh fruit—apricots, plums, apples, and mulberries by the sackful—for dessert. Jane felt very healthy on this diet, although most English people would have considered it starvation rations, and some Frenchmen would have thought it reason for suicide. She smiled at her husband. "A little more Béarnaise sauce with your steak?"

"No, thank you." He held out his cup. "Perhaps another drop of the Château Cheval-Blanc." Jane gave him more tea, and he pretended to taste it as if it were wine, chewing and gargling. "The nineteen sixty-two is an underrated vintage, following as it did the unforgettable sixty-one, but I have always felt that its relative amiability and impeccable good manners give almost as much pleasure as the perfection of elegance which is the austere mark of its highbrow predecessor."

Jane grinned. He was beginning to feel like himself again.

Chantal cried, and Jane felt an immediate answering twinge in her breasts. She picked up the baby and began to feed her. Jean-Pierre carried on eating. Jane said: "Leave some butter for Fara."

"Okay." He took the remains of their supper outside, and returned with a bowl of mulberries. Jane ate while Chantal suckled. Soon the baby fell asleep, but Jane knew she would wake again in a few minutes and want more.

Jean-Pierre pushed away the bowl and said: "I got another complaint about you today."

"From whom?" Jane said sharply.

Jean-Pierre looked defensive but stubborn. "Mohammed Khan."

"But he wasn't speaking for himself."

"Perhaps not."

"What did he say?"

"That you have been teaching the village women to be barren."

Jane sighed. It was not just the stupidity of the village menfolk that annoyed her, but also Jean-Pierre's accommodating attitude to their complaints. She wanted him to defend her, not defer to her accusers. "Abdullah Karim is behind it, of course," she said. The mullah's wife was often at the riverside, and no doubt she reported to her husband everything she heard.

"You may have to stop," said Jean-Pierre.

"Stop what?" Jane could hear the dangerous tone in her own voice.

"Telling them how to avoid pregnancy."

That was not a fair description of what Jane taught the women, but she was not willing to defend herself or apologize. "Why should I stop?" she said.

"It's creating difficulties," said Jean-Pierre with a patient air that irritated Jane. "If we offend the mullah grievously we may have to leave Afghanistan. More important, it would give the Médecins pour la Liberté organization a bad name, and the rebels might refuse other doctors. This is a holy war, you know—spiritual health is more important than the physical kind. They could decide to do without us."

There were other organizations sending idealistic young French doctors to Afghanistan, but Jane did not say that. Instead she said flatly: "We'll just have to take that risk."

"Shall we?" he said, and she could see that he was getting angry. "And why should we?"

"Because there is really only one thing of permanent value that we can give these people, and that is information. It's all very well to patch their wounds and give them drugs to kill germs, but they will never have enough surgeons or enough drugs. We can improve their health permanently by teaching them basic nutrition, hygiene and health care. Better to offend Abdullah than to stop doing that."

"Still, I wish you hadn't made an enemy of that man."

"He hit me with a stick!" Jane shouted furiously. Chantal began to cry. Jane forced herself to be calm. She rocked Chantal for a moment, then began to feed her. Why couldn't Jean-Pierre see how cowardly his attitude was? How could he be intimidated by the threat of expulsion from this godforsaken country? Jane sighed. Chantal turned her face away from Jane's breast and made discontented noises. Before the argument could continue they heard distant shouting.

Jean-Pierre frowned, listening, then got up. A man's voice came from their courtyard. Jean-Pierre picked up a shawl and draped it over Jane's shoulders. She pulled it together in the front. This was a compromise: it was not really sufficient covering, by Afghan standards, but she refused point-blank to scuttle out of the room like a second-class citizen if a man walked into her house while she was feeding her baby; and anyone who objected, she had announced, had better not come to see the doctor.

Jean-Pierre called out in Dari: "Come in."

It was Mohammed Khan. Jane was in a mood to tell him just what she thought of him and the rest of the village men, but she hesitated when she saw the strain on his handsome face. For once he hardly looked at her. "The convoy was ambushed," he said without preamble. "We lost twenty-seven men—and all the supplies."

Jane closed her eyes in pain. She had traveled with such a convoy when she first came to the Five Lions Valley, and she could not help but picture the ambush: the moonlit line of brown-skinned men and scrawny horses stretched out unevenly along a stony trail through a narrow, shadowy valley; the beat of the rotor blades in a sudden crescendo; the flares, the grenades, the machine-gun fire; the panic as the men tried to take cover on the bare hillside; the hopeless shots fired at the invulnerable helicopters; and then at last the shouts of the wounded and the screams of the dying.

She thought suddenly of Zahara: her husband had been with the convoy. "What—what about Ahmed Gul?"

"He came back."

"Oh, thank God," Jane breathed.

"But he's wounded."

"Who from this village died?"

"None. Banda was lucky. My brother, Matullah, is all right, and so is Al-ishan Karim, the brother of the mullah. There are three other survivors—two of them wounded."

Jean-Pierre said: "I'll come right away." He stepped into the front room of the house, the room that had once been the shop, and then the clinic, and was now the medical storeroom.

Jane put Chantal down in her makeshift cradle in the corner and hastily tidied herself up. Jean-Pierre would probably need her help, and if he did not, then Zahara could use some sympathy.

Mohammed said: "We have almost no ammunition."

Jane felt little regret about that. She was revolted by the war, and she would shed no tears if the rebels were obliged for a while to stop killing poor miserable homesick seventeen-year-old Russian soldier boys.

Mohammed went on: "We have lost four convoys in a year. Only three got through."

"How are the Russians able to find them?" asked Jane.

Jean-Pierre, who was listening in the next room, spoke through the open doorway. "They must have intensified their surveillance of the passes by low-flying helicopters—or perhaps even by satellite photography."

Mohammed shook his head. "The Pushtuns betray us."

Jane thought this was possible. In the villages through which they passed, the convoys were sometimes seen as a magnet for Russian raids, and it was conceivable that some villagers might buy their safety by telling the Russians where the convoys were—although it was not clear to Jane just how they would pass the information to the Russians.

She thought of what she had been hoping for from the ambushed convoy. She had asked for more antibiotics, some hypodermic needles and a lot of sterile dressings. Jean-Pierre had written out a long list of drugs. The organization *Médecins pour la Liberté* had a liaison man in Peshawar, the city in northwest Pakistan where the guerrillas bought their weapons. He might have got the basic supplies locally, but he would have had the drugs flown from Western Europe. What a waste. It might be months before replacements arrived. In Jane's view that was a far greater loss than the ammunition.

Jean-Pierre came back in, carrying his bag. The three of them went out into the courtyard. It was dark. Jane paused to give instructions to Fara about changing Chantal, then hurried after the two men.

She caught up with them as they approached the mosque. It was not an impressive building. It had none of the gorgeous colors or exquisite decoration familiar from coffee-table books about Islamic art. It was an open-sided building, its mat roof supported by stone columns, and Jane thought it looked like a glorified bus shelter, or perhaps the veranda of a ruined colonial mansion. An archway through the middle of the building led to a walled yard. The villagers treated it with small reverence. They prayed there, but they also used it as a meeting hall, marketplace, schoolroom and guest house. And tonight it would be a hospital.

Oil lamps suspended from hooks in the stone columns now lit the verandalike mosque building. The villagers formed a crowd to the left of the archway. They were subdued: several women were sobbing quietly, and the voices of two men could be heard, one asking questions and the other answering. The crowd parted to admit Jean-Pierre, Mohammed and Jane.

The six survivors of the ambush were huddled in a group on the beaten-earth floor. The three uninjured ones squatted on their haunches, still wearing their round Chitrali caps, looking dirty, dispirited and exhausted. Jane recognized Matullah Khan, a younger version of his brother, Mohammed; and Alishan Karim, thinner than his brother the mullah, but just as mean-looking. Two of the wounded men sat on the floor with their backs to the wall, one with a filthy, bloodstained bandage around his head and the other with his arm in an improvised sling. Jane did not know either of them. She automatically assessed their wounds: at first glance they appeared slight.

The third injured man, Ahmed Gul, was lying flat on a stretcher made from two sticks and a blanket. His eyes were closed and his skin was gray. His wife, Zahara, squatted behind him, cradling his head in her lap, stroking his hair and weeping silently. Jane could not see his wounds, but she could tell they must be serious.

Jean-Pierre called for a table, hot water and towels, then got down on his knees beside Ahmed. After a few seconds he looked up at the other guerrillas and said in Dari: "Was he in an explosion?"

"The helicopters had rockets," said one of the uninjured. "One went off beside him."

Jean-Pierre reverted to French and spoke to Jane: "He's in a bad way. It's a miracle he survived the journey."

Jane could see bloodstains on Ahmed's chin: he had been coughing blood, a sign that he had internal injuries.

Zahara looked pleadingly at Jane. "How is he?" she asked in Dari.

"I'm sorry, my friend," answered Jane as gently as she could. "He's bad."

Zahara nodded resignedly: she had known it, but the confirmation brought fresh tears to her handsome face.

Jean-Pierre said to Jane: "Check the others for me—I don't want to lose a minute here."

Jane examined the other two wounded men. "The head wound is just a scratch," she said after a moment.

"Deal with it," said Jean-Pierre. He was supervising the lifting of Ahmed onto a table.

She looked at the man with his arm in a sling. He was more seriously hurt: it looked as if a bullet had smashed a bone. "This must have hurt," she said to the guerrilla in Dari. He grinned and nodded. These men were made of cast iron. "The bullet broke the bone," she said to Jean-Pierre.

Jean-Pierre did not look up from Ahmed. "Give him a local anesthetic, clean the wound, take out the bits and give him a clean sling. We'll set the bone later."

She began to prepare the injection. When Jean-Pierre needed her assistance he would call. It looked as if it might be a long night.

Ahmed died a few minutes after midnight, and Jean-Pierre felt like crying—not with sadness, for he hardly knew Ahmed, but with sheer frustration, for he knew he could have saved the man's life, if only he had had an anesthetist and electricity and an operating theater.

He covered the dead man's face, then looked at the wife, who had been standing motionless, watching, for hours. "I'm sorry," he said to her. She nodded. He was glad she was calm. Sometimes they accused him of not trying everything: they seemed to think he knew so much that there was nothing he couldn't cure, and he wanted to scream *I am not God* at them; but this one seemed to understand.

He turned away from the corpse. He was weary to his bones. He had been working on mangled bodies all day, but this was the first patient he had lost. The people who had been watching him, mostly relatives of the dead man, came forward now to deal with the body. The widow began to wail, and Jane led her away.

Jean-Pierre felt a hand on his shoulder. He turned to see Mohammed, the guerrilla who organized the convoys. He felt a stab of guilt.

Mohammed said: "It's the will of Allah."

Jean-Pierre nodded. Mohammed took out a pack of Pakistani cigarettes and lit one. Jean-Pierre began to gather up his instruments and put them into his bag. Without looking at Mohammed he said: "What will you do now?"

"Send another convoy immediately," Mohammed said. "We must have ammunition."

Jean-Pierre was suddenly alert, despite his fatigue. "Do you want to look at the maps?"

"Yes."

Jean-Pierre closed his bag, and the two men walked away from the mosque. The stars illuminated their way through the village to the shopkeeper's house. In the living room, Fara was asleep on a rug beside Chantal's cradle. She awoke instantly and stood up. "You can go home now," Jean-Pierre told her. She left without speaking.

Jean-Pierre put his bag down on the floor, then picked up the cradle gently and carried it into the bedroom. Chantal stayed asleep until he put the cradle down; then she began to cry. "Now what is it?" he murmured to her. He looked at his wristwatch and realized she probably wanted feeding. "Mama's coming soon," he told her. This had no effect. He lifted her out of the cradle and began to rock her. She became quiet. He carried her back into the living room.

Mohammed was standing, waiting. Jean-Pierre said: "You know where they are."

Mohammed nodded and opened a painted wooden chest. He took out a thick bundle of folded maps, selected several and spread them on the floor.

Jean-Pierre rocked Chantal and looked over Mohammed's shoulder. "Where was the ambush?" he asked.

Mohammed pointed to a spot near the city of Jalalabad.

The trails followed by Mohammed's convoys were not shown on these or any other maps. However, Jean-Pierre's maps showed some of the valleys, plateaus and seasonal streams where there *might* be trails. Sometimes Mohammed knew from memory what was there. Sometimes he had to guess, and he would discuss with Jean-Pierre the precise interpretation of contour lines or the more obscure terrain features such as moraines.

Jean-Pierre suggested: "You could swing more to the north around Jalalabad." Above the plain in which the city stood, there was a maze of valleys like a cobweb stretched between the Konar and Nuristan rivers.

Mohammed lit another cigarette—like most of the guerrillas, he was a heavy smoker—and shook his head dubiously as he exhaled. "There have been too many ambushes in that area," he said. "If they are not betraying us already they soon will. No, the next convoy will swing *south* of Jalalabad."

Jean-Pierre frowned. "I don't see how that's possible. To the south, there's nothing but open country all the way from the Khyber Pass. You'd be spotted."

"We won't use the Khyber Pass," said Mohammed. He put his finger on the map, then traced the Afghanistan-Pakistan border southward. "We will cross the border at Teremengal." His finger reached the town he had named, then traced a route from there to the Five Lions Valley.

Jean-Pierre nodded, hiding his jubilation. "It makes a lot of sense. When will the new convoy leave here?"

Mohammed began to fold up the charts. "The day after tomorrow. There is no time to lose." He replaced the maps in the painted chest, then went to the door.

Jane came in just as he was leaving. He said, "Good night," to her in an absentminded way. Jean-Pierre was glad the handsome guerrilla no longer had the hots for Jane since her pregnancy. She was definitely oversexed, in Jean-Pierre's opinion, and quite capable of letting herself be seduced; and for her to have an affair with an Afghan would have caused endless trouble.

Jean-Pierre's medical bag was on the floor, where he had left it, and Jane bent down to pick it up. His heart missed a beat. He took the bag from her quickly. She gave him a mildly surprised look. "I'll put this away," he said. "You see to Chantal. She needs feeding." He gave the baby to her.

He carried the bag and a lamp into the front room as Jane settled down to feed Chantal. Cartons of medical supplies were stacked on the dirt floor.

Already-opened boxes were arranged on the shopkeeper's crude wooden shelves. Jean-Pierre put his medical bag on the blue tiled counter and took out a black plastic object about the size and shape of a portable telephone. This he put in his pocket.

He emptied his bag, putting the instruments for sterilization to one side and stowing the unused items on the shelves.

He returned to the living room. "I'm going down to the river to bathe," he said to Jane. "I'm too dirty to go to bed."

She gave him the dreamy, contented smile she often wore when feeding the baby. "Be quick," she said.

He went out.

The village was going to sleep, at last. Lamps still burned in a few houses, and he heard from one window the sound of a woman weeping bitterly, but most places were quiet and dark. Passing the last house in the village, he heard a woman's voice raised in a high, mournful song of bereavement, and for a moment he felt the crushing weight of the deaths he had caused; then he put the thought out of his mind.

He followed a stony path between two barley fields, looking around constantly and listening carefully: the men of the village would now be at work. In one field he heard the hiss of scythes, and on a narrow terrace he saw two men weeding by lamplight. He did not speak to them.

He reached the river, crossed the ford and climbed the winding path up the opposite cliff. He knew he was quite safe, yet he felt increasingly tense as he ascended the steep path in the faint light.

After ten minutes he reached the high point he was seeking. He took the radio from his pocket and extended its telescopic antenna. It was the latest and most sophisticated small transmitter the KGB had, but even so the terrain here was so inimical to radio transmission that the Russians had built a special relay station, on a hilltop just inside the territory they controlled, to pick up his signals and pass them on.

He pressed the TALK button and spoke in English and in code. "This is Simplex. Come in, please."

He waited, then called again.

After the third try he got a crackly, accented reply. "*Here is Butler. Go ahead, Simplex.*"

"Your party was a big success."

"*I repeat: The party was a big success,*" came the reply.

"Twenty-seven people attended and one more came later."

"*I repeat: Twenty-seven attended and one came later.*"

"In preparation for the next one, I need three camels." In code that meant "Meet me three days from today."

"*I repeat: You need three camels.*"

"I will see you at the mosque." That, too, was code: "the mosque" was a place some miles away where three valleys met.

"*I repeat: At the mosque.*"

"Today is Sunday." That was not code: it was a precaution against the possibility that the dullard who was taking all this down might not realize it was after midnight, with the consequence that Jean-Pierre's contact would arrive a day early at the rendezvous.

"*I repeat: Today is Sunday.*"

"Over and out."

Jean-Pierre collapsed the antenna and returned the radio to his pocket; then he made his way down the cliff to the riverside.

He stripped off his clothes quickly. From the pocket of the shirt he took a nailbrush and a small piece of soap. Soap was a scarce commodity, but he as doctor had priority.

He stepped gingerly into the Five Lions River, knelt down, and splashed icy water all over himself. He soaped his skin and his hair, then picked up the brush and began to scrub himself: his legs, his belly, his chest, his face, his arms and his hands. He worked especially hard on his hands, soaping them again and again. Kneeling in the shallows, naked and shivering beneath the stars, he scrubbed and scrubbed as if he would never stop.

CHAPTER SEVEN

"The child has measles, gastroenteritis and ringworm," said Jean-Pierre. "It is also dirty and undernourished."

"Aren't they all?" said Jane.

They were speaking French, as they normally did together, and the child's mother looked from one to the other as they spoke, wondering what they were saying. Jean-Pierre observed her anxiety and spoke to her in Dari, saying simply: "Your son will get well."

He crossed to the other side of the cave and opened his drugs case. All children brought to the clinic were automatically vaccinated against tuberculosis. As he prepared the BCG injection, he watched Jane out of the corner of his eye. She was giving the boy small sips of rehydration drink—a mixture of glucose, salt, baking soda and potassium chloride dissolved in clean water—and, between sips, was gently washing his grimy face. Her movements were quick and graceful, like those of a craftsman—a potter molding clay, perhaps, or a bricklayer wielding a trowel. He observed her narrow hands as she touched the frightened child with light, reassuring caresses. He liked her hands.

He turned away as he took the needle out, so that the child should not see it; then he held it concealed by his sleeve and turned again, waiting for Jane. He studied her face as she cleaned the skin of the boy's right shoulder and swabbed a patch with alcohol. It was an impish face, with big eyes, a turned-up nose and a wide mouth that smiled more often than not. Now her expression was serious, and she was moving her jaw from side to side, as if grinding her teeth—a sign that she was concentrating. Jean-Pierre knew all of her expressions and none of her thoughts.

He speculated often—almost continually—about what she was thinking, but he was afraid to ask her, for such conversations could so easily wander into forbidden territory. He had to be constantly on his guard, like an unfaithful husband, for fear that something he said—or even the expression on his face—might betray him. Any talk of truth and dishonesty, or trust and betrayal, or freedom and tyranny, was taboo; and so were any subjects which might lead to these, such as love, war and politics. He was wary even when talking of quite innocent topics. Consequently there was a peculiar lack of intimacy in their marriage. Making love was weird. He found that he could not reach a climax unless he closed his eyes and pretended he was somewhere else. It was a relief to him that he had not had to perform for the last few weeks because of the birth of Chantal.

"Ready when you are," Jane said, and he realized she was smiling at him.

He took the child's arm and said in Dari: "How old are you?"

"Five."

As the boy spoke, Jean-Pierre stuck the needle in. The child immediately began to wail. The sound of its voice made Jean-Pierre think of himself at the age of five, riding his first bicycle and falling off and crying just like that, a sharp howl of protest at an unexpected pain. He stared at the screwed-up face of his five-year-old patient, remembering how much it had hurt and how angry he had felt, and he found himself thinking: How did I get *here* from *there?*

He released the child and it went to its mother. He counted out thirty 250-gram capsules of griseofulvin and handed them to the woman. "Make him take one every day until they are all gone," he said in simple Dari. "Don't give them to anyone else—he needs them all." That would deal with the ringworm. The measles and the gastroenteritis would take their own course. "Keep him in bed until the spots disappear, and make sure he drinks a lot."

The woman nodded.

"Does he have any brothers and sisters?" Jean-Pierre asked.

"Five brothers and two sisters," the woman said proudly.

"He should sleep alone, or they will get sick too." The woman looked dubious: she probably had only one bed for all her children. There was nothing Jean-Pierre could do about that. He went on: "If he is not better when the tablets are finished, bring him back to me." What the child really needed was the one thing neither Jean-Pierre nor its mother could provide—plenty of good, nutritious food.

The two of them left the cave, the thin, sick child and the frail, weary mother. They had probably come several miles, she carrying the boy most of the way, and now they would walk back. The boy might die anyway. But not of tuberculosis.

There was one more patient: the *malang*. He was Banda's holy man. Half mad, and often more-than-half naked, he wandered the Five Lions Valley from Comar, twenty-five miles upstream of Banda, to Charikar in the Russian-controlled plain sixty miles to the southwest. He spoke gibberish and saw visions. The Afghans believed *malangs* to be lucky, and not only tolerated their behavior, but gave them food and drink and clothing.

He came in, wearing rags around his loins and a Russian officer's cap. He clutched his middle, miming pain. Jean-Pierre shook out a handful of diamorphine pills and gave them to him. The madman ran off, clutching his synthetic heroin tablets.

"He must be addicted to that stuff by now," Jane said. There was a distinct note of disapproval in her voice.

"He is," Jean-Pierre admitted.

"Why do you give it to him?"

"The man has an ulcer. What else should I do—operate?"

"You're the doctor."

Jean-Pierre began to pack his bag. In the morning he had to hold a clinic in Cobak, six or seven miles away across the mountains—and he had a rendezvous to keep on the way.

The crying of the five-year-old had brought an air of the past into the cave, like a smell of old toys, or a strange light that makes you rub your eyes. Jean-Pierre felt faintly disoriented by it. He kept seeing people from his childhood, their faces superimposed on the things around him, like scenes from a film cast by a misaligned projector onto the backs of the audience instead of on the screen. He saw his first teacher, the steel-rimmed Mademoiselle Médecin; Jacques Lafontaine, who had given him a bloody nose for calling him *con*; his mother, thin and ill-dressed and always distraught; and most of all his father, a big, beefy, angry man on the other side of a barred partition.

He made an effort to concentrate on the equipment and drugs he might need at Cobak. He filled a flask with purified water to drink while he was away. He would be fed by the villagers there.

He took his bags outside and loaded them onto the bad-tempered old mare he used for such trips. This animal would walk all day in a straight line but was highly reluctant to turn corners; on account of which Jane had named it Maggie, after Prime Minister Margaret Thatcher.

Jean-Pierre was ready. He went back into the cave and kissed Jane's soft mouth. As he turned to leave, Fara came in with Chantal. The baby was crying. Jane unbuttoned her shirt and put Chantal to her breast immediately. Jean-Pierre touched his daughter's pink cheek and said: "*Bon appétit.*" Then he went out.

He led Maggie down the mountain to the deserted village and headed southwest, following the riverbank. He walked quickly and tirelessly under the hot sun: he was used to it.

As he left his doctor persona behind and thought ahead to his rendezvous, he began to feel anxious. Would Anatoly be there? He might have been delayed. He might even have been captured. If captured, had he talked? Had he betrayed Jean-Pierre under torture? Would there be a party of guerrillas waiting for Jean-Pierre, merciless and sadistic and bent on revenge?

For all their poetry and their piety they were barbarians, these Afghans. Their national sport was *buzkashi,* a dangerous and bloody game: the headless body of a calf was placed in the center of a field, and two opposing teams lined up on horseback, then, at a rifle shot, they all charged toward the carcass. The aim was to pick it up, carry it to a predetermined turning point about a mile away, and bring it back to the circle without allowing any of the opposing players to wrench it from your grasp. When the grisly object got ripped apart, as often happened, a referee was there to decide which team had control of the larger remnant: Jean-Pierre had come across a game in progress last winter, just outside the town of Rokha down the Valley, and he had watched it for a few minutes before realizing that they were not using a calf, but a man, *and the man was still alive.* Sickened, he had tried to stop the game, but someone had told him the man was a Russian officer, as if that were all the explanation anyone could possibly want. The players just ignored Jean-Pierre then, and there was nothing he could do to get the attention of fifty highly excited riders intent on their savage game. He had not stayed to watch the man die, but perhaps he should have, for the image that remained in his mind, and returned to him every time he worried about being found out, was of that Russian, helpless and bleeding, being torn to pieces alive.

The sense of the past was still with him, and as he looked at the khaki-colored rock walls of the gully through which he was striding, he saw scenes from his childhood alternating with nightmares about being caught by the guerrillas. His earliest memory was of the trial, and of the overwhelming sense of outrage and injustice he had felt when they had sent his papa to jail. He could hardly read, but he could make out his father's name in the newspaper headlines. At that age—he must have been four—he did not know what it meant to be a hero of the Resistance. He knew his father was a Communist, as were his father's friends, the priest and the cobbler and the man behind the counter, in the village post office; but he thought they called him Red Roland because of his ruddy complexion. When his father was convicted of treason and sentenced to five years in jail, they had told Jean-Pierre that it had to do with Uncle Abdul, a frightened brown-skinned man who had stayed in the house for several weeks, and who was from the FLN, but Jean-Pierre did not know what the FLN was and thought they meant the elephant in the zoo. The only thing he understood clearly and always believed was that the police were cruel and the judges were dishonest and the people were fooled by the newspapers.

As the years went by he understood more and suffered more and his sense of outrage grew. When he went to school the other boys said his father was a traitor. He told them that, on the contrary, his father had fought bravely and risked his life in the war, but they did not believe him. He and his mother went to live in another village for a while, but somehow the neighbors found out who they were and told their children not to play with Jean-Pierre. But the worst part was visiting the prison. His father changed visibly, becoming thin, pale and sickly; but worse than that was to see him confined, dressed in a drab uniform, cowed and frightened, saying "sir" to strutting bullies with truncheons. After a while the smell of the prison began to make Jean-Pierre nauseous, and he would throw up as soon as he entered its doors; and his mother stopped taking him.

It was not until Papa came out of prison that Jean-Pierre talked to him at length and finally understood it all, and saw that the injustice of what had happened was even more gross than he had thought. After the Germans invaded France the French Communists, being already organized in cells, had played a leading role in the Resistance. When the war was over his father had carried on the fight against right-wing tyranny. At that time Algeria had been a French colony. Its people were oppressed and exploited but struggling courageously for their freedom. Young Frenchmen were conscripted into the army and forced to fight against the Algerians in a cruel war in which the atrocities committed by the French Army reminded many people of the work of the Nazis. The FLN, which Jean-Pierre would always associate with the image of a mangy old elephant in a provincial zoo, was the *Front de Libération Nationale*, the National Liberation Front of the Algerian people.

Jean-Pierre's father was one of 121 well-known people who signed a petition in favor of freedom for the Algerians. France was at war, and the petition was called seditious, for it might be construed as encouraging French soldiers to desert. But Papa had done worse than that: he had taken a suitcase full of money collected from French people for the FLN and had carried it across the border into Switzerland, where he had put it into a bank; and he had sheltered Uncle Abdul, who was not an uncle at all, but an Algerian wanted by the DST, the secret police.

These were the kinds of things he had done in the war against the Nazis, he had explained to Jean-Pierre. He was still fighting the same fight. The enemy had never been the Germans, just as the enemy now was not the French people: it was the capitalists, the owners of property, the rich and privileged, the ruling class who would use any means, no matter how vicious, to protect their position. They were so powerful they controlled half the world—but nevertheless there was hope for the poor, the powerless and the oppressed, for in Moscow the people ruled, and throughout the rest of the world the working class looked to the Soviet Union for help, guidance and inspiration in the battle for freedom.

As Jean-Pierre grew older the picture became tarnished, and he found out that the Soviet Union was not a workers' paradise; but he learned nothing to change his basic conviction that the Communist movement, guided from Moscow, was the only hope for the oppressed people of the world, and the only means of destroying the judges and the police and the newspapers which had so brutally betrayed his papa.

The father had succeeded in handing the torch on to the son. And, as if he knew this, Papa had gone into a decline. He never regained his red face. He no longer went to demonstrations, organized fund-raising dances, or wrote letters to the local newspapers. He held a series of undemanding clerical jobs. He belonged to the Party, of course, and to a trade union, but he did not resume the chairmanship of committees, the taking of minutes, the preparation of agendas. He still played chess and drank anisette with the priest and the cobbler and the man who ran the village post office, but their political discussions, which had once been passionate, were now lackluster, as if the revolution for which they had worked so hard had been indefinitely postponed. Within a few years Papa died. It was only then that Jean-Pierre discovered he had contracted tuberculosis in jail, and had never recovered. They took away his freedom, they broke his spirit and they ruined his health. But the worst thing they did to him was to brand him a traitor. He was a hero who had risked his life for his fellowmen, but he died convicted of treason.

They'd regret it now, Papa, if they knew what revenge I'm taking, Jean-Pierre thought as he led his bony mare up an Afghan mountainside. Because of the intelligence I have provided, the Communists here have been able to strangle Masud's supply lines. Last winter he was unable to stockpile weapons and ammunition. This summer, instead of launching attacks on the air base and the power stations and the supply trucks on the highway, he is struggling to defend himself against government raids on *his* territory. Single-handedly, Papa, I have almost destroyed the effectiveness of this barbarian who wants to take his country back to the dark ages of savagery, underdevelopment and Islamic superstition.

Of course, strangling Masud's supply lines was not enough. The man was already a figure of national stature. Furthermore, he had the brains and the strength of character to graduate from rebel leader to legitimate president. He was a Tito, a De Gaulle, a Mugabe. He had to be not just neutralized, but destroyed—taken by the Russians, dead or alive.

The difficulty was that Masud moved about quickly and silently, like a deer in a forest, suddenly emerging from the undergrowth and then disappearing again just as abruptly. But Jean-Pierre was patient, and so were the Russians: there would come a time, sooner or later, when Jean-Pierre would know for certain exactly where Masud was going to be for the next twenty-four hours—perhaps if he were wounded, or planning to attend a funeral—and then Jean-Pierre would use his radio to transmit a special code, and the hawk would strike.

He wished that he could tell Jane what he was really doing here. He might even convince her that it was right. He would point out that their medical work was useless, for helping the rebels served only to perpetuate the misery of poverty and ignorance in which the people lived, and to delay the moment when the Soviet Union would be able to grab this country by the scruff of the neck, as it were, and drag it kicking and screaming into the twentieth century. She might well understand that. However, he knew instinctively that she would not forgive him for deceiving her as he had. In fact she would be enraged. He could imagine her, remorseless, implacable, proud. She would leave him immediately, the way she had left Ellis Thaler. She would be doubly furious at having been deceived in exactly the same way by two successive men.

So, in his terror of losing her, he continued to deceive her, like a man on a precipice paralyzed by fright.

She knew *something* was wrong, of course; he could tell by the way she looked at him sometimes. But she felt it was a problem in their relationship, he was sure—it did not occur to her that his whole life was a monumental pretense.

Complete safety was not possible, but he took every precaution against discovery by her or by anyone else. When using the radio he spoke in code, not because the rebels might be listening in—they had no radios—but because the Afghan Army might, and it was so riddled with traitors that it had no secrets from Masud. Jean-Pierre's radio was small enough to be concealed in the false bottom of his medical bag, or in the pocket of his shirt or waistcoat when he was not carrying the bag. Its disadvantage was that it was powerful enough only for very short conversations. It would have taken a very long broadcast to dictate full details of the routes and timing of the convoys—especially in code—and would have required a radio and battery pack a great deal larger. Jean-Pierre and Monsieur Leblond had decided against that. In consequence, Jean-Pierre had to meet with his contact to pass on his information.

He crested a rise and looked down. He was at the head of a small valley. The trail he was on led down to another valley, running at right angles to this one and bifurcated by a tumbling mountain stream that glittered in the afternoon sun. On the far side of the stream another valley led up into the mountains toward Cobak, his ultimate destination. Where the three valleys met, on the near side of the river, was a little stone hut. The region was dotted with such primitive buildings. Jean-Pierre imagined they had been put up by the nomads and traveling merchants who used them at night.

He set off down the hill, leading Maggie. Anatoly was probably there already. Jean-Pierre did not know his real name or rank, but assumed he was in the KGB and guessed, from something he had once said about generals, that he was a colonel. Whatever his rank, he was no desk man. Between here and Bagram were fifty miles of mountain country, and Anatoly walked it, alone, taking a day and a half. He was an Oriental Russian with high cheekbones and yellow skin, and in Afghan clothes he passed as an Uzbak, a member of the Mongoloid ethnic group of north Afghanistan. This explained his hesitant Dari—the Uzbaks had their own language. Anatoly was brave: he did not speak the Uzbak tongue, of course, so there was a chance he might be unmasked; and he, too, knew that the guerrillas played *buzkashi* with captured Russian officers.

The risk to Jean-Pierre of these meetings was a little less. His constant traveling to outlying villages to hold clinics was only mildly odd. However, suspicion might be aroused if anyone noticed that he happened to bump into the same wandering Uzbak more than once or twice. And, of course, if somehow an Afghan who spoke French should overhear the doctor's conversation with that wandering Uzbak, Jean-Pierre could only hope to die fast.

His sandals made no noise on the footpath, and Maggie's hooves sank silently into the dusty earth, so as he neared the hut he whistled a tune, in case anyone other than Anatoly should be inside: he was careful not to startle Afghans, who were all armed and jumpy. He ducked his head and entered. To his surprise, the cool interior of the hut was empty. He sat down with his back to the stone wall and settled to wait. After a few minutes he closed his eyes. He was tired, but too tense to sleep. This was the worst part of what he was doing: the combination of fear and boredom which overcame him during these long waits. He had learned to accept delays, in this country without wristwatches, but he had never acquired the imperturbable patience of the Afghans. He could not help but imagine the various disasters which might have overtaken Anatoly. How ironic it would be if Anatoly had trodden on a Russian antipersonnel mine and blown his foot off. Those mines actually injured more livestock than humans, but they were no less effective for that: the loss of a cow could kill an Afghan family as surely as if their house had been bombed with them all inside. Jean-Pierre no longer laughed when he saw a cow or a goat with a rough-hewn wooden leg.

In his reverie he sensed the presence of someone else, and opened his eyes to see Anatoly's Oriental face inches from his own.

"I could have robbed you," said Anatoly in fluent French.

"I wasn't asleep."

Anatoly sat down, cross-legged, on the dirt floor. He was a squat, muscular figure in baggy cotton shirt and trousers with a turban, a checked scarf and a mud-colored woolen blanket, called a *pattu*, around his shoulders. He let the scarf drop from his face and smiled, showing tobacco-stained teeth. "How are you, my friend?"

"Well."

"And your wife?"

There was something sinister in the way Anatoly always asked about Jane. The Russians had been dead against the idea of his bringing Jane to Afghanistan, arguing that she would interfere with his work. Jean-Pierre had pointed out that he had to take a nurse with him anyway—it was the policy of *Médecins pour la Liberté* always to send pairs—and that he would probably sleep with whoever accompanied him, unless she looked like King Kong. In the end the Russians had agreed, but reluctantly. "Jane is fine," he said. "She had the baby six weeks ago. A girl."

"Congratulations!" Anatoly seemed genuinely pleased. "But wasn't it a little early?"

"Yes. Fortunately there were no complications. In fact the village midwife delivered the baby."

"Not you?"

"I wasn't there. I was with you."

"My God." Anatoly looked horrified. "That I should have kept you away on such an important day . . ."

Jean-Pierre was pleased by Anatoly's concern, but he did not show it. "It couldn't be anticipated," he said. "Besides, it was worth it: you hit the convoy I told you of."

"Yes. Your information is very good. Congratulations again."

Jean-Pierre felt a glow of pride, but he tried to appear matter-of-fact. "Our system seems to be working very well," he said modestly.

Anatoly nodded. "What was their reaction to the ambush?"

"Increasing desperation." It occurred to Jean-Pierre, as he spoke, that another advantage of meeting his contact in person was that he could give this kind of background information, feelings and impressions, stuff which was not concrete enough to be sent by radio in code. "They're constantly running out of ammunition now."

"And the next convoy—when will it depart?"

"It left yesterday."

"They *are* desperate. Good." Anatoly reached inside his shirt and brought out a map. He unfolded it on the floor. It showed the area between the Five Lions Valley and the Pakistan border.

Jean-Pierre concentrated hard, recalling the details he had memorized during his conversation with Mohammed, and began to trace for Anatoly the route the convoy would follow on its way back from Pakistan. He did not know exactly when they would return, for Mohammed did not know how long they would spend in Peshawar buying what they needed. However, Anatoly had people in Peshawar who would let him know when the Five Lions convoy departed, and from that he would be able to work out their timetable.

Anatoly made no notes, but memorized every word Jean-Pierre said. When they had finished they went over the whole thing again, with Anatoly repeating it to Jean-Pierre as a check.

The Russian folded the map and put it back inside his shirt. "And what of Masud?" he said quietly.

"We haven't seen him since last I spoke to you," said Jean-Pierre. "I've only seen Mohammed—and he is never quite sure where Masud is or when he will appear."

"Masud is a fox," said Anatoly with a rare flash of emotion.

"We will catch him," said Jean-Pierre.

"Oh, we will catch him. He knows the hunt is in full cry, so he covers his tracks. But the hounds have his scent, and he cannot elude us forever—we are so many, and so strong, and our blood is up." He suddenly became conscious that he was revealing his feelings. He smiled and became practical again. "Batteries," he said, and he brought a battery pack out of his shirt.

Jean-Pierre took the little radio transceiver from the concealed compartment in the bottom of his medical bag, extracted the old batteries and exchanged them for new ones. They did this every time they met, to be sure that Jean-Pierre should not lose contact simply by running out of power. Anatoly would carry the old ones all the way back to Bagram, for there was no point in taking the risk of throwing away Russian-made batteries here in the Five Lions Valley, where there were no electrical appliances.

As Jean-Pierre was putting the radio back into his medical bag, Anatoly said: "Have you got anything in there for blisters? My feet—" Then he stopped suddenly, frowned and cocked his head, listening.

Jean-Pierre tensed. So far they had never been observed together. It was bound to happen sooner or later, they knew, and they had planned what they would do, how they would act like strangers sharing a resting place and continue their conversation when the intruder had left—or, if the intruder showed signs of staying long, they would leave together, as if by chance they happened to be heading in the same direction. All that had been previously agreed, but nevertheless Jean-Pierre now felt his guilt must be written all over his face.

In the next instant he heard a footfall outside, and the sound of someone breathing hard; and then a shadow darkened the sunlit entrance, and Jane walked in.

"Jane!" he said.

Both men sprang to their feet.

Jean-Pierre said: "What is it? Why are you here?"

"Thank God I caught up with you," she said breathlessly.

Out of the corner of his eye, Jean-Pierre saw Anatoly turn away, as an Afghan would turn away from a brazen woman. The gesture helped Jean-

Pierre recover from the shock of seeing Jane. He looked around quickly. Anatoly had put away the maps several minutes earlier, fortunately. But the radio—the radio was sticking out an inch or two from the medical bag. However, Jane had not seen it—yet.

"Sit down," said Jean-Pierre. "Catch your breath." He sat down at the same time and used the movement as an excuse to shift his bag so that the radio poked out from the side facing him and away from Jane. "What's the matter?" he said.

"A medical problem I can't solve."

Jean-Pierre's tension eased a fraction: he had been afraid she might have followed him because she suspected something. "Have some water," he said. He reached into his bag with one hand, and with the other pushed the radio in while he rummaged. When the radio was concealed he drew out his flask of purified water and handed it to her. His heartbeat began to return to normal. He was recovering his presence of mind. The evidence was now out of sight. What else was there to make her suspicious? She might have heard Anatoly speaking French—but that was not uncommon: if an Afghan had a second language it was often French, and an Uzbak might speak French better than he spoke Dari. What had Anatoly been saying when she walked in? Jean-Pierre remembered: he had been asking for blister ointment. That was perfect. Afghans always asked for medicine when they met a doctor, even if they were in perfect health.

Jane drank from the flask and began to speak. "A few minutes after you left, they brought in a boy of eighteen with a very bad thigh wound." She took another sip. She was ignoring Anatoly, and Jean-Pierre realized she was so concerned about the medical emergency that she had hardly noticed the other man. "He was hurt in the fighting near Rokha, and his father had carried him all the way up the Valley—it took them two days. The wound was badly gangrenous by the time they arrived. I gave him six hundred milligrams of crystalline penicillin, injected into the buttock. Then I cleaned out the wound."

"Exactly correct," said Jean-Pierre.

"A few minutes later he broke out in a cold sweat and became confused. I took his pulse: it was rapid but weak."

"Did he go pale or gray, and have difficulty breathing?"

"Yes."

"What did you do?"

"I treated him for shock—raised his feet, covered him with a blanket and gave him tea—then I came after you." She was close to tears. "His father carried him for two days—I can't let him die."

"He needn't," said Jean-Pierre. "Allergic shock is a rare but quite well-known reaction to penicillin injections. The treatment is half a milliliter of adrenaline, injected into a muscle, followed by an antihistamine—say, six milliliters of diphenhydramine. Would you like me to come back with you?" As he made the offer he glanced at Anatoly, but the Russian showed no reaction.

Jane sighed. "No," she said. "There will be someone else dying on the far side of the hill. You go to Cobak."

"If you're sure."

"Yes."

A match flared as Anatoly lit a cigarette. Jane glanced at him, then looked at Jean-Pierre again. "Half a milliliter of adrenaline and then six milliliters of diphenhydramine." She stood up.

"Yes." Jean-Pierre stood up with her and kissed her. "Are you sure you can manage?"

"Of course."

"You must hurry."

"Yes."

"Would you like to take Maggie?"

Jane considered. "I don't think so. On that path, walking is faster."

"Whatever you think best."

"Good-bye."

"Good-bye, Jane."

Jean-Pierre watched her go out. He stood still for a while. Neither he nor Anatoly said anything. After a minute or two he went to the doorway and looked out. He could see Jane, two or three hundred yards away, a small, slight figure in a thin cotton dress, striding determinedly up the Valley, alone in the dusty brown landscape. He watched her until she disappeared into a fold in the hills.

He came back inside and sat down with his back to the wall. He and Anatoly looked at one another. "Jesus Christ Almighty," said Jean-Pierre. "That was close."

CHAPTER EIGHT

T he boy died.

He had been dead almost an hour when Jane arrived, hot and dusty and exhausted to the point of collapse. The father was waiting for her at the mouth of the cave, looking numb and reproachful. She could tell from his resigned posture and his calm brown eyes that it was all over. He said nothing. She went into the cave and looked at the boy. Too tired to feel angry, she was overwhelmed by disappointment. Jean-Pierre was away and Zahara was deep in mourning, so she had no one with whom to share her grief.

She wept later as she lay in her bed on the roof of the shopkeeper's house, with Chantal, on a tiny mattress beside her, murmuring from time to time in a sleep of contented ignorance. She wept for the father as much as for the dead boy. Like her, he had driven himself beyond ordinary exhaustion in trying to save the boy. How much greater his sadness would be. Her tears blurred the stars before she fell asleep.

She dreamed that Mohammed came to her bed and made love to her while the whole village looked on; then he told her that Jean-Pierre was having an affair with Simone, the wife of the fat journalist Raoul Clermont, and that the two lovers met in Cobak when Jean-Pierre was supposed to be holding a clinic.

The next day she ached all over, as a result of having run most of the way to the little stone hut. It was fortunate, she reflected as she went about her routine chores, that Jean-Pierre had stopped—to rest, presumably—at the little stone hut, giving her a chance to catch up with him. She had been so relieved to see Maggie tethered outside, and to find Jean-Pierre in the hut with that funny little Uzbak man. The two of them had jumped out of their skins when she walked in. It had been almost comical. It was the first time she had ever seen an Afghan stand up when a woman came in.

She walked up the mountainside with her medicine case and opened the cave clinic. As she dealt with the usual cases of malnutrition, malaria, infected wounds and intestinal parasites, she thought over yesterday's crisis. She had never heard of allergic shock before. No doubt people who had to give penicillin injections were normally taught what to do about it, but her training had been so rushed that a lot of things had been left out. In fact the medical details had been almost entirely skimped, on the grounds that Jean-Pierre was a fully qualified doctor and would be around to tell her what to do.

What an anxious time that had been, sitting in classrooms, sometimes with trainee nurses, sometimes on her own, trying to absorb the rules and procedures of medicine and health education, wondering what awaited her in Afghanistan. Some of her lessons had been the opposite of reassuring. Her first task, she had been told, would be to build an earth closet for herself. Why? Because the fastest way of improving the health of people in underdeveloped countries was to stop them using the rivers and streams as toilets, and this could be impressed upon them by setting an example. Her teacher, Stephanie, a bespectacled fortyish earth-mother type in dungarees and sandals, had also emphasized the dangers of prescribing medicines too generously. Most illnesses and minor injuries would get better without medical help, but primitive (and not-so-primitive) people always wanted pills and potions. Jane recalled that the little Uzbak man had been asking Jean-Pierre for blister ointment. He must have been walking long distances all his life, yet because he had met a doctor he said his feet hurt. The snag about overprescribing—apart from the waste of medicines—was that a drug given for a trivial ailment might cause the patient to develop tolerance, so that when he was seriously ill the treatment would not cure him. Stephanie had also advised Jane to try to work with, rather than against, traditional healers in the community. She had been successful with Rabia, the midwife, but not with Abdullah, the mullah.

Learning the language had been the easiest part. In Paris, before she ever thought of coming to Afghanistan, she had been studying Farsi, the Persian language, with the object of improving her usefulness as an interpreter. Farsi and Dari were dialects of the same language. The other main language in Afghanistan was Pashto, the tongue of the Pushtuns, but Dari was the language of the Tajiks, and the Five Lions Valley was in Tajik territory. Those few Afghans who traveled—the nomads, for example—usually spoke both Pashto and Dari. If they had a European language, it was English or French. The Uzbak man in the stone hut had been speaking French to Jean-Pierre. It was the first time Jane had heard French spoken with an Uzbak accent. It sounded the same as a Russian accent.

Her mind kept returning to the Uzbak during the day. The thought of him nagged her. It was a feeling she sometimes got when she knew there was something important she was supposed to do but could not remember what it was. There had been something odd about him, perhaps.

At noon she closed the clinic, fed and changed Chantal, then cooked a lunch of rice and meat sauce and shared it with Fara. The girl had become utterly devoted to Jane, eager to do anything to please her, reluctant to go home at night. Jane was trying to treat her more as an equal, but this seemed to serve only to increase her adoration.

In the heat of the day Jane left Chantal with Fara and went down to her secret place, the sunny ledge hidden below an overhang on the mountainside. There she did her postnatal exercises, determined to get her figure back. As she clenched her pelvic-floor muscles, she kept visualizing the Uzbak man, rising to his feet in the little stone hut, and the expression of astonishment on his Oriental face. For some reason she felt a sense of impending tragedy.

When she realized the truth it did not come in a sudden flash of insight, but more like an avalanche, starting small but growing inexorably until it swamped everything.

No Afghan would complain of blisters on his feet, even in pretense, for they had no knowledge of such things: it was as unlikely as a Gloucestershire farmer saying he had beriberi. And no Afghan, no matter how surprised, would react by standing up when a woman walked in. If he was not Afghan, then what was he? His accent told her, though few people would have recognized it: it was only because she was a linguist who spoke both Russian and French that she was able to recognize that he had been speaking French with a Russian accent.

So Jean-Pierre had met a Russian disguised as an Uzbak in a stone hut at a deserted location.

Was it an accident? That was possible, barely, but she pictured her husband's face when she had walked in, and now she could read the expression which at the time she had not noticed: a look of guilt.

No, it was no accidental encounter—it was a rendezvous. Perhaps it was not the first. Jean-Pierre was constantly traveling to outlying villages to hold clinics—indeed, he was unnecessarily scrupulous about keeping to his schedule of visits, a foolish insistence in a country without calendars and diaries—but not so foolish if there was another schedule, a clandestine series of secret meetings.

And *why* did he meet the Russian? That, too, was obvious, and hot tears welled up in Jane's eyes as she realized that his purpose must be treachery. He gave them information, of course. He told them about the convoys. He always knew the routes because Mohammed used his maps. He knew the approximate timing because he saw the men leaving, from Banda and from other villages in the Five Lions Valley. He gave this information to the Russians, obviously; and that was why the Russians had become so successful at ambushing convoys in the last year; that was why there were so many grieving widows and sad orphans in the Valley now.

What's wrong with me? she thought in a sudden fit of self-pity, and fresh tears rolled down her cheeks. First Ellis, then Jean-Pierre—why do I pick these bastards? Is there something about a secretive man that appeals to me? Is it the challenge of breaking down his defenses? Am I that crazy?

She remembered Jean-Pierre arguing that the Soviet invasion of Afghanistan was justified. At some point he had changed his mind, and she thought she had convinced him that he was wrong. Obviously the change had been faked. When he decided to come to Afghanistan to spy for the Russians, he had adopted an anti-Soviet point of view as part of his cover.

Was his love also faked?

The question alone was heartbreaking. She buried her face in her hands. It was almost unthinkable. She had fallen in love with him, married him, kissed his sour-faced mother, got used to his way of making love, survived their first row, struggled to make their partnership work, and given birth to his child in fear and pain—had she done all that for an illusion, a cardboard cutout of a husband, a man who cared for her not at all? It was like walking and running so many miles to ask how to cure the eighteen-year-old boy and then returning to find him already dead. It was worse than that. It was, she imagined, how the boy's father had felt, having carried his son for two days only to see him die.

There was a sensation of fullness in her breasts, and she realized it must be time for Chantal's feed. She put on her clothes, wiped her face on her sleeve and headed back up the mountain. As her immediate grief receded and she began to think more clearly, it seemed to her that she had felt a vague dissatisfaction throughout their year of marriage, and now she could understand why. In a way she had all along *sensed* Jean-Pierre's deceit. Because of that barrier between them, they had failed to become intimate.

When she reached the cave, Chantal was complaining loudly and Fara was rocking her. Jane took the baby and held her to her breast. Chantal began to suck. Jane felt the initial discomfort, like a cramp, in her stomach, and then a sensation in her breast which was pleasant and rather erotic.

She wanted to be alone. She told Fara to go and take her siesta in her mother's cave.

Feeding Chantal was soothing. Jean-Pierre's treachery came to seem less than cataclysmic. She felt sure his love for her was not faked. What would be the point? Why would he have brought her here? She was of no use to him in his spying. It must have been because he loved her.

And if he loved her, all other problems could be solved. He would have to stop working for the Russians, of course. For the moment she could not quite see herself confronting him—would she say, "All is revealed!" for example? No. But the words would come to her when she needed them. Then he would have to take her and Chantal back to Europe—

Back to Europe. When she realized they would have to go home, she was flooded by a sense of relief. It took her by surprise. If anyone had asked her how she liked Afghanistan, she would have said that what she was doing was fascinating and worthwhile and she was coping very well indeed and even enjoying it. But now that the prospect of returning to civilization was in front of her, her resilience crumbled, and she admitted to herself that the harsh landscape, the bitter winter weather, the alien people, the bombing and the endless stream of maimed and mangled men and boys had strained her nerves to the breaking point.

The truth is, she thought, that it's *awful* here.

Chantal stopped sucking and dropped off to sleep. Jane put her down, changed her and moved her to her mattress, all without waking her. The baby's unshakable equanimity was a great blessing. She slept through all kinds of crises—no amount of noise or movement would wake her if she was full and comfortable. However, she was sensitive to Jane's moods, and often woke when Jane was distressed, even when there was not much noise.

Jane sat cross-legged on her mattress, watching her sleeping baby, thinking about Jean-Pierre. She wished he were here now so she could talk to him right away. She wondered why she was not more angry—not to say outraged—that he had been betraying the guerrillas to the Russians. Was it because she was reconciled to the knowledge that all men were liars? Had she come to believe that the only innocent people in this war were the mothers, the wives and the daughters on both sides? Was it that being a wife and a mother had altered her personality, so that such a betrayal no longer outraged her? Or was it just that she loved Jean-Pierre? She did not know.

Anyway, it was time to think about the future, not the past. They would go back to Paris, where there were postmen and bookshops and tap water. Chantal would have pretty clothes, and a pram, and disposable diapers. They would live in a small apartment in an interesting neighborhood where the only real danger to life would be the taxi drivers. Jane and Jean-Pierre would start again, and this time they would really get to know one another. They would work to make the world a better place by gradual and legitimate means, without intrigue or treachery. Their experience in Afghanistan would help them to get jobs in Third World development, perhaps with the World Health Organization. Married life would be as she had imagined it, with the three of them doing good and being happy and feeling safe.

Fara came in. Siesta time was over. She greeted Jane respectfully, looked at Chantal, then, seeing that the baby was asleep, sat cross-legged on the ground, waiting for instructions. She was the daughter of Rabia's eldest son, Ismael Gul, who was away at present, with the convoy—

Jane gasped. Fara looked inquiringly at her. Jane made a deprecatory motion with her hand, and Fara looked away.

Her father is with the convoy, Jane thought.

Jean-Pierre had betrayed that convoy to the Russians. Fara's father would die in the ambush—unless Jane could do something to prevent it. But what? A runner could be sent to meet the convoy at the Khyber Pass and divert it onto a new route. Mohammed could arrange that. But Jane would have to tell him how she knew the convoy was due to be ambushed— and then Mohammed would undoubtedly kill Jean-Pierre, probably with his bare hands.

If one of them has to die, let it be Ismael rather than Jean-Pierre, thought Jane.

Then she thought of the other thirty or so men from the Valley who were with the convoy, and the thought struck her: Shall they *all* die to save my husband—Kahmir Khan with the wispy beard; and scarred old Shahazai Gul; and Yussuf Gul, who sings so beautifully; and Sher Kador, the goat boy;

and Abdur Mohammed with no front teeth; and Ali Ghanim who has four-teen children?

There had to be another way.

She went to the mouth of the cave and stood looking out. Now that the siesta was over, the children had come out of the caves and resumed their games among the rocks and thorny bushes. There was nine-year-old Mousa, the only son of Mohammed—even more spoiled now that he had only one hand—swaggering with the new knife that his doting father had given him. She saw Fara's mother, toiling up the hill with a bundle of fire-wood on her head. There was the mullah's wife, washing out Abdullah's shirt. She did not see Mohammed or his wife, Halima. She knew he was here in Banda, for she had seen him in the morning. He would have eaten with his wife and children in their cave—most families had a cave to themselves. He would be there now, but Jane was reluctant to seek him out openly, for that would scandalize the community, and she needed to be discreet.

What shall I tell him? she thought.

She considered a straightforward appeal: *Do this for me, because I ask it.* It would have worked on any Western man who had fallen in love with her, but Muslim men did not seem to have a romantic idea of love—what Mo-hammed felt for her was more like a rather tender kind of lust. It certainly did not put him at her disposal. And she wasn't sure he still felt it anyway. What, then? He did not owe her anything. She had never treated him or his wife. But she had treated Mousa—she had saved the boy's life. Mo-hammed owed her a debt of honor.

Do this for me, because I saved your son. It might work.

But Mohammed would ask why.

More women were appearing, fetching water and sweeping out their caves, tending to animals and preparing food. Jane knew she would see Mo-hammed shortly.

What shall I say to him?

The Russians know the route of the convoy.

How did they find out?

I don't know, Mohammed.

Then what makes you so sure?

I can't tell you. I overheard a conversation. I got a message from the British Secret Service. I have a hunch. I saw it in the cards. I had a dream.

That was it: a dream.

She saw him. He stepped from his cave, tall and handsome, wearing traveling clothes: the round Chitrali cap, like Masud's, the type most of the guerrillas sported; the mud-colored *pattu,* which served as cloak, towel, blanket and camouflage; and the calf-length leather boots he had taken from the corpse of a Russian soldier. He walked across the clearing with the stride of one who has a long way to go before sundown. He took the footpath down the mountainside, toward the deserted village.

Jane watched his tall figure disappear. It's now or never, she thought; and she followed him. At first she walked slowly and casually, so that it would not be obvious she was going after Mohammed; then, when she was out of sight of the caves, she broke into a run. She slithered and stumbled down the dusty trail, thinking: I wonder what all this running is doing to my insides. When she saw Mohammed ahead of her she called out to him. He stopped, turned and waited for her.

"God be with you, Mohammed Khan," she said when she caught up with him.

"And with you, Jane Debout," he said politely.

She paused, catching her breath. He watched her, wearing an expression of amused tolerance. "How is Mousa?" she said.

"He is well and happy, and learning to use his left hand. He will kill Russians with it one day."

This was a little joke: the left hand was traditionally used for "dirty" jobs, the right for eating. Jane smiled in acknowledgment of his wit, then said: "I'm so glad we were able to save his life."

If he thought her ungracious he did not show it. "I am forever in your debt," he said.

That was what she had been angling for. "There is something you could do for me," she said.

His expression was unreadable. "If it is within my power . . ."

She looked around for somewhere to sit. They were standing near a bombed house. Stones and earth from the front wall had spilled across the pathway, and they could see inside the building, where the only furnishings left were a cracked pot and, absurdly, a color picture of a Cadillac pinned to a wall. Jane sat on the rubble and, after a moment's hesitation, Mohammed sat beside her.

"It is within your power," she said. "But it will cause you some small trouble."

"What is it?"

"You may think it the whim of a foolish woman."

"Perhaps."

"You'll be tempted to deceive me, by agreeing to my request and then 'forgetting' to carry it out."

"No."

"I ask you to deal truthfully with me, whether you refuse or not."

"I shall."

Enough of that, she thought. "I want you to send a runner to the convoy and order them to change their homeward route."

He was quite taken aback—he had probably been expecting some trivial, domestic request. "But why?" he said.

"Do you believe in dreams, Mohammed Khan?"

He shrugged. "Dreams are dreams," he said evasively.

Perhaps that was the wrong approach, she thought, a vision might be better. "While I lay alone in my cave, in the heat of the day, I thought I saw a white pigeon."

He was suddenly attentive, and she knew she had said the right thing: Afghans believed that white pigeons were sometimes inhabited by spirits.

Jane went on: "But I must have been dreaming, for the bird tried to speak to me."

"Ah!"

He took that as a sign that she had had a vision, not a dream, Jane thought. She went on: "I couldn't understand what it was saying, although I listened as hard as I could. I think it was speaking Pashto."

Mohammed was wide-eyed. "A messenger from Pushtun territory . . ."

"Then I saw Ismael Gul, the son of Rabia, the father of Fara, standing behind the pigeon." She put her hand on Mohammed's arm and looked into his eyes, thinking: I could turn you on like an electric light, you vain, foolish man. "There was a knife in his heart, and he was weeping tears of blood. He pointed to the handle of the knife, as if he wanted me to pull it out of his chest. The handle was encrusted with jewels." Somewhere in the back of her mind she was thinking: Where did I get this stuff? "I got up from my bed and walked to him. I was afraid, but I had to save his life. Then, as I reached out to grasp the knife . . ."

"What?"

"He vanished. I think I woke up."

Mohammed closed his wide-open mouth, recovered his poise and frowned importantly, as if carefully considering the interpretation of the dream. Now, Jane thought, it is time to pander to him a little bit.

"It may be all foolishness," she said, arranging her face into a little-girl expression, all ready to defer to his superior masculine judgment. "That's why I ask you to do this *for me*, for the person who saved your son's life, to give me peace of mind."

He immediately looked a little haughty. "There is no need to invoke a debt of honor."

"Does that mean you'll do it?"

He answered with a question. "What kind of jewels were in the handle of the knife?"

Oh, God, she thought, what is the correct answer supposed to be? She thought to say "Emeralds," but they were associated with the Five Lions Valley, so it might imply that Ismael had been killed by a traitor in the Valley. "Rubies," she said.

He nodded slowly. "Did Ismael not speak to you?"

"He seemed to be trying to speak, but unable to."

He nodded again, and Jane thought: Come *on*, make up your bloody *mind*. At last he said: "The omen is clear. The convoy must be diverted."

Thank God for that, thought Jane. "I'm so relieved," she said truthfully. "I didn't know what to do. Now I can be sure Ahmed will be saved." She wondered what she could do to nail Mohammed down and make it impossible for him to change his mind. She could not make him swear an oath. She wondered whether to shake his hand. Finally she decided to seal his promise with an even older gesture: she leaned forward and kissed his mouth, quickly but softly, not giving him a chance either to refuse or to respond. "Thank you!" she said. "I know you are a man of your word." She stood up. Leaving him seated, looking a little dazed, she turned and ran up the path toward the caves.

At the top of the rise she stopped and looked back. Mohammed was striding down the hill, already some distance from the bombed cottage, his head high and his arms swinging. He got a big charge from that kiss, Jane thought. I should be ashamed. I played on his superstition, his vanity and his sexuality. As a feminist I ought not to exploit his preconceptions—psychic woman, submissive woman, coquettish woman—to manipulate him. But it worked. It worked!

She walked on. Next she had to deal with Jean-Pierre. He would be home around dusk: he would have waited until midafternoon, when the sun was a little less hot, before starting on his journey, just as Mohammed had. She felt that Jean-Pierre would be easier to handle than Mohammed had been. For one thing, she could tell the truth with Jean-Pierre. For another, he was in the wrong.

She reached the caves. The little encampment was busy now. A flight of Russian jets soared across the sky. Everyone stopped work to watch them, although they were too high and too far away for bombing. When they had gone the small boys stuck out their arms like wings and ran around making jet-engine sounds. In their imaginary flights, Jane wondered, who were they bombing?

She went into the cave, checked on Chantal, smiled at Fara and took out the journal. Both she and Jean-Pierre wrote in it almost every day. It was primarily a medical record, and they would take it back to Europe with them for the benefit of others who would follow them to Afghanistan. They had been encouraged to record personal feelings and problems, too, so that others would know what to expect; and Jane had written quite full notes on her pregnancy and the birth of Chantal; but it was a highly censored account of her emotional life that had been logged.

She sat with her back to the cave wall and the book on her knee, and wrote the story of the eighteen-year-old boy who had died of allergic shock. It made her feel sad but not depressed—a healthy reaction, she told herself.

She added brief details of today's minor cases; then, idly, she leafed backward through the volume. The entries in Jean-Pierre's slapdash, spidery handwriting were highly abbreviated, consisting almost entirely of symptoms, diagnoses, treatments and results: *Worms*, he would write, or *Malaria*; then *Cured* or *Stable* or sometimes *Died*. Jane tended to write sentences such as *She felt better this morning* or *The mother has tuberculosis*. She read about the early days of her pregnancy, sore nipples and thickening thighs and nausea in the morning. She was interested to see that almost a year ago she had written *I'm frightened of Abdullah*. She had forgotten that.

She put the journal away. She and Fara spent the next couple of hours cleaning and tidying up the cave clinic; then it was time to go down into the village and prepare for the night. As she walked down the mountainside and then busied herself in the shopkeeper's house, Jane considered how to handle her confrontation with Jean-Pierre. She knew what to do—she would take him for a walk, she thought—but she was not sure exactly what to say.

She still had not made up her mind when he arrived a few minutes later. She wiped the dust from his face with a damp towel and gave him green tea in a china cup. He was pleasantly tired, rather than exhausted, she knew: he was capable of walking much longer distances. She sat with him while he drank his tea, trying not to stare at him, thinking: You lied to me. When he had rested for a little while, she said: "Let's go out, like we used to."

He was a little surprised. "Where do you want to go?"

"Anywhere. Don't you remember, last summer, how we used to go out just to enjoy the evening?"

He smiled. "Yes, I do." She loved him when he smiled like that. He said: "Will we take Chantal?"

"No." Jane did not want to be distracted. "She'll be fine with Fara."

"All right," he said, faintly bemused.

Jane told Fara to prepare their evening meal—tea, bread and yogurt—then she and Jean-Pierre left the house. The daylight was fading and the evening air was mild and fragrant. This was the best time of day in summer. As they strolled through the fields to the river, she recalled how she had felt on this same pathway last summer: anxious, confused, excited, and determined to succeed. She was proud that she had coped so well, but glad the adventure was about to end.

She began to feel tense as the moment of confrontation drew nearer, even though she kept telling herself that she had nothing to hide, nothing to feel guilty about and nothing to fear. They waded across the river at a place where it spread wide and shallow over a rock shelf; then they climbed a steep, winding path up the face of the cliff on the other side. At the top they sat on the ground and dangled their legs over the precipice. A hundred feet below them, the Five Lions River hurried along, jostling boulders and foaming angrily through the rapids. Jane looked over the Valley. The cultivated ground was crisscrossed with irrigation channels and stone terrace walls. The bright green-and-gold colors of ripening crops made the fields look like shards of colored glass from a smashed toy. Here and there the picture was blemished by bomb damage—fallen walls, blocked ditches, and craters of mud amid the waving grain. The occasional round cap or dark turban showed that some of the men were already at work, bringing in their crops as the Russians parked their jets and put away their bombs for the night. Scarved heads or smaller figures were women and older children, who would help while the light lasted. On the far side of the Valley the farmland struggled to climb the lower slopes of the mountain, but soon surrendered to the dusty rock. From the cluster of houses off to the left the smoke of a few cooking fires rose in pencil-straight lines until the light breeze untidied it. The same breeze brought unintelligible snatches of conversation from the women bathing beyond a bend in the river upstream. Their voices were subdued, and Zahara's hearty laugh was no longer heard, for she was in mourning. And all because of Jean-Pierre. . . .

The thought gave Jane courage. "I want you to take me home," she said abruptly.

At first he misunderstood her. "We've only just got here," he said irritably; then he looked at her and his frown cleared. "Oh," he said.

There was a note of imperturbability in his voice which Jane found ominous, and she realized that she might not get her way without a struggle. "Yes," she said firmly. "Home."

He put his arm around her. "This country gets one down at times," he said. He was not looking at her but at the rushing river far below their feet. "You're especially vulnerable to depression at the moment, just after the birth. In a few weeks' time, you'll find—"

"Don't patronize me!" she snapped. She was not going to let him get away with that kind of nonsense. "Save your bedside manner for your patients."

"All right." He took his arm away. "We decided, before we came, that we would stay here for two years. Short tours are inefficient, we agreed, because of the time and money wasted in training, traveling and settling down. We were determined to make a real impact, so we *committed* ourselves to a two-year stint—"

"And then we had a baby."

"It wasn't my idea!"

"Anyway, I've changed my mind."

"You're not *entitled* to change your mind."

"You don't own me!" she said angrily.

"It's out of the question. Let us stop discussing it."

"We've only just begun," she said. His attitude infuriated her. The conversation had turned into an argument about her rights as an individual, and somehow she did not want to win by telling him that she knew about his spying, not yet anyway; she wanted him to admit that she was free to make her own decisions. "You have no right to ignore me or override my wishes," she said. "I want to leave this summer."

"The answer is no."

She decided to try reasoning with him. "We've been here a year. We *have* made an impact. We've also made considerable sacrifices, more than we anticipated. Haven't we done enough?"

"We agreed on two years," he said stubbornly.

"That was a long time ago, and before we had Chantal."

"Then the two of you should go, and leave me here."

For a moment Jane considered that. To travel on a convoy to Pakistan carrying a baby was difficult and dangerous. Without a husband it would be a nightmare. But it was not impossible. However, it would mean leaving

Jean-Pierre behind. He would be able to continue betraying the convoys, and every few weeks more husbands and sons from the Valley would die. And there was another reason why she could not leave him behind: it would destroy their marriage. "No," she said. "I can't go alone. You must come, too."

"I will not," he said angrily. "I will not!"

Now she *had* to confront him with what she knew. She took a deep breath. "You'll just have to," she began.

"I don't have to," he interrupted. He pointed his forefinger at her, and she looked into his eyes and saw something there that frightened her. "You can't force me to. Don't try."

"But I *can*—"

"I advise you not to," he said, and his voice was terribly cold.

Suddenly he seemed a stranger to her, a man she did not know. She was silent for a moment, thinking. She watched a pigeon rise up from the village and fly toward her. It homed in on the cliff face a little way below her feet. I don't know this man! she thought in a panic. After a whole year I still don't know who he is! "Do you love me?" she asked him.

"Loving you doesn't mean I have to do everything you want."

"Is that a yes?"

He stared at her. She met his gaze unflinchingly. Slowly the hard, manic light went out of his eyes, and he relaxed. At last he smiled. "It's a yes," he said. She leaned toward him, and he put his arm around her again. "Yes, I love you," he said softly. He kissed the top of her head.

She rested her cheek on his chest and looked down. The pigeon she had watched flew off again. It was a white pigeon, like the one in her invented vision. It floated away, gliding effortlessly down toward the far bank of the river. Jane thought: Oh, God, what do I do now?

It was Mohammed's son, Mousa—now known as Left Hand—who was the first to spot the convoy when it returned. He came racing into the clearing in front of the caves, yelling at the top of his voice: "They're back! They're back!" Nobody needed to ask who *they* were.

It was midmorning, and Jane and Jean-Pierre were in the cave clinic. Jane looked at Jean-Pierre. The faintest hint of a puzzled frown crossed his face: he was wondering why the Russians had not acted on his intelligence and ambushed the convoy. Jane turned away from him so that he should not see the triumph she felt. She had saved their lives! Yussuf would sing tonight, and Sher Kador would count his goats, and Ali Ghanim would kiss each of his fourteen children. Yussuf was one of Rabia's sons: saving his life repaid Rabia for helping to bring Chantal into the world. All the mothers and daughters who would have been in mourning could now rejoice.

She wondered how Jean-Pierre felt. Was he angry, or frustrated, or disappointed? It was hard to imagine someone being disappointed because people had *not* been killed. She stole a glance at him, but his face was blank. I wish I knew what's going on in his mind, she thought.

Their patients melted away within minutes: everybody was going down to the village to welcome the travelers home. "Shall we go down?" Jane said.

"You go," Jean-Pierre said. "I'll finish up here, then follow you."

"All right," said Jane. He wanted some time to compose himself, she guessed, so that he could pretend to be delighted at their safe return when he saw them.

She picked up Chantal and took the steep footpath toward the village. She could feel the heat of the rock through the thin soles of her sandals.

She still had not confronted Jean-Pierre. However, this could not go on indefinitely. Sooner or later he would learn that Mohammed had sent a runner to divert the convoy from its prearranged route. Naturally he would then ask Mohammed why this had been done, and Mohammed would tell him about Jane's "vision." But Jean-Pierre knew Jane did not believe in visions. . . .

Why am I afraid? she asked herself. I'm not the guilty one—he is. Yet I feel as if his secret is something I must be ashamed of. I should have spoken to him about it immediately, that evening we walked up to the top of the cliff. By nursing it to myself for so long, I, too, have become a deceiver. Perhaps that's it. Or perhaps it's the peculiar look in his eyes sometimes. . . .

She had not given up her determination to go home, but so far she had failed to think of a way to persuade Jean-Pierre to go. She had dreamed up a dozen bizarre schemes, from faking a message to say that his mother was dying, to poisoning his yogurt with something that would give him the symptoms of an illness which would force him to return to Europe for treatment. The simplest, and least far-fetched, of her ideas was to threaten to tell Mohammed that Jean-Pierre was a spy. She would never do it, of course, for to unmask him would be as good as killing him. But would Jean-Pierre *think* she might carry out the threat? Probably not. It would take a hard, pitiless, stone-hearted man to believe her capable of virtually killing her husband—and if Jean-Pierre were that hard and pitiless and stone-hearted, he might kill Jane.

She shivered despite the heat. This talk of killing was grotesque. When two people take such delight in one another's bodies as we do, she thought, how can they possibly do each other violence?

As she reached the village she began to hear the random, exuberant gunfire that signified an Afghan celebration. She made her way to the mosque—everything happened at the mosque. The convoy was in the courtyard, men and horses and baggage surrounded by smiling women and squealing children. Jane stood at the edge of the crowd, watching. It was worth it, she thought. It was worth the worry and the fear, and it was worth manipulating Mohammed in that undignified way, in order to see this, the men safely reunited with their wives and mothers and sons and daughters.

What happened next was probably the greatest shock of her life.

There in the crowd, among the caps and turbans, appeared a head of curly blond hair. At first she did not recognize it, even though its familiarity tugged at her heartstrings. Then it emerged from the crowd, and she saw, hiding behind an incredibly bushy blond beard, the face of Ellis Thaler.

Jane's knees suddenly felt weak. Ellis? Here? It was impossible.

He walked toward her. He was wearing the loose pajamalike cotton clothes of the Afghans, and a dirty blanket around his broad shoulders. The little of his face that was still visible above the beard was deeply tanned, so that his sky blue eyes were even more striking than usual, like cornflowers in a field of ripe wheat.

Jane was struck dumb.

Ellis stood in front of her, his face solemn. "Hello, Jane."

She realized she no longer hated him. A month ago she would have cursed him for deceiving her and spying on her friends; but now her anger had gone. She would never like him, but she could tolerate him. And it was nice to hear English spoken for the first time in more than a year.

"Ellis," she said weakly. "What in heaven's name are you doing here?"

"The same as you," he said.

What did that mean? Spying? No, Ellis did not know what Jean-Pierre was.

Ellis saw Jane's confused expression and said: "I mean I'm here to help the rebels."

Would he find out about Jean-Pierre? Jane was suddenly afraid for her husband. Ellis might kill him—

"Who does the baby belong to?" Ellis said.

"Me. And Jean-Pierre. Her name is Chantal." Jane saw that Ellis suddenly looked terribly sad. She realized he had been hoping to find her unhappy with her husband. Oh, God, I think he's still in love with me, she thought. She tried to change the subject. "But how will you help the rebels?"

He hefted his bag. It was a large, sausage-shaped thing of khaki canvas, like an old-fashioned soldier's kit bag. "I'm going to teach them how to blow up roads and bridges," he said. "So, you see, in this war I'm on the same side as you."

But not the same side as Jean-Pierre, she thought. What will happen now? The Afghans did not for one moment suspect Jean-Pierre, but Ellis was trained in the ways of deception. Sooner or later he would guess what was going on. "How long are you going to be here?" she asked him. If it was a short stay he might not have time to develop suspicions.

"For the summer," he said imprecisely.

Perhaps he would not spend much time around Jean-Pierre. "Where will you live?" she asked him.

"In this village."

"Oh."

He heard the disappointment in her voice and gave a wry smile. "I guess I shouldn't have expected you to be *glad* to see me. . . ."

Jane's mind was racing ahead. If she could make Jean-Pierre quit, he would be in no further danger. Suddenly she felt able to confront him. Why is that? she wondered. It's because I'm not afraid of him anymore. Why am I not afraid of him? Because Ellis is here.

I hadn't realized I was afraid of my husband.

"On the contrary," she said to Ellis, thinking: how cool I am! "I'm happy you're here."

There was a silence. Ellis clearly did not know what to make of Jane's reaction. After a moment he said: "Uh, I have a lot of explosives and stuff somewhere in this zoo. I'd better get to it."

Jane nodded. "Okay."

Ellis turned away and disappeared into the melee. Jane walked slowly out of the courtyard, feeling a little stunned. Ellis was *here*, in the Five Lions Valley, and apparently still in love with her.

As she reached the shopkeeper's house, Jean-Pierre came out. He had stopped there on his way to the mosque, probably to put away his medical bag. Jane was not sure what to say to him. "The convoy brought someone you know," she began.

"A European?"

"Yes."

"Well, who?"

"Go and see. You'll be surprised."

He hurried off. Jane went inside. What would Jean-Pierre do about Ellis? she wondered. Well, he would want to tell the Russians. And the Russians would want to kill Ellis.

The thought made her angry. "There is to be no more killing!" she said aloud. "I will not permit it!" Her voice made Chantal cry. Jane rocked her and she became quiet.

What am I going to do about it? thought Jane.

I have to stop him getting in touch with the Russians.

How?

His contact can't meet him here in the village. So all I have to do is keep Jean-Pierre here.

I'll say to him: You must promise not to leave the village. If you refuse I'll tell Ellis that you're a spy and *he* will make sure you don't leave the village.

Suppose Jean-Pierre makes the promise, then breaks it?

Well, I would *know* he had gone out of the village, and I would *know* he was meeting his contact, and I could then warn Ellis.

Has he any other way of communicating with the Russians?

He must have some means of getting in touch with them in an emergency.

But there are no phones here, no mail, no courier service, no carrier pigeons—

He must have a radio.

If he has a radio there's no way I can stop him.

The more she thought about it, the more convinced she was that he had a radio. He needed to arrange those meetings in stone huts. In theory they might have all been scheduled before he left Paris, but in practice that was almost impossible: what would happen when he had to break an appointment, or when he was late, or when he needed to meet his contact urgently?

He *must* have a radio.

What can I do if he has a radio?

I can take it away from him.

She put Chantal down in her cradle and looked around the house. She went into the front room. There on the tiled counter in the middle of what had been the shop was Jean-Pierre's medical bag.

It was the obvious place. No one was allowed to open the bag except Jane, and she never had any reason to.

She undid the clasp and went through the contents, taking them out one by one.

There was no radio.

It was not going to be that easy.

He *must* have one, she thought, and I *must* find it: if I don't, either Ellis will kill him or he will kill Ellis.

She decided to search the house.

She checked through the medical supplies on the shopkeeper's shelves, looking in all the boxes and packets whose seals had been broken, hurrying for fear he would come back before she was finished. She found nothing.

She went into the bedroom. She rummaged through his clothes, then in the winter bedding, which was stored in a corner. Nothing. Moving faster, she went into the living room and looked around frantically for possible hiding places. The map chest! She opened it. Only the maps were there. She closed the lid with a bang. Chantal stirred but did not cry, even though it was almost time for her feed. You're a good baby, thought Jane, thank God! She looked behind the food cupboard and lifted the rug in case there was a concealed hole in the floor.

Nothing.

It had to be here somewhere. She could not imagine that he would take the risk of hiding it *outside* the house, for there would be a terrible danger of its being found by accident.

She went back into the shop. If only she could find his radio everything would be all right—he would have no option but to give in.

His bag was so much the obvious place, for he took it with him wherever he went. She picked it up. It was heavy. She felt around inside it yet again. It had a thick base.

Suddenly she was inspired.

The bag could have a false bottom.

She probed the base with her fingers. It must be here, she thought; it *must*.

She pushed her fingers down beside the base and lifted.

The false bottom came up easily.

With her heart in her mouth, she looked inside.

There, in the hidden compartment, was a black plastic box. She took it out.

That's it, she thought; he calls them on this little radio.

Why does he meet them as well?

Perhaps he cannot tell them secrets over the radio for fear that someone is listening. Perhaps the radio is only for arranging meetings, and for emergencies.

Like when he can't leave the village.

She heard the back door open. Terrified, she dropped the radio to the floor and spun around, looking into the living room. It was only Fara with a broom. "Oh, Christ," she said aloud. She turned back, her heart racing.

She had to get rid of the radio before Jean-Pierre returned.

But how? She could not throw it away—it would be found.

She had to smash it.

With what?

She did not have a hammer.

A stone, then.

She hurried through the living room and into the courtyard. The courtyard wall was made of rough stones held together with sandy mortar. She reached up and wiggled one of the top row of stones. It seemed firm. She tried the next, and the next. The fourth stone seemed a little loose. She reached up and tugged at it. It moved a little. "Come on, come on," she cried. She pulled hard. The rough stone cut into the skin of her hands. She gave a mighty heave and the stone came loose. She jumped back as it fell to the ground. It was about the size of a can of beans: just right. She picked it up in both hands and hurried back into the house.

She went into the front room. She picked up the black plastic radio transmitter from the floor and placed it on the tiled counter. Then she lifted the stone above her head and brought it down with all her might on the radio.

The plastic casing cracked.

She would have to hit it harder.

She lifted the stone and brought it down again. This time the casing broke, revealing the innards of the instrument: she saw a printed circuit, a loudspeaker cone and a pair of batteries with Russian script on them. She took out the batteries and threw them on the floor, then started to smash the mechanism.

She was grabbed from behind suddenly, and Jean-Pierre's voice shouted: "What are you doing?"

She struggled against his grip, got free for a moment and struck another blow at the little radio.

He grasped her shoulders and hurled her aside. She stumbled and fell to the floor. She landed awkwardly, twisting her wrist.

He stared at the radio. "It's ruined!" he said. "It's irreparable!" He grabbed her by the shirt and hauled her to her feet. "You don't know what you've done!" he screamed. There was despair and hot rage in his eyes.

"Let me go!" she shouted at him. He had no right to act like this when it was *he* who had lied to *her*. "How *dare* you manhandle me!"

"How *dare* I?" He let go of her shirt, drew back his arm and punched her hard. The blow landed in the middle of her abdomen. For a split second she was simply paralyzed with shock; then the pain came, deep inside where she was still sore from having had Chantal, and she cried out and bent over with her hands clutching her middle.

Her eyes were shut tight, so she did not see the second blow coming.

His punch landed full on her mouth. She screamed. She could hardly believe he was doing this to her. She opened her eyes and looked at him, terrified that he would hit her again.

"How *dare* I?" he screamed. "How *dare* I?"

She fell to her knees on the dirt floor, and began to sob with shock and pain and misery. Her mouth hurt so much she could hardly speak. "Please don't hit me," she managed. "Don't hit me again." She held a hand in front of her face defensively.

He knelt down, shoved her hand aside and thrust his face into hers. "How long have you known?" he hissed.

She licked her lips. They were swelling already. She dabbed at them with her sleeve, and it came away bloody. She said: "Since I saw you in the stone hut . . . on the way to Cobak."

"But you didn't see anything!"

"He spoke with a Russian accent, and said he had blisters. I figured it out from there."

There was a pause while that sank in. "Why now?" he said. "Why didn't you break the radio before?"

"I didn't dare to."

"And now?"

"Ellis is here."

"So?"

Jane summoned up what little courage she had left. "If you don't stop this . . . spying . . . I'll tell Ellis, and he will stop you."

He took her by the throat. "And what if I strangle you, you bitch?"

"If any harm comes to me . . . Ellis will want to know why. He's still in love with me."

She stared at him. Hatred burned in his eyes. "Now I'll never get him!" he said. She wondered who he meant. Ellis? No. Masud? Could it be that

Jean-Pierre's ultimate purpose was to kill Masud? His hands were still around her throat. She felt his grip tighten. She watched his face fearfully.

Then Chantal cried.

Jean-Pierre's expression changed dramatically. The hostility went from his eyes, and the fixed, taut look of anger crumpled; and finally, to Jane's amazement, he put his hands over his eyes and began to cry.

She gazed at him with incredulity. She found herself feeling pity for him, and thought: Don't be a fool—the bastard just beat you up. But despite herself she was touched by his tears. "Don't cry," she said quietly. Her voice was surprisingly gentle. She touched his cheek.

"I'm sorry," he said. "I'm sorry for what I did to you. My life's work . . . all for nothing."

She realized with astonishment and a trace of self-disgust that she was no longer angry with him, despite her swollen lips and the continuing pain in her tummy. She gave in to the sentiment, and put her arms around him, patting his back as if comforting a child.

"Just because of Anatoly's accent," he mumbled. "Just because of that."

"Forget Anatoly," she said.

"We'll leave Afghanistan and go back to Europe. We'll go with the next convoy." He took his hands from his face and looked at her. "When we get back to Paris . . ."

"Yes?"

"When we're home . . . I still want us to be together. Can you forgive me? I love you—truly, I always loved you. And we're married. And there's Chantal. Please, Jane—please don't leave me. Please?"

To her surprise she felt no hesitation. He was the man she loved, her husband, the father of her child; and he was in trouble and appealing for help. "I'm not going anywhere," she replied.

"Promise," he said. "Promise you won't leave me."

She smiled at him with her bleeding mouth. "I love you," she said. "I promise I won't leave you."

CHAPTER NINE

E llis was frustrated, impatient and angry. He was frustrated because he had been in the Five Lions Valley for seven days and still had not met Masud. He was impatient because it was a daily purgatory for him to see Jane and Jean-Pierre living together and working together and sharing the pleasure of their happy little baby girl. And he was angry because he and nobody else had got himself into this wretched situation.

They had said he would meet Masud today, but the great man had not shown up so far. Ellis had walked all day yesterday to get here. He was at the southwestern end of the Five Lions Valley, in Russian territory. He had left Banda accompanied by three guerrillas—Ali Ghanim, Matullah Khan and Yussuf Gul—but they had accumulated two or three more at each village, and now they were thirty altogether. They sat in a circle, underneath a fig tree near the top of a hill, eating figs and waiting.

At the foot of the hill on which they sat, a flattish plain began and stretched south—all the way to Kabul, in fact, although that was fifty miles away and they could not see it. In the same direction, but much closer, was the Bagram air base, just ten miles away: its buildings were not visible, but they could see the occasional jet rising into the air. The plain was a fertile mosaic of fields and orchards, crisscrossed with streams all feeding into the Five Lions River as it flowed, wider and deeper now but just as fast, toward the capital city. A rough road ran past the foot of the hill and went up the

Valley as far as the town of Rokha, which was the northernmost limit of
Russian territory here. There was not much traffic on the road: a few peasant carts and an occasional armored car. Where the road crossed the river
there was a new Russian-built bridge.

Ellis was going to blow up the bridge.

The lessons in explosives, which he was giving in order to mask for as
long as possible his real mission, were hugely popular, and he had been
obliged to limit the numbers attending. This was despite his hesitant Dari.
He remembered a little Farsi from Tehran, and he had picked up a lot of
Dari on his way here with the convoy, so that he could talk about the landscape, food, horses and weapons, but he still could not say such things as
The indentation in the explosive material has the effect of focusing the blast. Nevertheless the idea of blowing things up appealed so much to the Afghan
machismo that he always had an attentive audience. He could not teach
them the formulas for calculating the amount of TNT required for a job, or
even show them how to use his idiot-proof U.S. Army computing tape, for
none of them had done elementary school arithmetic and most of them
could not read. Nevertheless he was able to show them how to destroy
things more decisively and at the same time use less matériel—which was
very important to them, for all ordnance was in short supply. He had also
tried to get them to adopt basic safety precautions, but in this he had failed:
to them caution was cowardly.

Meanwhile he was tortured by Jane.

He was jealous when he saw her touch Jean-Pierre; he was envious when
he saw the two of them in the cave clinic, working together so efficiently
and harmoniously; and he was consumed by lust when he caught a glimpse
of Jane's swollen breast as she fed her baby. He would lie awake at night,
under his sleeping bag in the house of Ismael Gul, where he was staying,
and he would turn constantly, sometimes sweating and sometimes shivering, unable to get comfortable on the floor of packed earth, trying not to
hear the muffled sounds of Ismael and his wife making love a few yards away
in the next room; and the palms of his hands seemed to itch to touch Jane.

He had nobody to blame but himself for all this. He had volunteered for
the mission in the foolish hope that he might win Jane back. It was unpro-
fessional, as well as immature. All he could do was get out of here as quickly
as possible.

And he could do nothing until he met Masud.

He stood up and walked around restlessly, careful nonetheless to stay in
the shade of the tree so that he would not be visible from the road. A few

yards away there was a mass of twisted metal where a helicopter had crashed. He saw a thin piece of steel about the size and shape of a dinner plate, and that gave him an idea. He had been wondering how to demonstrate the effect of shaped charges and now he saw a way.

He took from his kit bag a small, flat piece of TNT and a pocketknife. The guerrillas clustered closer around him. Among them was Ali Ghanim, a small, misshapen man—twisted nose, deformed teeth, and a slightly hunched back—who was said to have fourteen children. Ellis carved the name *Ali* into the TNT in Persian script. He showed it to them. Ali recognized his name. "Ali," he said, grinning and showing his hideous teeth.

Ellis placed the explosive, carved side down, on the piece of steel. "I hope this works," he said with a smile, and they all smiled back, although none of them spoke English. He took a coil of blasting fuse from his capacious bag and cut off a four-foot length. He got out his cap box, took a blasting cap and inserted the end of the fuse into the cylindrical cap. He taped the cap to the TNT.

He looked down the hill to the road. He could see no traffic. He carried his little bomb across the hillside and put it down about fifty yards away. He lit the fuse with a match, then walked back to the fig tree.

The fuse was slow-burning. Ellis wondered, while he waited, whether Masud was having him watched and weighed up by the other guerrillas. Was the leader waiting for assurance that Ellis was a serious person whom the guerrillas could respect? Protocol was always important in an army, even a revolutionary one. But Ellis could not pussyfoot around much longer. If Masud did not show today, Ellis would have to drop all this explosives nonsense, confess to being an envoy from the White House, and demand a meeting with the rebel leader immediately.

There was an unimpressive bang and a small cloud of dust. The guerrillas looked disappointed at such a feeble blast. Ellis retrieved the piece of metal, using his scarf to hold it in case it was hot. The name *Ali* was cut through it in ragged-edge letters of Persian script. He showed it to the guerrillas, and they burst into excited chatter. Ellis was pleased: it was a vivid demonstration of the point that the explosive was *more* powerful where it was indented, contrary to what common sense would suggest.

The guerrillas suddenly went quiet. Ellis looked around and saw another group of seven or eight men approaching over the hill. Their rifles and round Chitrali caps marked them as guerrillas. As they came nearer, Ali stiffened, almost as if he were about to salute. Ellis said: "Who is it?"

"Masud," Ali replied.

"Which one is he?"

"The one in the middle."

Ellis studied the central figure in the group. Masud looked just like the others at first: a thin man of average height, dressed in khaki clothes and Russian boots. Ellis scrutinized his face. He was light-skinned, with a sparse mustache and the wispy beard of a teenager. He had a long nose with a hooked point. His alert dark eyes were surrounded by heavy lines which made him look at least five years older than his reputed age of twenty-eight. It was not a handsome face, but there was in it an air of lively intelligence and calm authority that distinguished him from the men around him.

He came directly to Ellis with his hand outstretched. "I am Masud."

"Ellis Thaler." Ellis shook his hand.

"We're going to blow up this bridge," Masud said in French.

"You want to get started?"

"Yes."

Ellis packed his equipment into his kit bag while Masud went around the group of guerrillas, shaking hands with some, nodding to others, embracing one or two, speaking a few words to each.

When they were ready they went down the hill in a straggle, hoping—Ellis presumed—that if they were seen they would be taken for a group of peasants rather than a unit of the rebel army. When they reached the foot of the hill they were no longer visible from the road, although anyone overhead in a helicopter would have noticed them: Ellis presumed they would take cover if they heard a chopper. They headed for the river, following a footpath through the cultivated fields. They passed several small houses and were seen by the people working in the fields, some of whom ignored them studiously while others waved and called out greetings. The guerrillas reached the river and walked along its bank, gaining what cover they could from the boulders and sparse vegetation at the water's edge. When they were about three hundred yards from the bridge, a small convoy of army trucks began to cross it, and they all hid while the vehicles rumbled by, heading for Rokha. Ellis lay beneath a willow tree and found Masud beside him. "If we destroy the bridge," Masud said, "we will cut their supply line to Rokha."

After the trucks had gone they waited a few minutes, they walked the rest of the way to the bridge and clustered beneath, invisible from the road.

At its midpoint the bridge was twenty feet above the river, which seemed to be about ten feet deep here. Ellis saw that it was a simple stringer bridge—two long steel girders, or stringers, supporting a flat slab of concrete road and stretching from one bank to the other without intermediate support. The concrete was dead load—the girders took the strain. Break them and the bridge was ruined.

Ellis set about his preparations. His TNT was in one-pound yellow blocks. He made a stack of ten blocks and taped them together. Then he made three more identical stacks, using all his explosive. He was using TNT because that was the substance most often found in bombs, shells, mines and hand grenades, and the guerrillas got most of their supplies from unexploded Russian ordnance. Plastic explosive would have been more suitable for their needs, for it could be stuffed into holes, wrapped around girders and generally molded into any shape required—but they had to work with the materials they could find and steal. They could occasionally get a little *plastique* from the Russian engineers by trading it for marijuana grown in the Valley, but the transaction—which involved intermediaries in the Afghan regular army—was risky and supplies were limited. All this Ellis had been told by the CIA's man in Peshawar, and it had turned out to be right.

The girders above him were I-beams spaced about eight feet apart. Ellis said in Dari: "Somebody find me a stick this long," indicating the space between the beams. One of the guerrillas walked along the riverbank and uprooted a young tree. "I need another one just the same," Ellis said.

He put a stack of TNT on the lower lip of one of the I-beams and asked a guerrilla to hold it in place. He put another stack on the other I-beam in a similar position; then he forced the young tree between the two stacks so that it kept them both where they were.

He waded through the river and did exactly the same at the other end of the bridge.

He described everything he was doing in a mixture of Dari, French and English, letting them pick up what they could—the most important thing was for them to see what he was doing, and its results. He fused the charges with Primacord, the high-explosive detonating cord that burned at 21,000 feet per second, and he connected the four stacks so that they would explode simultaneously. He then made a ring main by looping the Primacord back on itself. The effect, he explained to Masud in French, would be that the cord burned down to the TNT from both ends, so that if somehow the cable was severed in one place the bomb would still go off. He recommended this as a routine precaution.

He felt oddly happy as he worked. There was something soothing about mechanical tasks and the dispassionate calculation of poundage of explosive. And now that Masud had shown up at last, he could get on with his mission.

He trailed the Primacord through the water so that it was less visible—it would burn perfectly well underwater—and brought it out onto the riverbank. He attached a blasting cap to the end of the Primacord, then added a four-minute length of ordinary, slow-burning blasting fuse.

"Ready?" he said to Masud.

Masud said: "Yes."

Ellis lit the fuse.

They all walked away briskly, heading upstream along the riverbank. Ellis felt a certain secret boyish glee about the enormous bang he was about to create. The others seemed excited, too, and he wondered whether he was as bad at concealing his enthusiasm as they were. It was while he was looking at them in this way that their expressions altered dramatically, and they all became alert suddenly, like birds listening for worms in the ground; and then Ellis heard it—the distant rumble of tank tracks.

The road was not visible from where they were, but one of the guerrillas quickly shinnied up a tree. "Two," he reported.

Masud took Ellis's arm. "Can you destroy the bridge while the tanks are on it?" he said.

Oh, shit, thought Ellis, this is a test. "Yes," he said rashly.

Masud nodded, smiling faintly. "Good."

Ellis scrambled up the tree alongside the guerrilla and looked across the fields. There were two black tanks trundling heavily along the narrow stony road from Kabul. He felt very tense: this was his first sight of the enemy. With their armor plating and their enormous guns they looked invulnerable, especially by contrast with the ragged guerrillas and their rifles; and yet the Valley was littered with the remains of tanks the guerrillas had destroyed with homemade mines, well-placed grenades and stolen rockets.

There were no other vehicles with the tanks. It was not a patrol, then, or a raiding party; the tanks were probably being delivered to Rokha after being repaired at Bagram, or perhaps they had just arrived from the Soviet Union.

He began calculating.

The tanks were going at about ten miles per hour, so they would reach the bridge in a minute and a half. The fuse had been burning for less than a minute: it had at least three minutes to go. At present the tanks would be across the bridge and a safe distance away before the explosion. He had to shorten the fuse.

He dropped from the tree and started to run, thinking: How the hell many years is it since the last time I was in a combat zone?

He heard footsteps behind him and glanced back. Ali was running right behind him, grinning horribly, and two more men were close on his heels. The others were taking cover along the riverbank.

A moment later he reached the bridge and dropped to one knee beside his slow-burning fuse, slipping the kit bag off his shoulder as he did so. He continued to calculate while he fumbled the bag open and rooted around for his pocketknife. The tanks were now a minute away, he thought. Blasting fuse burned at the rate of a foot every thirty to forty-five seconds. Was this particular reel slow, average or fast? He seemed to recall that it was fast. Say a foot, then, for a thirty-second delay. In thirty seconds he could run about a hundred and fifty yards—enough for safety, just barely.

He opened the pocketknife and handed it to Ali, who had knelt down beside him. Ellis grabbed the fuse wire at a point a foot from where it was joined to the blasting cap, and held it with both hands for Ali to cut. He held the severed end in his left hand and the burning fuse in his right. He was not sure whether it was time yet to relight the severed end. He had to see how far away the tanks were.

He scrambled up the embankment, still holding both pieces of fuse wire. Behind him, the Primacord trailed in the river. He poked his head up over the parapet of the bridge. The great black tanks rolled steadily closer. How soon? He was guessing wildly. He counted seconds, measuring their progress; and then, not calculating but hoping for the best, he put the burning end of the disconnected blasting fuse to the cut end that was still connected with the bombs.

He put the burning fuse down carefully on the ground and started to run. Ali and the other two guerrillas followed him.

At first they were hidden from the tanks by the riverbank, but as the tanks came closer the four running men were clearly visible. Ellis was counting slow seconds as the rumble of the tanks turned into a roar.

The gunners in the tanks hesitated only momentarily: Afghans running away could be presumed to be guerrillas, and therefore suitable for target practice. There was a double *boom* and two shells flew over Ellis's head. He changed direction, running off to the side, away from the river, thinking: The gunner adjusts his range . . . now he swings the barrel toward me . . . he aims . . . *now*. He dodged again, veering back toward the river, and a second later heard another *boom*. The shell landed close enough to spatter him with earth and stones. The next one will hit me, he thought, unless the damn bomb goes off first. Shit. Why did I have to show Masud how fucking macho I am? Then he heard a machine gun open up. It's hard to aim straight from a moving tank, he thought; but perhaps they will stop. He visualized the spray of machine-gun bullets waving toward him, and he began to bob and weave. He realized all of a sudden that he could guess exactly what the Russians would do: they would stop the tanks where they got the clearest view of the fleeing guerrillas, and that would be on the bridge. But would the bomb go off before the machine gunners hit their targets? He ran harder, his heart pounding and his breath coming in great gulps. I don't want to die, even if she loves him, he thought. He saw bullets chip a boulder almost in his path. He swerved suddenly, but the stream of fire followed him. It seemed hopeless: he was an easy target. He heard one of the guerrillas behind him cry out; then he was hit, twice in succession he felt a burning pain across his hip, then an impact, like a heavy blow, in his right buttock. The second slug paralyzed his leg momentarily, and he stumbled and fell, bruising his chest, then rolled over onto his back. He sat up, ignoring the pain, and tried to move. The two tanks had stopped on the bridge. Ali, who had been right behind him, now put his hands under Ellis's armpits and tried to lift him. The pair of them were sitting ducks: the gunners in the tanks could not miss.

Then the bomb went off.

It was beautiful.

The four simultaneous explosions sheared the bridge at both ends, leaving the midsection—with two tanks on it—totally unsupported. At first it fell slowly, its broken ends grinding; then it came free and dropped, spectacularly, into the rushing river, landing flat with a monster splash. The waters parted majestically, leaving the riverbed visible for a moment, then came together again with a sound like a thunderclap.

When the noise died away, Ellis heard the guerrillas cheering.

Some of them emerged from cover and ran toward the half-submerged tanks. Ali lifted Ellis to his feet. The feeling returned to his legs in a rush, and he realized that he was hurting. "I'm not sure I can walk," he said to Ali in Dari. He took a step, and would have fallen if Ali had not been holding him. "Oh, shit," Ellis said in English. "I think I've got a bullet in my ass."

He heard shots. Looking up, he saw the surviving Russians trying to escape from the tanks, and the guerrillas picking them off as they emerged. They were cold-blooded bastards, these Afghans. Looking down, he saw that the right leg of his trousers was soaked with blood. That would be from the surface wound, he surmised: he felt that the bullet was still plugging the other wound.

Masud came up to him, smiling broadly. "That was well done, the bridge," he said in his heavily accented French. "Magnificent!"

"Thanks," said Ellis. "But I didn't come here to blow up bridges." He felt weak and a little dizzy, but now was the time to state his business. "I came to make a deal."

Masud looked at him curiously. "Where are you from?"

"Washington. The White House. I represent the President of the United States."

Masud nodded, unsurprised. "Good. I'm glad."

It was at that moment that Ellis fainted.

He made his pitch to Masud that night.

The guerrillas rigged up a stretcher and carried him up the Valley to Astana, where they stopped at dusk. Masud had already sent a runner on to Banda to fetch Jean-Pierre, who would arrive sometime tomorrow to take the bullet out of Ellis's backside. Meanwhile they all settled down in the courtyard of a farmhouse. Ellis's pain had dulled, but the journey had made him weaker. The guerrillas had put primitive dressings on his wounds.

An hour or so after arrival he was given hot, sweet green tea, which revived him somewhat, and a little later they all had mulberries and yogurt for supper. It was usually like that with the guerrillas, Ellis had observed while traveling with the convoy from Pakistan to the Valley: an hour or two after they arrived somewhere, food would appear. Ellis did not know whether they bought it, commandeered it, or received it as a gift, but he guessed that it was given to them free, sometimes willingly and sometimes reluctantly.

When they had eaten, Masud sat near Ellis, and in the next few minutes most of the other guerrillas casually moved off, leaving Masud and two of his lieutenants alone with Ellis. Ellis knew he had to talk to Masud now, for there might not be another chance for a week. Yet he felt too feeble and exhausted for this subtle and difficult task.

Masud said: "Many years ago, a foreign country asked the King of Afghanistan for five hundred warriors to help in a war. The Afghan king sent five men from our Valley, with a message saying that it is better to have five lions than five hundred foxes. This is how our Valley came to be called the Valley of the Five Lions." He smiled. "You were a lion today."

Ellis said, "I heard a legend saying there used to be five great warriors, known as the Five Lions, each of whom guarded one of the five ways into the Valley. And I heard that this is why they call you the Sixth Lion."

"Enough of legends," Masud said with a smile. "What do you have to tell me?"

Ellis had rehearsed this conversation, and in his script it did not begin so abruptly. Clearly, Oriental indirection was not Masud's style. Ellis said: "I have first to ask you for your assessment of the war."

Masud nodded, thought for a few seconds and said: "The Russians have twelve thousand troops in the town of Rokha, the gateway to the Valley. Their dispositions are as always: first minefields, then Afghan troops, then Russian troops to stop the Afghans running away. They are expecting another twelve hundred men as reinforcements. They plan to launch a major offensive up the Valley within two weeks. Their aim is to destroy our forces."

Ellis wondered how Masud got such precise intelligence, but he was not so tactless as to ask. Instead he said: "And will the offensive succeed?"

"No," said Masud with quiet confidence. "When they attack, we melt into the hills, so there is no one here for them to fight. When they stop, we harass them from the high ground and cut their lines of communication. Gradually we wear them down. They find themselves spending vast resources to hold territory which gives them no military advantage. Finally they retreat. It is always so."

It was a textbook account of guerrilla war, Ellis reflected. There was no question that Masud could teach the other tribal leaders a lot. "How long do you think the Russians can go on making such futile attacks?"

Masud shrugged. "It is in God's hands."

"Will you ever be able to drive them out of your country?"

"The Vietnamese drove the Americans out," Masud said with a smile.

"I know—I was there," said Ellis. "Do you know *how* they did it?"

"One important factor, in my opinion, is that the Vietnamese were receiving from the Russians supplies of the most modern weapons, especially portable surface-to-air missiles. This is the only way guerrilla forces can fight back against aircraft and helicopters."

"I agree," said Ellis. "More important, the United States government agrees. We would like to help you get hold of better weapons. But we would need to see you make real progress against your enemy with those weapons. The American people like to see what they're getting for their money. How soon do you think the Afghan resistance will be able to launch unified, countrywide assaults on the Russians, the way the Vietnamese did toward the end of the war?"

Masud shook his head dubiously. "The unification of the Resistance is at a very early stage."

"What are the main obstacles?" Ellis held his breath, praying that Masud would give the expected answer.

"Mistrust between different fighting groups is the main obstacle."

Ellis breathed a clandestine sigh of relief.

Masud went on: "We are different tribes, different nations, and we have different commanders. Other guerrilla groups ambush my convoys and steal my supplies."

"Mistrust," Ellis repeated. "What else?"

"Communications. We need a regular network of messengers. Eventually we must have radio contact, but that is far in the future."

"Mistrust, and inadequate communications." This was what Ellis had hoped to hear. "Let's talk about something else." He felt terribly tired: he had lost quite a lot of blood. He fought off a powerful desire to close his eyes. "You here in the Valley have developed the art of guerrilla warfare more successfully than they have anywhere else in Afghanistan. Other leaders still waste their resources defending lowland territory and attacking strong positions. We would like you to train men from other parts of the country in modern guerrilla tactics. Would you consider that?"

"Yes—and I think I see where you're heading," said Masud. "After a year or so there would be in each zone of the Resistance a small cadre of men who had been trained in the Five Lions Valley. They could form a communications net. They would understand one another—they would trust me. . . ." His voice tailed off, but Ellis could see from his face that he was still unwinding the implications in his head.

"All right," said Ellis. He had run out of energy, but he was almost done. "Here's the deal. If you can get the agreement of other commanders and set up that training program, the U.S. will supply you with RPG-7 rocket launchers, ground-to-air missiles and radio equipment. But there are two other commanders in particular who must be part of the agreement. They are Jahan Kamil, in the Pich Valley, and Amal Azizi, the commander of Faizabad."

Masud grinned ruefully. "You picked the toughest."

"I know," said Ellis. "Can you do it?"

"Let me think about it," said Masud.

"All right." Exhausted, Ellis lay back on the cold ground and shut his eyes. A moment later he was asleep.

CHAPTER TEN

J ean-Pierre walked aimlessly through the moonlit fields in the depths of a black depression. A week ago he had been fulfilled and happy, master of the situation, doing useful work while he waited for his big chance. Now it was all over, and he felt worthless, a failure, a might-have-been.

There was no way out. He ran over the possibilities again and again, but he always ended up with the same conclusion: he had to leave Afghanistan.

His usefulness as a spy was over. He had no means of contacting Anatoly; and, even if Jane had not smashed the radio, he was unable to leave the village to meet Anatoly, for Jane would immediately know what he was doing and would tell Ellis. He might have been able to silence Jane somehow (*Don't think about it, don't even think about it*) but if anything happened to her Ellis would want to know why. It all came down to Ellis. I'd like to kill Ellis, he thought, if I had the nerve. But how? I have no gun. What would I do, cut his throat with a scalpel? He's much stronger than I am—I could never overcome him.

He thought about how it had gone wrong. He and Anatoly had become careless. They should have met in a place from which they had a good view of the approaches all around, so that they could have been forewarned of any approach. But who would have thought that Jane might follow him? He was the victim of the most appallingly bad luck: that the wounded boy was allergic to penicillin; that Jane had heard Anatoly speak; that she was able to recognize a Russian accent; and that Ellis had turned up to give her courage. It *was* bad luck. But the history books do not remember the men who *almost* achieved greatness. I did my best, Papa, he thought; and he could almost hear his father's reply: I'm not interested in whether you did your best. I want to know whether you succeeded or failed.

He was approaching the village. He decided to turn in. He was sleeping badly, but there was nothing else to do but go to bed. He headed for home.

Somehow the fact that he still had Jane was not much consolation. Her discovery of his secret seemed to have made them less intimate, not more. A new distance had grown up between them, even though they were planning their return home and even talking about their new life back in Europe.

At least they still hugged one another in bed at night. That was something.

He went into the shopkeeper's house. He had expected Jane to be in bed already, but to his surprise she was still up. She spoke as soon as he walked in. "A runner came for you from Masud. You have to go to Astana. Ellis is wounded."

Ellis wounded. Jean-Pierre's heart beat faster. "How?"

"Nothing serious. I gather he's got a bullet in his bum."

"I'll go first thing in the morning."

Jane nodded. "The runner will go with you. You can be back by nightfall."

"I see." Jane was making sure he had no opportunity of meeting with Anatoly. Her caution was unnecessary: Jean-Pierre had no way of arranging such a meeting. Besides, Jane was guarding against a minor peril and overlooking a major one. Ellis was *wounded*. That made him *vulnerable*. Which changed everything.

Now Jean-Pierre could kill him.

Jean-Pierre was awake all night, thinking about it. He imagined Ellis lying on a mattress under a fig tree, gritting his teeth against the pain of a smashed bone, or perhaps pale and weak from loss of blood. He saw himself preparing an injection. "This is an antibiotic to prevent infection of the wound," he would say; then he would inject him with an overdose of digitalis, which would give him a heart attack.

A natural heart attack was unlikely, but by no means impossible, in a man of thirty-four years, especially one who had been exercising strenuously after a long period of relatively sedentary work. Anyway, there would be no inquest, no postmortem, and no suspicions: in the West they would not doubt that Ellis had been wounded in action and had died of his wounds. Here in the Valley, everyone would accept Jean-Pierre's diagnosis. He was trusted as much as any of Masud's closest lieutenants—quite naturally, for he had sacrificed as much as any of them for the cause, it must seem to them. No, the only doubter would be Jane. And what could she do?

He was not sure. Jane was a formidable opponent when she was backed up by Ellis; but Jane alone was not. Jean-Pierre might be able to persuade her to stay in the Valley for another year: he could promise not to betray the convoys, then find a way to reestablish contact with Anatoly and just wait for his chance to pinpoint Masud for the Russians.

He gave Chantal her bottle at two a.m., then went back to bed. He did not even try to sleep. He was too anxious, too excited and too frightened. As he lay there waiting for the sun to rise, he thought of all the things that could go wrong: Ellis might refuse treatment; he, Jean-Pierre, might get the dosage wrong; Ellis might have suffered a mere scratch and be walking around normally; Ellis and Masud might even have left Astana already.

Jane's sleep was troubled by dreams. She tossed and turned beside him, occasionally muttering incomprehensible syllables. Only Chantal slept well.

Just before dawn Jean-Pierre got up, lit the fire and went to the river to bathe. When he came back, the runner was in his courtyard, drinking tea made by Fara and eating yesterday's leftover bread. Jean-Pierre took some tea, but could not eat anything.

Jane was feeding Chantal on the roof. Jean-Pierre went up and kissed them both good-bye. Every time he touched Jane he remembered how he had punched her, and he felt his whole being shudder with shame. She seemed to have forgiven him, but he could not forgive himself.

He led his old mare through the village and down to the riverside; then, with the runner at his side, he headed downstream. Between here and Astana there was a road, or what passed for a road in Five Lions: a strip of rocky earth, eight or ten feet wide and more or less flat, suitable for wooden carts or army jeeps although it would destroy an ordinary car within minutes. The Valley was a series of narrow rocky gorges broadening out at intervals to form small cultivated plains, a mile or two long and less than a mile wide, where the villagers scraped a living from the unwilling soil by hard work and clever irrigation. The road was good enough for Jean-Pierre to ride on the downhill stretches. (The horse was not good enough for him to ride uphill.)

The Valley must have been an idyllic place once upon a time, he thought as he rode south in the bright morning sunshine. Watered by the Five Lions River, made secure by its high valley walls, organized according to ancient traditions, and undisturbed except by a few butter carriers from Nuristan and the occasional ribbon salesman from Kabul, it must have been a throwback to the Middle Ages. Now the twentieth century had overtaken it with a vengeance. Almost every village had suffered some bomb damage: a water mill ruined, a meadow pitted with craters, an ancient wooden aqueduct smashed to splinters, a rubble-and-mortar bridge reduced to a few stepping-stones in the fast-moving river. The effect of all this on the economic life of the Valley was evident to Jean-Pierre's careful scrutiny. This house was a butcher's shop, but the wooden slab out front was bare of meat. This patch of weeds had once been a vegetable garden, but its owner had fled to Pakistan. There was an orchard, with fruit rotting on the ground when it should have been drying on a roof and ready to be stored for the long, cold winter: the woman and children who used to tend the orchard were dead, and the husband was a full-time guerrilla. That heap of mud and stones had been a mosque, and the villagers had decided not to rebuild it because it would probably get bombed again. All this waste and destruction happened because men such as Masud tried to resist the tide of history, and bamboozled the ignorant peasants into supporting them. With Masud out of the way, all this would end.

And with Ellis out of the way, Jean-Pierre could deal with Masud.

He wondered, as they approached Astana toward noon, whether he would find it difficult to stick the needle in. The idea of killing a patient was so grotesque that he did not know how he would react. He had seen patients die, of course; but even then he was consumed by regret that he could not save them. When he had Ellis helpless before him, and the needle in his hand, would he be tortured by doubt, like Macbeth, or vacillate, like Raskolnikov in *Crime and Punishment?*

They went through Sangana, with its cemetery and sandy beach, then followed the road around a bend in the river. There was a stretch of farmland in front of them and a cluster of houses up on the hillside. A minute or two later a boy of eleven or twelve approached them across the fields and led them not to the village on the hill, but to a large house at the edge of the farmland.

Still, Jean-Pierre felt no doubts, no hesitation, just a kind of anxious apprehension, like the hour before an important exam.

He took his medical bag off the horse, gave the reins to the boy, and went into the courtyard of the farmhouse.

Twenty or more guerrillas were scattered around, squatting on their haunches and staring into space, waiting with aboriginal patience. Masud was not there, Jean-Pierre noticed on looking around, but two of his closest aides were. Ellis was in a shady corner, lying on a blanket.

Jean-Pierre knelt down beside him. Ellis was evidently in some pain from the bullet. He was lying on his front. His face was taut, his teeth gritted. His skin was pale, and there was perspiration on his forehead. His breathing sounded harsh.

"It hurts, eh?" said Jean-Pierre in English.

"Fuckin'-A well told," said Ellis through his teeth.

Jean-Pierre pulled the sheet off him. The guerrillas had cut away his clothes and had put a makeshift dressing on the wound. Jean-Pierre removed the dressing. He could see immediately that the injury was not grave. Ellis had bled a lot, and the bullet still lodged in his muscle obviously hurt like hell, but it was well away from any bones or major blood vessels—it would heal fast.

No, it won't, Jean-Pierre reminded himself. It won't heal at all.

"First I'll give you something to ease the pain," he said.

"I'd appreciate that," Ellis said fervently.

Jean-Pierre pulled the blanket up. Ellis had a huge scar, shaped like a cross, on his back. Jean-Pierre wondered how he had got it.

I'll never know, he thought.

He opened his medical bag. Now I'm going to kill Ellis, he thought. I've never killed anyone, not even by accident. What is it like to be a murderer? People do it every day, all over the world: men kill their wives, women kill their children, assassins kill politicians, burglars kill householders, public executioners kill murderers. He took a large syringe and began to fill it with digitoxin: the drug came in small vials and he had to empty four of them to get a lethal dose.

What would it be like to watch Ellis die? The first effect of the drug would be to increase Ellis's heart rate. He would feel this, and it would make him anxious and uncomfortable. Then, as the poison affected the timing mechanism of his heart, he would get extra heartbeats, one small one after each normal beat. Now he would feel terribly sick. Finally the heartbeats would become totally irregular, the upper and lower chambers of the heart would beat independently, and Ellis would die in agony and terror. What will I do, Jean-Pierre thought, when he cries out in pain, asking me, the doctor, to help him? Will I let him know that I want him to die? Will he guess that I have poisoned him? Will I speak soothing words, in my best bedside manner, and try to ease his passing? *Just relax, this is a normal side effect of the painkiller, everything is going to be all right.*

The injection was ready.

I can do it, Jean-Pierre realized. I can kill him. I just don't know what will happen to me afterward.

He bared Ellis's upper arm and, from sheer force of habit, swabbed a patch with alcohol.

At that moment Masud arrived.

Jean-Pierre had not heard him approach, so he seemed to come from nowhere, making Jean-Pierre jump. Masud put a hand on his arm. "I startled you, *Monsieur le docteur*," he said. He knelt down at Ellis's head. "I have considered the proposal of the American government," he said in French to Ellis.

Jean-Pierre knelt there, frozen in position with the syringe in his right hand. What proposal? What the hell was this? Masud was talking openly, as if Jean-Pierre was just another of his comrades—which he was, in a way—but Ellis . . . Ellis might suggest they talk in private.

Ellis raised himself on to one elbow with an effort. Jean-Pierre held his breath. But all Ellis said was: "Go on."

He's too exhausted, thought Jean-Pierre, and he's in too much pain to think of elaborate security precautions; and besides, he has no more reason to suspect me than does Masud.

"It is good," Masud was saying. "But I have been asking myself how I am going to fulfill my part of the bargain."

Of course! thought Jean-Pierre. The Americans have not sent a top CIA agent here just to teach a few guerrillas how to blow up bridges and tunnels. Ellis is here to make a deal!

Masud went on: "This plan to train cadres from other zones must be explained to the other commanders. This will be difficult. They will be suspicious—especially if I present the proposal. I think *you* must put it to them, and tell them what your government is offering them."

Jean-Pierre was riveted. A plan to train cadres from other zones! What the hell was the idea?

Ellis spoke with some difficulty. "I'd be glad to do that. You would have to bring them all together."

"Yes." Masud smiled. "I shall call a conference of all the Resistance leaders, to be held here in the Five Lions Valley, in the village of Darg, in eight days' time. I will send runners today, with the message that a representative of the United States government is here to discuss arms supplies."

A conference! Arms supplies! The shape of the deal was becoming clear to Jean-Pierre. But what should he do about it?

"Will they come?" Ellis asked.

"Many will," Masud replied. "Our comrades from the western deserts will not—it's too far, and they don't know us."

"What about the two we particularly want—Kamil and Azizi?"

Masud shrugged. "It is in God's hands."

Jean-Pierre was trembling with excitement. This would be the most important event in the history of the Afghan Resistance.

Ellis was fumbling in his kit bag, which was on the floor near his head. "I may be able to help you persuade Kamil and Azizi," he was saying. He drew from the bag two small packages and opened one. It contained a flat, rectangular piece of yellow metal. "Gold," said Ellis. "Each of these is worth about five thousand dollars."

It was a fortune: five thousand dollars was more than two years' income for the average Afghan.

Masud took the piece of gold and hefted it in his hand. "What's that?" he said, pointing to an indented figure in the middle of the rectangle.

"The seal of the President of the United States," said Ellis.

Clever, thought Jean-Pierre. Just the thing to impress tribal leaders and at the same time make them irresistibly curious to meet Ellis.

"Will that help to persuade Kamil and Azizi?" said Ellis.

Masud nodded. "I think they will come."

You bet your *life* they'll come, thought Jean-Pierre.

And suddenly he knew exactly what he had to do. Masud, Kamil and Azizi, the three great leaders of the Resistance, would be together in the village of Darg in eight days' time.

He had to tell Anatoly.

Then Anatoly could kill them all.

This is it, thought Jean-Pierre; this is the moment I've been waiting for ever since I came to the Valley. I've got Masud where I want him—and two other rebel leaders, too.

But how can I tell Anatoly?

There *must* be a way.

"A summit meeting," Masud was saying. He smiled rather proudly. "It will be a good start to the new unity of the Resistance, will it not?"

Either that, Jean-Pierre thought, or the beginning of the end. He lowered his hand, pointing the needle at the ground, and depressed the plunger, emptying the syringe. He watched the poison soak into the dusty earth. A new start, or the beginning of the end.

Jean-Pierre gave Ellis an anesthetic, took out the bullet, cleaned the wound, put a new dressing on it, and injected him with antibiotics to prevent infection. He then dealt with two guerrillas who also had minor wounds from the skirmish. By that time word had got around the village that the doctor was here, and a little cluster of patients gathered in the courtyard of the farmhouse. Jean-Pierre treated a bronchitic baby, three minor infections and a mullah with worms. Then he had lunch. Around midafternoon he packed his bag and climbed onto Maggie for the journey home.

He left Ellis behind. Ellis would be much better off staying where he was for a few days—the wound would heal faster if he lay still and quiet. Jean-Pierre was paradoxically anxious now that Ellis should remain in good health, for if he were to die the conference would be canceled.

As he rode the old horse up the Valley, he racked his brain for a means of getting in touch with Anatoly. Of course, he could simply turn around and ride down the Valley to Rokha, and give himself up to the Russians. Provided they did not shoot him on sight, he would be in Anatoly's presence in no time. But then Jane would know where he had gone and what he had done, and she would tell Ellis, and Ellis would change the time and place of the conference.

Somehow he had to send a letter to Anatoly. But who would deliver it?

There was a constant trickle of people passing through the Valley on the way to Charikar, the Russian-occupied town sixty or seventy miles away in the plain, or to Kabul, the capital city, a hundred miles away. There were dairy farmers from Nuristan with their butter and cheese; traveling merchants selling pots and pans; shepherds bringing small flocks of fat-tailed sheep to market; and families of nomads going about their mysterious nomadic business. Any of them might be bribed to take a letter to a post office, or even just to thrust it into the hands of a Russian soldier. Kabul was three days' journey, Charikar two. Rokha, where there were Russian soldiers but no post office, was only a day away. Jean-Pierre was fairly sure he could find someone to accept the commission. There was a danger, of course, that the letter would be opened and read, and Jean-Pierre would be found out, and tortured and killed. He might be prepared to take that risk. But there was another snag. When the messenger had taken the money, would he de-

liver the letter? There was nothing to stop him "losing" it on the way. Jean-
Pierre might never know what had happened. The whole scheme was just
too *uncertain*.

He had not resolved the problem when he reached Banda at dusk. Jane
was on the roof of the shopkeeper's house, catching the evening breeze,
with Chantal on her knee. Jean-Pierre waved to them, then went inside the
house and put his medical bag on the tiled counter in the storeroom. It was
when he was emptying the bag, at the moment he saw the diamorphine
pills, that he realized there was one person he could trust with the letter to
Anatoly.

He found a pencil in his bag. He took the paper wrapping from a package of cotton swabs and tore a neat rectangle out of it—there was no writing paper in the Valley. He wrote in French:

To Colonel Anatoly of the KGB—

It sounded oddly melodramatic, but he did not know how else to begin. He
did not know Anatoly's full name and he did not have an address.

He went on:

> *Masud has called a council of leaders of the Rebellion. They meet eight
> days from today, on Thursday 27 August, at Darg, which is the next vil-
> lage to the south of Banda. They will probably all sleep in the mosque that
> night and stay together all day Friday which is a holy day. The conference
> has been called for them to talk with a CIA agent known to me as Ellis
> Thaler, who arrived in the Valley a week ago.*
>
> *This is our chance!*

He added the date and signed it *Simplex*.

He did not have an envelope—he had not seen one of those since he
left Europe. He wondered what would be the best way to enclose the letter.
As he looked around, his eye fell on a carton of plastic containers for dis-
pensing tablets. They came with self-adhesive labels which Jean-Pierre
never used because he could not write the Persian script. He rolled his letter into a cylinder and put it in one of the containers.

He wondered how to mark it. At some point in its journey the package
would find its way into the hands of a lowly Russian soldier. Jean-Pierre
imagined a bespectacled, anxious clerk in a cold office, or perhaps a stupid
ox of a man on sentry duty outside a barbed-wire fence. No doubt the art of

buck-passing was as well developed in the Russian Army as it had been in the French when Jean-Pierre did his military service. He considered how he might make the thing look important enough to be handed to a superior officer. There was no point in writing *Important* or *KGB* or anything at all in French or English or even in Dari because the soldier would not be able to read the European or Persian letters. Jean-Pierre did not know any Russian script. It was ironic that the woman on the roof, whose voice he could hear singing a lullaby now, was a fluent speaker of Russian and could have told him how to write anything at all, had she been willing. In the end he wrote *Anatoly—KGB* in European letters and stuck the label on the container, then put the container into an empty drug box which was marked POISON! in fifteen languages and three international symbols. He tied up the box with string.

Moving quickly, he put everything back in his medical bag and replaced the items he had used at Astana. He took a handful of diamorphine tablets and put them in his shirt pocket. Finally he wrapped the POISON! box in a threadbare towel.

He left the house. "I'm going to the river to wash," he called up to Jane.

"Okay."

He walked quickly through the village, nodding curtly to one or two people, and headed out through the fields. He was full of optimism. All sorts of risks attended his plans, but he could once again hope for a great triumph. He skirted a clover field that belonged to the mullah and climbed down a series of terraces. A mile or so from the village, on a rocky outcrop of the mountain, was a solitary cottage that had been bombed. It was getting dark when Jean-Pierre came within sight of it. He walked slowly toward it, picking his way gingerly across the uneven ground, regretting that he had not brought a lamp.

He stopped at the pile of rubble that had once been the front of the house. He thought of going in, but the smell as well as the darkness dissuaded him. He called out: "Hey!"

A shapeless form rose from the ground at his feet and scared him. He jumped back, cursing.

The *malang* stood up.

Jean-Pierre peered at the skeletal face and matted beard of the mad fellow. Recovering his composure, he said in Dari: "God be with you, holy man."

"And with you, Doctor."

Jean-Pierre had caught him in a coherent phase. Good. "How is your belly?"

The man mimed a stomachache: as always, he wanted drugs. Jean-Pierre gave him one diamorphine pill, letting him see the others, then putting them back in his pocket. The *malang* ate his heroin and said: "I want more."

"You can have more," Jean-Pierre told him. "A lot more."

The man held out his hand.

"But you have to do something for me," said Jean-Pierre.

The *malang* nodded eagerly.

"You have to go to Charikar and give this to a Russian soldier." Jean-Pierre had decided on Charikar, despite the extra day's journey it involved, because he feared that Rokha, being a rebel town temporarily occupied by the Russians, might be in a state of confusion, and the package could get lost, whereas Charikar was permanently in Russian territory. And he had decided on a soldier, rather than a post office, as the destination because the *malang* might not be able to deal with the business of buying a stamp and mailing something.

He looked carefully at the man's unwashed face. He had been wondering whether the fellow would comprehend even these simple instructions, but the look of fear on his face at the mention of a Russian soldier indicated that he had understood perfectly.

Now, was there any way Jean-Pierre could ensure that the *malang* actually followed these orders? He, too, could throw the package away and come back swearing that he had carried out the task, for if he was intelligent enough to understand what he had to do, he might be capable of lying about it.

Jean-Pierre was inspired with an idea. "And buy a pack of Russian cigarettes," he said.

The *malang* held out empty hands. "No money."

Jean-Pierre knew he had no money. He gave him one hundred afghanis. That should ensure he actually went to Charikar. Was there a way to compel him to deliver the package?

Jean-Pierre said: "If you do this, I'll give you all the pills you want. But do not cheat me—for if you do, I shall know, and I will never give you pills again, and your bellyache will grow worse and worse and you will swell up and then your guts will burst like a grenade and you will die in agony. Do you understand?"

"Yes."

Jean-Pierre stared at him in the faint light. The whites of his mad eyes gleamed back. He seemed terrified. Jean-Pierre gave him the rest of the diamorphine pills. "Eat one every morning until you come back to Banda."

He nodded vigorously.

"Go now, and do not try to cheat me."

The man turned away and began to run along the rough path with his odd, animallike gait. Watching him disappear into the gathering darkness, Jean-Pierre thought: The future of this country is in your filthy hands, you poor mad wretch. May God go with you.

A week later the *malang* had not returned.

By Wednesday, the day before the conference, Jean-Pierre was distraught. Every hour, he told himself the man could be here within the next hour. At the end of each day, he said he would come tomorrow.

Aircraft activity in the Valley had increased, as if to add to Jean-Pierre's worries. All week the jets had been howling overhead to bomb the villages. Banda had been lucky: only one bomb had landed, and it had merely made a big hole in Abdullah's clover field; but the constant noise and danger made everyone irritable. The tension produced in Jean-Pierre's clinic a predictable crop of patients with stress symptoms: miscarriages, domestic accidents, unexplained vomiting and headaches. It was the children who got the headaches. In Europe, Jean-Pierre would have recommended psychiatry. Here, he sent them to the mullah. Neither psychiatry nor Islam would do much good, for what was wrong with the children was the war.

He went through the morning's patients mechanically, asking his routine questions in Dari, announcing his diagnoses to Jane in French, dressing wounds and giving injections and handing out plastic containers of tablets and glass bottles of colored medicine. It should have taken the *malang* two days to walk to Charikar. Allow him a day to work up the nerve to approach a Russian soldier and a night to get over it. Setting off the next morning, he had another two days' journey. He should have got back the day before yesterday. What had happened? Had he lost the package, and stayed away in fear and trembling? Had he taken all the pills at once and made himself ill? Had he fallen in the damn river and drowned? Had the Russians used him for target practice?

Jean-Pierre looked at his wristwatch. It was ten thirty. Any minute now the *malang* might arrive, bearing a pack of Russian cigarettes as proof that he had been to Charikar. Jean-Pierre wondered briefly how he would explain the cigarettes to Jane, for he did not smoke. He decided that no explanation was necessary for the acts of a lunatic.

He was bandaging a small boy from the next valley who had burned his hand on a cooking fire, when there came from outside the flurry of footsteps and greetings which meant someone had arrived. Jean-Pierre contained his eagerness and continued wrapping the boy's hand. When he heard Jane speak he looked around, and to his intense disappointment saw that it was not the *malang* but two strangers.

The first of them said: "God be with you, Doctor."

"And with you," said Jean-Pierre. In order to preempt a lengthy exchange of civilities he said: "What is the matter?"

"There has been a terrible bombing at Skabun. Many people are dead and many wounded."

Jean-Pierre looked at Jane. He still could not leave Banda without her permission, for she was afraid he would get in touch with the Russians somehow. But clearly he could not have contrived this summons. "Shall I go?" he said to her in French. "Or will you?" He really did not want to go, for it would mean an overnight stay in all probability, and he was desperate to see the *malang*.

Jane hesitated. Jean-Pierre knew she was thinking that if she went she would have to take Chantal. Besides, she knew she could not deal with major traumatic wounds.

"It's up to you," Jean-Pierre said.

"You go," she said.

"All right." Skabun was a couple of hours away. If he worked quickly and if there were not too many wounded, he might just get away at dusk, Jean-Pierre thought. He said: "I'll try to get back tonight."

She came over and kissed his cheek. "Thank you," she said.

He checked his bag quickly: morphine for the pain, penicillin to prevent wound infections, needles and surgical thread, plenty of dressings. He put a cap on his head and a blanket over his shoulders.

"I won't take Maggie," he said to Jane. "Skabun is not far and the trail is very bad." He kissed her again, then turned to the two messengers. "Let's go," he said.

They walked down to the village, then forded the river and climbed the steep steps on the far side. Jean-Pierre was thinking about kissing Jane. If he succeeded in his plan, and the Russians killed Masud, how would she react? She would know he had been behind it. But she would not betray him, he was sure. Would she still love him? He wanted her. Since they had been together he had suffered less and less from the black depressions which used to assault him regularly. Just by loving him she made him feel that he was all right. He wanted that. But he also wanted to succeed in this mission. He thought: I suppose I must want success more than happiness, and that is why I'm prepared to risk losing her for the sake of killing Masud.

The three of them walked southwest along the clifftop footpath with the rushing river loud in their ears. Jean-Pierre asked: "How many people dead?"

"Many people," said one of the messengers.

Jean-Pierre was used to this sort of thing. Patiently he said: "Five? Ten? Twenty? Forty?"

"A hundred."

Jean-Pierre did not believe him: there were not a hundred inhabitants in Skabun. "How many wounded?"

"Two hundred."

That was ludicrous. Did the man not know? Jean-Pierre wondered. Or was he exaggerating for fear that if he gave small numbers the doctor would turn around and go back? Perhaps it was just that he could not count beyond ten. "What kind of wounds?" Jean-Pierre asked him.

"Holes and cuts and bleeding."

Those sounded more like battle injuries. Bombing produced concussion, burns and compression damage from falling buildings. This man was obviously a poor witness. There was no point in questioning him further.

A couple of miles outside Banda they turned off the cliff path and headed north on a track unfamiliar to Jean-Pierre. "Is this the way to Skabun?" he asked.

"Yes."

It was obviously a shortcut he had never discovered. They were certainly heading in the right general direction.

A few minutes later they saw one of the little stone huts in which travelers could rest or spend the night. To Jean-Pierre's surprise, the messengers headed for its doorless entrance. "We haven't time to rest," he told them irritably. "Sick people are waiting for me."

Then Anatoly stepped out of the hut.

Jean-Pierre was dumbfounded. He did not know whether to be exultant because now he could tell Anatoly about the conference, or terrified that the Afghans would kill Anatoly.

"Don't worry," Anatoly said, reading his expression. "They're soldiers of the Afghan regular army. I sent them to fetch you."

"My God!" It was brilliant. There had been no bombing at Skabun—that had been a ruse, dreamed up by Anatoly for getting Jean-Pierre to come. "Tomorrow," Jean-Pierre said excitedly, "tomorrow something terribly important is happening—"

"I know, I know—I got your message. That's why I'm here."

"So you will get Masud . . . ?"

Anatoly smiled mirthlessly, showing his tobacco-stained teeth. "We will get Masud. Calm down."

Jean-Pierre realized he was behaving like an excited child at Christmastime. He suppressed his enthusiasm with an effort. "When the *malang* failed to come back, I thought . . ."

"He arrived in Charikar yesterday," said Anatoly. "God knows what happened to him on the way. Why didn't you use your radio?"

"It broke," said Jean-Pierre. He did not want to explain about Jane right now. "The *malang* will do anything for me because I supply him with heroin, to which he is addicted."

Anatoly looked hard at Jean-Pierre for a moment, and in his eyes there was something like admiration. "I'm glad you're on my side," he said.

Jean-Pierre smiled.

"I want to know more," said Anatoly. He put an arm around Jean-Pierre's shoulders and led him into the hut. They sat on the earth floor and Anatoly lit a cigarette. "How do you know about this conference?" he began.

Jean-Pierre told him about Ellis, about the bullet wound, about Masud talking to Ellis when Jean-Pierre was about to inject him, about the bars of gold and the training scheme and the promised weapons.

"This is fantastic," said Anatoly. "Where is Masud now?"

"I don't know. But he will arrive in Darg today, probably. Tomorrow at the latest."

"How do you know?"

"He called the meeting—how can he fail to come?"

Anatoly nodded. "Describe the CIA man."

"Well, five foot ten, a hundred and fifty pounds, blond hair and blue eyes, age thirty-four but looks a little older, college-educated."

"I'll put all that through the computer." Anatoly stood up. He went outside and Jean-Pierre followed him.

Anatoly took from his pocket a small radio transmitter. He extended its telescopic aerial, pressed a button and muttered into it in Russian. Then he turned back to Jean-Pierre. "My friend, you have succeeded in your mission," he said.

It's true, Jean-Pierre thought. I succeeded.

He said: "When will you strike?"

"Tomorrow, of course."

Tomorrow. Jean-Pierre felt a wave of savage glee. Tomorrow.

The others were looking up. He followed their gaze and saw a helicopter descending: Anatoly had presumably summoned it with his transmitter. The Russian was throwing caution to the wind now: the game was almost over, this was the last hand, and stealth and disguise were to be replaced by boldness and speed. The machine came down and landed, with difficulty, on a small patch of level ground a hundred yards away.

Jean-Pierre walked over to the helicopter with the other three men. He wondered where to go when they had departed. There was nothing for him to do at Skabun, but he could not return to Banda immediately without revealing that there had been no bombing victims for him to take care of. He decided he had better sit in the stone hut for a few hours, then return home.

He held out his hand to shake with Anatoly. "*Au revoir.*"

Anatoly did not take his hand. "Get in."

"What?"

"Get in the helicopter."

Jean-Pierre was flabbergasted. "Why?"

"You're coming with us."

"Where? To Bagram? To Russian territory?"

"Yes."

"But I can't—"

"Stop blustering and listen," Anatoly said patiently. "Firstly, your work is done. Your assignment in Afghanistan is over. You have achieved your goal. Tomorrow we will capture Masud. You can go home. Secondly, you are now a security risk. You know what we plan to do tomorrow. So for the sake of secrecy you cannot remain in rebel territory."

"But I wouldn't tell anyone!"

"Suppose they tortured you? Suppose they tortured your wife in front of your eyes? Suppose they were to tear your baby daughter limb from limb in front of your wife?"

"But what will happen to them if I go with you?"

"Tomorrow, in the raid, we will capture them and bring them to you."

"I can't believe this." Jean-Pierre knew that Anatoly was right, but the idea of not returning to Banda was so unexpected that it disoriented him. Would Jane and Chantal be safe? Would the Russians really pick them up? Would Anatoly let the three of them go back to Paris? How soon could they leave?

"Get in," Anatoly repeated.

The two Afghan messengers were standing on either side of Jean-Pierre, and he realized that he had no choice: if he refused to get in they would pick him up and put him in.

He climbed into the helicopter.

Anatoly and the Afghans jumped in after him, and the chopper lifted. Nobody closed the door.

As the helicopter rose, Jean-Pierre got his first aerial view of the Five Lions Valley. The white river zigzagging through the dun-colored land reminded him of the scar of an old knife wound on the brown forehead of Shahazai Gul, the brother of the midwife. He could see the village of Banda with its yellow-and-green patchwork fields. He looked hard at the hilltop where the caves were, but he saw no signs of occupation: the villagers had chosen their hiding place well. The helicopter went higher and turned, and he could no longer see Banda. He looked for other landmarks. I spent a year of my life there, he thought, and now I'll never see it again. He identified the village of Darg, with its doomed mosque. This Valley was the stronghold of the Resistance, he thought. By tomorrow it will be a memorial to a failed rebellion. And all because of me.

Suddenly the helicopter veered south and crossed the mountain, and within seconds the Valley was lost from view.

CHAPTER ELEVEN

When Fara learned that Jane and Jean-Pierre would be leaving with the next convoy, she cried for a whole day. She had developed a strong attachment to Jane and a great fondness for Chantal. Jane was pleased, but embarrassed: sometimes it seemed as if Fara preferred Jane to her own mother. However, Fara seemed to get used to the idea that Jane was leaving, and the next day she was her usual self, devoted as ever but no longer heartbroken.

Jane herself became anxious about the journey home. From the Valley to the Khyber Pass was a 150-mile trek. Coming in, it had taken fourteen days. She had suffered from blisters and diarrhea as well as the inevitable aches and pains. Now she had to do the return journey carrying a two-month-old baby. There would be horses, but for much of the way it would not be safe to ride them, for the convoys traveled by the smallest and steepest of mountain paths, often at night.

She made a sort of hammock of cotton, to be slung around her neck, for carrying Chantal. Jean-Pierre would have to carry whatever supplies they needed during the day, for—as Jane had learned on the journey in—horses and men walked at different speeds, the horses going faster than the men uphill and slower downhill, so that people got separated from the baggage for long periods.

Deciding *what* supplies to take was the problem that occupied her this afternoon, while Jean-Pierre was at Skabun. There would be a basic medical kit—antibiotics, wound dressings, morphine—which Jean-Pierre would put together. They would have to take some food. Coming in, they had had a lot of high-energy Western rations: chocolate and packet soups and the explorers' perennial favorite, Kendal Mint Cake. Going out, they would have only what they could find in the Valley: rice, dried fruit, dried cheese, hard bread and anything they could buy on the road. It was a good thing they did not have to worry about food for Chantal.

However, there were other difficulties with the baby. Mothers here did not use diapers, but left the baby's lower half uncovered, and washed the towel on which it lay. Jane thought it was a much healthier arrangement than the Western system, but it was no good for traveling. Jane had made three diapers out of towels, and had improvised a pair of waterproof underpants for Chantal out of the polythene wrappings from Jean-Pierre's medical supplies. She would have to wash a diaper every evening—in cold water, of course—and try to dry it overnight. If it did not dry, there was a spare one; and if both were damp, Chantal would get sore. No baby ever died of diaper rash, she told herself. The convoy certainly would not stop for a baby to sleep or be fed and changed, so Chantal would have to feed and doze in motion and be changed whenever the opportunity arose.

In some ways Jane was tougher than she had been a year ago. The skin of her feet was hard and her stomach was resistant to the commoner local bacteria. Her legs, which had hurt so badly on the incoming journey, were now used to walking many miles. But the pregnancy seemed to have made her prone to backache, and she was worried about carrying a baby all day. Her body seemed to have recovered from the trauma of childbirth. She felt she would be able to make love, although she had not told Jean-Pierre this—she was not sure why.

She had taken a lot of photographs, when she first arrived, with her Polaroid camera. She would leave the camera behind—it was a cheap one—but of course she wanted to take most of the photographs. She looked through them, wondering which to throw away. She had pictures of most of the villagers. Here were the guerrillas, Mohammed and Alishan and Kahmir and Matullah, striking ludicrously heroic poses and looking fierce. Here were the women, the voluptuous Zahara, wrinkled old Rabia, and dark-eyed Halima, all giggling like schoolgirls. Here were the children: Mohammed's three girls; his boy, Mousa; Sahara's toddlers, aged two, three, four and five; and the mullah's four children. She could not throw away any; she would have to take them all with her.

She was packing clothes into a bag while Fara swept the floor and

Chantal slept in the next room. They had come down from the caves early to get the work done. However, there was not much to pack: apart from Chantal's diapers, just one clean pair of knickers for herself and one for Jean-Pierre and a spare pair of socks for each of them. None of them would have a change of outer clothing. Chantal had no clothes anyway—she lived in a shawl, or nothing at all. For Jane and Jean-Pierre, one pair of trousers, a shirt, a scarf and a *pattu*-type blanket would suffice for the whole trip, and would probably be burned in a hotel in Peshawar in celebration of their return to civilization.

That thought would give her strength for the journey. She vaguely remembered thinking that Dean's Hotel in Peshawar was primitive, but it was difficult to recall what had been wrong with it. Was it *possible* she had complained that the air conditioner was noisy? The place had *showers*, for God's sake!

"Civilization," she said aloud, and Fara looked at her inquiringly. Jane smiled and said in Dari: "I'm happy because I'm going back to the big town."

"I like the big town," Fara said. "I went to Rokha once." She carried on sweeping. "My brother has gone to Jalalabad," she added in a tone of envy.

"When will he be back?" Jane asked, but Fara had become dumb and embarrassed, and after a moment Jane realized why: the sounds of whistling and a man's footsteps came from the courtyard, there was a tap on the door, and Ellis Thaler's voice said: "Anyone at home?"

"Come in," Jane called. He walked in, limping. Although she was no longer romantically interested in him, she had been concerned about his injury. He had remained in Astana to recover. He must have come back today. "How do you feel?" she asked him.

"Foolish," he said with a rueful grin. "It's an embarrassing place to get shot in."

"If embarrassed is all you feel, it must be getting better."

He nodded. "Is the doctor in?"

"He's gone to Skabun," Jane said. "There was a bad bombing raid and they sent for him. Anything I can do?"

"I just wanted to tell him that my convalescence is over."

"He'll be back tonight or tomorrow morning." She was observing Ellis's appearance: with his mane of blond hair and curly golden beard he looked like a lion. "Why don't you cut your hair?"

"The guerrillas told me to grow it, and not to shave."

"They always say that. The object of the exercise is to make Westerners less conspicuous. In your case it has the opposite effect."

"I'm going to look conspicuous in this country regardless of my haircut."

"That's true." It occurred to Jane that this was the first time she and Ellis had been together without Jean-Pierre. They had slipped very easily into their old conversational style. It was hard to remember how terribly angry she had been with him.

He was looking curiously at her packing. "What's that for?"

"For the journey home."

"How will you travel?"

"With a convoy, as we came."

"The Russians have taken a lot of territory during the last few days," he said. "Didn't you know?"

Jane felt a chill of apprehension. "What are you telling me?"

"The Russians have launched their summer offensive. They've advanced over big stretches of country through which the convoys ordinarily pass."

"Are you saying the route to Pakistan is closed?"

"The *regular* route is closed. You can't get from here to the Khyber Pass. There may be other routes—"

Jane saw her dream of returning home fade. "Nobody *told* me!" she said angrily.

"I guess Jean-Pierre didn't know. I've been with Masud a lot, so I'm right up-to-date."

"Yes," Jane said, not looking at him. Perhaps Jean-Pierre really did not know this. Or perhaps he knew but had not told her about it because he did not want to go back to Europe anyway. Whichever it was, she was not going to accept the situation. First, she would find out for certain whether Ellis was right. Then she would look at ways of solving the problem.

She went to Jean-Pierre's chest and took out his American maps of Afghanistan. They were rolled into a cylinder and fastened with an elastic band. Impatiently, she snapped the band and dropped the maps on the floor. Somewhere in the back of her mind a voice said: That may have been the only rubber band within a hundred-mile radius.

Calm down, she told herself.

She knelt on the floor and began to shuffle through the maps. They were on a very large scale, so she had to put several of them together to show all of the territory between the Valley and the Khyber Pass. Ellis looked over her shoulder. "These are good maps!" he said. "Where did you get them?"

"Jean-Pierre brought them from Paris."

"They're better than what Masud has."

"I know. Mohammed always uses these to plan the convoys. Right. Show me how far the Russians have advanced."

Ellis knelt on the rug beside her and traced a line across the map with his finger.

Jane felt a surge of hope. "It doesn't look to me as if the Khyber Pass is cut off," she said. "Why can't we go this way?" She drew an imaginary line across the map a little to the north of the Russian front.

"I don't know whether that's a route," Ellis said. "It may be impassable— you'd have to ask the guerrillas. But the other thing is that Masud's infor- mation is at least a day or two old, and the Russians are still advancing. A valley or pass might be open one day and closed the next."

"Damn!" She was *not* going to be defeated. She leaned over the map and peered closely at the border zone. "Look, the Khyber Pass isn't the only way across."

"A river valley runs all along the border, with mountains on the Afghan side. It may be that you can only reach those other passes from the south— which means from Russian-occupied territory."

"There's no point in speculating," Jane said. She put the maps together and rolled them up. "Someone must *know.*"

"I guess so."

She stood up. "There's got to be more than one way out of this bloody country," she said. She tucked the maps under her arm and went out, leav- ing Ellis kneeling on the rug.

The women and children had returned from the caves and the village had come to life. The smoke of cooking fires drifted over courtyard walls. In front of the mosque, five children were sitting in a circle playing a game called (for no apparent reason) Melon. It was a storytelling game, in which the teller stopped before the end and the next child had to carry on. Jane spotted Mousa, the son of Mohammed, sitting in the circle, wearing at his belt the rather wicked-looking knife his father had given him after the ac- cident with the mine. Mousa was telling the story. Jane heard: ". . . and the bear tried to bite the boy's hand off, but the boy drew his knife . . ."

She headed for Mohammed's house. Mohammed himself might not be there—she had not seen him for a long time—but he lived with his broth- ers, in the usual Afghan extended family, and they, too, were guerrillas—all the fit young men were—so if they were there they might be able to give her some information.

She hesitated outside the house. By custom she should stop in the courtyard and speak to the women, who would be there preparing the evening meal; and then, after an exchange of courtesies, the most senior woman might go into the house to inquire whether the menfolk would condescend to speak to Jane. She heard her mother's voice say: "Don't make an exhibition of yourself!" Jane said aloud: "Go to hell, Mother." She walked in, ignoring the women in the courtyard, and marched straight into the front room of the house—the men's parlor.

There were three men there: Mohammed's eighteen-year-old brother, Kahmir Khan, with a handsome face and a wispy beard; his brother-in-law, Matullah; and Mohammed himself. It was unusual for so many guerrillas to be at home. They all looked up at her, startled.

"God be with you, Mohammed Khan," Jane said. Without pausing to let him reply, she went on: "When did you get back?"

"Today," he replied automatically.

She squatted on her haunches like them. They were too astonished to say anything. She spread out her maps on the floor. The three men leaned forward reflexively to look at them: already they were forgetting Jane's breach of etiquette. "Look," she said. "The Russians have advanced this far—am I right?" She retraced the line Ellis had shown her.

Mohammed nodded agreement.

"So the regular convoy route is blocked."

Mohammed nodded again.

"What is the best way out now?"

They all looked dubious and shook their heads. This was normal: when talking of difficulties, they liked to make a meal of it. Jane thought it was because their local knowledge was the only power they had over foreigners such as she. Usually she was tolerant, but today she had no patience. "Why not this way?" she asked peremptorily, drawing a line parallel with the Russian front.

"Too close to the Russians," said Mohammed.

"Here, then." She traced a more careful route, following the contours of the land.

"No," he said again.

"Why not?"

"Here—" He pointed to a place on the map, between the heads of two valleys, where Jane had blithely run her finger over a mountain range. "Here there is no saddle." A saddle was a pass.

Jane outlined a more northerly route. "This way?"

"Worse still."

"There *must* be another way out!" Jane cried. She had a feeling they were enjoying her frustration. She decided to say something mildly offensive, to liven them up a bit. "Is this country a house with one door, cut off from the rest of the world just because you cannot get to the Khyber Pass?" The phrase *the house with one door* was a euphemism for the privy.

"Of course not," said Mohammed stiffly. "In summer there is the Butter Trail."

"Show me."

Mohammed's finger traced a complex route which began due east of the Valley, proceeding through a series of high passes and dried-up rivers, then turned north into the Himalayas, and finally crossed the border near the entrance to the uninhabited Waikhan Corridor before swinging southeast to the Pakistani town of Chitral. "This is how the people of Nuristan take their butter and yogurt and cheese to market in Pakistan." He smiled and touched his round cap. "That is where we get the hats." Jane recalled that they were called Chitrali caps.

"Good," said Jane. "We will go home that way."

Mohammed shook his head. "You cannot."

"And why not?"

Kahmir and Matullah gave knowing smiles. Jane ignored them. After a moment Mohammed said: "The first problem is the altitude. This route goes above the ice line. That means the snow never melts, and there is no running water, even in summer. Second is the landscape. The hills are very steep and the paths are narrow and treacherous. It is hard to find your way: even local guides get lost. But the worst problem of all is the people. That region is called Nuristan, but it used to be called Kafiristan, because the people were unbelievers, and drank wine. Now they are true believers, but still they cheat, rob and sometimes murder travelers. This route is no good for Europeans, impossible for women. Only the youngest and strongest men can use it—and even then, many travelers are killed."

"Will you send convoys that way?"

"No. We will wait until the southerly route is reopened."

She studied his handsome face. He was not exaggerating, she could tell: he was being dryly factual. She stood up and began to shuffle the maps together. She was bitterly disappointed. Her return home was postponed indefinitely. The strain of life in the Valley suddenly seemed insupportable, and she felt like crying.

She rolled her maps into a cylinder and forced herself to be polite. "You were away a long time," she said to Mohammed.

"I went to Faizabad."

"A long trip." Faizabad was a large town in the far north. The Resistance was very strong there: the army had mutinied and the Russians had never regained control. "Aren't you tired?"

It was a formal question, like *How do you do?* in English, and Mohammed gave the formal reply: "I'm still alive!"

She tucked her roll of maps under her arm and went out.

The women in the courtyard looked at her fearfully as she passed them. She nodded at Halima, Mohammed's dark-eyed wife, and got a nervous half-smile in return.

The guerrillas were doing a lot of traveling lately. Mohammed had been to Faizabad, Fara's brother had gone to Jalalabad. . . . Jane recalled that one of her patients, a woman from Dasht-i-Rewat, had said that her husband had been sent to Pagman, near Kabul. And Zahara's brother-in-law, Yussuf Gul, the brother of her dead husband, had been sent to the Logar Valley, on the far side of Kabul. All four places were rebel strongholds.

Something was going on.

Jane forgot her disappointment for a while as she tried to figure out what was happening. Masud had sent messengers to many—perhaps all—of the other Resistance commanders. Was it a coincidence that this happened so soon after Ellis's arrival in the Valley? If not, what could Ellis be up to? Perhaps the U.S. was collaborating with Masud in organizing a concerted offensive. If all the rebels acted together they could really achieve something—they could probably take Kabul temporarily.

Jane went into her house and dropped the maps in the chest. Chantal was still asleep. Fara was preparing food for supper: bread, yogurt and apples. Jane said: "Why did your brother go to Jalalabad?"

"He was sent," said Fara with the air of one who states the obvious.

"Who sent him?"

"Masud."

"What for?"

"I don't know." Fara looked surprised that Jane should ask such a question: who could be so foolish as to think that a man would tell his sister his reason for a journey?

"Did he have something to do there, or did he take a message, or what?"

"I don't know," Fara repeated. She was beginning to look anxious.

"Never mind," Jane said with a smile. Of all the women in the village, Fara was probably the least likely to know what was going on. Who was the most likely? Zahara, of course.

Jane picked up a towel and headed for the river.

Zahara was no longer in mourning for her husband, although she was a good deal less boisterous than she used to be. Jane wondered how soon she would marry again. Zahara and Ahmed had been the only Afghan couple Jane had come across who actually seemed to be in love. However, Zahara was a powerfully sensual woman who would have trouble living without a man for very long. Ahmed's younger brother, Yussuf, the singer, lived in the same house as Zahara, and was still unmarried at the age of eighteen: there was speculation among the village women that Yussuf might marry Zahara.

Brothers lived together, here; sisters were always separated. A bride routinely went to live with her husband in the home of the husband's parents. It was just one more way in which the men of this country oppressed their women.

Jane strode quickly along the footpath through the fields. A few men were working in the evening light. The harvest was coming to an end. It would soon be too late to take the Butter Trail anyway, Jane thought: Mohammed had said it was a summer-only route.

She reached the women's beach. Eight or ten village women were bathing in the river or in pools at the water's edge. Zahara was out in midstream, splashing a lot as usual but not laughing and joking.

Jane dropped her towel and waded into the water. She decided to be a little less direct with Zahara than she had been with Fara. She would not be able to fool Zahara, of course, but she would try to give the impression that she was gossiping rather than interrogating. She did not approach Zahara immediately. When the other women got out of the water, Jane followed a minute or two later, and dried herself with her towel in silence. It was not until Zahara and a few other women began to drift back toward the village that Jane spoke. "How soon will Yussuf be back?" she asked Zahara in Dari.

"Today or tomorrow. He went to the Logar Valley."

"I know. Did he go alone?"

"Yes—but he said he may bring someone home with him."

"Who?"

Zahara shrugged. "A wife, perhaps."

Jane was momentarily diverted. Zahara was too coolly indifferent. That meant she was worried: she did not want Yussuf to bring home a wife. It looked as if the village rumors were true. Jane hoped so. Zahara needed a man. "I don't think he has gone to get a wife," Jane said.

"Why?"

"Something important is happening. Masud has sent out many messengers. They can't all be after wives."

Zahara continued to try to look indifferent, but Jane could tell she was pleased. Was there any significance, Jane wondered, in the possibility that Yussuf might have gone to the Logar Valley to fetch someone?

Night was falling as they approached the village. From the mosque came a low chant: the eerie sound of the most bloodthirsty men in the world at prayer. It always reminded Jane of Josef, a young Russian soldier who had survived a helicopter crash just over the mountain from Banda. Some women had brought him to the shopkeeper's house—this was in the winter, before they moved the clinic to the cave—and Jean-Pierre and Jane had tended his wounds while a message was sent to Masud asking what should be done. Jane learned what Masud's reply had been one evening when Ali-shan Karim walked into the front room of the shopkeeper's house, where Josef lay in bandages, and put the muzzle of his rifle to the boy's ear and blew his head off. It had been about this time of day, and the sound of the men praying had been in the air while Jane washed the blood off the wall and scooped up the boy's brains from the floor.

The women climbed the last stretch of the footpath up from the river and paused in front of the mosque, finishing their conversations before going to their separate homes. Jane glanced into the mosque. The men were praying on their knees, with Abdullah, the mullah, leading them. Their weapons, the usual mixture of ancient rifles and modern submachine guns, were piled in a corner. The prayers were just finishing. As the men stood up, Jane saw that there were a number of strangers among them. She said to Zahara: "Who are they?"

"By their turbans, they must be from the Pich Valley and Jalalabad," Zahara replied. "They are Pushtuns—normally they are our enemies. Why are there here?" As she was speaking, a very tall man with an eye patch emerged from the crowd. "That must be Jahan Kamil—Masud's great enemy!"

"But there is Masud, talking to him," said Jane, and she added in English: "Just fancy that!"

Zahara imitated her. "Jass fencey hat!"

It was the first joke Zahara had made since her husband died. That was a good sign: Zahara was recovering.

The men began to come out, and the women scuttled away to their homes, all except Jane. She thought she was beginning to understand what was happening; and she wanted confirmation. When Mohammed came out she approached him and spoke to him in French. "I forgot to ask whether your trip to Faizabad was successful."

"It was," he said without pausing in his stride: he did not want his com-rades or the Pushtuns to see him answering a woman's questions.

Jane hurried alongside him as he headed for his house. "So the com-mander of Faizabad is here?"

"Yes."

Jane had guessed right: Masud had invited all the rebel commanders here. "What do you think of this idea?" she asked him. She was still fishing for details.

Mohammed looked thoughtful, and dropped his hauteur, as he always did when he got interested in the conversation. "Everything depends on what Ellis does tomorrow," he said. "If he impresses them as a man of honor, and wins their respect, I think they will agree to his plan."

"And you think his plan is good?"

"Obviously it will be a good thing if the Resistance is united and gets weapons from the United States."

So that was it! American weapons for the rebels, on condition they fought together against the Russians instead of fighting one another half the time.

They reached Mohammed's house, and Jane turned away with a wave. Her breasts felt full: it was time for Chantal to be fed. The right breast felt a little heavier, because at the last feed she had started with the left, and Chantal always emptied the first one more thoroughly.

Jane reached the house and went into the bedroom. Chantal lay naked on a folded towel inside her cradle, which was actually a cardboard box cut in half. She had no need of clothes in the warm air of the Afghan summer. At night she would be covered with a sheet—that was all. The rebels and the war, Ellis and Mohammed and Masud, all receded into the background as Jane looked at her baby. She had always thought small babies ugly, but Chantal seemed very pretty to her. As Jane watched, Chantal stirred, opened her mouth and cried. Jane's right breast immediately leaked milk in response, and a warm, damp patch spread on her shirt. She undid the but-tons and picked up Chantal.

Jean-Pierre said she should wash her breasts with surgical spirit before feeding, but she never did because she knew Chantal would not like the taste. She sat on a rug with her back to the wall and cradled Chantal in her right arm. The baby waved her fat little arms and moved her head from side to side, frantically seeking with her open mouth. Jane guided her to the nipple. The toothless gums clamped hard and the baby sucked fiercely. Jane winced at the first hard pull, then at the second. The third suck was gentler. A small, plump hand reached up and touched the round side of Jane's swollen breast, pressing it with a blind, clumsy caress. Jane relaxed.

Feeding her baby made her feel terribly tender and protective. Also, it was erotic. At first she had felt guilty about being turned on by it, but she soon decided that if it was natural it could not be bad, and settled down to enjoy it.

She was looking forward to showing Chantal off if they ever got back to Europe. Jean-Pierre's mother would tell her she was doing everything wrong, no doubt, and her own mother would want to have the baby christened, but her father would adore Chantal through an alcoholic haze, and her sister would be proud and enthusiastic. Who else? Jean-Pierre's father was dead. . . .

A voice came from the courtyard. "Anybody at home?"

It was Ellis. "Come in," Jane called. She did not feel she needed to cover herself: Ellis was not an Afghan, and anyway he had once been her lover.

He came in, saw her feeding the baby and did a double take. "Shall I leave?"

She shook her head. "You've seen my tits before."

"I don't think so," he said. "You must have changed them."

She laughed. "Pregnancy gives you great tits." Ellis had been married once, she knew, and had a child, although he gave the impression he no longer saw either the child or its mother. That was one of the things he would never talk about very much. "Don't you remember from when your wife was pregnant?"

"I missed it," he said, in that curt tone he used when he wanted you to shut up. "I was away."

She was too relaxed to respond in like manner. In fact she felt sorry for him. He had made a mess of his life, but it was not all his own fault; and he had certainly been punished for his sins—not the least by her.

"Jean-Pierre didn't come back," Ellis said.

"No." The sucking eased as Jane's breast emptied. She gently pulled her nipple from Chantal's mouth and lifted the baby to her shoulder, patting the narrow back to make her burp.

"Masud would like to borrow his maps," Ellis said.

"Of course. You know where they are." Chantal belched loudly. "Good girl," Jane said. She put the baby to her left breast. Hungry again after burping, Chantal began to suck. Giving in to an impulse, Jane said: "Why don't you see your child?"

He took the maps from the chest, closed its lid and straightened up. "I do," he said. "But not often."

Jane was shocked. I almost lived with him for six months, she thought, and I never really knew him. "A boy or a girl?"

"Girl."

"She must be . . ."

"Thirteen."

"My God." That was practically grown-up. Jane was suddenly intensely curious. Why had she never questioned him about all this? Perhaps she had not been interested before she had a child of her own. "Where does she live?"

He hesitated.

"Don't tell me," she said. She could read his face. "You were about to lie to me."

"You're right," he said. "But do you understand *why* I have to lie about it?"

She thought for a moment. "Are you afraid that your enemies will attack you through the child?"

"Yes."

"That's a good reason."

"Thank you. And thanks for these." He waved the maps at her, then went out.

Chantal had gone to sleep with Jane's nipple in her mouth. Jane disengaged her gently and lifted her to shoulder level. She burped without waking. The child could sleep through anything.

Jane wished Jean-Pierre had come back. She was sure he could do no harm, but all the same she would have felt easier if he had been under her eye. He could not contact the Russians because she had smashed his radio. There was no other means of communication between Banda and Russian territory. Masud could send messengers by runner, of course; but Jean-Pierre had no runners, and anyway if he sent someone the whole village would know about it. The only thing he could possibly do was to walk all the way to Rokha, and he had not had time for that.

As well as being anxious, she hated to sleep alone. In Europe she had not minded, but here she was frightened of the brutal, unpredictable tribesmen who thought it as normal for a man to beat his wife as for a mother to smack her child. And Jane was no ordinary woman in their eyes: with her liberated views and her direct gaze and her says-who attitude she was a symbol of forbidden sexual delights. She had not followed the conventions of sexual behavior, and the only other women they knew like that were whores.

When Jean-Pierre was there she always reached out to touch him just before falling asleep. He always slept curled up, facing away from her, and although he moved a lot in his sleep he never reached out for her. The only other man she had shared a bed with for a long period was Ellis, and he had been just the opposite: all night long he was touching her, hugging her and kissing her, sometimes while half-awake and sometimes when fast asleep. Twice or three times he had tried to make love to her, roughly, in his sleep: she would giggle and try to accommodate him, but after a few seconds he would roll off and start snoring, and in the morning he had no recollection of what he had done. How different he was from Jean-Pierre. Ellis touched her with clumsy affection, like a child playing with a beloved pet; Jean-Pierre touched her the way a violinist might handle a Stradivarius. They had loved her differently, but they had betrayed her the same way.

Chantal gurgled. She was awake. Jane laid her in her lap, supporting her head so that they could look directly at one another, and began to talk to her, partly in nonsense syllables and partly in real words. Chantal liked this. After a while Jane ran out of small talk and began to sing. She was in the middle of "Daddy's Gone to London in a Puffer Train" when she was interrupted by a voice from outside. "Come in," she called. She said to Chantal: "We have visitors all the time, don't we? It's like living in the National Gallery, isn't it?" She pulled the front of her shirt together to hide her cleavage.

Mohammed walked in and said in Dari: "Where is Jean-Pierre?"

"Gone to Skabun. Anything I can do?"

"When will he be back?"

"In the morning, I expect. Do you want to tell me what the problem is, or do you plan to continue talking like a Kabul policeman?"

He grinned at her. When she spoke disrespectfully to him he found her sexy, which was not the effect she intended. He said: "Alishan has arrived with Masud. He wants more pills."

"Ah, yes." Alishan Karim was the brother of the mullah, and he suffered from angina. Of course, he would not give up his guerrilla activities, so Jean-Pierre gave him trinitrin to take immediately before battle or other exertion. "I'll give you some pills," she said. She stood up and handed Chantal to Mohammed.

Mohammed took the baby automatically and then looked embarrassed.

Jane grinned at him and went into the front room. She found the tablets on a shelf beneath the shopkeeper's counter. She poured about a hundred into a container and returned to the living room. Chantal was staring, fascinated, at Mohammed. Jane took the baby and handed over the pills. "Tell Alishan to rest more," she said.

Mohammed shook his head. "He's not frightened of me," he said. "You tell him."

Jane laughed. Coming from an Afghan, that joke was almost feminist.

Mohammed said: "Why did Jean-Pierre go to Skabun?"

"There was a bombing there this morning."

"No, there wasn't."

"Of course there wa—" Jane stopped suddenly.

Mohammed shrugged. "I was there all day with Masud. You must be mistaken."

She tried to keep her face composed. "Yes. I must have misheard."

"Thank you for the pills." He went out.

Jane sat down heavily on a stool. There had been no bombing at Skabun. Jean-Pierre had gone to meet his contact. She did not see quite how he had arranged it, but she had no doubt whatsoever.

What was she to do?

If Jean-Pierre knew about the gathering tomorrow, and could tell the Russians about it, then the Russians would be able to attack—

They could wipe out the entire leadership of the Afghan Resistance in a single day.

She had to see Ellis.

She wrapped a shawl around Chantal—the air would be a little cooler now—and left the house, heading for the mosque. Ellis was in the courtyard with the rest of the men, poring over Jean-Pierre's maps with Masud and Mohammed and the man with the eye patch. Some guerrillas were passing around a hookah; others were eating. They stared in surprise as she walked in with her baby on her hip. "Ellis," she said. He looked up. "I need to talk to you. Would you come outside?"

He got up, and they went out through the arch and stood in front of the mosque.

"What is it?" he said.

"Does Jean-Pierre know about this gathering you have arranged, of all the Resistance leaders?"

"Yes—when Masud and I first talked about it, he was right there, taking the slug out of my ass. Why?"

Jane's heart sank. Her last hope had been that Jean-Pierre might not know. Now she had no choice. She looked around. There was no one else within earshot, and anyway they were speaking English. "I have something to tell you," she said, "but I want your promise that no harm will come to him."

He stared at her for a moment. "Oh, *shit*," he said fervently. "Oh fuck, oh shit. He works for them. Of course! Why didn't I guess? In Paris he must have led those motherfuckers to my apartment! He's been telling them about the convoys—that's why they've been losing so many! The *bastard*—" He stopped suddenly, and spoke more gently. "It must have been terrible for you."

"Yes," she said. Irresistibly her face crumpled, tears rushed to her eyes and she began to sob. She felt weak and foolish and ashamed of herself for crying, but she also felt as if a huge weight had been lifted from her.

Ellis put his arms around her and Chantal. "You poor thing," he said.

"Yes," she sobbed. "It was awful."

"How long have you known?"

"A few weeks."

"You didn't know when you married him."

"No."

"Both of us," he said. "We both did it to you."

"Yes."

"You mixed with the wrong crowd."

"Yes."

She buried her face in his shirt and cried without restraint, for all the lies and betrayals and spent time and wasted love. Chantal cried, too. Ellis held Jane close and stroked her hair until eventually she stopped shaking, began to calm down and wiped her nose on her sleeve. "I broke his radio, you see," she said, "and then I thought he had no way of getting in touch with them; but today he was called to Skabun to see to the bomb-wounded, but there was no bombing at Skabun today. . . ."

Mohammed came out of the mosque. Ellis let go of Jane and looked embarrassed. "What's happening?" he said to Mohammed in French.

"They're arguing," he said. "Some say this is a good plan and it will help us defeat the Russians. Others ask why Masud is considered the only good commander, and who is Ellis Thaler that he should judge Afghan leaders? You must come back and talk to them some more."

"Wait," Ellis said. "There's been a new development."

Jane thought: Oh, God, Mohammed will kill somebody when he hears this—

"There has been a leak."

"What do you mean?" Mohammed said dangerously.

Ellis hesitated, as if reluctant to spill the beans; and then he seemed to decide that he had no alternative. "The Russians may know about the conference—"

"Who?" Mohammed demanded. "Who is the traitor?"

"Possibly the doctor, but—"

Mohammed rounded on Jane. "How long have you known this?"

"You'll speak to me politely or not at all," she snapped back.

"Hold it," said Ellis.

Jane was not going to let Mohammed get away with his accusatory tone of voice. "I warned you, didn't I?" she said. "I told you to change the route of the convoy. I saved your damn life, so don't point your finger at *me*."

Mohammed's anger evaporated, and he looked a little sheepish.

Ellis said: "So that's why the route was changed." He looked at Jane with something like admiration.

Mohammed said: "Where is he now?"

"We're not sure," Ellis replied.

"When he comes back he must be killed."

"No!" said Jane.

Ellis put a restraining hand on her shoulder and said to Mohammed: "Would you kill a man who has saved the lives of so many of your comrades?"

"He must face justice," Mohammed insisted.

Mohammed had talked about *if* he comes back, and Jane realized she had been assuming that he would return. Surely he would not abandon her and their baby?

Ellis was saying: "If he is a traitor, and if he has succeeded in contacting the Russians, then he has told them about tomorrow's meeting. They will surely attack and try to take Masud."

"This is very bad," said Mohammed. "Masud must leave immediately. The conference will have to be called off—"

"Not necessarily," Ellis said. "Think. We could turn this to advantage."

"How?"

Ellis said: "In fact the more I think about it, the more I like it. This may turn out to have been the best thing that could possibly happen. . . ."

CHAPTER TWELVE

T hey evacuated the village of Darg at dawn. Masud's men went from house to house, gently waking the occupants and telling them that their village was to be attacked by the Russians today and they must go up the Valley to Banda, taking with them their more precious possessions. By sunrise a ragged line of women, children, old people and livestock was wending its way out of the village along the dirt road that ran beside the river.

Darg was different in shape from Banda. At Banda the houses were clustered at the eastern end of the plain, where the Valley narrowed and the ground was rocky. In Darg all the houses were crammed together on a thin shelf between the foot of the cliff and the bank of the river. There was a bridge just in front of the mosque, and the fields were on the other side of the river.

It was a good place for an ambush.

Masud had devised his plan during the night, and now Mohammed and Alishan made the dispositions. They moved around with quiet efficiency, Mohammed tall and handsome and gracious, Alishan short and mean-looking, both of them giving instructions in soft voices, imitating their leader's low-key style.

Ellis wondered, as he laid his charges, whether the Russians would come. Jean-Pierre had not reappeared, so it seemed certain that he had succeeded in contacting his masters; and it was almost inconceivable that they should resist the temptation to capture or kill Masud. But that was all circumstantial. And if they did not come, Ellis would look foolish, having caused Masud to set an elaborate trap for a no-show victim. The guerrillas would not make a pact with a fool. But if the Russians do come, Ellis thought, and if the ambush works, the boost to my prestige and Masud's might be enough to clinch the whole deal.

He was trying not to think about Jane. When he had put his arms around her and her baby, and she had wet his shirt with her tears, his passion for her had flared up anew. It was like throwing gasoline on a bonfire. He had wanted to stand there forever, with her narrow shoulders shaking under his arm and her head against his chest. Poor Jane. She was so honest, and her men were so treacherous.

He trailed his detonating cord in the river and brought its end out at his position, which was in a tiny one-room house on the riverbank a couple of hundred yards upstream of the mosque. He used his crimper to attach a blasting cap to the cord, then finished the assembly with a simple army-issue pull-ring firing device.

He approved of Masud's plan. Ellis had taught ambush and counterambush at Fort Bragg for a year between his two tours in Asia, and he would have given Masud's setup nine out of ten. The lost point was due to Masud's failure to provide an exit route for his troops in case the fight should go against them. Of course Masud might not consider that a mistake.

By nine o'clock everything was ready, and the guerrillas made breakfast. Even that was part of the ambush: they could all get into position in minutes, if not seconds, and then the village seen from the air would look more natural, as if the villagers had all rushed to hide from the helicopters, leaving behind their bowls and rugs and cooking fires; so that the commander of the Russian force would have no reason to suspect a trap.

Ellis ate some bread and drank several cups of green tea, then settled down to wait as the sun rose high over the Valley. There was always a lot of waiting. He remembered it in Asia. In those days he had often been high, on marijuana or speed or cocaine, and then the waiting hardly seemed to matter because he enjoyed it. It was funny, he thought, how he had lost interest in drugs after the war.

Ellis expected the attack either this afternoon or at dawn tomorrow. If he were the Russian commander he would reason that the rebel leaders had assembled yesterday and would leave tomorrow, and he would want to attack late enough to catch any latecomers, but not so late that some of them might have left already.

At around midmorning the heavy weapons arrived, a pair of Dashokas, 12.7mm antiaircraft machine guns, each pulled along the road on its two-wheeled mounting by a guerrilla. A donkey followed, loaded down with cases of 5–0 Chinese armor-piercing bullets.

Masud announced that one of the guns would be manned by Yussuf, the singer, who, according to village rumor, was likely to marry Jane's friend Zahara; the other by a guerrilla from the Pich Valley, one Abdur, whom Ellis did not know. Yussuf had already shot down three helicopters with his Kalashnikov, it was said. Ellis was skeptical about this: he had flown helicopters in Asia and he knew it was close to impossible to shoot one down with a rifle. However, Yussuf explained with a grin that the trick was to get above the target and fire down at it from a mountainside, a tactic that was not possible in Vietnam because the landscape was different.

Although Yussuf had a much bigger weapon today, he was going to use the same technique. The guns were dismounted, then taken, each carried by two men, up the steep steps cut into the cliffside that towered over the village. The mounts and the ammunition followed.

Ellis watched from below as they reassembled the guns. At the top of the cliff was a shelf ten or fifteen feet wide; then the mountainside continued up at a gentler slope. The guerrillas set up the guns about ten yards apart on the shelf and camouflaged them. The helicopter pilots would soon find out where the guns were, of course, but they would find it very difficult to knock them out where they were.

When that was done, Ellis went back to his position in the little one-room house by the riverside. His mind kept returning to the sixties. He had begun the decade as a schoolboy and ended a soldier. He had gone to Berkeley in 1967, confident that he knew what the future held for him: he wanted to be a producer of television documentaries, and since he was bright and creative, and this was California, where anybody could be anything if he worked hard, there had been no reason he could see why he should not achieve his ambition. Then he had been overtaken by peace and flower power, antiwar marches and love-ins, the Doors and bell-bottom jeans and LSD; and once again he had thought he knew what the future held: he was going to change the world. That dream had also been short-lived, and soon he was overtaken once again, this time by the mindless brutality of the army and the drugged horror of Vietnam. Whenever he looked back like this, he could see that it was the times when he felt confident and settled that life would hit him with the really big changes.

Midday passed without lunch. That would be because the guerrillas did not have any food. Ellis found it hard to get used to the essentially rather simple idea that when there was no food then nobody could have lunch. It occurred to him that this might be why nearly all the guerrillas were heavy smokers: tobacco deadened the appetite.

It was hot even in the shade. He sat in the doorway of the little house, trying to catch what breeze there was. He could see the fields, the river with its arched rubble-and-mortar bridge, the village with its mosque, and the overhanging cliff. Most of the guerrillas were in their positions, which provided them with shelter from the sun as well as cover. The majority of them were in houses close to the cliff, where it would be difficult for helicopters to strafe them; but inevitably some were in the more vulnerable forward positions, nearer the river. The rough stone façade of the mosque was pierced by three arched doorways, and one guerrilla sat cross-legged under each arch. They made Ellis think of guardsmen in sentry boxes. Ellis knew all three of them: there was Mohammed in the farthest arch; his brother Kahmir, with the wispy beard, in the middle; and in the nearest arch Ali Ghanim, the ugly man with the twisted spine and the family of fourteen children, the man who had been wounded with Ellis down on the plain. Each of the three had a Kalashnikov across his knees and a cigarette between his lips. Ellis wondered which of them would be alive tomorrow.

The first essay he had written in college had been about the wait before battle as handled by Shakespeare. He had contrasted two precombat speeches: the inspirational one in *Henry V* in which the King says: "Once more unto the breach, dear friends, once more; or close the wall up with our English dead"; and Falstaff's cynical soliloquy on honor in *1 Henry IV*: "Can honour set to a leg? No. Or an arm? No. . . . Honour hath no skill in surgery, then? No. . . . Who hath it? He that died o' Wednesday." The nineteen-year-old Ellis had got an A for that—his first, and his last, for afterward he was too busy arguing that Shakespeare and indeed the entire English course were "irrelevant."

His reverie was interrupted by a series of shouts. He did not understand the Dari words used, but he had no need to: he knew, from the urgency of tone, that the sentries on the surrounding hillsides had spotted distant helicopters, and had signaled to Yussuf on the clifftop, who had spread the word. There was a flurry of movement throughout the sun-baked village as guerrillas manned their posts, retreated farther into their cover, checked their weapons and lit fresh cigarettes. The three men in the archways of the mosque melted into its shadowy interior. Now the village seen from the air would appear deserted, as it normally would during the hottest part of the day, when most people rested.

Ellis listened hard and heard the menacing throb of approaching helicopter rotors. His bowels felt watery: nerves. This is how the slants felt, he thought, hiding in the dripping jungle, when they heard my helicopter gunship coming toward them through the rain clouds. You reap what you sow, baby.

He loosened the safety pins in the firing device.

The helicopters roared closer, but still he could not see them. He wondered how many there were: he could not tell from the noise. He saw something out of the corner of his eye, and turned to see a guerrilla dive into the river from the far bank and begin swimming across toward him. When the figure emerged near Ellis he could see that it was scarred old Shahazai Gul, the brother of the midwife. Shahazai's specialty was mines. He dashed past Ellis and took cover in a house.

For a few moments the village was still and there was nothing but the heart-stopping throb of rotor blades, and Ellis was thinking, Jesus, how the hell many of them have they sent? And then the first one flashed into view over the cliff, going *fast*, and wheeled down toward the village. It hesitated over the bridge like a giant hummingbird.

It was an Mi-24, known in the West as a Hind (the Russians called them Hunchbacks because of the bulky twin turboshaft engines mounted on top of the passenger cabin). The gunner sat low in the nose with the pilot behind and above him, like children playing piggyback; and the windows all around the flight deck looked like the multifaceted eye of a monstrous insect. The helicopter had a three-wheeled undercarriage and short, stubby wings with underslung rocket pods.

How the hell could a few ragged tribesmen fight against machinery like that?

Five more Hinds followed in rapid succession. They overflew the village and the ground all around it, scouting, Ellis presumed, for enemy positions. This was a routine precaution—the Russians had no reason to expect heavy resistance, for they believed their attack would be a surprise.

A second type of helicopter began to appear, and Ellis recognized the Mi-8, known as the Hip. Larger than the Hind but less fearsome, it could carry twenty or thirty men, and its purpose was troop transport rather than assault. The first one hesitated over the village, then dropped suddenly sideways and came down in the barley field. It was followed by five more. A hundred and fifty men, Ellis thought. As the Hips landed, the troops jumped out and lay flat, pointing their guns toward the village but not shooting.

To take the village they had to cross the river, and to cross the river they had to take the bridge. But they did not know that. They were just being cautious: they expected the element of surprise to enable them to prevail easily.

Ellis worried that the village might appear *too* deserted. By now, a couple of minutes after the first helicopter appeared, there would normally be a few people visible, running away. He strained his hearing for the first shot. He was no longer scared. He was concentrating too hard on too many things to feel fear. From the back of his mind came the thought: It's always like this once it starts.

Shahazai had laid mines in the barley field, Ellis recalled. Why had none of them exploded yet? A moment later he had the answer. One of the soldiers stood up—an officer presumably—and shouted an order. Twenty or thirty men scrambled to their feet and ran toward the bridge. Suddenly there was a deafening bang, loud even over the whirlwind of helicopter noise, then another and another as the ground seemed to explode under the soldiers' running feet—Ellis thought, Shahazai pepped up his mines with extra TNT—and clouds of brown earth and golden barley obscured them, all but one man who was thrown high in the air and fell slowly, turning over and over like an acrobat until he hit the ground and crumpled in a heap. As the echoes died there was another sound, a deep, stomach-thudding drumbeat that came from the clifftop as Yussuf and Abdur opened fire. The Russians retreated in disarray as the guerrillas in the village started firing their Kalashnikovs across the river.

Surprise had given the guerrillas a tremendous initial advantage, but it would not last forever: the Russian commander would rally his troops. But before he could achieve anything he had to clear the approach to the bridge.

One of the Hips in the barley field blew apart, and Ellis realized that Yussuf and Abdur must have hit it. He was impressed: although the Dashoka had a range of a mile, and the helicopters were less than half a mile away, it took good shooting to destroy one at this distance.

The Hinds—the humpbacked gunships—were still in the air, circling above the village. Now the Russian commander brought them into action. One of them swooped low over the river and shelled Shahazai's minefield. Yussuf and Abdur fired at it but missed. Shahazai's mines exploded harmlessly, one after another. Ellis thought anxiously: I wish the mines had knocked out more of the enemy—twenty or so men out of a hundred and fifty isn't much. The Hind rose again, driven off by Yussuf; but another one descended and strafed the minefield again. Yussuf and Abdur poured a constant stream of fire at it. Suddenly it lurched, part of a wing fell off and it nose-dived into the river; and Ellis thought: Nice shooting, Yussuf! But the approach to the bridge was clear, and the Russians still had more than a hundred men and ten helicopters, and Ellis realized with a chill of fear that the guerrillas could lose this battle.

The Russians took heart then, and most of them—eighty or more men, Ellis estimated—began moving toward the bridge on their bellies, firing constantly. They can't be as dispirited or undisciplined as the American newspapers say, Ellis thought, unless this is an elite outfit. Then he realized that the soldiers all seemed white-skinned. There were no Afghans in this force. It was just like Vietnam, where the Arvins were always kept out of anything really important.

Suddenly there was a lull. The Russians in the barley field and the guerrillas in the village exchanged fire across the river in a desultory fashion, the Russians shooting more or less at random, the guerrillas using their ammunition sparingly. Ellis looked up. The Hinds in the air were going after Yussuf and Abdur on the cliff. The Russian commander had correctly identified the heavy machine guns as his main target.

As a Hind swooped toward the clifftop gunners, Ellis had a moment of admiration for the pilot, for flying directly at the guns: he knew how much nerve that took. The aircraft veered away: they had missed one another.

Their chances were roughly equal, Ellis thought: it was easier for Yussuf to aim accurately, because he was stationary whereas the aircraft was moving; but by the same token he was the easier target because he was still. Ellis recalled that in the Hind the wing-mounted rockets were fired by the pilot, while the gunner operated the machine gun in the nose. It would be hard for a pilot to aim accurately in such terrifying circumstances, Ellis thought; and since the Dashokas had a greater range than the helicopter's four-barrel Gatling-type gun, perhaps Yussuf and Abdur had a slight edge.

I hope so, for the sake of all of us, Ellis thought.

Another Hind descended toward the cliff like a hawk falling on a rabbit, but the guns drummed and the helicopter exploded in midair. Ellis felt like cheering—which was ironic, for he knew so well the terror and barely controlled panic of the helicopter crew under fire.

Another Hind swooped. The gunners were a fraction wide this time, but they shot off the helicopter's tail, and it went out of control and crashed into the face of the cliff, and Ellis thought: Jesus Christ, we may yet get them all! But the note of the guns had changed, and after a moment Ellis realized that only one was firing. The other had been knocked out. Ellis peered through the dust and saw a Chitrali cap moving up there. Yussuf was still alive. Abdur had been hit.

The three remaining Hinds circled and repositioned. One climbed high above the battle: the Russian commander must be in that one, Ellis thought. The other two descended on Yussuf in a pincer movement. That was smart thinking, Ellis thought anxiously, for Yussuf could not shoot at both of them at once. Ellis watched them come down. When Yussuf aimed at one, the other swooped lower. Ellis noticed that the Russians flew with their doors open, just as the Americans had in Vietnam.

The Hinds pounced. One dived at Yussuf and veered away, but he scored a direct hit and it burst into flames; then the second was swooping, rocket pods and guns blazing away, and Ellis thought, Yussuf doesn't stand a chance! and then the second Hind seemed to hesitate in midair. Had it been hit? It fell suddenly, going twenty or thirty feet straight down—*When your engine cuts out*, the instructor in flight school had said, *your helicopter will glide like a grand piano*—and crashed on the ledge just a few yards from Yussuf; but then its engine seemed to catch again, and to Ellis's surprise it began to lift. It's tougher than a goddamn Huey, he thought; helicopters have improved in the last ten years. Its gunner had been blazing away all the time, but now he stopped. Ellis saw why and his heart sank. A Dashoka came tumbling over the edge of the cliff in a welter of camouflage, bushes and branches; and it was followed immediately by a limp mud-colored bundle that was Yussuf. As he fell down the face of the cliff, he bounced off a jagged outcrop halfway, and his round Chitrali cap came off. A moment later he disappeared from Ellis's view. He had almost won the battle single-handed: there would be no medal for him, but his story would be told beside campfires in the cold Afghan mountains for a hundred years.

The Russians had lost four of their six Hinds, one Hip, and about twenty-five men; but the guerrillas had lost both their heavy guns, and now they had no defense as the two remaining Hinds began to strafe the village. Ellis huddled inside his hut, wishing it were not made of mud. The strafing was a softening-up tactic: after a minute or two, as if at a signal, the Russians in the barley field rose from the ground and rushed the bridge.

This is it, Ellis thought; this is the end, one way or another.

The guerrillas in the village fired on the charging troops, but they were inhibited by the air cover and few Russians fell. Almost all the Russians

were on their feet now, eighty or ninety men, firing blindly across the river
as they ran. They were yelling enthusiastically, encouraged by the thinness
of the defense. The guerrillas' shooting became a little more accurate as the
Russians reached the bridge, and several more fell, but not enough to halt
the charge. Seconds later the first of them had crossed the river and were
diving for cover among the houses of the village.

There were about sixty men on or near the bridge when Ellis pulled the
handle of the firing device.

The ancient stonework of the bridge blew up like a volcano.

Ellis had laid his charges to kill, not for a neat demolition, and the explosion sprayed lethal chunks of masonry like a burst from a giant machine
gun, taking out all the men on the bridge and many still in the barley field.
Ellis ducked back into his hut as rubble rained on the village. When it
stopped he looked out again.

Where the bridge had been, there was just a low pile of stones and bodies in a grisly mélange. Part of the mosque and two village houses had also
collapsed. And the Russians were in full retreat.

As he watched, the twenty or thirty men still left alive scrambled into
the open doors of the Hips. Ellis did not blame them. If they stayed in the
barley field, with no cover, they would be wiped out slowly by the guerrillas in good positions in the village; and if they tried to cross the river they
would be picked off in the water like fish in a barrel.

Seconds later, the three surviving Hips took off from the field to join the
two Hinds in the air, and then, without a parting shot, the aircraft soared
away over the clifftop and disappeared.

As the beat of their rotors faded, he heard another noise. After a moment he realized that it was the sound of men cheering. We won, he
thought. Hell, we won. And he started cheering, too.

CHAPTER THIRTEEN

"And where have all the guerrillas gone?" Jane asked.

"They scattered," Ellis replied. "This is Masud's technique. He melts away into the hills before the Russians can catch their breath. They may come back with reinforcements—they could even be at Darg now—but they will find nobody to fight. The guerrillas have gone, all but these few."

There were seven wounded men in Jane's clinic. None of them would die. Twelve more had been treated for minor wounds and sent on their way. Only two men had died in the battle, but by a heartbreaking stroke of bad luck one of them was Yussuf. Zahara would be in mourning again—and again it was because of Jean-Pierre.

Jane felt depressed, despite Ellis's euphoria. I must stop brooding, she thought. Jean-Pierre has gone, and he isn't coming back, and there's no point in grieving. I should think positively. I should take an interest in other people's lives.

"What about your conference?" she asked Ellis. "If all the guerrillas have gone away . . ."

"They all agreed," Ellis said. "They were so euphoric, after the success of the ambush, that they were ready to say yes to anything. In a way the ambush proved what some of them had doubted: that Masud is a brilliant leader and that by uniting under him they can achieve great victories. It also established my macho credentials, which helped."

"So you've succeeded."

"Yes. I even have a treaty, signed by all the rebel leaders and witnessed by the mullah."

"You must be proud." She reached out and squeezed his arm, then withdrew her hand quickly. She was so glad he was here to keep her from being alone that she felt guilty about having been angry with him for such a long time. But she was afraid she might accidentally give him the mistaken impression that she still cared for him in the old way, which would be awkward.

She turned away from him and looked around the cave. The bandages and syringes were in their boxes and the drugs were in her bag. The wounded guerrillas were comfortable on rugs or blankets. They would stay in the cave all night: it was too difficult to move them all down the hill. They had water and a little bread, and two or three of them were well enough to get up and make tea. Mousa, the one-handed son of Mohammed, was squatting in the mouth of the cave, playing a mysterious game in the dust with the knife his father had given him: he would stay with the wounded men, and in the unlikely event that one of them should need medical attention during the night, the boy would run down the hill and fetch Jane.

Everything was in order. She wished them good night, patted Mousa on the head and went outside. Ellis followed. Jane felt a hint of cold in the evening breeze. It was the first sign of the end of summer. She looked up at the distant mountaintops of the Hindu Kush, from where the winter would come. The snowy peaks were pink with the reflection of the setting sun. This was a beautiful country: that was too easy to forget, especially on busy days. I'm glad I've seen it, she thought, even though I can't wait to go home.

She walked down the hill with Ellis at her side. She glanced at him now and again. The sunset made his face appear bronzed and craggy. She realized that he probably had not slept much the night before. "You look tired," she said.

"It's a long time since I was in a real war," he replied. "Peace makes you soft."

He was very matter-of-fact about it. At least he did not relish the slaughter, as the Afghan men did. He had told her the bare fact that he had blown up the bridge at Darg, but one of the wounded guerrillas had given her the details, explaining how the timing of the explosion had turned the tide of the battle and graphically describing the carnage.

Down in the village of Banda, there was an air of celebration. Men and women stood talking animatedly in groups, instead of retiring to their courtyards. The children were playing noisy war games, ambushing imaginary Russians in imitation of their older brothers. Somewhere a man was singing to the beat of a drum. The thought of spending the evening alone suddenly seemed unbearably dreary to Jane, and on impulse she said to Ellis: "Come and have tea with me—if you don't mind my feeding Chantal."

"I'd like that," he said.

The baby was crying as they entered the house, and as always Jane's body responded: one of her breasts sprang a sudden leak. She said hurriedly: "Sit down, and Fara will bring you some tea." Then she darted into the other room before Ellis could see the embarrassing stain on her shirt. She undid her buttons quickly and picked up the baby. There was the usual moment of blind panic as Chantal sought the nipple, then she began to suck, painfully hard at first and then more gently. Jane felt awkward about going back into the other room. Don't be silly, she told herself; you asked him, and he said it was okay, and in any case you spent practically every night in his bed at one time. . . . All the same, she felt herself flush slightly as she walked through the door.

Ellis was looking at Jean-Pierre's maps. "This was the cleverest thing," he said. "He knew all the routes because Mohammed always used his maps." He looked up at her, saw her expression and said hastily: "But let's not talk about that. What will you do now?"

She sat on the cushion with her back against the wall, her favorite position for nursing. Ellis did not seem embarrassed by her exposed breast, and she began to feel more comfortable. "I have to wait," she said. "As soon as the route to Pakistan is open and the convoys begin again, I'll go home. What about you?"

"The same. My work here is over. The agreement will have to be supervised, of course, but the Agency has people in Pakistan who can do that."

Fara brought the tea. Jane wondered what Ellis's next job would be: plotting a coup in Nicaragua, or blackmailing a Soviet diplomat in Washington, or perhaps assassinating an African Communist? She had questioned him, when they were lovers, about going to Vietnam, and he had told her that everybody had expected him to dodge the draft, but he was a contrary son of a bitch and so he did the opposite. She was not sure she believed that, but even if it was true it did not explain why he had remained in this violent line of work even after he got out of the army. "So what will you do when you get home?" she asked. "Go back to devising cute ways of killing Castro?"

"The Agency is not supposed to do assassinations," he said.

"But it does."

"There's a lunatic element that gives us a bad name. Unfortunately, presidents can't resist the temptation to play secret-agent games, and that encourages the nutcase faction."

"Why don't you turn your back on them all and join the human race?"

"Look. America is full of people who believe that other countries as well as their own have a right to be free—but they're the type of people who turn their backs and join the human race. In consequence, the Agency employs too many psychopaths and too few decent, compassionate citizens. Then, when the Agency brings down a foreign government at the whim of a president, they all ask how this kind of thing can possibly happen. The answer is because they let it. My country is a democracy, so there's nobody to blame but me when things are wrong; and if things are to be put right, I have to do it, because it's my responsibility."

Jane was unconvinced. "Would you say that the way to reform the KGB is to join it?"

"No, because the KGB is not ultimately controlled by the people. The Agency is."

"Control isn't that simple," said Jane. "The CIA tells lies to the people. You can't control them if you have no way of knowing what they're doing."

"But in the end it's our Agency and our responsibility."

"You could work to abolish it instead of joining it."

"But we need a central intelligence agency. We live in a hostile world and we need information about our enemies."

Jane sighed. "But look what it leads to," she said. "You're planning to send more and bigger guns to Masud so that he can kill more people faster. And that's what you people *always* end up doing."

"It's *not* just so that he can kill more people faster," Ellis protested. "The Afghans are fighting for their freedom—and they're fighting *against* a bunch of murderers—"

"They're *all* fighting for their freedom," Jane interrupted. "The PLO, the Cuban exiles, the Weathermen, the IRA, the white South Africans and the Free Wales Army."

"Some are right and some aren't."

"And the CIA knows the difference?"

"It ought to—"

"But it doesn't. Whose freedom is Masud fighting for?"

"The freedom of all Afghans."

"Bullshit," Jane said fiercely. "He's a Muslim fundamentalist, and if he ever takes power the first thing he'll do is clamp down on women. He will never give them the vote—he wants to take away what few rights they have. And how do you think he will treat his opponents, given that his political hero is the Ayatollah Khomeini? Will scientists and teachers have academic freedom? Will gay men and women have sexual freedom? What will happen to the Hindus, the Buddhists, the atheists and the Plymouth Brethren?"

Ellis said: "Do you *seriously* think Masud's regime would be worse than that of the Russians?"

Jane thought for a moment. "I don't know. The only thing that's certain is that Masud's regime will be an Afghan tyranny instead of a Russian tyranny. And it's not worth killing people to exchange a local dictator for a foreigner."

"The Afghans seem to think it is."

"Most of them have never been asked."

"I think it's obvious. However, I don't normally do this sort of work anyway. Usually I'm more of a detective type."

This was something about which Jane had been curious for a year. "What exactly was your mission in Paris?"

"When I spied on all our friends?" He smiled thinly. "Didn't Jean-Pierre tell you?"

"He said he didn't really know."

"Perhaps he didn't. I was hunting terrorists."

"Among our friends?"

"That's where they are usually to be found—among dissidents, dropouts and criminals."

"Was Rahmi Coskun a terrorist?" Jean-Pierre had said that Rahmi got arrested because of Ellis.

"Yes. He was responsible for the Turkish Airlines firebombing in the Avenue Félix Faure."

"Rahmi? How do you know?"

"He told me. And when I had him arrested he was planning another bombing."

"He told you that, too?"

"He asked me to help him with the bomb."

"My God." Handsome Rahmi, with the smoldering eyes and passionate hatred of his wretched country's government . . .

Ellis had not finished. "Remember Pepe Gozzi?"

Jane frowned. "Do you mean the funny little Corsican who had a Rolls-Royce?"

"Yes. He supplied guns and explosives to every nutcase in Paris. He'd sell to anyone who could afford his prices, but he specialized in 'political' customers."

Jane was flabbergasted. She had assumed that Pepe was somewhat disreputable, purely on the grounds that he was both rich and Corsican; but she had supposed that at worst he was involved in some everyday crime such as smuggling or dope dealing. To think that he sold guns to murderers! Jane was beginning to feel as if she had been living in a dream, while intrigue and violence went on in the real world all around her. *Am I so naïve?* she thought.

Ellis plowed on. "I also pulled in a Russian who had financed a lot of assassinations and kidnappings. Then Pepe was interrogated and spilled the beans on half the terrorists in Europe."

"That's what you were doing, all the time we were lovers," Jane said dreamily. She recalled the parties, the rock concerts, the demonstrations, the political arguments in cafés, the endless bottles of *vin rouge ordinaire* in attic studios. . . . Since their breakup she had assumed vaguely that he had been writing little reports on all the radicals, saying who was influential, who was extreme, who had money, who had the largest following among students, who had Communist Party connections, and so on. It was hard now to accept the idea that he had been after real criminals, and that he had actually found some among their friends. "I can't believe it," she said in amazement.

"It was a great triumph, if you want to know the truth."

"You probably shouldn't be telling me."

"I shouldn't. But when I've lied to you in the past, I have regretted doing so—to put it mildly."

Jane felt awkward and did not know what to say. She shifted Chantal to her left breast, then, catching Ellis's eye, covered her right breast with her shirt. The conversation was becoming uncomfortably personal, but she was intensely curious to know more. She could see now how he justified himself—although she did not agree with his reasoning—but still she wondered about his motivation. *If I don't find out now,* she thought, *I may never get another chance.* She said: "I don't understand what makes a man decide to spend his life doing this sort of thing."

He glanced away. "I'm good at it and it's worth doing and the pay's terrific."

"And I expect you liked the pension plan and the canteen menu. It's all right—you don't have to explain yourself to me if you don't want to."

He gave her a hard look, as if he were trying to read her thoughts. "I do want to tell you," he said. "Are you sure you want to hear it?"

"Yes. Please."

"It's to do with the war," he began, and suddenly Jane knew he was about to say something he had never told to anyone else. "One of the terrible things about flying in Vietnam was that it was so hard to differentiate between Vietcong and civilians. Whenever we gave air support to ground troops, say, or mined a jungle trail, or declared a free-fire zone, we knew that we would kill more women and children and old men than guerrillas. We used to say they had been sheltering the enemy, but who knows? And who cares? We killed them. *We were the terrorists then*. And I'm not talking about isolated cases—although I saw atrocities too—I'm talking about our regular everyday tactics. And there was no justification, you see; that was the kicker. We did all those terrible things in a cause that turned out to be all lies and corruption and self-deceit. We were on the wrong side." His face was drawn, as if he were in pain from some persistent internal injury. In the restless lamplight his skin was shadowed and sallow. "There's no excuse, you see, no forgiveness."

Gently, Jane encouraged him to say more. "So why did you stay?" she asked him. "Why volunteer for a second tour?"

"Because I didn't see all of that so clearly then; because I was fighting for my country and you can't walk away from a war; because I was a good officer, and if I had gone home my job might have been taken over by some jerk and my men would have got killed: and none of these reasons is good enough, of course, so at some point I asked myself 'What are you going to do about it?' I wanted . . . I didn't realize it at the time, but I wanted to do something to redeem myself. In the sixties we would have called it a guilt trip."

"Yes, but . . ." He looked so uncertain and vulnerable that she found it hard to ask him direct questions, but he needed to talk and she wanted to hear it, so she plowed on. "But why *this*?"

"I was in Intelligence, toward the end, and they offered me the chance to continue in the same line of work in the civilian world. They said I would be able to work undercover because I was familiar with that milieu. They knew about my radical past, you see. It seemed to me that by catching terrorists I might be able to undo some of the things I had done. So I became a counterterrorist expert. It sounds simplistic when I put it into words—but I've been successful, you know. The Agency doesn't like me because I sometimes refuse a mission, such as the time they killed the President of Chile, and agents aren't supposed to refuse missions; but I've been responsible for incarcerating some very nasty people, and I'm proud of myself."

Chantal was asleep. Jane laid her in the box that was her cradle. She said to Ellis: "I suppose I ought to say that . . . that I seem to have misjudged you."

He smiled. "Thank God for that."

For a moment she was seized by nostalgia as she thought of the time—was it only a year and a half ago?—when she and Ellis had been happy and none of *this* had happened: no CIA, no Jean-Pierre, no Afghanistan. "You can't wipe it out, though, can you?" she said. "Everything that has happened—your lies, my anger."

"No." He was sitting on the stool, studying her intently, looking up at her as she stood in front of him. He held out his arms, hesitated, then rested his hands on her hips in a gesture which might have been brotherly affection or something more. Then Chantal said: "Mumumumummmm . . ." Jane turned around and looked at her, and Ellis let his hands fall. Chantal was wide awake, waving her arms and legs in the air. Jane picked her up, and she burped immediately.

Jane turned back to face Ellis. He had folded his arms across his chest and was watching her, smiling. Suddenly she did not want him to leave. On impulse, she said: "Why don't you have supper with me? It's only bread and curds, though."

"All right."

She held Chantal out to him. "Let me go and tell Fara." He took the baby and she went out into the courtyard. Fara was heating water for Chantal's bath. Jane tested the temperature with her elbow and found it just right. "Make bread for two people, please," she said in Dari. Fara's eyes widened, and Jane realized it was shocking for a woman alone to invite a man to supper. To hell with all that, she thought. She picked up the pot of water and carried it back into the house.

Ellis was sitting on the big cushion under the oil lamp, dandling Chantal on his knee, saying a rhyme in a low voice. His big hairy hands encircled her tiny pink body. She was looking up at him, gurgling happily and kicking her fat feet. Jane stopped in the doorway, transfixed by the scene, and a thought came unbidden into her mind: Ellis should have been Chantal's father.

Is that true? she asked herself as she looked at them. Do I really wish it?

Ellis finished the rhyme and looked up at her and smiled a little sheepishly, and she thought: Yes, I really do.

They walked up the mountainside at midnight, Jane leading the way, Ellis following with his big down sleeping bag under his arm. They had bathed Chantal, eaten their meager supper of bread and curds, fed Chantal again, and settled the baby down for the night on the roof, where she was now fast asleep beside Fara, who would protect her with her life. Ellis had wanted to take Jane away from the house where she had been someone else's wife, and Jane had felt the same, so she had said: "I know a place where we can go."

Now she turned off the mountain path and led Ellis across the sloping, stony ground to her secret retreat, the concealed ledge where she had sun-bathed naked and oiled her tummy before Chantal was born. She found it easily in the moonlight. She looked down into the village, where the embers of cooking fires glowed in the courtyards and a few lamps still flickered behind glassless windows. She could just about make out the shape of her house. In a few hours, as soon as day began to break, she would be able to see the sleeping forms of Chantal and Fara on the roof. She would be glad: this was the first time she had left Chantal at night.

She turned around. Ellis had completely unzipped the sleeping bag and was spreading it on the ground like a blanket. Jane felt awkward and uncomfortable. The surge of warmth and lust which had overcome her in the house, when she watched him saying a nursery rhyme to her baby, had gone. All her old feelings had returned, momentarily: the urge to touch him, her love of the way he smiled when he felt self-conscious, the need to feel his big hands on her skin, the obsessive wish to see him naked. A few weeks before Chantal was born she had lost her desire for sex, and it had not come back until that moment. But that mood had been dissipated, bit by bit, in the succeeding hours, as they had made clumsy practical arrangements to be alone, for all the world like a pair of teenagers trying to get away from their parents for a petting session.

"Come and sit down," Ellis said.

She sat beside him on the sleeping bag. They both looked down at the darkened village. They were not touching. There was a moment of strained silence. "Nobody else has ever been here," Jane remarked, just for something to say.

"What did you use it for?"

"Oh, I just used to lie in the sun and think about nothing," she said.

Then she thought, Oh, what the hell, and she said: "No, that's not quite true, I used to masturbate."

He laughed, then put his arm around her and hugged her. "I'm glad you still haven't learned to mince your words," he said.

She turned her face to him. He kissed her mouth softly. He likes me for my faults, she thought: my tactlessness and my quick temper and my cursing, my willfulness and my being opinionated. "You don't want to change me," she said.

"Oh, Jane, I've missed you." He closed his eyes and spoke in a murmur. "Most of the time I didn't even realize that I was missing you." He lay back, pulling her with him, so that she ended up leaning over him. She kissed his face lightly. The awkward feeling was going rapidly. She thought: Last time I kissed him he had no beard. She felt his hands move: he was unbuttoning her shirt. She was not wearing a bra—she did not have one big enough—and her breasts felt very naked. She slipped her hand inside his shirt and touched the long hairs around his nipple. She had almost forgotten what men felt like. For months her life had been full of the soft voices and smooth faces of women and babies: now suddenly she wanted to feel rough skin and hard thighs and bristly cheeks. She twined her fingers in his beard and pushed his mouth open with her tongue. His hands found her swollen breasts, she felt a pang of pleasure—and then she knew what was going to happen and was powerless to stop it, for even as she pulled abruptly away from him, she felt both her nipples spurt warm milk over his hands, and she flushed with shame and said: "Oh, God, I'm sorry, how disgusting. I can't help it—"

He silenced her with a finger over her lips. "It's all right," he said. He caressed her breasts as he spoke, and they became slippery all over. "It's normal. It always happens. It's sexy."

It *can't* be sexy, she thought, but he shifted his position and brought his face to her chest and started to kiss her breasts and stroke them at the same time, and gradually she relaxed and started to enjoy the sensation. Eventually she felt another sharp pang of pleasure as they leaked again, but this time she did not mind. Ellis said: "Aaah," and the rough surface of his tongue touched her tender nipples, and she thought: If he sucks them I'll come.

It was as if he had read her mind. He closed his lips around one long nipple, pulled it into his mouth and sucked it while holding the other between finger and thumb, squeezing gently and rhythmically. Helplessly Jane yielded to the sensation. And as her breasts squirted milk, one into his hand

and the other into his mouth, the feeling was so exquisite that she shuddered uncontrollably and moaned: "Oh God oh God oh God" until it died away and she slumped on top of him.

For a while there was nothing in her mind but what she could feel: his warm breath on her wet breasts, his beard scratching her skin, the cool night air wafting over her heated cheeks, the nylon sleeping bag and the hard ground beneath. After a while his muffled voice said: "I'm suffocating."

She rolled off him. "Are we weird?" she said.

"Yes."

She giggled. "Have you ever done that before?"

He hesitated, then said: "Yes."

"What . . ." She still felt faintly embarrassed. "What does it taste like?"

"Warm and sweet. Like canned milk. Did you come?"

"Didn't you notice?"

"I wasn't sure. It's hard to tell with girls, sometimes."

She kissed him. "I came. A little one, but unmistakable. A boobinal orgasm."

"I almost came."

"Really?" She ran her hand down his body. He had on the thin cotton pajamalike shirt and trousers that Afghans all wore. She could feel his ribs and his hipbones: he had lost the soft underskin fat which all but the thinnest Westerners had. Her hand encountered his prick, standing upright inside the trousers, and she said: "Ahhh," and grasped it. "It feels good," she said.

"Also at this end."

She wanted to give him as much pleasure as he had given her. She sat upright, untied the drawstring of his trousers and took out his prick. Stroking it gently, she bent over and kissed the end. Then the imp of mischief seized her and she said: "How many girls have you had since me?"

"Just keep doing that and I'll tell you."

"Okay." She resumed stroking and kissing. He was silent. "Okay," she said after a minute, "how many?"

"Wait, I'm still counting."

"Bastard!" she said, and bit his prick.

"Ouch! Not many, really . . . I swear!"

"What do you do when you haven't got a girl?"

"Take three guesses."

She was not to be put off. "Do you do it with your hand?"

"Aw, shucks, Miz Janey, I'se bashful."

"You do," she said triumphantly. "What do you think about while you're doing it?"

"Would you believe Princess Diana?"

"No."

"Now I *am* embarrassed."

Jane was consumed with curiosity. "You have to tell the truth."

"Pam Ewing."

"Who the hell is she?"

"You *have* been out of touch. She's Bobby Ewing's wife, on *Dallas*."

Jane remembered the television show and the actress, and she was astonished. "You can't be serious."

"You asked for the truth."

"But she's made of plastic!"

"We're talking *fantasy* here."

"Can't you fantasize a liberated woman?"

"Fantasy is no place for politics."

"I'm shocked." She hesitated. "How do you do it?"

"What?"

"What you do. With your hand."

"Kind of like what you're doing, but harder."

"Show me."

"I'm not just embarrassed now," he said. "I'm mortified."

"Please. Please show me. I've always wanted to see a man do that. I've never had the nerve to ask before—if you turn me down I may never know." She took his hand and placed it where hers had been.

After a moment he started to move his hand slowly. He made several rather halfhearted strokes; then he sighed, closed his eyes and started to rub it in earnest.

"You're so rough with it!" she exclaimed.

He stopped. "I can't do this . . . unless you do it too."

"It's a deal," she said eagerly. Quickly she slipped off her trousers and panties. She knelt beside him and started to stroke herself.

"Come closer," he said. His voice sounded a little hoarse. "I can't see you."

He was lying flat on his back. She shuffled closer until she was kneeling upright beside his head, with the moonlight silvering her nipples and her pubic hair. He started to rub his prick again, faster this time, and he stared at her hand as if transfixed as she caressed herself.

"Oh, Jane," he said.

She began to enjoy the familiar darts of pleasure spreading from her fingertips. She saw Ellis's hips start to move up and down in rhythm with his hand. "I want you to come," she said. "I want to see it shoot out." Part of her was shocked at herself, but that part was swamped by excitement and desire.

He groaned. She looked at his face. His mouth was open and he was breathing hard. His eyes were fixed on her cunt. She stroked the lips with her middle finger. "Put your finger in," he breathed. "I want to see your finger go inside."

That was something she did not normally do. She pushed her fingertip inside. It felt smooth and slippery. She put it all the way in. He gasped, and because he was so excited by what she was doing, she got turned on, too. She turned her gaze back to his prick. His hips jerked faster as he fucked his hand. She moved her finger in and out of her cunt with mounting pleasure. Suddenly he arched his back, thrusting his pelvis high in the air and groaning, and a streak of white semen shot out from him. Involuntarily Jane cried, "Oh, my God!"; then as she gazed, fascinated, at the tiny hole in the end of his organ, another jet came, and another, and a fourth, spurting up into the air, gleaming in the moonlight and landing on his chest and her arm and in her hair; and then when he collapsed, she herself was racked by spasms of pleasure fired by her fast-moving finger until she, too, was exhausted.

She slumped, lying beside him on the sleeping bag with her head on his thigh. His prick was still stiff. She leaned over weakly and kissed it. She could taste a trace of salty semen on the end. She felt his face nuzzle between her thighs in response.

For a while they were quiet. The only sounds were their breathing and the rushing river on the far side of the Valley. Jane looked at the stars. They were very bright, and there were no clouds. The night air was becoming cooler. We'll have to get inside this sleeping bag before too long, she thought. She looked forward to falling asleep close to him.

"Are we weird?" said Ellis.

"Oh, yes," she said.

His prick had fallen sideways and lay on his belly. She teased the red-gold hair of his groin with her fingertips. She had almost forgotten what it was like to make love to Ellis. He was so different from Jean-Pierre. Jean-Pierre liked a lot of preparation: bath oil, scent, candlelight, wine, violins. He was a fastidious lover. He liked her to wash before making love, and he always hurried to the bathroom afterward. He would never touch her while she had her period, and he certainly would not have sucked her breasts and swallowed the milk as Ellis had. Ellis would do *anything*, she thought, and the more unhygienic the better. She grinned in the dark. It occurred to her that she had never been completely convinced that Jean-Pierre actually *liked* performing oral sex, good at it though he was. With Ellis there was no doubt.

The thought made her want him to do it. She opened her thighs invitingly. She felt him kiss her, his lips brushing the wiry hair; then his tongue started to probe lasciviously between the folds of her lips. After a while he rolled her onto her back, knelt between her thighs, and lifted her legs over his shoulders. She felt utterly naked, terribly open and vulnerable and yet greatly cherished. His tongue moved in a long, slow curve, starting at the base of her spine—Oh, God, she thought, I remember how he does this—licking along the cleft of her buttocks, pausing to push deep into her vagina, then lifting to tease the sensitive skin where the lips met and the tingling clitoris between them. After seven or eight long licks she held his head over her clitoris, making him concentrate on that, and she began to lift and lower her hips, telling him by the pressure of her fingertips on his temples to lick harder or more lightly, higher or lower, left or right. She felt his hand on her cunt, pushing into the moist interior, and guessed what he was going to do: a moment later he withdrew his hand, and then pushed a wet finger slowly into her anus. She remembered how shocked she had been the first time he did that, and how quickly she had grown to like it. Jean-Pierre would never do that in a million years. As the muscles of her body began to tense for the climax, the thought came to her that she had missed Ellis more than she had ever admitted to herself; indeed, the reason she had been so angry with him for so long was that she had continued to love him all along, and she loved him still; and as she admitted it, a terrible weight lifted from her mind and she started to come, shaking like a tree in a gale, and Ellis, knowing what she liked, thrust his tongue deep inside her while she ground her sex frantically against his face.

It seemed it would go on forever. Each time the sensations eased, he would thrust his finger deeper into her ass, or lick her clitoris, or bite the lips of her cunt, and it would start all over again; until, out of sheer exhaustion, she pleaded: "Stop, stop, I've no energy left—it will kill me," and at last he lifted his face from her cunt and lowered her legs to the ground.

He leaned over her, resting his weight on his hands, and kissed her mouth. The smell of her cunt was in his beard. She lay prone, too tired to open her eyes, too tired even to kiss him back. She felt his hand on her cunt, opening it, then his prick nosing in, and she thought, He got hard again quickly, and then, It's been so long oh God it feels good.

He began to move in and out, slowly at first and then faster. She opened her eyes. His face was above hers and he was gazing at her. Then he bent his neck and looked down to where their bodies were joined. His eyes widened and his mouth opened as he watched his prick going in and out of her cunt, and the sight so inflamed him that she wished she could see it, too. Suddenly he slowed his pace, thrusting deeper, and she remembered that he did this before the climax. He looked into her eyes. "Kiss me while I come," he said, and he lowered his cunt-smelling lips to hers. She thrust her tongue into his mouth. She loved it when he came. His back arched and his head lifted, and he gave a cry like a wild animal, and she felt him spurt inside her.

When it was over he lowered his head to her shoulder and moved his lips gently against the soft skin of her neck, whispering words which she could not make out. After a minute or two he gave a deep sigh of contentment, kissed her mouth, then raised himself to his knees and kissed each of her breasts in turn. Finally he kissed her cunt. Her body responded instantly, and she moved her hips to push against his lips. Knowing that she was getting turned on yet again, he began to lick; and, as always, the thought of him licking her cunt while it was still dripping with his semen almost drove her mad, and she came immediately, crying his name until the spasm passed.

He slumped beside her at last. Automatically they moved into the position they had always lain in after making love: his arm around her, her head on his shoulder, her thigh lying across his hips. He yawned hugely, and she giggled at him. They touched one another lethargically, she reaching down to toy with his limp penis, he moving his fingers in and out of her sopping cunt. She licked his chest and tasted salt perspiration on his skin. She looked at his neck. The moon highlighted the lines and furrows, betraying his age. He's ten years older than me, Jane thought. Maybe that's why he's such a great fuck, because he's older. "Why are you such a great fuck?" she said aloud. He did not reply; he was asleep. So she said: "I love you, dear, sleep well," and then she closed her eyes.

After a year in the Valley, Jean-Pierre found the city of Kabul bewildering and frightening. The buildings were too tall, the cars went too fast and there were too many people. He had to cover his ears as enormous Russian trucks roared by in convoy. Everything assaulted him with the shock of the new: apartment blocks, schoolgirls in uniform, streetlights, elevators, table-cloths, and the taste of wine. After twenty-four hours he was still jumpy. It was ironic: he was a Parisian!

He had been given a room in the unmarried officers' quarters. They had promised him that he would get an apartment as soon as Jane arrived with Chantal. Meanwhile he felt as if he were living in a cheap hotel. The building probably had been a hotel before the Russians came. If Jane were to arrive now—she was due at any time—the three of them would have to make the best of it here for the rest of the night. I can't complain, thought Jean-Pierre; I'm not a hero—yet.

He stood at his window, looking over Kabul at night. For a couple of hours the power had been out all over the city, due presumably to the urban counterparts of Masud and his guerrillas, but a few minutes ago it had come back on again, and there was a faint glow over the city center, which had street lighting. The only noise was the howl of engines as army cars, trucks and tanks hurtled through the city, hurrying to their mysterious destinations. What was so urgent, at midnight in Kabul? Jean-Pierre had done military service, and he thought that if the Russian Army was anything like the French, the kind of task done on the double in the middle of the night was something like moving five hundred chairs from a barracks to a hall on the other side of town in preparation for a concert that was to take place in two weeks' time and would probably get canceled.

He could not smell the night air, for his window was nailed shut. His door was not locked, but there was a Russian sergeant with a pistol sitting blank-faced on a straight-backed chair at the end of the corridor, next to the toilet, and Jean-Pierre felt that if he wanted to leave, the sergeant would probably prevent him.

Where was Jane? The raid on Darg must have been over by nightfall. For a helicopter to go from Darg to Banda and pick up Jane and Chantal would be the work of a few minutes. The helicopter could get from Banda to Kabul in under an hour. But perhaps the attacking force was returning to Bagram, the air base near the mouth of the Valley, in which case Jane might have had to come from Bagram to Kabul by road, no doubt accompanied by Anatoly.

She would be so glad to see her husband that she would be ready to forgive his deceit, see his point of view about Masud, and let bygones be bygones, Jean-Pierre thought. For a moment he wondered whether that was wishful thinking. No, he decided; he knew her quite well, and she was basically under his thumb.

And she would *know*. Only a few people would share the secret and comprehend the magnitude of what he had achieved: he was glad she would be one of them.

He hoped Masud had been captured, rather than killed. If he had been captured, the Russians could put him on trial, so that all the rebels would know for sure he was finished. Death was almost as good, provided they had the body. If there were no body, or an unrecognizable corpse, the rebels' propagandists in Peshawar would put out press releases claiming that Masud was still alive. Of course, it would become clear in the end that he was dead, but the impact would be softened a little. Jean-Pierre hoped they had the body.

He heard footsteps in the corridor. Would it be Anatoly, or Jane—or both? It sounded like a masculine tread. He opened the door and saw two rather large Russian soldiers and a third, smaller man in an officer's uniform. No doubt they had come to take him to wherever Anatoly and Jane were. He was disappointed. He looked inquiringly at the officer, who made a gesture with his hand. The two soldiers stepped through the door rudely. Jean-Pierre went back a pace, a protest rising to his lips, but before he could speak, the nearer of the two grabbed him by the shirt and smashed a huge fist into his face.

Jean-Pierre let out a howl of pain and fear. The other soldier kicked him in the groin with a heavy boot. The pain was excruciating, and Jean-Pierre sank to his knees, knowing that the most terrible moment of his life had arrived.

The two soldiers pulled him upright and held him standing, one at each arm, and the officer came in. Through a haze of tears Jean-Pierre saw a short, thickset young man with some kind of deformity which made one side of his face appear flushed and swollen and gave him a permanent sneer. He carried a truncheon in his gloved hand.

For the next five minutes the two soldiers held Jean-Pierre's squirming, shuddering body while the officer smashed the wooden truncheon repeatedly into his face, his shoulders, his knees, his shins, his belly and his groin—always his groin. Every blow was carefully placed and viciously delivered, and there was always a pause between blows, so that the agony of the last could fade just enough to allow Jean-Pierre to dread the next for a second before it came. Every blow made him scream in pain, and every pause made him scream in anticipation of the next blow. At last there was a longer pause, and Jean-Pierre began to babble, not knowing whether they could understand him or not: "Oh, please, don't hit me, please, don't hit me again, sir, I'll do anything, what is it you want, please don't hit me no don't hit me—"

"Enough!" said a voice in French.

Jean-Pierre opened his eyes and tried to peer through the blood streaming down his face at this savior who had said *Enough*. It was Anatoly.

The two soldiers slowly let Jean-Pierre sink to the ground. His body felt as if it was on fire. Every move was agony. Every bone felt broken, his balls felt crushed, his face seemed to have swollen enormously. He opened his mouth, and blood came out. He swallowed, and spoke through smashed lips. "Why . . . why have they done this?"

"You know why," said Anatoly.

Jean-Pierre shook his head from side to side slowly and tried to keep from descending into utter madness. "I risked my life for you . . . I gave everything . . . why?"

"You set a trap," Anatoly said. "Eighty-one men died today because of you."

The raid must have gone wrong, Jean-Pierre realized, and somehow he was being blamed. "No," he said, "not I—"

"You expected to be miles away when the trap was sprung," Anatoly went on. "But I surprised you by making you get into the helicopter and come with me. So you are here to take your punishment—which will be painful and very, very prolonged." He turned away.

"No," said Jean-Pierre. "Wait!"

Anatoly turned back.

Jean-Pierre fought to think despite the pain. "I came here . . . I risked my life . . . I gave you information on the convoys . . . you attacked the convoys . . . did far more damage than the loss of eighty men . . . not logical, it's not logical." He gathered his strength for one coherent sentence. "If I had known of a trap I could have warned you yesterday and begged for mercy."

"Then how did they know we would attack the village?" Anatoly demanded.

"They must have guessed. . . ."

"How?"

Jean-Pierre racked his confused brains. "Was Skabun bombed?"

"I think not."

That was it, Jean-Pierre realized; someone had found out that there had been no bombing at Skabun. "You should have bombed it," he said.

Anatoly looked thoughtful. "Somebody there is very good at making connections."

It was Jane, thought Jean-Pierre, and for a second he hated her.

Anatoly said: "Has Ellis Thaler got any distinguishing marks?"

Jean-Pierre wanted to pass out, but he was afraid they would hit him again. "Yes," he said miserably. "A big scar on his back shaped like a cross."

"Then it *is* him," said Anatoly in a near-whisper.

"Who?"

"John Michael Raleigh, age thirty-four, born in New Jersey, eldest son of a builder. He was a dropout from the University of California at Berkeley and a captain in the U.S. Marines. He has been a CIA agent since 1972. Marital status: divorced once, one child, whereabouts of the family a closely guarded secret." He waved his hand as if to brush such details aside. "There's no doubt it was he who outguessed me at Darg today. He's brilliant and very dangerous. If I could have my pick of all the agents of the Western imperialist nations to catch I would choose him. In the last ten years he has done us irreparable damage on at least three occasions. Last year in Paris he destroyed a network that had taken seven or eight years of patient work to develop. The year before that he found an agent we had planted in the Secret Service in *nineteen sixty-five*—a man who could have assassinated a president one day. And now—now we have him here."

Jean-Pierre, kneeling on the floor and hugging his battered body, let his head fall forward and closed his eyes in despair. All along he had been far out of his depth, blithely pitting himself against the grand masters of this merciless game, a naked child in a den of lions.

He had had such high hopes. Working alone, he was to have dealt the Afghan Resistance a blow from which it would never recover. He would have changed the course of history in this area of the globe. And he would have taken his revenge on the smug rulers of the West; he would have deceived and dismayed the establishment that had betrayed and killed his father. But instead of that triumph, he had been defeated. It had all been snatched from him at the last moment—by Ellis.

He heard Anatoly's voice like a background murmur. "We can be sure he achieved what he wanted with the rebels. We don't know the details, but the outline is enough: a unity pact among the bandit leaders in exchange for American arms. That kind of thing could keep the rebellion going for years. We've got to stop it before it gets started."

Jean-Pierre opened his eyes and looked up. "How?"

"We have to catch this man before he can return to the United States. That way nobody will know that he arranged the treaty, the rebels will never get their arms, and the whole thing will fizzle out."

Jean-Pierre listened, fascinated despite the pain. Could it be that there was still a chance of wreaking his revenge?

"Catching him would almost make up for losing Masud," Anatoly went on, and Jean-Pierre's heart leaped with new hope. "Not only would we have neutralized the single most dangerous agent the imperialists have, but think of it: a real live CIA man caught here in Afghanistan. . . . For three years the American propaganda machine has been saying that the Afghan bandits are freedom fighters waging a heroic David-and-Goliath struggle against the might of the Soviet Union. Now we have *proof* of what we have been saying all along—that Masud and the others are mere lackeys of American imperialism. We can put Ellis on trial. . . ."

"But the Western newspapers will deny everything," said Jean-Pierre. "The capitalist press—"

"Who cares about the West? It is the nonaligned countries, the Third World waverers, and the Muslim nations in particular whom we want to impress."

It *was* possible, Jean-Pierre realized, to turn this into a triumph; and it would still be a triumph for him personally, because it was he who had alerted the Russians to the presence of a CIA agent in the Five Lions Valley.

"Now," said Anatoly, "*where* is Ellis tonight?"

"He moves around with Masud," said Jean-Pierre. Catching Ellis was easier said than done: it had taken Jean-Pierre a whole year to pin down Masud.

"I don't see why he should continue to be with Masud," said Anatoly. "Did he have a base?"

"Yes—he lived with a family in Banda, theoretically. But he was rarely there."

"Nevertheless, that is obviously the place to begin."

Yes, of course, thought Jean-Pierre. If Ellis is not at Banda, somebody there may know where he has gone. . . . Somebody like Jane. If Anatoly went to Banda looking for Ellis, he might at the same time find Jane. Jean-Pierre's pain seemed to ease as he realized that he might get his revenge on the establishment, capture Ellis, who had stolen his triumph, *and* get Jane and Chantal back. "Will I go with you to Banda?" he asked.

Anatoly considered. "I think so. You know the village and the people—it may be useful to have you on hand."

Jean-Pierre struggled to his feet, gritting his teeth against the agony in his groin. "When do we go?"

"Now," said Anatoly.

CHAPTER FOURTEEN

E llis was hurrying to catch a train, and he was panicking even though he knew he was dreaming. First he could not park his car—he was driving Gill's Honda—then he could not find the ticket window. Having decided to get on the train without a ticket, he found himself pushing through a dense crowd of people in the vast concourse of Grand Central Station. At that point he remembered that he had dreamed this dream before, several times, and quite recently; and he never caught the train. The dreams always left him with an unbearable feeling that all happiness had passed him by, permanently, and now he was terrified that the same thing would happen again. He shoved through the crowd with increasing violence, and at last reached the gate. This was where he had previously stood watching the rear end of the train disappear into the distance, but today, it was in the station. He ran along the platform and jumped aboard just as it started to move.

He was so delighted to have caught the train that he felt almost high. He took his seat, and it did not seem at all strange that he was in a sleeping bag with Jane. Outside the train's windows, dawn was breaking over the Five Lions Valley.

There was no sharp division between sleep and wakefulness. The train gradually faded until all that was left was the sleeping bag and the Valley and Jane and the sense of delight. At some point during the short night they had zipped up the bag, and now they lay very close together, hardly

able to move. He could feel her warm breath on his neck, and her enlarged breasts were squashed against his ribs. Her bones prodded him, her
hip and her knee, her elbow and her foot, but he liked it. They had always
slept close together, he remembered. The antique bed in her Paris apartment had been too small for anything else anyway. His own bed had been
bigger, but even there they had slept entangled. She always claimed that
he molested her during the night, but he never remembered it in the
morning.

It was a long time since he had slept all night with a woman. He tried
to recall who was the last one, and realized it was Jane: the girls he had
taken to his apartment in Washington had never stayed for breakfast.

Jane was the last and the *only* person with whom he had had such uninhibited sex. He ran over in his mind the things they had done last
night, and he began to get an erection. There seemed to be no limit to the
number of times he could get hard with her. In Paris they had sometimes
stayed in bed all day, getting up only to raid the fridge or open some wine,
and he would come five or six times, while she just lost count of her or-
gasms. He had never thought of himself as a sexual athlete, and subse-
quent experience proved that he was not, except with her. She freed
something that was imprisoned, when he was with other women, by fear
or guilt or something. No one else had done that to him, although one
woman had come close: a Vietnamese with whom he had had a brief,
doomed affair in 1970.

It was obvious that he had never stopped loving Jane. For the past year
he had done his work, dated women, visited Petal and gone to the super-
market like an actor playing a part, pretending for the sake of verisimilitude
that this was the real him, but knowing in his heart of hearts that it was not.
He would have mourned her forever if he had not come to Afghanistan.

It seemed to him that he was often blind to the most important facts
about himself. He had not realized, back in 1968, that he wanted to fight
for his country; he had not realized that he did not want to marry Gill; in
Vietnam he had not realized that he was against the war. Each of these revelations had astonished him and overturned his whole life. Self-deceit was
not necessarily a bad thing, he believed: he could not have survived the war
without it, and what would he have done if he had never come to
Afghanistan other than tell himself he did not want Jane?

Do I have her now? he wondered. She had not said much, except *I love
you, dear, sleep well* just as he was falling asleep. He thought it the most de-
lightful thing he had ever heard.

"What are you smiling about?"

He opened his eyes and looked at her. "I thought you were asleep," he replied.

"I've been watching you. You looked so happy."

"Yes." He took a deep breath of the cool morning air and raised himself on his elbow to look across the Valley. The fields were almost colorless in the dawn light, and the sky was pearl gray. He was on the point of telling her what he was happy about when he heard a buzzing noise. He cocked his head to listen.

"What is it?" she said.

He put a finger to her lips. A moment later she heard it. In a few seconds the noise swelled until it was unmistakably the sound of helicopters. Ellis had a sense of impending disaster. "Oh, shit," he said feelingly.

The aircraft came into view over their heads, emerging from behind the mountain: three hunchbacked Hinds bristling with armament and one big troop-carrying Hip.

"Get your head in," Ellis snapped at Jane. The sleeping bag was brown and dusty, like the ground all around them: if they could stay under it they might be invisible from the air. The guerrillas employed the same principle in hiding from aircraft—they covered themselves with the mud-colored blankets, called *pattus*, they all carried.

Jane burrowed down into the sleeping bag. The bag had a flap at its open end to hold a pillow, although there was no pillow in it at the moment. If they got the flap above them it would cover their heads. Ellis held Jane tight and rolled over, and the pillowcase flopped over. Now they were practically invisible.

They lay on their stomachs, he half on top of her, and looked down at the village. The helicopters seemed to be descending.

Jane said: "They aren't going to land *here*, surely?"

Ellis said slowly: "I think they are. . . ."

Jane started to get up, saying: "I've got to go down—"

"No!" Ellis held her shoulders, using his weight to force her down. "Wait—just wait a few seconds and see what will happen—"

"But Chantal—"

"Wait!"

She gave up the struggle, but he continued to hold her tightly. On the roofs of the houses, sleepy people were sitting up, rubbing their eyes and staring dazedly at the huge machines beating the air like giant birds above them. Ellis located Jane's house. He could see Fara, standing up and wrapping a sheet around herself. There beside her was the tiny mattress on which Chantal lay hidden by bedding.

The helicopters circled cautiously. They're aiming to land here, Ellis thought, but they're wary after the ambush at Darg.

The villagers were galvanized. Some ran out of their houses, while others ran in. Children and livestock were rounded up and herded indoors. Several people tried to flee, but one of the Hinds flew low over the pathways out of the village and forced them back.

The scene convinced the Russian commander that there was no ambush here. The troop-carrying Hip and one of the three Hinds made their ungainly descent and landed in a field. Seconds later, soldiers emerged from the Hip, jumping out of its huge belly like insects.

"It's no good," Jane cried. "I'll have to go down now."

"Listen!" said Ellis. "She's in no danger—whatever the Russians want, they're not after babies. But they might be after you."

"I must be with her—"

"Stop panicking," he shouted. "If you're with her she *will* be in danger. If you stay here she's safe. Don't you see? Rushing to her is the worst thing you could possibly do."

"Ellis, I *can't*—"

"*You* must."

"Oh, God!" She closed her eyes. "Hold me tight."

He gripped her shoulders and squeezed.

The troops encircled the little village. Only one house was outside their net: the home of the mullah, which was four or five hundred yards from the other houses, on the footpath that led up the mountainside. As Ellis noticed this, a man came scurrying out of the house. He was close enough for Ellis to see his henna-dyed beard: it was Abdullah. Three children of different sizes and a woman carrying a baby followed him out of the house and ran behind him up the mountain path.

The Russians saw him immediately. Ellis and Jane pulled the sleeping bag farther over their heads as the airborne helicopter veered away from the village and came to hover over the path. There was a burst from the machine gun low in the nose of the helicopter, and dust exploded in a neatly stitched line at Abdullah's feet. He stopped short, looking almost comical as he nearly fell over; then he turned around and ran back, waving his hands and yelling at his family to return. When they approached the house another warning burst from the machine gun prevented them from entering, and after a moment the whole family headed downhill toward the village.

Occasional shots could be heard through the oppressive beat of the rotor blades, but the soldiers appeared to be firing into the air to subdue the villagers. They were entering houses and driving out the occupants. The Hind that had rounded up the mullah and his family now began to circle the village, very low, as if looking for more strays.

"What are they going to do?" said Jane in an unsteady voice.

"I'm not sure."

"Is this a . . . reprisal?"

"God forbid."

"What, then?" she persisted.

Ellis felt like saying *How the fuck should I know?* but instead he said: "They may be having another try at capturing Masud."

"But he never stays near the scene of a battle."

"They may hope he's getting careless, or lazy, or that he might be wounded. . . ." In truth Ellis did not know what was happening, but he feared a My Lai–style massacre. The villagers were being herded into the courtyard of the mosque by soldiers who seemed to be treating them roughly but not brutally.

Suddenly Jane cried: "Fara!"

"What is it?"

"What's she doing?"

Ellis located the roof of Jane's house. Fara was kneeling beside Chantal's tiny mattress, and Ellis could just see a little pink head peeping out. Chantal appeared still to be asleep. Fara would have given her a bottle at some time in the middle of the night, but although Chantal was not yet hungry the noise of the helicopters could have wakened her. Ellis hoped she would stay asleep.

He saw Fara place a cushion beside Chantal's head, then pull the sheet up over the baby's face.

"She's hiding her," said Jane. "The cushion props open the cover to let air in."

"She's a clever girl."

"I wish I was *there*."

Fara rumpled the sheet, then draped another sheet untidily over Chantal's body. She paused for a moment, studying the effect. From a distance the baby looked exactly like a hastily abandoned pile of bedding. Fara seemed satisfied with the illusion, for she went to the edge of the roof and descended the steps into the courtyard.

"She's leaving her," said Jane.

"Chantal is as safe as she could possibly be in the circumstances—"

"I know, I know!"

Fara was pushed into the mosque with the others. She was one of the last to go in. "All the babies are with their mothers," said Jane. "I think Fara should have taken Chantal. . . ."

"No," said Ellis. "Wait. You'll see." He still did not know what would happen, but if there was going to be a massacre Chantal was safest where she was.

When everyone seemed to be within the walls of the mosque, the soldiers began to search the village again, running in and out of the houses, firing into the air. *They* were not short of ammunition, Ellis thought. The helicopter that had stayed in the air flew low and scanned the outskirts of the village in ever-increasing circles, as if searching.

One of the soldiers went into the courtyard of Jane's house.

Ellis felt her go rigid. "It'll be all right," he said into her ear.

The soldier entered the building. Ellis and Jane stared fixedly at the door. A few seconds later he came out and quickly ran up the outside staircase.

"Oh, God, save her," whispered Jane.

He stood on the roof, glanced at the rumpled bedding, looked around at the other nearby roofs, and returned his attention to Jane's. Fara's mattress was nearest to him. Chantal was just beyond it. He poked Fara's mattress with his toe.

Suddenly he turned away and ran down the stairs.

Ellis breathed again and looked at Jane. She was ghastly white. "I told you it would be all right," he said. She began to shake.

Ellis looked at the mosque. He could see only a part of the courtyard inside. The villagers appeared to be sitting down in rows, but there was some movement to and fro. He tried to guess what was going on in there. Were they being interrogated about Masud and his whereabouts? There were only three people down there who might know, three guerrillas who were from Banda and who had not melted into the hills with Masud yesterday: Shahazai Gul, the one with the scar; Alishan Karim, the brother of Abdullah, the mullah; and Sher Kador, the goat boy. Shahazai and Alishan were both in their forties, and could easily play the part of cowed old men. Sher Kador was only fourteen. All three could say plausibly that they knew nothing of Masud. It was fortunate that Mohammed was not here: the Russians would not have believed in his innocence so readily. The guerrillas' weapons were skillfully hidden in places where the Russians would not look: in the roof of a privy, among the leaves of a mulberry tree, deep in a hole in the riverbank.

"Oh, look!" Jane gasped. "The man in front of the mosque!"

Ellis looked. "The Russian officer in the peaked hat?"

"Yes. I know who that is—I've seen him before. It's the man who was in the stone hut with Jean-Pierre—it's Anatoly."

"His contact," Ellis breathed. He looked hard, trying to make out the man's features: at this distance he seemed somewhat Oriental. What was he like? He had ventured alone into rebel territory to meet with Jean-Pierre, so he must be brave. Today he was certainly angry, for he had led the Russians into a trap at Darg. He would want to strike back fast, to recover the initiative—

Ellis's speculations were abruptly cut off as another figure emerged from the mosque, a bearded man in an open-neck white shirt and dark Western-style trousers. "Jesus Christ Almighty," Ellis said. "It's Jean-Pierre."

"Oh!" Jane cried out.

"Now what the hell is going on?" muttered Ellis.

"I thought I'd never see him again," said Jane. Ellis looked at her. Her face wore an odd expression. After a moment he realized it was a look of remorse.

He returned his attention to the scene in the village. Jean-Pierre was speaking to the Russian officer and gesticulating, pointing up the mountainside.

"He's standing oddly," said Jane. "I think he's hurt himself."

"Is he pointing toward us?" Ellis asked.

"He doesn't know about this place—nobody does. Can he see us?"

"No."

"We can see him," she said dubiously.

"But he's standing upright against a plain background. We're lying flat, peeping out from under a blanket, against a mottled hillside. He couldn't spot us unless he knew where to look."

"Then he must be pointing toward the caves."

"Yes."

"He must be telling the Russians to look there."

"Yes."

"But that's *awful*. How could he . . ." Her voice tailed off, and after a pause she said: "But of course that's what he's been doing ever since he got here—betraying people to the Russians."

Ellis noticed that Anatoly appeared to be speaking into a walkie-talkie.

A moment later one of the circling Hinds roared over Ellis and Jane's hooded heads to land, audible but out of sight, on the hilltop.

Jean-Pierre and Anatoly were walking away from the mosque. Jean-Pierre was limping. "He *is* hurt," said Ellis.

"I wonder what happened."

It looked to Ellis as if Jean-Pierre had been beaten up, but he did not say so. He was wondering what was going on in Jane's mind. There was her husband, walking with a KGB officer—a colonel, Ellis thought, from the uniform. Here she was, in a makeshift bed with another man. Did she feel guilty? Ashamed? Disloyal? Or unrepentant? Did she hate Jean-Pierre, or was she merely disappointed in him? She had been in love with him: was there any love left? He said: "How do you *feel* about him?"

She gave Ellis a long, hard look, and for a moment he thought she was going to get mad, but it was only that she was taking his question very seriously. Finally she said: "Sad." She turned her gaze back to the village.

Jean-Pierre and Anatoly were heading for Jane's house, where Chantal lay concealed on the roof.

Jane said: "I think they're looking for me."

Her expression was drawn and scared as she stared at the two men down below. Ellis did not think the Russians had come all this way with so many men and machines just for Jane, but he did not say so.

Jean-Pierre and Anatoly walked through the courtyard of the shopkeeper's house and entered the building.

"Don't cry, little girl," whispered Jane.

It was a miracle the baby was still asleep, Ellis thought. Perhaps she was not: perhaps she was awake and crying, but her cries were drowned by the noise of the helicopters. Perhaps the soldier had not heard her because there had been a chopper directly overhead at that moment. Perhaps the more sensitive ears of her father would hear sounds which had failed to catch the attention of an uninterested stranger. Perhaps—

The two men came out of the house.

They stood in the courtyard for a moment, talking intently. Jean-Pierre limped across to the wooden staircase which led to the roof. He mounted the first step with evident difficulty, then got down again. There was another short exchange of words, and the Russian mounted the stairs.

Ellis held his breath.

Anatoly reached the top of the stair and stepped onto the roof. Like the soldier before him, he glanced at the scattered bedding, looked around at other house and then returned his attention to this one. Like the soldier, he poked at Fara's mattress with the toe of his boot. Then he knelt down beside Chantal.

Gently, he drew back the sheet.

Jane gave an inarticulate cry as Chantal's pink face came into view.

If they're after Jane, Ellis thought, they will take Chantal, for they know she would give herself up in order to be reunited with her baby.

Anatoly stared at the tiny bundle for several seconds.

"Oh, God, I can't stand this. I can't stand it," Jane groaned.

Ellis held her tight and said: "Wait, wait and see."

He strained his eyes to make out the expression on the baby's face, but the distance was too great.

The Russian appeared to be thinking.

Suddenly he seemed to make up his mind.

He dropped the sheet, tucked it in around the baby, stood up and walked away.

Jane burst into tears.

From the roof Anatoly spoke to Jean-Pierre, shaking his head in negation. Then he descended into the courtyard.

"Now why did he do that?" Ellis mused, thinking aloud. The shake of the head meant that Anatoly was lying to Jean-Pierre, saying *There is nobody on the roof.* The implication was that Jean-Pierre would have wanted to take the baby, but Anatoly did not. That meant that Jean-Pierre wanted to find Jane, but the Russian was not interested in her.

So what *was* he interested in?

It was obvious. He was after Ellis.

"I believe I may have fucked up," Ellis said, mainly to himself. Jean-Pierre wanted Jane and Chantal, but Anatoly was looking for him. Anatoly wanted revenge for yesterday's humiliation; he wanted to prevent Ellis returning to the West with the treaty the rebel commanders had signed; and he wanted to put Ellis on trial to prove to the world that the CIA was behind the Afghan rebellion. I should have thought of all this yesterday, Ellis reflected bitterly, but I was flushed with success and thinking only about Jane. Besides, Anatoly could not *know* I was here—I might have been in Darg, or Astana, or hiding out in the hills with Masud—so it must have been a long shot. But it had almost worked. Anatoly had good instincts. He was a formidable opponent—and the battle was not yet over.

Jane was weeping. Ellis stroked her hair and made soothing noises while he watched Jean-Pierre and Anatoly walk back toward the helicopters, which were still standing in the fields with their rotors churning the air.

The Hind that had landed on the hilltop near the caves took off again and rose over Ellis's and Jane's heads. Ellis wondered whether the seven wounded guerrillas in the cave clinic had been interrogated or taken prisoner or both.

It ended very quickly. The soldiers came out of the mosque at the double and piled into the Hip as fast as they had emerged. Jean-Pierre and Anatoly boarded one of the Hinds. The ugly aircraft took off, one by one, lifting giddily until they were higher than the hill and then speeding southward in a straight line.

Ellis, knowing what was in Jane's mind, said: "Just wait a few more seconds, until all the choppers have gone—don't spoil everything now."

She nodded tearful acquiescence.

The villagers began to trickle out of the mosque, looking scared. The last helicopter took off and headed south. Jane scrambled out of the sleeping bag, pulled on her trousers, shrugged into her shirt and ran off down the hillside, slipping and stumbling and buttoning her shirt as she went. Ellis watched her go, feeling that somehow she had spurned him, knowing that the feeling was irrational, unable nevertheless to shake it. He would not follow her yet, he decided. He would leave her alone for her reunion with Chantal.

She went out of sight beyond the mullah's house. Ellis looked down at the village. It was beginning to return to normal. He could hear voices raised in excited cries. The children were running around playing helicopters or pointing imaginary guns and herding chickens into courtyards to be interrogated. Most of the adults were walking slowly back to their homes, looking cowed.

Ellis remembered the seven wounded guerrillas and the boy with one hand in the cave clinic. He decided he would check on them. He pulled on his clothes, rolled up his sleeping bag and set off up the mountain path.

He recalled Allen Winderman, in his gray suit and his striped tie, picking over a salad in a Washington restaurant and saying: "What are the chances that the Russians would catch our man?" *Slender*, Ellis had said. *If they can't catch Masud, why would they be able to catch an undercover agent sent to meet Masud?* Now he knew the answer to that question: Because of Jean-Pierre. "Goddam Jean-Pierre," said Ellis aloud.

He reached the clearing. There was no noise coming from the cave clinic. He hoped the Russians had not taken the child, Mousa, as well as the wounded guerrillas—Mohammed would be inconsolable.

He went into the cave. The sun was up now and he could see quite clearly. They were all there, lying still and quiet. "Are you all right?" Ellis asked in Dari.

There was no reply. None of them moved.

"Oh, God," Ellis whispered.

He knelt beside the nearest guerrilla and touched the bearded face. The man was lying in a pool of blood. He had been shot in the head at point-blank range.

Moving quickly, Ellis checked each of them.

They were all dead.

And so was the child.

CHAPTER FIFTEEN

Jane dashed through the village in a blind panic, pushing people aside, cannoning into walls, stumbling and falling and getting up again, sobbing and panting and moaning all at the same time. "She must be all right," she told herself, repeating it like a litany; but just the same her brain kept asking *Why didn't Chantal wake up?* and *What did Anatoly do?* and *Is my baby hurt?*

She stumbled into the courtyard of the shopkeeper's house and climbed the steps two at a time to the roof. She fell on her knees and pulled the sheet off the little mattress. Chantal's eyes were closed. Jane thought: Is she breathing? Is she breathing? Then the baby's eyes opened, she looked at her mother, and—for the first time ever—she smiled.

Jane snatched her up and hugged her fiercely, feeling as if her heart would burst. Chantal cried at the sudden squeeze, and Jane cried, too, awash with joy and relief because her little girl was still here, still alive and warm and squalling, and because she had just smiled her first smile.

After a while Jane calmed down, and Chantal, sensing the change, became quiet. Jane rocked her, patting her back rhythmically and kissing the top of her soft bald head. Eventually Jane remembered that there were other people in the world, and she wondered what had happened to the villagers in the mosque, and whether they were all right. She went down into her courtyard, and there she met Fara.

Jane looked at the girl for a moment—silent, anxious Fara, timid and so easily shocked: where had she found the courage and presence of mind and sheer nerve to conceal Chantal under a rumpled sheet while the Russians were landing their helicopters and firing their rifles a few yards away? "You saved her," Jane said.

Fara looked frightened, as if it had been an accusation.

Jane shifted Chantal to her left hip and put her right arm around Fara, hugging her. "You saved my baby!" she said. "Thank you! Thank you!"

Fara beamed with pleasure for a moment, then burst into tears.

Jane soothed her, patting her back as she had patted Chantal's. As soon as Fara was quiet Jane said: "What happened in the mosque? What did they do? Is anyone hurt?"

"Yes," said Fara dazedly.

Jane smiled: you couldn't ask Fara three questions one after another and expect a sensible answer. "What happened when you went into the mosque?"

"They asked where the American was."

"Whom did they ask?"

"Everyone. But nobody knew. The doctor asked me where you and the baby were, and I said I didn't know. Then they picked out three of the men: first my uncle Shahazai, then the mullah, then Alishan Karim, the mullah's brother. They asked them again, but it was no use, for the men did not know where the American had gone. So they beat them."

"Are they badly hurt?"

"Just beaten."

"I'll take a look at them." Alishan had a heart condition, Jane recalled anxiously. "Where are they now?"

"Still in the mosque."

"Come with me." Jane went into the house and Fara followed. In the front room Jane found her nursing bag on the old shopkeeper's counter. She added some nitroglycerin pills to her regular kit and went out again. As she headed for the mosque, still clutching Chantal tightly, she said to Fara: "Did they hurt you?"

"No. The doctor seemed very angry, but they didn't beat me."

Jane wondered whether Jean-Pierre had been angry because he guessed that she was spending the night with Ellis. It occurred to her that the whole village was guessing the same thing. She wondered how they would react. This might be the final proof that she was the Whore of Babylon.

Still, they would not shun her yet, not while there were injured people to be attended to. She reached the mosque and entered the courtyard. Abdullah's wife saw her, bustled over importantly, and led her to where he lay on the ground. At first glance he looked all right, and Jane was worried about Alishan's heart, so she left the mullah—ignoring his wife's indignant protests—and went to Alishan, who was lying nearby.

He was gray-faced and breathing with difficulty, and he had one hand on his chest: as Jane had feared, the beating had brought on an attack of angina. She gave him a tablet, saying: "Chew, don't swallow it."

She handed Chantal to Fara and examined Alishan quickly. He was badly bruised, but no bones were broken. "How did they beat you?" she asked him.

"With their rifles," he answered hoarsely.

She nodded. He was lucky: the only real damage they had done was to subject him to the stress that was so bad for his heart, and he was already recovering from that. She dabbed iodine on his cuts and told him to lie where he was for an hour.

She returned to Abdullah. However, when the mullah saw her approach he waved her away with an angry roar. She knew what had infuriated him: he thought he was entitled to priority treatment, and he was insulted that she had seen Alishan first. Jane was not going to make excuses. She had told him before that she treated people in order of urgency, not status. Now she turned away. There was no point in insisting on examining the old fool. If he was well enough to yell at her, he would live.

She went to Shahazai, the scarred old fighter. He had already been ex-amined by his sister Rabia, the midwife, who was bathing his cuts. Rabia's herbal ointments were not quite as antiseptic as they should be, but Jane thought they probably did more good than harm on balance, so she con-tented herself with making him wiggle his fingers and toes. He was all right.

We were lucky, Jane thought. The Russians came, but we escaped with minor injuries. Thank God. Perhaps now we can hope they will leave us alone for a while—maybe until the route to the Khyber Pass is open again. . . .

"Is the doctor a Russian?" Rabia asked abruptly.

"No." For the first time, Jane wondered just exactly what had been in Jean-Pierre's mind. If he had found me, she thought, what would he have said to me? "No, Rabia, he's not a Russian. But he seems to have joined their side."

"So he is a traitor."

"Yes, I suppose he is." Now Jane wondered what was in old Rabia's mind.

"Can a Christian divorce her husband for being a traitor?"

In Europe she can divorce him for a good deal less, thought Jane, so she said: "Yes."

"Is this why you have now married the American?"

Jane saw how Rabia was thinking. Spending the night on the mountainside with Ellis had, indeed, confirmed Abdullah's accusation that she was a Western whore. Rabia, who had long been Jane's leading supporter in the village, was planning to counter that accusation with an alternative interpretation, according to which Jane had been rapidly divorced from the traitor under strange Christian laws unknown to True Believers and was now married to Ellis under those same laws. So be it, Jane thought. "Yes," she said, "that is why I have married the American."

Rabia nodded, satisfied.

Jane almost felt as if there were an element of truth in the mullah's epithet. She had, after all, moved from one man's bed to another's with indecent rapidity. She felt a little ashamed, then caught herself: she had never let her behavior be ruled by other people's expectations. Let them think what they like, she said to herself.

She did not consider herself married to Ellis. Do I feel divorced from Jean-Pierre? she asked herself. The answer was no. However, she *did* feel that her obligations to him had ended. After what he's done, she thought, I don't owe him anything. It should have come as some kind of relief to her, but in fact she just felt sad.

Her musings were interrupted. There was a flurry of activity over at the mosque entrance, and Jane turned around to see Ellis walk in carrying something in his arms. As he came nearer she could see that his face was a mask of rage, and it flashed through her mind that she had seen him like that once before: when a careless taxi driver had made a sudden U-turn and knocked down a young man on a motorcycle, injuring him quite badly. Ellis and Jane had witnessed the whole thing and called the ambulance—in those days she had known nothing of medicine—and Ellis had said over and over again: "So unnecessary, it was so unnecessary."

She made out the shape of the bundle in his arms: it was a child, and she realized that his expression meant that the child was dead. Her first, shameful reaction was to think, Thank God it's not my baby; then, when she looked closely, she saw that it was the one child in the village who sometimes seemed like her own—one-handed Mousa, the boy whose life she had saved. She felt the dreadful sense of disappointment and loss that came when a patient died after she and Jean-Pierre had fought long and hard for

his life. But this was especially painful, for Mousa had been brave and determined in coping with his disability; and his father was so proud of him.
Why him? thought Jane as the tears came to her eyes. Why him?

The villagers clustered around Ellis, but he looked at Jane.

"They are all dead," he said, speaking Dari so that the others could understand. Some of the women began to weep.

"How?" Jane said.

"Shot by the Russians, each one."

"Oh, my God." Only last night she had said *None of them will die*—of
their wounds, she had meant, but nonetheless she had foreseen each of
them getting better, quickly or slowly, and returning to full health and
strength under her care. Now—all dead. "But why did they kill the child?"
she cried.

"I think he annoyed them."

Jane frowned, puzzled.

Ellis shifted his burden slightly so that Mousa's hand came into view.
The small fingers were rigidly grasping the handle of the knife his father
had given him. There was blood on the blade.

Suddenly a great wail was heard, and Halima pushed through the crowd.
She took the body of her son from Ellis and sank to the ground with the
dead child in her arms, screaming his name. The women gathered around
her. Jane turned away.

Beckoning Fara to follow her with Chantal, Jane left the mosque and
walked slowly home. Just a few minutes ago she had been thinking that
the village had had a lucky escape. Now seven men and a boy were dead.
Jane had no tears left, for she had cried too much: she just felt weak with
grief.

She went into the house and sat down to feed Chantal. "How patient
you have been, little one," she said as she put the baby to her breast.

A minute or two later Ellis came in. He leaned over her and kissed her.
He looked at her for a moment, then said: "You seem angry with me."

Jane realized that she was. "Men are so bloody," she said bitterly. "That
child obviously tried to attack armed Russian troops with his hunting
knife—who taught him to be foolhardy? Who told him it was his role in life
to kill Russians? When he threw himself at the man with the Kalashnikov,
who was his role model? Not his mother. It's his father; it's Mohammed's
fault that he died; Mohammed's fault and yours."

Ellis looked astonished. "Why mine?"

She knew she was being harsh, but she could not stop. "They beat Abdullah, Alishan and Shahazai in an attempt to make them tell where you were," she said. "They were looking for you. That was the object of the exercise."

"I know. Does that make it my fault that they shot the little boy?"

"It happened because you're here, where you don't belong."

"Perhaps. Anyway, I have the solution to *that* problem. I'm leaving. My presence brings violence and bloodshed, as you are so quick to point out. If I stay, not only am I liable to get caught—for we were very lucky last night—but my fragile little scheme to start these tribes working together against their common enemy will fall apart. It's worse than that, in fact. The Russians would put me on public trial for the maximum propaganda. 'See how the CIA attempts to exploit the internal problems of a Third World country.' That sort of thing."

"You really are a big cheese, aren't you?" It seemed odd that what happened here in the Valley, among this small group of people, should have such great global consequences. "But you can't go. The route to the Khyber Pass is blocked."

"There's another way: the Butter Trail."

"Oh, Ellis . . . it's very hard—and dangerous." She thought of him climbing those high passes in the bitter winds. He might lose his way and freeze to death in the snow, or be robbed and murdered by the bandits. "Please don't do that."

"If I had another choice I'd take it."

So she would lose him again, and she would be alone. The thought made her miserable. That was surprising. She had only spent one night with him. What had she expected? She was not sure. More, anyway, than this abrupt parting. "I didn't think I'd lose you again so soon," she said. She moved Chantal to the other breast.

He knelt in front of her and took her hand. "You haven't thought this situation through," he said. "Think about Jean-Pierre. Don't you know he wants you back?"

Jane considered that. Ellis was right, she realized. Jean-Pierre would now be feeling humiliated and emasculated: the only thing that would heal his wounds would be to have her back, in his bed and in his power. "But what would he do with me?" she said.

"He will want you and Chantal to live out the rest of your lives in some mining town in Siberia, while he spies in Europe and visits you every two or three years for a holiday between assignments."

"What could he do if I were to refuse?"

"He could make you. Or he could kill you."

Jane remembered Jean-Pierre punching her. She felt nauseous. "Will the Russians help him to find me?" she said.

"Yes."

"But why? Why should they care about me?"

"First because they owe him. Second because they figure you will keep him happy. Third because you know too much. You know Jean-Pierre intimately and you've seen Anatoly: you could provide good descriptions of both of them for the CIA's computer, if you were able to get back to Europe."

So there would be more bloodshed, Jane thought; the Russians would raid villages, interrogate people, and beat and torture them to find out where she was. "That Russian officer . . . Anatoly, his name is. He saw Chantal." Jane hugged her baby tighter for a moment as she remembered those dreadful seconds. "I thought he was going to pick her up. Didn't he realize that, if he had taken her, I would have given myself up just to be with her?"

Ellis nodded. "That puzzled me at the time. But I'm more important to them than you are; and I think he decided that, while he wants eventually to capture you, in the meantime he has another use for you."

"What use? What could they want me to do?"

"Slow me down."

"By making you stay here?"

"No, by coming with me."

As soon as he said it she realized he was right, and a sense of doom settled over her like a shroud. She had to go with him, she and her baby; there was no alternative. If we die, we die, she thought fatalistically. So be it. "I suppose I have a better chance of escaping from here with you than of escaping from Siberia alone," she said.

Ellis nodded. "That's about it."

"I'll start packing," said Jane. There was no time to lose. "We'd better leave first thing tomorrow morning."

Ellis shook his head. "I want to be out of here in an hour."

Jane panicked. She had been planning to leave, of course, but not so suddenly; and now she felt she did not have time to *think*. She began to rush around the little house, throwing clothes and food and medical supplies indiscriminately into an assortment of bags, terrified that she would forget something crucial but too rushed to pack sensibly.

Ellis understood her mood and stopped her. He held her shoulders, kissed her forehead and spoke calmly to her. "Tell me something," he said. "Do you happen to know what the highest mountain in Britain is?"

She wondered if he was crazy. "Ben Nevis," she said. "It's in Scotland."

"How high is it?"

"Over four thousand feet."

"Some of the passes we're going to climb are sixteen and seventeen thousand feet high—that's *four times* as high as the highest mountain in Britain. Although the distance is only a hundred and fifty miles, it's going to take us at least two weeks. So stop; think; and plan. If you take a little more than an hour to pack, too bad—it's better than going without the antibiotics."

She nodded, took a deep breath and started again.

She had two saddlebags that could double as backpacks. Into one she put clothes: Chantal's diapers, a change of underwear for all of them, Ellis's quilted down coat from New York, and the fur-lined raincoat, complete with hood, that she had brought from Paris. She used the other bag for medical supplies and food—iron rations for emergencies. There was no Kendal Mint Cake, of course, but Jane had found a local substitute, a cake made of dried mulberries and walnuts, almost indigestible but packed with concentrated energy. They also had a lot of rice and a lump of hard cheese. The only souvenir Jane took was her collection of Polaroid photographs of the villagers. They also took their sleeping bags, a saucepan and Ellis's military kit bag, which contained some explosives and blasting equipment—their only weapon. Ellis lashed all the baggage to Maggie, the unidirectional mare.

Their hurried leave-taking was tearful. Jane was embraced by Zahara, old Rabia the midwife, and even Halima, Mohammed's wife. A sour note was introduced by Abdullah, who passed by just before they left and spat on the ground, hurrying his family along; but a few seconds later his wife came back, looking frightened but determined, and pressed into Jane's hand a present for Chantal, a primitive rag doll with a miniature shawl and veil.

Jane hugged and kissed Fara, who was inconsolable. The girl was thirteen: soon she would have a husband to adore. In a year or two she would marry and move into the home of her husband's parents. She would have eight or ten children, perhaps half of whom would live past the age of five. Her daughters would marry and leave home. Those of her sons who survived the fighting would get married and bring their wives home. Eventually, when the family grew too large, the sons and the daughters-in-law and

the grandchildren would begin to move out to start new extended families
of their own. Then Fara would become a midwife, like her grandmother
Rabia. I hope, Jane thought, that she'll remember a few of the lessons I
taught her.

Ellis was embraced by Alishan and Shahazai, and then they left, to cries
of "God go with you!" The village children accompanied them to the bend
in the river. Jane paused there and looked back for a moment at the little
huddle of mud-colored houses that had been her home for a year. She knew
she would never come back; but she had a feeling that, if she survived, she
would be telling stories of Banda to her grandchildren.

They walked briskly along the riverbank. Jane found herself straining
her ears for the sound of helicopters. How soon would the Russians start
looking for them? Would they send a few helicopters to hunt more or less
at random, or would they take the time to organize a really thorough search?
Jane did not know which to hope for.

It took them less than an hour to reach Dasht-i-Rewat, "The Plain with
a Fort," a pleasant village where the cottages with their shaded courtyards
were dotted along the northern bank of the river. Here it was that the cart
track—the pitted, snaking, now-you-see-it-now-you-don't dirt path that
passed for a road in the Five Lions Valley—came to an end. Any wheeled
vehicles robust enough to survive the road had to stop here, so the village
did a little business horse trading. The fort mentioned in the name was up
a side valley, and was now a prison, run by the guerrillas, housing a few captured government troops, a Russian or two, and the occasional thief. Jane
had visited it once, to treat a miserable nomad from the western desert who
had been conscripted into the regular army, had contracted pneumonia in
the cold Kabul winter, and had deserted. He was being "reeducated" before
being allowed to join the guerrillas.

It was midday, but neither of them wanted to stop and eat. They hoped
to reach Saniz, ten miles away at the head of the Valley, by nightfall; and
although ten miles was no great distance on level ground, in this landscape
it could take many hours.

The last stretch of the road wound in and out between the houses on
the north bank. The south bank was a cliff two hundred feet high. Ellis led
the horse and Jane carried Chantal in the sling she had devised, which enabled her to feed Chantal without stopping. The village ended at a water
mill close to the mouth of the side valley called the Riwat, which led to the
prison. After they had passed that point, they were not able to walk so fast.
The ground began to slope up, gradually at first and then more steeply. They

climbed steadily under the hot sun. Jane covered her head with her *pattu*, the brown blanket all travelers carried. Chantal was shaded by the sling. Ellis wore his Chitrali cap, a gift from Mohammed.

When they reached the summit of the pass she noted, with some satisfaction, that she was not even breathing hard. She had never been this fit in her life—and she probably never would be so again. Ellis was not only panting but perspiring, she observed. He was in quite good shape, but he was not as hardened to hours of walking as she was. It made her feel rather smug, until she remembered he had suffered two bullet wounds just nine days ago.

Beyond the pass, the track ran along the mountainside, high above the Five Lions River. Here, the river was sluggish. Where it was deep and still the water appeared bright green, the color of the emeralds which were found all around Dasht-i-Riwat and taken to Pakistan to be sold. Jane had a fright when her hypersensitive ears picked up the sound of distant aircraft: there was nowhere to hide on the bare clifftop, and she was seized by a sudden desire to jump off the cliff into the river a hundred feet below. But it was only a flight of jets, too high to see anyone on the ground. Nevertheless, from then on Jane scanned the terrain constantly for trees, bushes and hollows in which they might hide. A devil inside her said *You don't have to do this, you could go back, you could give yourself up and be reunited with your husband*, but somehow it seemed an academic question, a technicality.

The path was still climbing, but more gently, so they made better speed. They were delayed, every mile or two, by the tributaries which came rushing in from the side valleys to join the main river. The track would dive down to a log bridge or a ford, and Ellis would have to drag the unwilling Maggie into the water, with Jane yelling and throwing stones at her from behind.

An irrigation channel ran the full length of the gorge, on the cliffside high above the river. Its purpose was to enlarge the cultivable area in the plain. Jane wondered how long ago it was that the Valley had had time and men and peace enough to carry out such a big engineering project: hundreds of years, perhaps.

The gorge narrowed and the river below was littered with granite boulders. There were caves in the limestone cliffs: Jane noted them as possible hiding places. The landscape became bleak and a cold wind blew down the Valley, making Jane shiver for a moment despite the sunshine. The rocky terrain and the sheer cliffs suited birds: there were scores of Asian magpies.

At last the gorge gave way to another plain. Far to the east, Jane could see a range of hills, and above the hills were visible the white mountains of Nuristan. Oh, my God, that's where we're going, Jane thought; and she was afraid.

In the plain stood a small cluster of poor houses. "I guess this is it," said Ellis. "Welcome to Saniz."

They walked onto the plain, looking for a mosque or one of the stone huts for travelers. As they drew level with the first of the houses, a figure stepped out of it, and Jane recognized the handsome face of Mohammed. He was as surprised as she. Her surprise gave way to horror when she realized she was going to have to tell him that his son had been killed.

Ellis gave her time to collect her thoughts by saying in Dari: "Why are you here?"

"Masud is here," Mohammed replied. Jane realized that this must be a guerrilla hideout. Mohammed went on: "Why are *you* here?"

"We're going to Pakistan."

"This way?" Mohammed's face became grave. "What happened?"

Jane knew she had to be the one to tell him, for she had known him longer. "We bring bad news, my friend Mohammed. The Russians came to Banda. They killed seven men—and a child. . . ." He guessed, then, what she was going to say, and the look of pain on his face made Jane want to cry. "Mousa was the child," she finished.

Mohammed composed himself rigidly. "How did my son die?"

"Ellis found him," said Jane.

Ellis, struggling to find the Dari words he needed, said: "He died . . . knife in hand, blood on knife."

Mohammed's eyes widened. "Tell me everything."

Jane took over, because she could speak the language better. "The Russians came at dawn," she began. "They were looking for Ellis and for me. We were up on the mountainside, so they didn't find us. They beat Alishan and Shahazai and Abdullah, but they didn't kill them. Then they found the cave. The seven wounded mujahideen were there, and Mousa was with them, to run to the village if they needed help in the night. When the Russians had gone, Ellis went to the cave. All the men had been killed, and so had Mousa—"

"How?" Mohammed interrupted. "How was he killed?"

Jane looked at Ellis. Ellis said: "Kalashnikov," using a word that needed no translation. He pointed to his heart to show where the bullet had struck.

Jane added: "He must have tried to defend the wounded men, for there was blood on the point of his knife."

Mohammed swelled with pride even as the tears came to his eyes. "He attacked them—grown men, armed with guns—he went for them with his knife! The knife his father gave him! The one-handed boy is now surely in the warrior's heaven."

To die in a holy war was the greatest possible honor for a Muslim, Jane recalled. Little Mousa would probably become a minor saint. She was glad that Mohammed had that comfort, but she could not help thinking cynically: This is how warlike men assuage their consciences—by talk of glory.

Ellis embraced Mohammed solemnly, saying nothing.

Jane suddenly remembered her photographs. She had several of Mousa. Afghans loved photos, and Mohammed would be overjoyed to have one of his son. She opened one of the bags on Maggie's back and rummaged through the medical supplies until she found the cardboard box of Polaroids. She located a picture of Mousa, took it out and repacked the bag. Then she handed the picture to Mohammed.

She had never seen an Afghan man so profoundly moved. He was unable to speak. For a moment it seemed that he would weep. He turned away, trying to control himself. When he turned back, his face was composed but wet with tears. "Come with me," he said.

They followed him through the little village to the edge of the river, where a group of fifteen or twenty guerrillas were squatting around a cooking fire. Mohammed strode into the group and without preamble began to tell the story of Mousa's death, with tears and gesticulations.

Jane turned away. She had seen too much grief.

She looked around her anxiously. Where will we run to if the Russians come? she wondered. There was nothing but the fields, the river and the few hovels. But Masud seemed to think it was safe. Perhaps the village was just too small to attract the attention of the army.

She did not have the energy to worry anymore. She sat on the ground with her back to a tree, grateful to rest her legs, and began to feed Chantal. Ellis tethered Maggie and unloaded the bags, and the horse began to graze on the rich greenery beside the river. It's been a long day, Jane thought, and a terrible day. And I didn't get much sleep last night. She smiled a secret smile as she remembered the night.

Ellis got out Jean-Pierre's maps and sat beside Jane to study them in the rapidly fading evening light. Jane looked over his shoulder. Their planned route continued up the Valley to a village called Comar, where they would turn southeast into a side valley which led to Nuristan. This valley was also called Comar, and so was the first high pass they would en-counter. "Fifteen thousand feet," said Ellis, pointing to the pass. "This is where it gets cold."

Jane shivered.

When Chantal had drunk her fill, Jane changed her diaper and washed the old one in the river. She returned to find Ellis deep in conversation with Masud. She squatted beside them.

"You have made the right decision," Masud was saying. "You must get out of Afghanistan, with our treaty in your pocket. If the Russians catch you, all is lost."

Ellis nodded agreement. Jane thought: I've never seen Ellis like this before—he treats Masud with deference.

Masud went on: "However, it is a journey of extraordinary difficulty. Much of the trail is above the ice line. Sometimes the path is hard to find in the snow, and if you get lost there, you die."

Jane wondered where all this was leading. It seemed to her ominous that Masud was carefully addressing Ellis, not her.

"I can help you," Masud went on. "But, like you, I want to make a deal."

"Go on," said Ellis.

"I will give you Mohammed as a guide, to take you through Nuristan and into Pakistan."

Jane's heart leaped. Mohammed as a guide! It would make a world of dif-ference to the journey.

"What is my part of the bargain?" Ellis asked.

"You go alone. The doctor's wife and the child stay here."

It was heartbreakingly clear to Jane that she must agree to this. It was foolhardy for the two of them to try to make it alone—they would probably both die. This way she could at least save Ellis's life. "You *must* say yes," she told him.

Ellis smiled at her and looked at Masud. "It's out of the question," he said.

Masud stood up, visibly offended, and walked back to the circle of guerrillas.

Jane said: "Oh, Ellis, was that wise?"

"No," he said. He held her hand. "But I'm not going to let you go that easily."

She squeezed his hand. "I . . . I've made you no promises."

"I know," he said. "When we get back to civilization, you're free to do whatever you like—live with Jean-Pierre, if that's what you want, and if you can find him. I'll settle for the next two weeks, if that's all I can get. Anyway, we may not live that long."

That was true. Why agonize over the future, she thought, when we probably don't have a future?

Masud came back, smiling again. "I'm not a good negotiator," he said. "I'll give you Mohammed anyway."

CHAPTER SIXTEEN

They took off half an hour before dawn. One by one, the helicopters lifted from the concrete apron and disappeared into the night sky beyond the range of the floodlights. In turn, the Hind Jean-Pierre and Anatoly were in struggled into the air like an ungainly bird and joined the convoy. Soon the lights of the air base were lost from view, and once again Jean-Pierre and Anatoly were flying over the mountaintops toward the Five Lions Valley.

Anatoly had worked a miracle. In less than twenty-four hours he had mounted what was probably the largest operation in the history of the Afghan war—and he was in command of it.

He had spent most of yesterday on the phone to Moscow. He had had to galvanize the slumbering bureaucracy of the Soviet Army by explaining, first to his superiors in the KGB and then to a series of military bigwigs, just how important it was to catch Ellis Thaler. Jean-Pierre had listened, not understanding the words but admiring the precise combination of authority, calm and urgency in Anatoly's tone of voice.

Formal permission was given late in the afternoon, and then Anatoly had faced the challenge of putting it into practice. To get the number of helicopters he wanted he had begged favors, called in old debts, and scattered threats and promises from Jalalabad to Moscow. When a general in Kabul had refused to release his machines without a written order, Anatoly had called the KGB in Moscow and persuaded an old friend to sneak a look at the general's private file, then called the general and threatened to cut off his supply of child pornography from Germany.

The Soviets had six hundred helicopters in Afghanistan: by three a.m. five hundred of them were on the tarmac at Bagram, under Anatoly's command.

Jean-Pierre and Anatoly had spent the last hour bent over maps, deciding where each helicopter should go and giving the appropriate orders to a stream of officers. The deployments were precise, thanks to Anatoly's compulsive attention to detail and Jean-Pierre's intimate knowledge of the terrain.

Although Ellis and Jane had not been in the village yesterday when Jean-Pierre and Anatoly went to find them, it was almost certain they had heard about the raid and had now gone into hiding. They would not be in Banda. They might be living in a mosque in another village—short-term visitors normally slept in the mosques—or, if they felt the villages were unsafe, they might move into one of the little one-room stone huts for travelers which dotted the countryside. They could be anywhere in the Valley, or they could be in one of the many little side valleys.

Anatoly had covered all these possibilities.

Helicopters would land at every village in the Valley and at every hamlet in every side valley. The pilots would overfly all the trails and footpaths. The troops—more than a thousand men—were instructed to search every building and look under large trees and inside caves. Anatoly was determined not to fail again. Today they would *find* Ellis.

And Jane.

The interior of the Hind was cramped and bare. There was nothing in the passenger cabin but a bench fixed to the fuselage opposite the door. Jean-Pierre shared it with Anatoly. They could see the flight deck. The pilot's seat was raised two or three feet off the floor, with a step beside it for access. All the money had been spent on the armament, speed and maneuverability of the aircraft and none on comfort.

As they flew north, Jean-Pierre brooded. Ellis had pretended to be his friend while working all the time for the Americans. Using that friendship, he had ruined Jean-Pierre's scheme for catching Masud, thereby destroying a year's painstaking work. And finally, Jean-Pierre thought, he seduced my wife.

His mind went in circles, always returning to that seduction. He stared out into the darkness, watching the lights of the other helicopters, and imagined the two lovers as they must have been the night before,

lying on a blanket under the stars in some field, playing with one another's bodies and whispering endearments. He wondered whether Ellis
was good in bed. He had asked Jane which of them was the better lover,
but she said neither was better—they were just different. Was that what
she said to Ellis? Or did she murmur *You're the best, baby, the very best?*
Jean-Pierre was beginning to hate her as well. How *could* she go back to
a man who was nine years older than she, a crass American and a CIA
spook?

Jean-Pierre looked at Anatoly. The Russian sat still and blank-faced,
like a stone statue of a Chinese mandarin. He had got very little sleep during the previous forty-eight hours, but he did not look tired, just dogged.
Jean-Pierre was seeing a new side to the man. In their meetings over the
past year Anatoly had been relaxed and affable, but now he was taut, un-
emotional and tireless, driving himself and his colleagues relentlessly. He
was calmly obsessed.

When dawn broke they could see the other helicopters. It was an awe-
some sight: they were like a vast cloud of giant bees swarming over the
mountains. The noise of their buzzing must have been deafening on the
ground.

As they approached the Valley, they began to divide into smaller groups.
Jean-Pierre and Anatoly were with the flight going to Comar, the northernmost village of the Valley. For the last stretch of the journey they followed the river. The rapidly brightening morning light revealed tidy ranks
of sheaves in the wheatfields: the bombing had not completely disrupted
farming here in the upper Valley.

The sun was in their eyes as they descended to Comar. The village was
a cluster of houses peeping over a heavy wall on the hillside. It reminded
Jean-Pierre of perched hill villages in the south of France, and he felt a pang
of homesickness. Wouldn't it be good to go home, and hear French spoken
properly, and eat fresh bread and tasty food, or get into a taxi and go to a
cinema!

He shifted his weight in the hard seat. Right now it would be good just
to get out of the helicopter. He had been in pain more or less constantly
since the beating. But worse than the pain was the memory of the humiliation, the way he had screamed and wept and begged for mercy: each time
he thought of that, he flinched physically and wished he could hide. He
wanted revenge for that. He felt he would never sleep peacefully until he
had evened the score. And there was only one way that would satisfy him.
He wanted to see Ellis beaten, in the same way, by the same brute soldiers,

until he sobbed and screamed and pleaded for mercy, but with one extra re-
finement: Jane would be watching.

•

By the middle of the afternoon, failure stared them in the face yet again.

They had searched the village of Comar, all the hamlets around it, all
the side valleys in the area, and each of the single farmhouses in the almost-
barren land to the north of the village. Anatoly was in constant touch with
the commanders of the other squads by radio. They had conducted equally
thorough searches throughout the entire Valley. They had found arms
caches in a few caves and houses; they had fought skirmishes with several
groups of men, presumably guerrillas, especially in the hills around Saniz,
but the skirmishes had been notable only for greater-than-normal Russian
casualties due to the guerrillas' new expertise with explosives; they had
looked at the naked faces of all veiled women and examined the skin color
of every tiny baby; and still they had not found Ellis or Jane or Chantal.

Jean-Pierre and Anatoly finished up at a horse station in the hills above
Comar. The place had no name: it was a handful of bare stone houses and
a dusty meadow where malnourished nags grazed the sparse grass. The only
male inhabitant seemed to be the horse dealer, a barefoot old man wearing
a long shirt with a voluminous hood to keep off flies. There were also a couple of young women and a huddle of frightened children. Clearly the young
men were guerrillas, and were away somewhere with Masud. The hamlet
did not take long to search. When they were done, Anatoly sat in the dust
with his back to a stone wall, looking thoughtful. Jean-Pierre sat down beside him.

Across the hills they could see the distant white peak of Mesmer, almost
twenty thousand feet high, which had attracted climbers from Europe in
the old days. Anatoly said: "See if you can get some tea."

Jean-Pierre looked around and saw the old man in the hood lurking
nearby. "Make tea," he shouted at him in Dari. The man scurried away. A
moment later Jean-Pierre heard him shouting at the women. "Tea is coming," he said to Anatoly in French.

Anatoly's men, seeing that they were to stay here awhile, killed the engines of their helicopters and sat around in the dust, waiting patiently.

Anatoly stared into the distance. Weariness showed on his flat face.
"We are in trouble," he said.

Jean-Pierre found it ominous that he said *we*.

Anatoly went on: "In our profession, it is wise to minimize the importance of a mission until one is certain of success, at which point one begins to exaggerate it. In this case I could not follow that pattern. In order to secure the use of five hundred helicopters and a thousand men, I had to persuade my superiors of the overwhelming importance of catching Ellis Thaler. I had to make very clear to them the dangers that face us if he escapes. I succeeded. And their anger at me for *not* catching him will now be all the greater. Your future, of course, is tied to mine."

Jean-Pierre had not previously thought of it that way. "What will they do?"

"My career will simply stop. My salary will stay the same but I will lose all privileges. No more Scotch whisky, no more Rive Gauche for my wife, no more family holidays on the Black Sea, no more denim jeans and Rolling Stones records for my children . . . but I could live without those things. What I couldn't stand would be the sheer boredom of the kind of job given to failures in my profession. They would send me to a small town in the Far East where there is really no security work to do. I know how our men spend their time and justify their existence in such places. You have to ingratiate yourself with mildly discontented people, get them to trust you and talk to you, encourage them to make remarks critical of the government and the Party, then arrest them for subversion. It's such a waste of time. . . ." He seemed to realize he was rambling, and tailed off.

"And me?" said Jean-Pierre. "What will happen to me?"

"You'll become a nobody," said Anatoly. "You won't work for us anymore. They might let you stay in Moscow, but most likely they would send you back."

"If Ellis gets away, I can never go back to France—they would kill me."

"You have committed no crime in France."

"Nor had my father, but they killed him."

"Maybe you could go to some neutral country—Nicaragua, say, or Egypt."

"Shit."

"But let us not give up hope," Anatoly said a little more brightly. "People cannot vanish into thin air. Our fugitives are *somewhere*."

"If we can't find them with a thousand men, I don't suppose we can find them with ten thousand," said Jean-Pierre gloomily.

"We shan't have a thousand, let alone ten thousand," said Anatoly. "From now on we have to use our brains, and minimal resources. All our credit is spent. Let's try a different approach. Think: somebody must have helped them hide. That means that somebody knows where they are."

Jean-Pierre considered. "If they had help it was probably from the guerrillas—the people least likely to tell."

"Others may *know* about it."

"Perhaps. But will they tell?"

"Our fugitives must have *some* enemies," Anatoly persisted.

Jean-Pierre shook his head. "Ellis hasn't been here long enough to make enemies, and Jane is a heroine—they treat her like Joan of Arc. Nobody dislikes her—oh!" Even as he was speaking, he realized it was not true.

"Well?"

"The mullah."

"Aaah."

"Somehow she irritated him beyond reason. It was partly that her cures were more effective than his, but not only that, for mine were, too, but he never disliked me particularly."

"He probably called her a Western whore."

"How did you guess?"

"They always do. Where does this mullah live?"

"Abdullah lives in Banda, in a house about half a kilometer outside the village."

"Will he talk?"

"He probably hates Jane enough to give her away to us," said Jean-Pierre reflectively. "But he couldn't be *seen* to do it. We can't just land in the village and pick him up—everyone would know what had happened and he would clam up. I'd have to meet him in secret somehow. . . ." Jean-Pierre wondered what kind of danger he might put himself in if he continued thinking along this line. Then he thought of the humiliation he had suffered: revenge was worth any risk. "If you drop me near the village I can make my way to the path between the village and his house and hide there until he comes along."

"What if he doesn't 'come along' all day?"

"Yes . . ."

"We'll just have to make sure he does." Anatoly frowned. "We'll round up all the villagers in the mosque, as we did before—then just let them go. Abdullah will almost certainly go back to his house."

"But will he be alone?"

"Hmmm. Suppose we let the women go first, and order them to return to their homes. Then, when the men are released they will all want to check on their wives. Does anyone else live near Abdullah?"

"No."

"Then he *should* hurry along that footpath all alone. You step out from behind a bush—"

"And he slits my throat from ear to ear."

"He carries a knife?"

"Did you ever meet an Afghan who didn't?"

Anatoly shrugged. "You can take my pistol."

Jean-Pierre was pleased, and a little surprised, to be trusted that much, even though he did not know how to use a gun. "I suppose it may serve as a threat," he said anxiously. "I'll need some native clothes, just in case I'm seen by someone other than Abdullah. What if I meet someone who knows me? I'll have to cover my face with a scarf or something. . . ."

"That's easy," said Anatoly. He shouted something in Russian, and three of the soldiers jumped to their feet. They disappeared into the houses and emerged a few seconds later with the old horse dealer. "You can take his clothes," said Anatoly.

"Good," said Jean-Pierre. "The hood will hide my face." He switched to Dari and shouted at the old man: "Take off your clothes."

The man began to protest: nakedness was terribly shameful to Afghans. Anatoly shouted an abrupt command in Russian, and the soldiers threw the man on the ground and pulled off his shirt. They all laughed uproariously to see his stick-thin legs poking out of his ragged shorts. They let him go and he scuttled away with his hands over his genitals, which made them laugh all the more.

Jean-Pierre was too nervous to find it funny. He took off his European-style shirt and trousers and donned the old man's hooded shirt.

"You smell of horse piss," said Anatoly.

"It's even worse from inside," Jean-Pierre replied.

They climbed into their helicopter. Anatoly took the pilot's headset and spoke into the radio microphone at length in Russian. Jean-Pierre was very uneasy about what he was about to do. Suppose three guerrillas were to come over the mountain and catch him threatening Abdullah with the gun? He was known by literally everyone in the Valley. The news that he had visited Banda with the Russians would have spread rapidly. Without doubt most people now knew that he had been a spy. He must be Public Enemy Number One. They would tear him apart.

Perhaps we're being too clever, he thought. Maybe we should just land and pull Abdullah in and beat the truth out of him.

No, we tried that yesterday and it didn't work. This is the only way.

Anatoly gave the headset back to the pilot, who took his seat and began to warm up the helicopter. While they were waiting, Anatoly took out his gun and showed it to Jean-Pierre. "This is a nine-millimeter Makarov," he said over the noise of the rotors. He flipped a catch in the heel of the grip and drew out the magazine. It contained eight rounds. He pushed the magazine back in. He pointed to another catch on the left-hand side of the pistol. "This is the safety catch. When the red dot is covered, the catch is in the 'safe' position." Holding the gun in his left hand, he used his right hand to pull back the slide above the grip. "This is how the pistol is cocked." He released it and it sprang back into position. "When you fire, give a long pull on the trigger to recock the gun." He handed the weapon to Jean-Pierre.

He really trusts me, Jean-Pierre thought, and for a moment a glow of pleasure took the chill off his fear.

The helicopters took off. They followed the Five Lions River southwest, going down the Valley. Jean-Pierre was thinking that he and Anatoly made a good team. Anatoly reminded him of his father: a clever, determined, brave man with an unshakable commitment to world communism. If we succeed here, Jean-Pierre thought, we will probably be able to work together again, on some other battlefield. The thought pleased him inordinately.

At Dasht-i-Rewat, where the lower Valley began, the helicopter turned southeast, following the tributary Rewat upstream into the hills, in order to approach Banda from behind the mountain.

Anatoly used the pilot's headset again, then came over to shout in Jean-Pierre's ear. "They are all in the mosque already. How long will it take the wife to reach the mullah's house?"

"Five or ten minutes," Jean-Pierre yelled back.

"Where do you want to be dropped off?"

Jean-Pierre considered. "All the villagers are in the mosque, right?"

"Yes."

"Did they check the caves?"

Anatoly went back to the radio and asked. He returned and said: "They checked the caves."

"Okay. Drop me there."

"How long will it take you to reach your hiding place?"

"Give me ten minutes; then release the women and children, then wait another ten minutes and release the men."

"Right."

The helicopter descended into the shadow of the mountain. The afternoon was waning, but there was still an hour or so before nightfall. They landed behind the ridge, a few yards from the caves. Anatoly said to Jean-Pierre: "Don't go yet. Let us check the caves again."

Through the open door, Jean-Pierre saw another Hind land. Six men got out and ran over the ridge.

"How will I signal you to come down and pick me up afterward?" Jean-Pierre asked.

"We'll wait for you here."

"What will you do if some of the villagers come up here before I return?"

"Shoot them."

That was something else Anatoly had in common with Jean-Pierre's father: ruthlessness.

The reconnaissance party came back over the ridge and one of the men waved an all-clear sign.

"Go," said Anatoly.

Jean-Pierre opened the door and jumped out of the helicopter, still holding Anatoly's pistol in his hand. He hurried away from its beating blades with his head bent. When he reached the ridge he looked back: both aircraft were still there.

He crossed the familiar clearing in front of his old cave clinic and looked down into the village. He could just see into the courtyard of the mosque. He was unable to identify any of the figures he saw there, but it was just possible that one of them might glance up at the wrong moment and see him—their eyesight might be better than his—so he pulled the hood forward to obscure his face.

His heart beat faster as he got farther away from the safety of the Russian helicopters. He hurried down the hill and past the mullah's house. The Valley seemed oddly quiet despite the ever-present noise of the river and the distant whisper of helicopter blades. It was the absence of children's voices, he realized.

He turned a corner and found that he was out of sight of the mullah's house. Beside the footpath was a clump of camel grass and juniper bushes. He went behind it and crouched down. He was well hidden, but he had a clear view of the path. He settled down to wait.

He considered what he would say to Abdullah. The mullah was a hysterical woman hater: maybe he could use that.

A sudden burst of high voices from far down in the village told him that Anatoly had given instructions for the women and children to be released from the mosque. The villagers would wonder what the whole exercise had been for, but they would attribute it to the notorious craziness of armies everywhere.

A few minutes later the mullah's wife came up the footpath, carrying her baby and followed by three older children. Jean-Pierre tensed: was he really well hidden here? Would the children run off the path and stumble into his bush? What a humiliation that would be—to be foiled by children. He remembered the gun in his hand. Could I shoot children? he wondered.

They went past and turned the corner toward their house.

Soon afterward the Russian helicopters began to take off from the wheatfield: that meant the men had been released. Right on schedule, Abdullah came puffing up the hill, a tubby figure in a turban and a pin-striped English jacket. There must be a huge trade in used clothes between Europe and the East, Jean-Pierre had decided, for so many of these people wore clothes which had undoubtedly been made in Paris or London and had been discarded, perhaps because they became unfashionable, long before they were worn out. This is it, thought Jean-Pierre, as the comical figure drew level; this clown in a stockbroker's jacket could hold the key to my future. He got to his feet and stepped out from the bushes.

The mullah started and gave a cry of shock. He looked at Jean-Pierre and recognized him. "You!" he said. His hand went to his belt. Jean-Pierre showed him the gun. Abdullah looked frightened.

"Don't be afraid," Jean-Pierre said in Dari. The unsteadiness of his voice betrayed his jumpiness, and he made an effort to bring it under control. "No one knows I am here. Your wife and children passed without seeing me. They are safe."

Abdullah looked suspicious. "What do you want?"

"My wife is an adulteress," said Jean-Pierre, and although he was deliberately playing on the mullah's prejudices, his anger was not entirely faked. "She has taken my child and left me. She has gone whoring after the American."

"I know," said Abdullah, and Jean-Pierre could see him beginning to swell with righteous indignation.

"I have been searching for her, in order to bring her back and punish her."

Abdullah nodded enthusiastically, and malice showed in his eyes: he liked the idea of punishing adulteresses.

"But the wicked couple have gone into hiding." Jean-Pierre spoke slowly and carefully: at this point every nuance counted. "You are a man of God. Tell me where they are. No one will ever know how I found out, except you and me and God."

"They have gone away," Abdullah spat, and saliva wetted his red-dyed beard.

"Where?" Jean-Pierre held his breath.

"They have left the Valley."

"But where did they go?"

"To Pakistan."

To Pakistan! What was the old fool talking about? "The routes are closed!" Jean-Pierre yelled in exasperation.

"Not the Butter Trail."

"Mon Dieu," Jean-Pierre whispered in his native tongue. "The Butter Trail." He was awestruck by their courage, and at the same time bitterly disappointed, for it would be impossible to find them now. "Did they take the baby?"

"Yes."

"Then I'll never see my daughter again."

"They will all die in Nuristan," Abdullah said with satisfaction. "A Western woman with a baby will never survive those high passes, and the American will die trying to save her. Thus God punishes those who escape man's justice."

Jean-Pierre realized he should get back to the helicopter as quickly as possible. "Go back to your house now," he told Abdullah.

"The treaty will die with them, for Ellis has the paper," Abdullah added. "This is a good thing. Although we need the American weapons, it is dangerous to make pacts with infidels."

"Go!" said Jean-Pierre. "If you don't want your family to see me, make them stay inside for a few minutes."

Abdullah looked momentarily indignant at being given orders, but he seemed to realize he was at the wrong end of the gun for protests, and he hurried away.

Jean-Pierre wondered whether they would all die in Nuristan, as Abdullah had gloatingly predicted. That was not what he wanted. It would not give him revenge or satisfaction. He wanted his daughter back. He wanted Jane alive and in his power. He wanted Ellis to suffer pain and humiliation.

He gave Abdullah time to get inside his house, then drew the hood over his face and set off disconsolately up the hill. He kept his face averted as he passed the house in case one of the children should look out.

Anatoly was waiting for him in the clearing in front of the caves. He held out his hand for the pistol and said: "Well?"

Jean-Pierre gave him back his gun. "They've escaped us," he said. "They've left the Valley."

"They can't have *escaped* us," said Anatoly angrily. "Where have they gone?"

"To Nuristan." Jean-Pierre pointed in the direction of the helicopters. "Shouldn't we leave?"

"We can't talk in the helicopter."

"But if the villagers come—"

"To hell with the villagers! Stop acting defeated! What are they doing in Nuristan?"

"They're heading for Pakistan by a route known as the Butter Trail."

"If we know their route we can find them."

"I don't think so. There is one route, but it has variations."

"We'll overfly them all."

"You can't follow these paths from the air. You can hardly follow them from the *ground* without a native guide."

"We can use maps—"

"What maps?" said Jean-Pierre. "I've seen your maps, and they're no bet-ter than my American ones, which are the best available—and they do not show these trails and passes. Don't you know there are regions of the world that have never been properly charted? You're in one of them now!"

"I know—I'm in Intelligence, remember?" Anatoly lowered his voice. "You're too easily discouraged, my friend. Think. If Ellis can find a native guide to show him the route, then I can do the same."

Was it possible? Jean-Pierre wondered. "But there is more than one way to go."

"Suppose there are ten variations. We need ten native guides to lead ten search parties."

Jean-Pierre's enthusiasm rose rapidly as he realized that he might yet get Jane and Chantal back and see Ellis captured. "It might not be that bad," he said enthusiastically. "We can simply inquire along the way. Once we are out of this godforsaken Valley, people may be less tight-lipped. The Nuris-tanis aren't as involved in the war as these people."

"Good," said Anatoly abruptly. "It is getting dark. We've got a lot to do tonight. We start early in the morning. Let's go!"

CHAPTER SEVENTEEN

J ane woke up frightened. She did not know where she was or who she was with or whether the Russians had caught her. For a second she stared up at the exposed underside of a wattle roof, thinking, Is this a prison? Then she sat up abruptly, her heart hammering, and saw Ellis in his sleeping bag, slumbering with his mouth open, and she remembered, We're out of the Valley. We escaped. The Russians don't know where we are and they can't find us.

She lay down again and waited for her heartbeat to return to normal.

They were not following the route Ellis had originally planned. Instead of going north to Comar and then east along the Comar Valley into Nuristan, they had turned back south from Saniz and gone east along the Aryu Valley. Mohammed had suggested this because it got them out of the Five Lions Valley much more quickly, and Ellis had agreed.

They had left before dawn and walked uphill all day, Ellis and Jane taking turns carrying Chantal, Mohammed leading Maggie. At midday they had stopped in the mud-hut village of Aryu and bought bread from a suspicious old man with a snapping dog. Aryu village had been the limit of civilization: after that, there had been nothing for miles but the boulder-strewn river and the great bare ivory-colored mountains on either side, until they had reached this place at the weary end of the afternoon.

Jane sat up again. Chantal lay beside her, breathing evenly and radiating heat like a hot-water bottle. Ellis was in his own sleeping bag: they could have zipped the two bags together to make one, but Jane had been afraid that Ellis might roll onto Chantal in the night, so they had slept separately and contented themselves with lying close together and reaching out to touch one another now and again. Mohammed was in the adjoining room.

Jane got up carefully, trying not to disturb Chantal. As she put on her shirt and stepped into her trousers, she felt twinges of pain in her back and her legs: she was hardened to walking, but not all day, climbing without respite, on such rough terrain.

She put on her boots without tying the laces and went outside. She blinked against the bright cold light of the mountains. She was in an upland meadow, a vast green field with a stream winding through it. To one side of the meadow the mountain rose steeply, and sheltered here at the foot of the slope was a handful of stone houses and some cattle pens. The houses were empty and the cattle had gone: this was a summer pasture, and the cowherds had left for their winter quarters. It was still summer in the Five Lions Valley, but at this altitude autumn came in September.

Jane walked over to the stream. It was sufficiently far from the stone houses for her to slip out of her clothes without fear of offending Mohammed. She ran into the stream and quickly immersed herself in the water. It was searingly cold. She got out again immediately, her teeth chattering uncontrollably. "To hell with *this*," she said aloud. She would stay dirty until she got back to civilization, she resolved.

She put her clothes back on—there was only one towel, and that was reserved for Chantal—and ran back to the house, picking up a few sticks on the way. She laid the sticks over the remains of last night's fire and blew on the embers until the wood caught. She held her frozen hands to the flames until they felt normal again.

She put a pan of water on the fire for washing Chantal. While she was waiting for it to warm up, the others woke, one by one: first Mohammed, who went outside to wash; then Ellis, who complained that he ached all over; and finally Chantal, who demanded to be fed and was satisfied.

Jane felt oddly euphoric. She should have been anxious, she thought, about taking her two-month-old baby into one of the world's wild places; but somehow that anxiety was swamped by her happiness. Why am I happy? she asked herself, and the answer came out of the back of her mind: because I'm with Ellis.

Chantal also seemed happy, as if she were imbibing contentment with her mother's milk. They had been unable to buy food last night, because the cowherds had left and there was nobody else from whom to buy it. However, they had some rice and salt, which they had boiled—not without difficulty because it took forever to boil water at this altitude. Now for breakfast there was cold leftover rice. That brought Jane's spirits down a little.

She ate while Chantal fed, then washed and changed her. The spare diaper, washed in the stream yesterday, had dried by the fire overnight. Jane put it on Chantal and took the dirty diaper to the stream. She would attach it to the baggage and hope that the wind and the heat of the horse's body would dry it. What would Mummy say about her granddaughter wearing one diaper all day? She would be horrified. Never mind. . . .

Ellis and Mohammed loaded the horse and got her pointed in the right direction. Today would be harder than yesterday. They had to cross the mountain range that for centuries had kept Nuristan more or less isolated from the rest of the world. They would climb the Aryu Pass, fourteen thousand feet high. Much of the way they would have to struggle through snow and ice. They hoped to reach the Nuristan village of Linar: it was only ten miles away as the crow flies, but they would be doing well to get there by late afternoon.

The sunlight was bright when they set off, but the air was cold. Jane was wearing heavy socks and mittens and an oiled sweater under her fur-lined coat. She carried Chantal in the sling between her sweater and her coat, with the top buttons of the coat undone to let air in.

They left the meadow, following the Aryu River upstream, and immediately the landscape became harsh and hostile again. The cold cliffs were bare of vegetation. Once Jane saw, far in the distance, a huddle of nomads' tents on a bleak slope: she did not know whether to be glad there were other humans around or frightened of them. The only other living thing she saw was a bearded vulture floating in the bitter wind.

There was no visible pathway. Jane was immeasurably glad that Mohammed was with them. At first he followed the river, but when it narrowed and petered out, he carried on with undiminished confidence. Jane asked him how he knew the way, and he told her that the route was marked by piles of stones at intervals. She had not noticed them until he pointed them out.

Soon there was a thin layer of snow on the ground, and Jane's feet got cold despite her heavy socks and her boots.

Amazingly, Chantal slept much of the time. Every couple of hours they stopped for a few minutes' rest, and Jane took the opportunity to feed her, wincing as she exposed her tender breasts to the freezing air. She told Ellis that she thought Chantal was being remarkably good, and he said: "Unbelievably. Unbelievably."

At midday they stopped within sight of the Aryu Pass for a welcome half-hour rest. Jane was already tired, and her back hurt. She was also starvingly hungry—she wolfed the mulberry-and-walnut cake they had for lunch.

The approach to the pass was terribly daunting. Looking at that steep climb, Jane lost heart. I think I'll sit here a little longer, she thought; but it was cold, and she began to shiver, and Ellis noticed and stood up. "Let's go, before we're frozen to the spot," he said brightly, and Jane thought: I wish you wouldn't be so bloody cheerful.

She stood up with an effort of will.

Ellis said: "Let me carry Chantal."

Jane handed the baby over gratefully. Mohammed led the way, heaving on Maggie's reins. Wearily, Jane forced herself to follow. Ellis brought up the rear.

The slope was steep and the ground slippery with snow. After a few minutes Jane was more tired than she had been before they stopped to rest. As she stumbled along, panting and aching, she recalled saying to Ellis *I suppose I have a better chance of escaping from here with you than of escaping from Siberia alone.* Perhaps I can't manage either, she thought now. I didn't know it was going to be like this. Then she caught herself. Of course you knew, she said to herself; and you know it's going to get worse before it gets better. Snap out of it, you pathetic creature. At that moment she slipped on an icy rock and fell sideways. Ellis, just behind her, caught her arm and held her upright. She realized that he was watching her carefully, and she felt a surge of love for him. Ellis cherished her in a way Jean-Pierre never had. Jean-Pierre would have walked on ahead, assuming that if she needed help she would ask for it; and if she had complained about that attitude, he would have asked whether she wanted to be treated as an equal or not.

They were almost at the summit. Jane leaned forward to take the incline, thinking: Just a little more, just a little more. She felt dizzy. In front of her, Maggie skidded on the loose rocks and then scampered up the last few feet, forcing Mohammed to run alongside. Jane plodded after her, counting the steps. At last she reached the level ground. She stopped. Her head was spinning. Ellis's arm went around her, and she closed her eyes and leaned on him.

"From now on it's downhill all day," he said.

She opened her eyes. She could never have imagined such a cruel land-scape: nothing but snow, wind, mountains and loneliness forever and ever. "What a godforsaken place this is," she said.

They looked at the view for a minute; then Ellis said: "We must keep going."

They walked on. The way down was steeper. Mohammed, who had been heaving on Maggie's reins all the way up, now hung on to her tail to act as a brake and prevent the horse slithering out of control down the slippery slope. The cairns were hard to distinguish among the litter of loose snow-covered rocks, but Mohammed showed no hesitation about which way to go. Jane thought she should offer to take Chantal, to give Ellis a reprieve, but she knew she could not carry her.

As they descended, the snow thinned and then cleared, and the track was visible. Jane kept hearing an odd whistling sound, and eventually found the energy to ask Mohammed what it was. In reply he used a Dari word she did not know. He did not know the French equivalent. In the end he pointed, and Jane saw a small squirrellike animal scuttling out of the way: a marmot. Afterward she saw several more, and wondered what they found to eat up here.

Soon they were walking alongside another brook, heading downstream now, and the endless gray-and-white rock was relieved by a little coarse grass and a few low bushes on the banks of the stream; but still the wind hurtled up the gorge and penetrated Jane's clothing like needles of ice.

Just as the climb had become relentlessly worse, so the descent got eas-ier and easier: the path growing smoother, the air warmer, and the land-scape friendlier. Jane was still exhausted but she no longer felt oppressed and downcast. After a couple of miles they reached the first village in Nuristan. The men there wore thick sleeveless sweaters with a striking black-and-white pattern, and spoke a language of their own which Mo-hammed could barely understand. However, he managed to buy bread with some of Ellis's Afghan money.

Jane was tempted to plead with Ellis that they stop here for the night, for she felt desperately weary; but there were still several hours of daylight left, and they had agreed they would try to reach Linar today, so she bit her tongue and forced her aching legs to walk on.

To her immense relief the remaining four or five miles were easier, and they arrived well before nightfall. Jane sank to the ground underneath an enormous mulberry tree and simply sat still for a while. Mohammed lit a fire and began to make tea.

Mohammed somehow let it be known that Jane was a Western nurse, and later, while she was feeding and changing Chantal, a little group of patients gathered, waiting at a respectful distance. Jane summoned her energy and saw them. There were the usual infected wounds, intestinal parasites and bronchial complaints, but there were fewer malnourished children here than in the Five Lions Valley, presumably because the war had not much affected this remote wilderness.

As a result of the impromptu clinic, Mohammed got a chicken, which he boiled in their saucepan. Jane would have preferred to go to sleep, but she made herself wait for the food and ate ravenously when it came. It was stringy and tasteless, but she was hungrier than she had ever been in her life.

Ellis and Jane were given a room in one of the village houses. There was a mattress for them and a crude wooden crib for Chantal. They joined their sleeping bags together and made love with weary tenderness. Jane enjoyed the warmth and the lying down almost as much as the sex. Afterward, Ellis fell asleep instantly. Jane lay awake for a few minutes. Her muscles seemed to hurt more now that she was relaxing. She thought about lying on a real bed in an ordinary bedroom, with streetlights shining through the curtains and car doors slamming outside, and a bathroom with a flush toilet and a hot-water tap, and a shop on the corner where you could buy cotton balls and Pampers and Johnson's No More Tears baby shampoo. We escaped from the Russians, she thought, as she drifted off to sleep; maybe we really will make it home. Maybe we really will.

Jane woke when Ellis did, sensing his sudden tension. He lay rigid beside her for a moment, not breathing, listening to the sound of two dogs barking. Then he slipped out of bed fast.

The room was pitch-dark. She heard a match scrape; then a candle flickered in the corner. She looked at Chantal: the baby was sleeping peacefully. "What is it?" she said to Ellis.

"I don't know," he whispered. He pulled on his jeans, stepped into his boots, and put on his coat; then he went out.

Jane threw on some clothes and followed him. In the next room, moonlight coming through the open door revealed four children in a row in a bed, all staring wide-eyed over the edge of their shared blanket. Their parents were asleep in another room. Ellis was in the doorway, looking out.

Jane stood beside him. Up on the hill she could see, by the moonlight, a lone figure, running toward them.

"The dogs heard him," Ellis whispered.

"But who is he?" said Jane.

Suddenly there was another figure beside them. Jane gave a start, then recognized Mohammed. The blade of a knife glinted in his hand.

The figure came closer. His gait seemed familiar to Jane. Suddenly Mohammed gave a grunt and lowered the knife. "Ali Ghanim," he said.

Jane now recognized the distinctive stride of Ali, who ran that way because his back was slightly twisted. "But why?" she whispered.

Mohammed stepped forward and waved. Ali saw him, waved back and ran to the hut where the three of them stood. He and Mohammed embraced.

Jane waited impatiently for Ali to catch his breath. At last he said: "The Russians are on your trail."

Jane's heart sank. She had thought they had escaped. What had gone wrong?

Ali breathed hard for a few seconds longer, then went on: "Masud has sent me to warn you. The day you left, they searched the whole Five Lions Valley for you, with hundreds of helicopters and thousands of men. Today, having failed to find you, they sent search parties to follow each valley leading to Nuristan."

"What's he saying?" Ellis interrupted.

Jane held up a hand to stop Ali while she translated for Ellis, who could not follow Ali's rapid, breathless speech.

Ellis said: "How did they know we had gone to Nuristan? We might have decided to hide out anywhere in the damn country."

Jane asked Ali. He did not know.

"Is there a search party in this valley?" Jane asked Ali.

"Yes. I overtook them just before the Aryu Pass. They may have reached the last village by nightfall."

"Oh, no," said Jane despairingly. She translated for Ellis. "How can they move so much faster than us?" she said. Ellis shrugged, and she answered the question herself: "Because they're not slowed down by a woman with a baby. Oh, shit."

Ellis said: "If they start early in the morning they'll catch us tomorrow."

"What can we do?"

"Leave now."

Jane felt the weariness in her bones, and she was filled with an irrational resentment against Ellis. "Can't we hide somewhere?" she said irritably.

"Where?" said Ellis. "There's only one road here. The Russians have enough men to search all the houses—there aren't many. Besides, the local people aren't necessarily on our side. They might easily tell the Russians where we're hiding. No, our only hope is to stay ahead of the searchers."

Jane looked at her watch. It was two a.m. She felt ready to give up.

"I'll load the horse," Ellis said. "You feed Chantal." He switched to Dari and said to Mohammed: "Will you make some tea? And give Ali something to eat."

Jane went back into the house, finished dressing, then fed Chantal. While she was doing that, Ellis brought her sweet green tea in a pottery bowl. She drank it gratefully.

As Chantal sucked, Jane wondered how much Jean-Pierre had to do with this relentless pursuit of her and Ellis. She knew he had helped with the raid on Banda, for she had seen him. When they searched the Five Lions Valley, his local knowledge would be invaluable. He must know they were hunting down his wife and baby like dogs chasing rats. How could he bring himself to help them? His love must have been changed to hatred by his seething resentment and jealousy.

Chantal had had enough. How pleasant it must be, Jane thought, to know nothing of passion or jealousy or betrayal, to have no feelings but warm or cold and full or empty. "Enjoy it while you may, little girl," she said.

Hurriedly, she buttoned her shirt and pulled her heavy oiled sweater down over her head. She put the sling around her neck, made Chantal comfortable inside it, then shrugged into her coat and went outside.

Ellis and Mohammed were studying the map by the light of a lantern. Ellis showed Jane their route. "We follow the Linar down to where it empties into the Nuristan River. Then we turn uphill again, following the Nuristan north. Then we take one of these side valleys—Mohammed won't be sure which one until he gets there—and head for the Kantiwar Pass. I'd like to get out of the Nuristan Valley today—that will make it more difficult for the Russians to follow us, for they won't be sure which side valley we've taken."

"How far is it?" said Jane.

"It's only fifteen miles—but whether that's easy or tough depends on the terrain, of course."

Jane nodded. "Let's get going," she said. She was proud of herself for sounding more cheerful than she felt.

They set off in the moonlight. Mohammed set a fast pace, and whipped the horse mercilessly with a leather strap when she hung back. Jane had a slight headache and an empty, nauseous feeling in her stomach. However, she was not sleepy, but rather nervously tense and bone-weary.

She found the track scary by night. Sometimes they walked in the sparse grass beside the river, which was all right; but then the trail would hairpin up the mountainside to continue on the cliff edge hundreds of feet above, where the ground was covered with snow, and Jane was terrified of slipping and falling to her death with her baby in her arms.

Sometimes there was a choice: the path forked, one way going up and the other down. Since none of them knew which route to take, they let Mohammed guess. The first time, he stayed low and turned out to be right: the track led them across a little beach, where they had to wade through a foot of water, but it saved them a long diversion. However, the second time they had to choose they again took the riverbank, but this time they regretted it: after a mile or so the path led straight into a sheer rock face, and the only way around it would have been to swim. Wearily they retraced their steps to the fork and then climbed the cliff path.

At the next opportunity they descended to the riverbank again. This time the path led them to a ledge which ran along the face of the cliff about a hundred feet above the river. The horse became nervous, probably because the path was so narrow. Jane was frightened, too. The starlight was not enough to illuminate the river below, so the gorge seemed like a bottomless black pit beside her. Maggie kept stopping, and Mohammed would have to pull on the reins to make her go again.

When the path turned blindly around an abutment in the cliff, Maggie refused to go around the corner and became skittish. Jane backed away, wary of the horse's shuffling rear feet. Chantal began to cry, either because she sensed the moment of tension or because she had not gone back to sleep after her two a.m. feed. Ellis gave Chantal to Jane and went forward to help Mohammed with the horse.

Ellis offered to take the reins, but Mohammed refused ungraciously: the tension was getting to him. Ellis contented himself with pushing the beast from behind and yelling *hup* and *git* at it. Jane was just thinking that it was almost funny when Maggie reared, Mohammed dropped the reins and stumbled, and the mare backed into Ellis and knocked him off his feet and kept coming.

Fortunately Ellis fell to the left, against the cliff wall. When the horse backed into Jane she was on the wrong side of it, with her feet at the edge of the path as it pushed past her. She grabbed hold of a bag that was lashed to its harness, holding on like grim death in case it should nudge her sideways over the precipice. "You stupid beast!" she screamed. Chantal, squashed between Jane and the horse, screamed, too. Jane was carried along for several feet, afraid to loose her hold. Then, taking her life in her hands, she let go of the bag, reached out with her right hand and grabbed the bridle, got a firm footing, pushed past the horse's forequarter to stand beside her head, tugged hard on the bridle and said, "Stop!" in a loud voice.

Somewhat to Jane's surprise, Maggie stopped.

Jane turned around. Ellis and Mohammed were getting to their feet. "Are you all right?" she asked them in French.

"Just about," said Ellis.

"I lost the lantern," said Mohammed.

Ellis said in English: "I just hope the fucking Russians have the same problems."

Jane realized that they had not seen how the horse had almost pushed her over the edge. She decided not to tell them. She found the leading rein and gave it to Ellis. "Let's keep going," she said. "We can lick our wounds later." She walked past Ellis and said to Mohammed: "Lead the way."

Mohammed cheered up after a few minutes without Maggie. Jane wondered whether they really needed a horse, but she decided they did: there was too much baggage for them to carry, and all of it was essential—indeed they probably should have brought more food.

They hurried through a silent, sleeping hamlet, just a handful of houses and a waterfall. In one of the cottages a dog barked hysterically until someone silenced it with a curse. Then they were in the wilderness again.

The sky was turning from black to gray, and the stars had gone: it was getting light. Jane wondered what the Russians were doing. Perhaps the officers would now be rousing the men, shouting to wake them and kicking those who were slow to climb out of their sleeping bags. A cook would be making coffee while the commanding officer studied his map. Or perhaps they had got up early, an hour ago, while it was still dark, and had set out within minutes, marching in single file alongside the river Linar; perhaps they had already passed through the village of Linar; perhaps they had taken all the right forks and were even now just a mile or so behind their quarry.

Jane walked a little faster.

The ledge meandered along the cliff and then dropped down to the riverbank. There were no signs of agriculture, but the mountain slopes on either side were thickly wooded, and as the light brightened, Jane identified the trees as holly oak. She pointed them out to Ellis, saying: "Why can't we hide in the woods?"

"As a last resort, we could," he said. "But the Russians would soon realize we had stopped, because they would question villagers and be told we had not passed through; so they would turn back and start searching intensively."

Jane nodded resignedly. She was just looking for excuses to stop.

Just before sunrise they rounded a bend and stopped short: a landslide had filled the gorge with earth and loose rock, blocking it completely.

Jane felt like bursting into tears. They had walked two or three miles along the bank and that narrow ledge: to turn back meant an extra five miles, including the section that had frightened Maggie so.

The three of them stood for a moment looking at the blockage. "Could we climb it?" said Jane.

"The horse can't," said Ellis.

Jane was angry at him for stating the obvious. "One of us could go back with the horse," she said impatiently. "The other two could rest while waiting for the horse to catch up."

"I don't think it's wise to get separated."

Jane resented his my-decision-is-final tone of voice. "Don't assume we'll all do what *you* happen to think is wise," she snapped.

He looked startled. "All right. But I also think that mound of earth and stones might shift if someone tried to climb it. In fact I might as well say that I'm not going to try it, regardless of what you two might decide."

"So you won't even discuss it. I see." Furious, Jane turned around and started back along the track, leaving the two men to follow her. Why was it, she wondered, that men slipped into that bossy, know-it-all mode whenever there was a physical or mechanical problem?

Ellis was not without his faults, she reflected. He could be woolly-minded: for all his talk about being an antiterrorist expert, still he worked for the CIA, which was probably the largest group of terrorists in the world. There was undeniably a side of him that liked danger, violence and deceit. Don't pick a macho romantic, she thought, if you want a man to respect you.

One thing that could be said for Jean-Pierre was that he never patronized women. He might neglect you, deceive you or ignore you, but he would never condescend to you. Perhaps it was because he was younger.

She passed the place where Maggie had reared. She did not wait for the men: they could cope with the damn horse themselves this time.

Chantal was complaining, but Jane made her wait. She strode on until she reached a point where there seemed to be a pathway up to the clifftop. There she sat down and unilaterally declared a rest. Ellis and Mohammed caught up with her a minute or two later. Mohammed got some mulberry-

and-walnut cake out of the baggage and handed it around. Ellis did not
speak to Jane.

After the break they climbed the hillside. When they reached the top
they emerged into sunshine, and Jane began to feel a little less angry. After
a while Ellis put his arm around her and said: "I apologize for assuming
command."

"Thank you," Jane said stiffly.

"Do you think that maybe you might have overreacted a little bit?"

"No doubt I did. Sorry."

"You bet. Let me take Chantal."

Jane handed the baby over. As the weight was lifted, she realized that
her back was aching. Chantal had never *seemed* heavy, but the burden told
over a long distance. It was like carrying a full shopping bag for ten miles.

The air became milder as the sun climbed the morning sky. Jane opened
her coat and Ellis took his off. Mohammed retained his Russian uniform
greatcoat, with characteristic Afghan indifference to all but the most severe
changes in the weather.

Toward noon they emerged from the narrow gorge of the Linar into the
broad Nuristan Valley. Here the way was once again quite clearly marked,
the path being almost as good as the cart track which ran up the Five Lions
Valley. They turned north, going upstream and uphill.

Jane felt terribly tired and discouraged. After getting up at two a.m. she
had walked for ten hours—but they had only covered four or five miles.
Ellis wanted to do another ten miles today. It was Jane's third consecutive
day on the march, and she knew she could not continue until nightfall.
Even Ellis was wearing the bad-tempered expression which, Jane knew, was
a sign he was weary. Only Mohammed seemed tireless.

In the Linar Valley they had seen no one outside the villages, but here
there were a few travelers, most of them wearing white robes and white turbans. The Nuristanis looked with curiosity at the two pale, exhausted Westerners, but greeted Mohammed with wary respect, no doubt because of the
Kalashnikov slung over his shoulder.

As they trudged uphill beside the Nuristan River, they were overtaken
by a black-bearded, bright-eyed young man carrying ten fresh fish speared
on a pole. He spoke to Mohammed in a mixture of languages—Jane recognized some Dari and the occasional Pashto word—and they understood one
another well enough for Mohammed to buy three of the fish.

Ellis counted out the money, and said to Jane: "Five hundred afghanis
per fish—how much is that?"

"Five hundred afghanis is fifty French francs—five pounds."

"Ten bucks," said Ellis. "Expensive fish."

Jane wished he would stop jabbering: it was as much as she could do to put one foot in front of the other, and he was talking about the price of fish.

The young man, whose name was Halam, said he had caught the fish in Lake Mundol, farther down the valley, although he had probably bought them, for he did not look like a fisherman. He slowed his pace to walk with them, talking volubly, apparently not much concerned about whether they understood him or not.

Like the Five Lions Valley, the Nuristan was a rocky canyon which broadened, every few miles, into small cultivated plains with terraced fields. The most noticeable difference was the forest of holly oak which covered the mountainsides like the wool on a sheep's back, and which Jane thought of as her hiding place should all else fail.

They were making better time now. There were no infuriating diversions up the mountain, for which Jane was deeply thankful. In one place the road was blocked by a landfall, but this time Ellis and Jane were able to climb over it, and Mohammed and the horse forded the river and came back across a few yards upstream. A little later, when an abutment jutted into the stream, the road continued around the cliff face on a shaky wooden trestle which the horse refused to tread on, and once again Mohammed solved the problem by crossing in the water.

By this time Jane was near to collapse. When Mohammed came back across the river, she said: "I need to stop and rest."

Mohammed said: "We are almost at Gadwal."

"How far is it?"

Mohammed conferred with Halam in Dari and French, then said: "One half hour."

It seemed like forever to Jane. Of *course* I can walk for another half hour, she told herself, and tried to think of something other than the ache in her back and the need to lie down.

But then, when they turned the next bend, they saw the village.

It was a startling sight as well as a welcome one: the wooden houses scrambled up the steep mountainside like children clambering on one another's backs, giving the impression that if one house at the bottom were to collapse, the whole village would come tumbling down the hill and fall into the water.

As soon as they drew alongside the first house, Jane simply stopped and sat down on the riverbank. Every muscle in her body ached, and she hardly had the strength to take Chantal from Ellis, who sat beside her with a readiness that suggested he, too, was wiped out. A curious face looked out from the house, and Halam immediately began to talk to the woman, presumably telling her what he knew about Jane and Ellis. Mohammed tethered Maggie where she could graze the coarse grass on the riverbank, then squatted beside Ellis.

"We must buy bread and tea," Mohammed said.

Jane thought they all needed something more substantial. "What about the fish?" she said.

Ellis said: "It would take too long to clean and cook it. We'll have that for tonight. I don't want to spend more than half an hour here."

"All right," said Jane, although she was not sure she would be able to carry on after only half an hour. Perhaps some food would revive her, she thought.

Halam called to them. Jane looked up and saw him beckoning. The woman did the same: she was inviting them into her house. Ellis and Mohammed got to their feet. Jane put Chantal down on the ground, stood up, then bent down to pick up the baby. Suddenly her vision blurred at the edges and she seemed to lose her balance. For a moment she fought it, seeing only Chantal's tiny face surrounded by a haze; then her knees became weak and she sank to the ground, and everything went dark.

When she opened her eyes she saw a circle of anxious faces above her: Ellis, Mohammed, Halam and the woman. Ellis said: "How do you feel?"

"Foolish," she said. "What happened?"

"You fainted."

She sat upright. "I'll be all right."

"No, you won't," said Ellis. "You can't go any farther today."

Jane's head was clearing. She knew he was right. Her body would not take any more, and no effort of will would change that. She started to speak French so that Mohammed could understand. "But the Russians are sure to reach here today."

"We'll have to hide," said Ellis.

Mohammed said: "Look at these people. Do you think they could keep a secret?"

Jane looked at Halam and the woman. They were watching, riveted by the conversation even though they could not understand a word of it. The arrival of the foreigners was probably the most exciting event of the year. In a few minutes the whole of the village would be here. She studied Halam. Telling him not to gossip would be like telling a dog not to bark. The location of their hideout would be known all over Nuristan by nightfall. Was it possible to get away from these people, and sneak off up a side valley unobserved? Perhaps. But they could not live indefinitely without help from the local people—at some point their food would run out, and that would be about the time the Russians realized they had stopped and began searching the woods and canyons. Ellis had been right, earlier in the day, when he said their only hope was to stay ahead of their pursuers.

Mohammed drew heavily on his cigarette, looking thoughtful. He spoke to Ellis. "You and I will have to go on, and leave Jane behind."

"No," said Ellis.

Mohammed said: "The piece of paper you have, which bears the signatures of Masud, Kamil and Azizi, is more important than the life of any one of us. It represents the future of Afghanistan—the freedom for which my son died."

Ellis would have to go on alone, Jane realized. At least he could be saved. She was ashamed of herself for the terrible despair she felt at the thought of losing him. She should be trying to figure out how to help him, not wondering how she could keep him with her. Suddenly she had an idea. "I could divert the Russians," she said. "I could let myself be captured. Then, after a show of reluctance, I could give Jean-Pierre all sorts of false information about which way you were headed and how you were traveling. . . . If I sent them off completely the wrong way, you might gain several days' lead—enough to get you safely out of the country!" She became enthusiastic about the idea even while in her heart she was thinking, Don't leave me, please don't leave me.

Mohammed looked at Ellis. "It's the only way, Ellis," he said.

"Forget it," said Ellis. "It isn't going to happen."

"But, Ellis—"

"It isn't going to happen," Ellis repeated. "Forget it."

Mohammed shut up.

Jane said: "But what are we going to do?"

"The Russians won't catch up with us today," Ellis said. "We still have a lead—we got up so early this morning. We'll stay here tonight and start early again tomorrow. Remember, it isn't over until it's over. Anything could happen. Somebody back in Moscow could decide that Anatoly is out of his mind and order the search called off."

"Bullshit," said Jane in English, but secretly she was glad, against all reason, that he had refused to go on alone.

"I have an alternative suggestion," said Mohammed. "I will go back and divert the Russians."

Jane's heart leaped. Was it possible?

Ellis said: "How?"

"I will offer to be their guide and interpreter, and I will lead them south down the Nuristan Valley, away from you, to Lake Mundol."

Jane thought of a snag, and her heart sank again. "But they must have a guide already," she said.

"He may be a good man from the Five Lions Valley who has been forced to help the Russians against his will. In that case I will speak with him and arrange things."

"What if he won't help?"

Mohammed considered. "Then he is not a good man who has been forced to help them, but a traitor who willingly collaborates with the enemy for personal gain, in which case I will kill him."

"I don't want anyone killed for my sake," she said quickly.

"It's not for you," Ellis said harshly. "It's for me—I refused to go on alone."

Jane shut up.

Ellis was thinking about practicalities. He said to Mohammed: "You're not dressed like a Nuristani."

"I will change clothes with Halam."

"You don't speak the local language well."

"There are many languages in Nuristan. I will pretend to come from a district where they use a different tongue. The Russians speak none of these languages anyway, so they will never know."

"What will you do with your gun?"

Mohammed thought for a moment. "Will you give me your bag?"

"It's too small."

"My Kalashnikov is the type that has a folding butt."

"Sure," said Ellis. "You can have the bag."

Jane wondered whether it would attract suspicion, but decided not: Afghans' bags were as strange and varied as their clothes. All the same, Mohammed would surely arouse suspicion sooner or later. She said: "What will happen when they finally realize they are on the wrong trail?"

"Before that happens I will run away in the night, leaving them in the middle of nowhere."

"It's terribly dangerous," said Jane.

Mohammed tried to look heroically unconcerned. Like most of the guerrillas, he was genuinely brave but also ludicrously vain.

Ellis said: "If you time this wrong, and they suspect you before you've decided to leave them, they will torture you to find out which way we went."

"They will never take me alive," said Mohammed.

Jane believed him.

Ellis said: "But we will have no guide."

"I shall find you another one." Mohammed turned to Halam and began a rapid multilingual conversation. Jane gathered that Mohammed was proposing to hire Halam as a guide. She did not like Halam much—he was too good a salesman to be entirely trustworthy—but he was obviously a traveling man, so he was a natural choice. Most of the local people had probably never ventured outside their own valley.

"He says he knows the way," said Mohammed, reverting to French. Jane suffered a twinge of anxiety about the words *He says*. Mohammed went on: "He will take you to Kantiwar, and there he will find another guide to take you across the next pass, and in this way you will proceed to Pakistan. He will charge five thousand afghanis."

Ellis said: "It sounds like a fair price, but how many more guides will we have to hire at that rate before we reach Chitral?"

"Maybe five or six," said Mohammed.

Ellis shook his head. "We don't have thirty thousand afghanis. And we have to buy food."

"You will have to get food by holding clinics," Mohammed said. "And the way becomes easier once you are in Pakistan. Perhaps you will not need guides at the end."

Ellis looked dubious. "What do you think?" he asked Jane.

"There's an alternative," she said. "You could go on without me."

"No," he said. "That's not an alternative. We'll go on together."

CHAPTER EIGHTEEN

All the first day, the search parties found no trace of Ellis and Jane. Jean-Pierre and Anatoly sat on hard wooden chairs in a spartan, windowless office at the Bagram air base, monitoring the reports as they came in over the radio network. The search parties had left before dawn—again. There were six of them at the start: one for each of the five main side valleys leading east from the Five Lions, and one to follow the Five Lions River north to its source and beyond. Each of the parties included at least one Dari-speaking officer from the Afghan regular army. They landed their helicopters at six different villages in the Valley, and half an hour later all six parties had reported that they had found local guides.

"That was quick," said Jean-Pierre after the sixth reported in. "How did they do it?"

"Simple," said Anatoly. "They ask someone to be a guide. He says no. They shoot him. They ask someone else. It doesn't take long to find a volunteer."

One of the search parties tried to follow its assigned trail from the air, but the experiment was a failure. The trails were rather difficult to follow from the ground, impossible from the air. Furthermore, none of the guides had ever been in an aircraft before and the new experience was totally disorienting. So all the search parties went on foot, some with commandeered horses to carry their baggage.

Jean-Pierre did not expect any further news in the morning, for the fugitives had a full day's start. However, the soldiers would certainly move faster than Jane, especially as she was carrying Chantal—

Jean-Pierre felt a stab of guilt every time he thought of Chantal. His rage at what his wife was doing did not extend to his daughter, yet the baby was suffering, he felt sure: trekking all day, crossing passes above the snow line, blasted by icy winds. . . .

His mind turned, as it often did nowadays, to the question of what would happen if Jane died and Chantal survived. He pictured Ellis captured, alone, Jane's body found a mile or two back, dead of the cold, with the baby still miraculously alive in her arms. I would arrive back in Paris a tragic, romantic figure, thought Jean-Pierre, a widower with a baby daughter, a veteran of the war in Afghanistan. . . . How they would lionize me! I'm perfectly capable of bringing up a baby. What an intense relationship we would have as she grew older. I'd have to hire a nanny, of course, but I'd make sure she did not take the place of a mother in the child's affections. No, I would be both father and mother to her.

The more he thought about it, the more outraged he felt that Jane was risking Chantal's life. Surely she had forfeited all her parental rights by taking her baby on such an escapade. He thought he could probably get legal custody of the child in a European court on this basis. . . .

As the afternoon wore on, Anatoly grew bored and Jean-Pierre became tense. They were both tetchy. Anatoly held long conversations in Russian with other officers who came into the windowless little room, and their interminable jabbering got on Jean-Pierre's nerves. At first Anatoly had translated all the radio reports of the search parties, but now he would just say, "Nothing." Jean-Pierre had been plotting the routes of the parties on a set of maps, marking their locations with red pins, but by the end of the afternoon they were following trails or dried-up riverbeds which were not on the maps, and if their radio reports gave clues to their whereabouts, Anatoly was not passing them on.

The parties made camp at nightfall without reporting any signs of the fugitives. The searchers had been instructed to question the inhabitants of the villages through which they passed. The villagers were saying they had seen no foreigners. This was not surprising, for the searchers were still on the Five Lions side of the great passes leading to Nuristan. The people they were questioning were generally loyal to Masud: to them, helping the Russians was treason. Tomorrow, when the search parties passed into Nuristan, the people would be more cooperative.

Nevertheless, Jean-Pierre felt dispirited as he and Anatoly left the office at nightfall and walked across the concrete to the canteen. They ate a vile dinner of canned sausages and reconstituted mashed potatoes; then Anatoly went off moodily to drink vodka with some brother officers, leaving Jean-Pierre in the care of a sergeant who spoke only Russian. They played chess once, but—to Jean-Pierre's chagrin—the sergeant was far too good. Jean-Pierre retired early and lay awake on a hard army mattress, visualizing Jane and Ellis in bed together.

Next morning he was awakened by Anatoly, his Oriental face wreathed in smiles, all irritation gone, and Jean-Pierre felt like a bad child who has been forgiven, although as far as he knew he had done nothing wrong. They ate their breakfast porridge together in the canteen. Anatoly had already talked to each of the search parties, all of which had struck camp and set off again at dawn. "Today we will catch your wife, my friend," said Anatoly cheerfully, and Jean-Pierre felt a surge of happy optimism.

As soon as they reached the office, Anatoly radioed to the searchers again. He asked them to describe what they could see all around them, and Jean-Pierre used their descriptions of streams, lakes, depressions and moraines to guess their locations. They seemed to be moving terribly slowly in terms of kilometers per hour, but of course they were going uphill on difficult terrain, and the same factors would slow Ellis and Jane.

Each search party had a guide, and when they came to a place where the trail forked and both ways led to Nuristan, they would conscript an additional guide from the nearest village and split into two groups. By noon Jean-Pierre's map was spotted with little red pinheads like a case of measles.

In the middle of the afternoon there was an unexpected distraction. A bespectacled general on a five-day fact-finding tour of Afghanistan landed at Bagram and decided to find out how Anatoly was spending the Russian taxpayer's money. This Jean-Pierre learned in a few words from Anatoly seconds before the general burst into the little office, followed by anxious officers like ducklings hurrying after the mother duck.

Jean-Pierre was fascinated to see how masterfully Anatoly handled the visitor. He sprang to his feet, looking energetic but unruffled; shook the general's hand and gave him a chair; barked a series of orders through the open door; spoke rapidly but deferentially to the general for a minute or so; excused himself and spoke into the radio; translated for Jean-Pierre's benefit the reply that came crackling through the atmosphere from Nuristan; and introduced the general to Jean-Pierre in French.

The general began to ask questions, and Anatoly pointed to the pinheads on Jean-Pierre's map as he replied. Then, in the middle of it all, one of the search parties called in unbidden, an excited voice jabbering in Russian, and Anatoly shushed the general in midsentence to listen.

Jean-Pierre sat on the edge of his hard seat and longed for a translation. The voice stopped. Anatoly asked a question and got a reply.

"What did he see?" blurted Jean-Pierre, unable to keep silent any longer.

Anatoly ignored him for a moment and spoke to the general. At last he turned to Jean-Pierre. "They have found two Americans at a village called Atati in the Nuristan valley."

"Wonderful!" said Jean-Pierre. "It's them!"

"I suppose so," said Anatoly.

Jean-Pierre could not understand his lack of enthusiasm. "Of course it is! Your troops don't know the difference between American and English."

"Probably not. But they say there is no baby."

"No baby!" Jean-Pierre frowned. How could that be? Had Jane left Chantal behind in the Five Lions Valley, to be brought up by Rabia or Zahara or Fara? It seemed impossible. Had she hidden the baby with a family in this village—Atati—just a few seconds before being caught by the search party? That, too, seemed unlikely: Jane's instinct would be to keep the baby close to her in times of danger.

Was Chantal dead?

It was probably a mistake, he decided: some error of communication, atmospheric interference on the radio link, or even a purblind officer in the search party who simply had not seen the tiny baby.

"Let's not speculate," he said to Anatoly. "Let's go and see."

"I want you to go with the pickup squad," said Anatoly.

"Of course," said Jean-Pierre; then he was struck by Anatoly's phrasing. "Do you mean to say you're not coming?"

"Correct."

"Why not?"

"I'm needed here." Anatoly shot a glance at the general.

"All right." There were power games within the military bureaucracy, no doubt: Anatoly was afraid to leave the base while the general was still prowling around in case some rival should get a chance to slander him behind his back.

Anatoly picked up the desk phone and gave a series of orders in Russian. While he was still speaking, an orderly came into the room and beckoned Jean-Pierre. Anatoly put his hand over the mouthpiece and said: "They'll give you a warm coat—it's already winter in Nuristan. À bientôt."

Jean-Pierre went out with the orderly. They walked across the concrete apron. Two helicopters were waiting, rotors spinning: a bug-eyed Hind with rocket pods slung under its stubby wings, and a Hip, rather bigger, with a row of portholes along its fuselage. Jean-Pierre wondered what the Hip was for, then realized it was to bring back the search party. Just before they reached the machines, a soldier ran up to them with a uniform greatcoat and gave it to Jean-Pierre. He slung it over his arm and boarded the Hind.

They took off immediately. Jean-Pierre was in a fever of anticipation. He sat on the bench in the passenger cabin with half a dozen troops. They headed northeast.

When they were clear of the air base, the pilot beckoned Jean-Pierre. Jean-Pierre went forward and stood on the step so that the pilot could speak to him. "I will be your translator," the man said in hesitant French.

"Thank you. You know where we're headed?"

"Yes, sir. We have the coordinates, and I can speak by radio with the leader of the search party."

"Fine." Jean-Pierre was surprised to be treated with such deference. It seemed he had acquired honorary rank by association with a KGB colonel.

He wondered, as he returned to his seat, how Jane would look when he walked in. Would she be relieved? Defiant? Or just exhausted? Ellis would be angry and humiliated, of course. How should I act? wondered Jean-Pierre. I want to make them squirm, but I must remain dignified. What should I say?

He tried to visualize the scene. Ellis and Jane would be in the courtyard of some mosque, or sitting on the earth floor of a stone hut, possibly tied up, guarded by soldiers with Kalashnikovs. They would probably be cold, hungry and miserable. Jean-Pierre would stride in, wearing his Russian greatcoat, looking confident and commanding, followed by deferential junior officers. He would give them a long, penetrating look and say—

What would he say? *We meet again* sounded terribly melodramatic. *Did you really think you could escape from us?* was too rhetorical. *You never stood a chance* was better, but a little anticlimactic.

The temperature dropped fast as they headed into the mountains. Jean-Pierre put on his coat and stood by the open door, looking down. Below him was a valley something like the Five Lions, with a river at its center flowing in the shadows of the mountains. There was snow on the peaks and ridges to either side, but none in the valley itself.

Jean-Pierre went forward to the flight deck and spoke into the pilot's ear. "Where are we?"

"This is called the Sakardara Valley," the man replied. "As we go north its name changes to the Nuristan Valley. It takes us all the way to Atati."

"How much longer?"

"Twenty minutes."

It sounded like forever. Controlling his impatience with an effort, Jean-Pierre went back to sit on the bench among the troops. They sat still and quiet, watching him. They seemed afraid of him. Perhaps they thought he was in the KGB.

I *am* in the KGB, he thought suddenly.

He wondered what the troops were thinking about. Girlfriends and wives back home, perhaps? Their home would be his home, from now on. He would have an apartment in Moscow. He wondered whether he could possibly have a happy married life with Jane now. He wanted to install her and Chantal in his apartment while he, like these soldiers, would fight the good fight in foreign countries and look forward to going home on leave, to sleep with his wife again and see how his daughter had grown. I betrayed Jane and she betrayed me, he thought; perhaps we can forgive one another, if only for the sake of Chantal.

What had happened to Chantal?

He was about to find out. The helicopter lost height. They were almost there. Jean-Pierre stood up to look out of the door again. They were coming down to a meadow where a tributary joined the main river. It was a pretty spot with just a few houses sprawling up the hillside, each overlapping the one beneath in the Nuristani manner: Jean-Pierre remembered seeing photographs of such villages in coffee-table books about the Himalayas.

The helicopter touched down.

Jean-Pierre jumped to the ground. On the other side of the meadow, a group of Russian soldiers—the search party, undoubtedly—emerged from the lowest of a mound of wooden houses. Jean-Pierre waited impatiently for the pilot, his interpreter. Finally the man got out of the helicopter. "Let's go!" said Jean-Pierre, and started off across the field.

He restrained himself from breaking into a run. Ellis and Jane were probably in the house from which the search party was emerging, he thought, and he headed that way at a fast walk. He began to feel angry: long-suppressed rage was churning up inside him. To hell with being dignified, he thought; I'm going to tell this loathsome couple just what I think of them.

As he neared the search party, the officer at the head of the group began speaking. Ignoring him, Jean-Pierre turned to his pilot and said: "Ask him where they are."

The pilot asked, and the officer pointed to the wooden house. Without further ado Jean-Pierre went past the soldiers to the house.

His anger was at the boiling point as he stormed into the crude building. Several more of the search party stood in a group in one corner. They looked at Jean-Pierre, then made way for him.

In the corner were two people tied to a bench.

Jean-Pierre stared at them, shocked. His mouth fell open and the blood drained from his face. There was a thin, anemic-looking boy of eighteen or nineteen with long, dirty hair and a droopy mustache; and a large-bosomed blond girl with flowers in her hair. The boy looked at Jean-Pierre with relief and said in English: "Hey, man, will you help us? We are in *deep* shit."

Jean-Pierre felt as if he would explode. They were just a couple of hippies on the Katmandu trail, a species of tourist which had not quite died out despite the war. What a disappointment! Why did they have to be here just when the whole world was looking for a runaway Western couple?

Jean-Pierre certainly was not going to help a pair of drug-taking degenerates. He turned around and went out.

The pilot was just coming in. He saw the expression on Jean-Pierre's face and said: "What's the matter?"

"It's the wrong couple. Come with me."

The man hurried after Jean-Pierre. "The wrong people? These are not the Americans?"

"They're Americans, but they're not the people we're looking for."

"What are you going to do now?"

"I'm going to speak to Anatoly, and I need you to get him on the radio for me."

They crossed the field and climbed into the helicopter. Jean-Pierre sat in the gunner's seat and put on the headphones. He tapped his foot impatiently on the metal floor as the pilot talked interminably over the radio in Russian. At last Anatoly's voice came on, sounding very distant and punctuated by atmospheric crackling.

"Jean-Pierre, my friend, here is Anatoly. Where are you?"

"I'm at Atati. The two Americans they have captured are not Ellis and Jane. Repeat, they are not Ellis and Jane. They're just a couple of foolish kids looking for nirvana. Over."

"This does not surprise me, Jean-Pierre," Anatoly's voice came back.

"What?" Jean-Pierre interrupted, forgetting that communication was one-way.

"—have received a series of reports that Ellis and Jane have been seen in the Linar Valley. The search party has not made contact with them but we are hot on their trail. Over."

Jean-Pierre's anger about the hippies evaporated and some of his eagerness came back. "The Linar Valley—where is that? Over."

"Near where you are now. It runs into the Nuristan Valley fifteen or twenty miles south of Atati. Over."

So close! "Are you sure? Over."

"The search party got several reports in the villages they passed through. The descriptions fit Ellis and Jane. And they mention a baby. Over."

Then it *was* them. "Can we figure out where they are now? Over."

"Not yet. I'm on my way to join the search party. Then I'll get more details. Over."

"You mean you're not at Bagram? What happened to your, uh . . . visitor? Over."

"He left," Anatoly said briskly. "I'm in the air now and about to meet the team at a village called Mundol. It's in the Nuristan Valley, downstream of the point where the Linar joins the Nuristan, and it's near a big lake which is also called Mundol. Join me there. We'll spend the night there and then supervise the search in the morning. Over."

"I'll be there!" said Jean-Pierre elatedly. He was struck by a thought. "What are we going to do with these hippies? Over."

"I'll have them taken to Kabul for interrogation. We have some people there who will remind them of the reality of the material world. Let me speak to your pilot. Over."

"See you in Mundol. Over."

Anatoly began speaking in Russian to the copilot, and Jean-Pierre took off his headset. He wondered why Anatoly wanted to waste time interrogating a pair of harmless hippies. They obviously weren't spies. Then it occurred to him that the only person who really *knew* whether or not these two were Ellis and Jane was Jean-Pierre himself. It was possible—even if wildly unlikely—that Ellis and Jane might have persuaded him to let them go and tell Anatoly this search party had just captured a couple of hippies.

He was a suspicious bastard, that Russian.

Jean-Pierre waited impatiently for him to finish talking to the pilot. It sounded as if the search party down in Mundol was close to its quarry. Tomorrow, perhaps, Ellis and Jane would be caught. Their attempt to escape had always been more or less futile, in reality; but that did not stop Jean-Pierre worrying, and he would be in an agony of suspense until the two of them were bound hand and foot and locked in a Russian cell.

The pilot took off the headset and said: "We will take you to Mundol in this helicopter. The Hip will take the others back to base."

"Okay."

A few minutes later they were in the air, leaving the others to take their time. It was almost dark, and Jean-Pierre wondered whether it would prove difficult to find the village of Mundol.

Night fell rapidly as they headed downstream. The landscape below disappeared into darkness. The pilot spoke constantly on the radio, and Jean-Pierre imagined that the people on the ground at Mundol were guiding him. After ten or fifteen minutes, powerful lights appeared below. A kilometer or so beyond the lights, the moon glinted off the surface of a large body of water. The helicopter went down.

It landed near another helicopter in a field. A waiting trooper led Jean-Pierre across the grass to a village on a hillside. The silhouettes of the wooden houses were limned with moonlight. Jean-Pierre followed the trooper into one of the houses. There, sitting on a folding chair and wrapped in an enormous coat of wolf fur, was Anatoly.

He was in an ebullient mood. "Jean-Pierre, my French friend, we are close to success!" he said loudly. It was odd to see a man with an Oriental face being hearty and jovial. "Have some coffee—there's vodka in it."

Jean-Pierre accepted a paper cup from an Afghan woman who appeared to be waiting on Anatoly. He sat down on a folding chair like Anatoly's. They looked army, these chairs. If the Russians were carrying this much equipment—folding chairs and coffee and paper cups and vodka—perhaps they would not move faster than Ellis and Jane, after all.

Anatoly read his mind. "I brought a few little luxuries in my helicopter," he said with a smile. "The KGB has its dignity, you know."

Jean-Pierre could not read the expression on his face and did not know whether he was joking or not. He changed the subject. "What's the latest news?"

"Our fugitives definitely passed through the villages of Bosaydur and Linar today. At some point this afternoon the search party lost its guide— he just disappeared. He probably decided to go home." Anatoly frowned, as if bothered by that little loose end, then resumed his story. "Fortunately, they found another guide almost immediately."

"Employing your usual highly persuasive recruiting technique, no doubt," said Jean-Pierre.

"No, oddly enough. This one was a genuine volunteer, they tell me. He's here in the village somewhere."

"Of course, they're more likely to volunteer here in Nuristan," Jean-

Pierre mused. "They're hardly involved in the war—and in any case they're said to be totally without scruples."

"This new man claims actually to have seen the fugitives today, before he joined us. They passed him at the point where the Linar flows into the Nuristan. He saw them turn south, heading this way."

"Good!"

"Tonight, after the search party arrived here in Mundol, our man questioned some villagers and learned that two foreigners with a baby passed through this afternoon, going south."

"Then there's no doubt," said Jean-Pierre with satisfaction.

"None at all," Anatoly agreed. "We'll catch them tomorrow. For sure."

Jean-Pierre woke up on an inflatable mattress—another KGB luxury—on the dirt floor of the house. The fire had gone out during the night and the air was cold. Anatoly's bed, across the dim little room, was empty. Jean-Pierre did not know where the owners of the house had spent the night. After they had provided food and served it, Anatoly had sent them away. He treated the whole of Afghanistan as if it were his personal kingdom. Perhaps it was.

Jean-Pierre sat up and rubbed his eyes, then saw Anatoly standing in the doorway, looking at him speculatively. "Good morning," said Jean-Pierre.

"Have you ever been here before?" Anatoly asked without preamble.

Jean-Pierre's brain was still foggy with sleep. "Where?"

"Nuristan," Anatoly replied impatiently.

"No."

"Strange."

Jean-Pierre found this enigmatic style of conversation irritating so early in the morning. "Why?" he said tetchily. "Why is it strange?"

"I was talking to the new guide a few minutes ago."

"What's his name?"

"Mohammed, Muhammad, Mahomet, Mahmoud—one of those names a million other people have."

"What language did you use, with a Nuristani?"

"French, Russian, Dari and English—the usual mixture. He asked me who arrived in the second helicopter last night. I said: 'A Frenchman who can identify the fugitives,' or words to that effect. He asked your name, so I told him: I wanted to keep him going until I found out why he was so interested. But he didn't ask any more questions. It was almost as if he knew you."

"Impossible."

"I suppose so."

"Why don't you just ask him?" It was not like Anatoly to be diffident, Jean-Pierre thought.

"There is no point in asking a man a question until you have established whether he has any reason to lie to you." With that, Anatoly went out.

Jean-Pierre got up. He had slept in his shirt and underwear. He pulled on his trousers and boots, then draped the greatcoat over his shoulders and stepped outside.

He found himself on a rough wooden veranda overlooking the whole valley. Down below, the river coiled between the fields, broad and sluggish. Some way to the south it entered a long, narrow lake rimmed with mountains. The sun had not yet risen. A mist over the water obscured the far end of the lake. It was a pleasant scene. Of course, Jean-Pierre remembered, this was the most fertile and populous part of Nuristan: most of the rest was wilderness.

The Russians had dug a field latrine, Jean-Pierre noted with approval. The Afghan practice of using the streams from which they took their drinking water was the reason they all had worms. The Russians will really knock this country into shape once they get control of it, he thought.

He walked down to the meadow, used the latrine, washed in the river, and got a cup of coffee from a group of soldiers standing around a cooking fire.

The search party was ready to leave. Anatoly had decided last night that he would direct the search from here, remaining in constant radio contact with the searchers. The helicopters would stay ready to take him and Jean-Pierre to join the searchers as soon as they sighted their quarry.

While Jean-Pierre was sipping his coffee, Anatoly came across the field from the village. "Have you seen that damn guide?" he asked abruptly.

"No."

"He seems to have disappeared."

Jean-Pierre raised his eyebrows. "Just like the last one."

"These people are impossible. I'll have to ask the villagers. Come and translate."

"I don't speak their language."

"Maybe they'll understand your Dari."

Jean-Pierre walked with Anatoly back across the meadow to the village. As they climbed the narrow dirt path between the rickety houses, somebody called to Anatoly in Russian. They stopped and looked to the side. Ten or twelve men, some Nuristanis in white and some Russians in uniform, were crowded together on a veranda looking at something on the ground. They parted to let Anatoly and Jean-Pierre through. The thing on the floor was a dead man.

The villagers were jabbering in outraged tones and pointing to the body. The man's throat had been cut: the wound gaped horribly and the head hung loose. The blood had dried—he had probably been killed yesterday.

"Is this Mohammed, the guide?" Jean-Pierre asked.

"No," said Anatoly. He questioned one of the soldiers, then said: "This is the *previous* guide, the one who disappeared."

Jean-Pierre addressed the villagers slowly in Dari. "What is going on?"

After a pause, a wrinkled old man with a bad occlusion in his right eye replied in the same language. "He has been murdered!" he said accusingly.

Jean-Pierre began to question him and, bit by bit, the story emerged. The dead man was a villager from the Linar Valley who had been con-scripted as a guide by the Russians. His body, hastily concealed in a clump of bushes, had been found by a goatherd's dog. The man's family thought the Russians had murdered him, and they had brought the body here this morning in a dramatic attempt to find out why.

Jean-Pierre explained to Anatoly. "They're outraged because they think your men killed him," he finished.

"Outraged?" said Anatoly. "Don't they know there's a war on? People are getting killed every day—that's the whole idea."

"Obviously they don't see much action here. *Did* you kill him?"

"I'll find out." Anatoly spoke to the soldiers. Several of them answered together in animated tones. "We didn't kill him," Anatoly translated to Jean-Pierre.

"So who did? I wonder. Could the locals be murdering our guides for col-laborating with the enemy?"

"No," said Anatoly. "If they hated collaborators they wouldn't be mak-ing this fuss about one who got killed. Tell them we're innocent—calm them down."

Jean-Pierre spoke to the one-eyed man. "The foreigners did not kill this man. They want to know who murdered their guide."

The one-eyed man translated this, and the villagers reacted with con-sternation.

Anatoly looked thoughtful. "Perhaps the disappearing Mohammed killed this man in order to get the job of guide."

"Are you paying much?" Jean-Pierre asked.

"I doubt it." Anatoly asked a sergeant and translated the answer. "Five hundred afghanis a day."

"It's a good wage, to an Afghan, but hardly worth killing for—although they do say a Nuristani will murder you for your sandals if they're new."

"Ask them if they know where Mohammed is."

Jean-Pierre asked. There was some discussion. Most of the villagers were shaking their heads, but one man raised his voice above the others and pointed insistently to the north. Eventually the one-eyed man said to Jean-Pierre: "He left the village early this morning. Abdul saw him go north."

"Did he leave before or after this body was brought here?"

"Before."

Jean-Pierre told Anatoly, and added: "I wonder why he went away, then?"

"He's acting like a man guilty of *something*."

"He must have left immediately after he spoke to you this morning. It's almost as if he went because I had arrived."

Anatoly nodded thoughtfully. "Whatever the explanation is, I think he knows something we don't. We'd better go after him. If we lose a little time, too bad—we can afford it anyway."

"How long ago was it that you spoke to him?"

Anatoly looked at his watch. "A little over an hour."

"Then he can't have got far."

"Right." Anatoly turned away and gave a rapid series of orders. The soldiers were suddenly galvanized. Two of them got hold of the one-eyed man and marched him down toward the field. Another ran to the helicopters. Anatoly took Jean-Pierre's arm and they walked briskly after the soldiers. "We will take the one-eyed man, in case we need an interpreter," Anatoly said.

By the time they reached the field the two helicopters were cranking. Anatoly and Jean-Pierre boarded one of them. The one-eyed man was already inside, looking at once thrilled and terrified. He'll be telling the story of this day for the rest of his life, thought Jean-Pierre.

A few minutes later they were in the air. Both Anatoly and Jean-Pierre stood near the open door and looked down. A well-beaten path, clearly visible, led from the village to the top of the hill, then disappeared into the trees. Anatoly spoke into the pilot's radio, then explained to Jean-Pierre: "I have sent some troopers to beat those woods, just in case he decided to hide."

The runaway had almost certainly gone farther than this, Jean-Pierre thought, but Anatoly was being cautious—as usual.

They flew parallel with the river for a mile or so, then reached the mouth of the Linar. Had Mohammed continued up the valley, into the cold heart of Nuristan, or had he turned east, into the Linar Valley, heading for Five Lions?

Jean-Pierre said to the one-eyed man: "Where did Mohammed come from?"

"I don't know," said the man. "But he was a Tajik."

That meant he was more likely to be from the Linar Valley than the Nuristan. Jean-Pierre explained this to Anatoly, and Anatoly directed the pilot to turn left and follow the Linar.

This was a telling illustration, Jean-Pierre thought, of why the search for Ellis and Jane could not be conducted by helicopter. Mohammed had only an hour's start, and already they might have lost track of him. When the fugitives were a whole day ahead, as Ellis and Jane were, there were very many more alternative routes and places to hide.

If there was a track along the Linar Valley, it was not visible from the air. The helicopter pilot simply followed the river. The hillsides were bare of vegetation, but not yet snow-covered, so that if the fugitive were here, he would have nowhere to hide.

They spotted him a few minutes later.

His white robes and turban stood out clearly against the gray-brown ground. He was striding out along the clifftop with the steady, tireless pace of Afghan travelers, his possessions in a bag slung over his shoulder. When he heard the noise of the helicopters he stopped and looked back at them, then continued walking.

"Is that him?" said Jean-Pierre.

"I think so," said Anatoly. "We'll soon find out." He took the pilot's headset and spoke to the other helicopter. It went on ahead, passing over the figure on the ground, and landed a hundred meters or so in front of him. He walked toward it unconcernedly.

"Why don't we land, too?" Jean-Pierre asked Anatoly.

"Just a precaution."

The side door of the other helicopter opened and six troopers got out. The man in white walked toward them, unslinging his bag. It was a long bag, like a military kit bag, and the sight of it rang a bell in Jean-Pierre's memory; but before he could figure out what it reminded him of, Mohammed hefted the bag and pointed it at the troopers, and Jean-Pierre realized what he was about to do and opened his mouth to shout a useless warning.

It was like trying to shout in a dream, or run under water: events moved slowly, but he moved even slower. Before words could come he saw the snout of a machine gun emerge from the bag.

The sound of shooting was drowned by the noise of the helicopters, which gave the weird impression that it all took place in dead silence. One of the Russian troops clutched his belly and fell forward; another threw up his arms and fell back; and the face of a third exploded in blood and flesh. The other three got their weapons raised. One died before he could pull the trigger, but the other two unleashed a storm of bullets, and even as Anatoly was yelling, *"Niet! Niet! Niet! Niet!"* into the radio, the body of Mohammed was lifted off the ground and thrown backward to land in a bloody heap on the cold ground.

Anatoly was still shouting furiously into the radio. The helicopter went down fast. Jean-Pierre found himself trembling with excitement. The sight of battle had given him a high like cocaine, making him feel as if he wanted to laugh, or fuck, or run, or dance. The thought flashed across his mind: I used to want to *heal* people.

The helicopter touched down. Anatoly pulled off the headset, saying disgustedly: "Now we'll never know why that guide got his throat cut." He jumped out, and Jean-Pierre followed him.

They walked over to the dead Afghan. The front of his body was a mass of torn flesh, and most of his face had gone, but Anatoly said: "It's that guide, I'm sure. The build is right, the coloring is right, and I recognize the bag." He bent down and carefully picked up the machine gun. "But why is he carrying a machine gun?"

A piece of paper had fallen out of the bag and fluttered to the ground. Jean-Pierre picked it up and looked at it. It was a Polaroid photograph of Mousa. "Oh, my God," he said. "I think I understand this."

"What is it?" said Anatoly. "What do you understand?"

"The dead man is from the Five Lions Valley," Jean-Pierre said. "He is one of Masud's top lieutenants. This is a photograph of his son, Mousa. The photograph was taken by Jane. I also recognize the bag in which he concealed his gun: it used to belong to Ellis."

"So what?" said Anatoly impatiently. "What do you conclude from that?"

Jean-Pierre's brain was in overdrive, working things out faster than he could explain them. "Mohammed killed your guide in order to take his place," he began. "You had no way of knowing he was not what he claimed to be. The Nuristanis knew that he was not one of them, of course, but that didn't matter, because (a) they didn't know he was pretending to be a local and (b) even if they had they couldn't have told you because he was also your interpreter. In fact there was only one person who could possibly find him out. . . ."

"You," said Anatoly. "Because you knew him."

"He was aware of that danger and he was on the lookout for me. That's why this morning he asked you who it was that arrived after dark yesterday. You told him my name. He left immediately." Jean-Pierre frowned: something was not quite right. "But why did he stay out in the open? He could have concealed himself in the woods, or hidden in a cave: it would have taken us much longer to find him. It's as if he didn't expect to be pursued."

"Why should he?" said Anatoly. "When the first guide disappeared, we didn't send a search party after *him*—we just got another guide and carried on: no investigation, no pursuit. What was different this time—what went wrong for Mohammed—was that the local people found the body and accused us of murder. That made us suspicious of Mohammed. Even so, we considered forgetting about him and just pressing on. He was unlucky."

"He didn't know what a cautious man he was dealing with," said Jean-Pierre. "Next question: What was his motive in all this? Why did he go to so much trouble to substitute himself for the original guide?"

"Presumably to mislead us. Presumably, everything he told us was a lie. He did *not* see Ellis and Jane yesterday afternoon at the mouth of the Linar Valley. They did *not* turn south into the Nuristan. The villagers of Mundol did *not* confirm that two foreigners with a baby passed through yesterday heading south—Mohammed never even asked them the question. He *knew* where the fugitives were—"

"And he led us in the opposite direction, of course!" Jean-Pierre felt elated again. "The old guide disappeared just after the search party left the village of Linar, didn't he?"

"Yes. So we can assume that reports *up to* that point are true—therefore Ellis and Jane *did* pass through that village. Afterward, Mohammed took over and led us *south*—"

"Because Ellis and Jane went north!" said Jean-Pierre triumphantly.

Anatoly nodded grimly. "Mohammed gained them a day, at most," he said thoughtfully. "For that he gave his life. Was it worth it?"

Jean-Pierre looked again at the Polaroid photograph of Mousa. The cold wind made it flutter in his hand. "You know," he said, "I think Mohammed would answer: Yes, it was worth it."

CHAPTER NINETEEN

They left Gadwal in the deep darkness before dawn, hoping to steal a march on the Russians by setting out so early. Ellis knew how difficult it was for even the most capable officer to get a squad of soldiers moving before dawn: the cook had to make breakfast, the quartermaster had to strike camp, the radio operator had to check in with headquarters, and the men had to eat; and all those things took time. The one advantage Ellis had over the Russian commander was that he had no more to do than load the mare while Jane fed Chantal, then shake Halam awake.

Ahead of them was a long, slow climb up the Nuristan Valley for eight or nine miles and then up a side valley. The first part, in the Nuristan, should not be too difficult, Ellis thought, even in the dark, for there was a road of sorts. If only Jane could keep going, they should be able to get into the side valley during the afternoon and travel a few miles up it by nightfall. Once they were out of the Nuristan Valley it would be much more difficult to trail them, for the Russians would not know which side valley they had taken.

Halam led the way, wearing Mohammed's clothes, including his Chitrali cap. Jane followed, carrying Chantal, and Ellis brought up the rear, leading Maggie. The horse was now carrying one bag fewer: Mohammed had taken the kit bag and Ellis had not found a suitable container to replace it. He had been forced to leave most of his blasting equipment in Gadwal. However, he had kept some TNT, a length of Primacord, a few blasting caps and the pull-ring firing device, and had them stowed in the roomy pockets of his down coat.

Jane was cheerful and energetic. The rest yesterday afternoon had renewed her reserves of strength. She was marvelously tough, and Ellis felt proud of her, although when he thought about it he did not see why *he* should be entitled to feel proud of *her* strength.

Halam was carrying a candle lantern, which threw grotesque shadows on the cliff walls. He seemed disgruntled. Yesterday he had been all smiles, apparently pleased to be part of this bizarre expedition; but this morning he was grim-faced and taciturn. Ellis blamed the early start.

The path, such as it was, snaked along the cliffside, founding promontories that jutted out into the stream, sometimes hugging the water's edge and sometimes ascending to the clifftop. After less than a mile they came to a place where the track simply vanished: there was a cliff on the left and the river on the right. Halam said the path had been washed away in a rainstorm, and they would have to wait until light to find a way around.

Ellis was unwilling to lose any time. He took off his boots and trousers and waded into the ice-cold water. At its deepest it was only up to his waist, and he gained the far bank easily. He returned and led Maggie across, then came back for Jane and Chantal. Halam followed at last, but modesty prevented him from undressing, even in the dark, so he had to walk on with soaking-wet trousers, which made his mood worse.

They passed through a village in darkness, followed briefly by a couple of mangy dogs that barked at them from a safe distance. Soon after that, dawn cracked the eastern sky, and Halam snuffed the candle.

They had to ford the river several more times in places where the path was washed away or blocked by a landslide. Halam gave in and rolled his baggy trousers up over his knees. At one of these crossings they met a traveler coming from the opposite direction, a small, skeletal man leading a fat-tailed sheep which he carried across the river in his arms. Halam had a long conversation with him in some Nuristani language, and Ellis suspected, from the way they waved their arms, that they were talking about routes across the mountains.

After they parted from the traveler, Ellis said to Halam in Dari: "Don't tell people where we are going."

Halam pretended not to understand.

Jane repeated what Ellis had said. She spoke more fluently, and used emphatic gestures and nods as the Afghan men did. "The Russians will question all travelers," she explained.

Halam appeared to understand, but he did exactly the same thing with the next traveler they met, a dangerous-looking young man carrying a venerable Lee-Enfield rifle. During the conversation, Ellis thought he heard Halam say, "Kantiwar," the name of the pass for which they were heading; and a moment later the traveler repeated the word. Ellis was angered: Halam was fooling around with their lives. But the damage was done, so he suppressed the urge to interfere, and waited patiently until they moved on again.

As soon as the young man with the rifle was out of sight, Ellis said: "I said you are not to tell people where we are going."

This time Halam did not pretend incomprehension. "I told him nothing," he said indignantly.

"You did," said Ellis emphatically. "From now on you will not speak to other travelers."

Halam said nothing.

Jane said: "You will not talk to other travelers, do you understand?"

"Yes," Halam admitted reluctantly.

Ellis felt it was important to shut him up. He could guess why Halam wanted to discuss routes with other people: they might know of factors such as landslides, snowfalls or floods in the mountains that might block one valley and make another approach preferable. He had not really grasped the fact that Ellis and Jane were *running away* from the Russians. The existence of alternative routes was about the only factor in the fugitives' favor, for the Russians had to check every possible route. They would be working quite hard to eliminate some of those routes by interrogating people, especially travelers. The less information they could garner that way, the more difficult and lengthy their search would be, and the better the chances Ellis and Jane would evade them.

A little later they met a white-robed mullah with a red-dyed beard, and to Ellis's frustration Halam immediately opened a conversation with the man in exactly the same way as he had with the previous two travelers.

Ellis hesitated only for a moment. He went up to Halam, grabbed him in a painful double-arm lock and marched him off.

Halam struggled briefly, but soon stopped because it hurt. He called out something, but the mullah simply watched openmouthed, doing nothing. Looking back, Ellis saw that Jane had taken the reins and was following with Maggie.

After a hundred yards or so, Ellis released Halam saying: "If the Russians find me, they will kill me. This is why you must not talk to anyone."

Halam said nothing but went into a sulk.

After they had walked on awhile, Jane said: "I fear he'll make us suffer for that."

"I suppose he will," said Ellis. "But I had to shut him up somehow."

"I just think there may have been a better way to handle him."

Ellis suppressed a spasm of irritation. He wanted to say *So why didn't you do it, smart-ass?* but this was not the time to quarrel. Halam passed the next traveler with only the briefest of formal greetings, and Ellis thought: At least my technique was effective.

At first their progress was a lot slower than Ellis had anticipated. The meandering path, the uneven ground, the uphill gradient and the continual diversions meant that by midmorning they had covered only four or five miles as the crow flies, he estimated. Then, however, the way became easier, passing through the woods high above the river.

There was still a village or hamlet every mile or so, but now, instead of ramshackle wooden houses piled up the hillsides like collapsible chairs thrown haphazardly into a heap, there were box-shaped dwellings made of the same stone as the cliffs on whose sides they perched precariously, like seagulls' nests.

At midday they stopped in a village, and Halam got them invited into a house and given tea. It was a two-story building, the ground floor apparently being a storeroom, just like the medieval English houses Ellis remembered from ninth-grade history lessons. Jane gave the woman of the house a small bottle of pink medicine for her children's intestinal worms, and in return got pan-baked bread and delicious goat's-milk cheese. They sat on rugs on the mud floor around the open fire, with the poplar beams and willow laths of the roof visible above them. There was no chimney, so the smoke from the fire drifted up to the rafters and eventually seeped through the roof: that, Ellis surmised, was why the houses had no ceilings.

He would have liked to let Jane rest after eating, but he dared not risk it, for he did not know how close behind them the Russians might be. She looked tired but all right. Leaving immediately had the additional advantage that it prevented Halam getting into conversation with the villagers.

However, Ellis watched Jane carefully as they walked on up the valley. He asked her to lead the horse while he took Chantal, judging that carrying the baby was more tiring.

Each time they came upon an eastward-leading side valley, Halam would stop and study it carefully, then shake his head and walk on. Clearly he was not sure of the way, although he denied this hotly when Jane asked him. It was infuriating, especially when Ellis was so impatient to get out of the Nuristan Valley; but he consoled himself with the thought that if Halam was not sure which valley to take, then the Russians would not know which way the fugitives had gone.

He was beginning to wonder whether Halam might have gone past the turning when, at last, Halam stopped where a chattering stream flowed into the Nuristan River, and announced that their route lay up this valley. He seemed to want to stop for a rest, as if he was reluctant to leave familiar territory, but Ellis hurried them along.

Soon they were climbing through a forest of silver birch, and the main valley was lost to view behind them. Ahead of them they could see the mountain range they had to cross, an immense snow-covered wall filling a quarter of the sky, and Ellis kept thinking: even if we escape from the Russians, how can we possibly climb that? Jane stumbled once or twice and cursed, which Ellis took as a sign she was tiring rapidly, although she did not complain.

At dusk they emerged from the forest into a bare, bleak, uninhabited landscape. It seemed to Ellis that they might not find shelter in such territory, so he suggested they spend the night in an empty stone hut they had passed half an hour or so earlier. Jane and Halam agreed, and they turned back.

Ellis insisted that Halam build the fire inside the hut, not outside, so that the flame could not be seen from the air and there would be no telltale column of smoke. His caution was vindicated later, when they heard a helicopter drone overhead. That meant, he supposed, that the Russians were not far away; but in this country, what was a short distance for a helicopter could be an impossible journey on foot. The Russians might be just the other side of an impassable mountain—or only a mile down the track. It was fortunate that the landscape was too wild, and the path too difficult to discern from the air, for a helicopter search to be viable.

Ellis gave the horse some grain. Jane fed and changed Chantal, then fell asleep immediately. Ellis roused her to zip her into the sleeping bag; then he took Chantal's diaper down to the stream, washed it out and put it by the fire to dry. He lay beside Jane for a while, looking at her face in the flickering firelight while Halam snored on the other side of the hut. She looked absolutely drained, her face thin and taut, her hair dirty, her cheeks smudged with earth. She slept restlessly, wincing and grimacing and moving her mouth in silent speech. He wondered how much longer she could go on. It was the pace that was killing her. If they could move more slowly, she would be all right. If only the Russians would give up, or be recalled for some major battle in another part of this wretched country . . .

He wondered about the helicopter he had heard. Perhaps it was on a mission unconnected with Ellis. That seemed unlikely. If it had been part of a search party, then Mohammed's attempt to divert the Russians must have had very limited success.

He allowed himself to think about what would happen if they were captured. For him there would be a show trial, at which the Russians would prove to skeptical nonaligned countries that the Afghan rebels were no more than CIA stooges. The agreement between Masud, Kamil and Azizi would collapse. There would be no American arms for the rebels. Dispirited, the Resistance would weaken and might not last another summer.

After the trial Ellis would be interrogated by the KGB. He would make an initial show of resisting the torture, then pretend to break down and tell them everything; but what he told them would be all lies. They were prepared for that, of course, and they would torture him further; and this time he would act a more convincing breakdown, and tell them a mixture of fact and fiction that would be difficult for them to check out. That way he hoped to survive. If he did, he would be sent to Siberia. After a few years, he might hope to be exchanged for a Soviet spy captured in the States. If not, he would die in the camps.

What would grieve him most would be to be parted from Jane. He had found her, and lost her, and found her again—a piece of luck that still made him reel when he thought of it. To lose her a second time would be unbearable, unbearable. He lay staring at her for a long time trying not to go to sleep for fear she might not be there when he woke up.

Jane dreamed she was in the George V Hotel in Peshawar, Pakistan. The George V was in Paris, of course, but in her dream she did not notice this oddity. She called room service and ordered a fillet steak, medium rare, with mashed potatoes, and a bottle of Château Ausone 1971. She was terribly hungry, but she could not remember why she had waited so long before ordering. She decided to take a bath while they were preparing her dinner. The bathroom was warm and carpeted. She turned on the water and poured in some bath salts, and the room filled with scented steam. She could not understand how she had let herself get this dirty: it was a miracle they had admitted her into the hotel! She was about to step into the hot water when she heard someone calling her name. It must be room service, she thought, how annoying—now she would have to eat while she was still dirty, or let the food get cold. She was tempted to lie down in the hot water and ignore the voice—it was rude of them to call her "Jane" anyway; they should call her "Madame"—but it was a very persistent voice, and somehow familiar. In fact it was not room service, but Ellis, and he was shaking her shoulder, and with the most tragic sense of disappointment, she realized that the George V was a dream, and in reality she was in a cold stone hut in Nuristan, a million miles from a hot bath.

She opened her eyes and saw Ellis's face.

"You have to wake up," he was saying.

Jane felt almost paralyzed by lethargy. "Is it morning already?"

"No, it's the middle of the night."

"What time?"

"One thirty."

"Fuck." She felt angry with him for disturbing her sleep. "Why have you woken me?" she said irritably.

"Halam has gone."

"Gone?" She was still sleepy and confused. "Where? Why? Is he coming back?"

"He didn't tell me. I woke up to find he had gone."

"You think he's abandoned us?"

"Yes."

"Oh, God. How will we find our way without a guide?" Jane had a nightmare dread of getting lost in the snow with Chantal in her arms.

"I'm afraid it could be worse than that," said Ellis.

"What do you mean?"

"You said he would make us suffer for humiliating him in front of that mullah. Perhaps abandoning us is sufficient revenge. I hope so. But I assume he's headed back the way we came. He may run into the Russians. I don't think it will take them long to persuade him to tell them exactly where he left us."

"It's too much," said Jane, and a feeling almost like grief gripped her. It seemed as if some malign deity were conspiring against them. "I'm too tired," she said. "I'm going to lie here and sleep until the Russians come and take me prisoner."

Chantal had been stirring quietly, moving her head from side to side and making sucking noises, and now she started to cry. Jane sat up and picked her up.

"If we leave now we can still escape," Ellis said. "I'll load the horse while you feed her."

"All right," said Jane. She put Chantal to her breast. Ellis watched her for a second, smiling faintly, then went out into the night. Jane thought they could easily escape if they did not have Chantal. She wondered how Ellis felt about that. She was, after all, another man's child. But he did not seem to mind. He regarded Chantal as a part of Jane. Or was he hiding some resentment?

Would he like to be a father to Chantal? she asked herself. She looked at the tiny face, and wide blue eyes looked back at her. Who could fail to cherish this helpless little girl?

Suddenly she was completely uncertain about everything. She was not sure how much she loved Ellis; she did not know what she felt about Jean-Pierre, the husband who was hunting her; she could not figure out what her duty to her child was. She was frightened of the snow and the mountains and the Russians, and she had been tired and tense and cold for too long.

Automatically she changed Chantal, using the dry diaper from the fireside. She could not remember changing her last night. It seemed to her that she had fallen asleep after feeding her. She frowned, doubting her memory; then it came back to her that Ellis had roused her momentarily to zip her into the sleeping bag. He must have taken the soiled diaper down to the stream and washed it and wrung it out and hung it on a stick beside the fire to dry. Jane started to cry.

She felt very foolish, but she could not stop, so she carried on dressing Chantal with tears streaming down her face. Ellis came back in as she was making the baby comfortable in the carrying sling.

"Goddam horse didn't want to wake up either," he said; then he saw her face and said: "What is it?"

"I don't know why I ever left you," she said. "You're the best man I've ever known, and I never stopped loving you. Please forgive me."

He put his arms around her and Chantal. "Just don't do it again, that's all," he said.

They stood like that for a while.

Eventually Jane said: "I'm ready."

"Good. Let's go."

They went outside and set off uphill through the thinning woodland. Halam had taken the lantern, but the moon was out and they could see clearly. The air was so cold it hurt to breathe. Jane worried about Chantal. The baby was once again inside Jane's fur-lined coat, and she hoped that her body warmed the air Chantal was breathing. Could a baby come to harm by breathing cold air? Jane had no idea.

Ahead of them was the Kantiwar Pass, at fifteen thousand feet a good deal higher than the last pass, the Aryu. Jane knew she was going to be colder and more tired than she had ever been in her life, and perhaps more frightened, too, but her spirits were high. She felt she had resolved something deep inside herself. If I live, she thought, I want to live with Ellis. One of these days I'll tell him it was because he washed out a dirty diaper.

They soon left the trees behind and started across a plateau like a moonscape, with boulders and craters and odd patches of snow. They followed a line of huge flat stones like a giant's footpath. They were still climbing, although less steeply for the moment, and the temperature dropped steadily, the white patches increasing until the ground was a crazy chessboard.

Nervous energy kept Jane going for the first hour or so, but then, as she settled into the endless march, weariness overcame her again. She wanted to say *How far is it now?* and *Will we be there soon?* as she had when a child in the back of her father's car.

At some point on that sloping upland they crossed the ice line. Jane became aware of the new danger when the horse skidded, snorted with fear, almost fell and regained its balance. Then she noticed that the moonlight was reflecting off the boulders as if they were glazed: the rocks were like diamonds, cold and hard and glittering. Her boots gripped better than Maggie's hooves, but nevertheless, a little while later, Jane slipped and almost fell. From then on she was terrified she would fall and crush Chantal, and she trod ultracarefully, her nerves so taut she felt she might snap.

After a little more than two hours they reached the far side of the plateau and found themselves facing a steep path up a snow-covered mountainside. Ellis went first, pulling Maggie behind him. Jane followed at a safe distance in case the horse should slip backward. They went up the mountain in a zigzag.

The path was not clearly marked. They presumed it lay wherever the ground was lower than in neighboring areas. Jane longed for a more definite sign that this was the route: the remains of a fire, a clean-picked chicken carcass, even a discarded matchbox—anything that would indicate that other human beings had once passed this way. She began obsessively to imagine that they were completely lost, far from the path, wandering aimlessly through endless snows, and that they would continue to meander for days, until they ran out of food and energy and willpower, and lay down in the snow, all three of them, to freeze to death together.

Her back ached insupportably. With much reluctance she gave Chantal to Ellis and took the horse's reins from him, to transfer the strain to a different set of muscles. The wretched horse stumbled constantly now. At one point it slipped on an icy boulder and went down. Jane had to haul mercilessly on the bridle to get the animal to its feet. When the horse stood up finally Jane saw a dark stain on the snow where it had fallen: blood. Looking more closely, she saw a cut on its left knee. The injury did not appear serious: she made Maggie walk on.

Now that she was in the lead, she had to decide where the path lay, and the nightmare of getting irretrievably lost haunted every hesitation. At times the way seemed to fork and she had to guess, left or right? Often the ground was more or less uniformly level, so she just followed her nose until some kind of pathway reappeared. Once she found herself floundering in a snowdrift, and had to be pulled out by Ellis and the horse.

Eventually the path led her onto a ledge which wound far up the side of the mountain. They were very high: looking back across the plateau so far below made her a little dizzy. Surely they could not be far from the pass?

The ledge was steep and icy and only a few feet wide, and beyond the edge was a precipitous drop. Jane trod extra carefully, but all the same she stumbled several times, and once fell to her knees, bruising them. She ached so much all over that she hardly noticed the new pains. Maggie slipped constantly, until Jane no longer bothered to turn around when she heard her hooves skid, but simply pulled harder on the reins. She would have liked to readjust the horse's load so that the heavy bags were farther forward, which would have helped the animal's stability on the uphill climb; but there was no room on the ledge, and she was afraid that if she stopped she would not be able to start again.

The ledge narrowed and wound around an outcrop of cliffs. Jane gingerly took steps across the most slender section, but despite her caution— or perhaps because she was so nervous—she slipped. For a heart-stopping moment she thought she was going to fall over the edge; but she landed on her knees and steadied herself with both hands. From the corner of her eye she could see the snowy slopes hundreds of feet below. She started to shake, and controlled herself with an effort.

She stood up slowly and turned around. She had let go of the reins, which now dangled over the precipice. The horse stood watching her, stiff-legged and trembling, evidently terrified. When she reached for the bridle the horse took a panicky step backward. "Stop!" Jane cried; then she made her voice calm and said quietly: "Don't do that. Come to me. You'll be all right."

Ellis called to her from the other side of the outcrop, "What is it?"

"Hush," she called softly. "Maggie's frightened. Stay back." She was dreadfully aware that Ellis was carrying Chantal. She continued to murmur reassuringly to the horse as she stepped slowly toward it. It stared at her, wide-eyed, breath like smoke coming from its flared nostrils. She got within arm's length and reached for its bridle.

The horse jerked its head away, stepped backward, skidded and lost its balance.

As the horse's head jerked back, Jane caught the reins; but its legs slipped from beneath it, it fell to the right, the reins flew from Jane's hand, and to her unspeakable horror the horse slid slowly on its back to the lip of the ledge and fell over, neighing in terror.

Ellis appeared. "Stop!" he shouted at Jane, and she realized she was screaming. She closed her mouth with a snap. Ellis knelt down and peered over the edge, still clutching Chantal to his chest beneath his down coat. Jane controlled her hysteria and knelt beside him.

She expected to see the body of the horse embedded in the snow hundreds of feet below. In fact it had landed on a shelf just five or six feet down, and it was lying on its side with its feet sticking out into the void. "It's still alive!" Jane cried. "Thank God!"

"And our supplies are intact," said Ellis unsentimentally.

"But how can we get the animal back up here?"

Ellis looked at her and said nothing.

Jane realized they could not possibly get the horse back up onto the path. "But we can't leave her behind to die in the cold!" Jane said.

"I'm sorry," said Ellis.

"Oh, God, it's unbearable."

Ellis unzipped his down coat and unslung Chantal. Jane took her and put her inside her own coat. "I'll get the food first," said Ellis.

He lay flat on his belly along the lip of the ledge and then swung his feet over. Loose snow flurried over the prone horse. Ellis lowered himself slowly, feet searching for the shelf. He touched firm ground, slid his elbows off the ledge and carefully turned around.

Jane watched him, petrified. Between the horse's rump and the face of the cliff there was not room enough for both of Ellis's feet side by side: he had to stand, with his feet one behind the other, like a figure in an ancient

Egyptian wall painting. He bent at the knees and slowly lowered himself into a crouch; then he reached for the complex web of leather straps holding the canvas bag of emergency rations.

At that moment the horse decided to get up.

It bent its front legs and somehow managed to get them under its forequarters; then, with the familiar snakelike wriggle of a horse getting to its feet, it lifted its front end and tried to swing its rear legs back onto the ledge.

It almost succeeded.

Then its back feet slid away, it lost its balance, and its rear end fell sideways. Ellis grabbed the food bag. Inch by inch the horse slipped away, kicking and struggling. Jane was terrified it would injure Ellis. Inexorably the animal slithered over the edge. Ellis jerked at the food bag, no longer trying to save the horse, but hoping to snap the leather straps and hold on to the food. So determined was he that Jane feared he would let the horse pull him over the edge. The animal slid faster, dragging Ellis to the brink. At the last second he let go of the bag with a cry of frustration, and the horse made a noise like a scream and dropped away, tumbling over and over as it fell into the void, taking with it all their food, their medical supplies, their sleeping bag and Chantal's spare diaper.

Jane burst into tears.

A few moments later Ellis scrambled up onto the ledge beside her. He put his arms around her and knelt there with her for a minute while she cried for the horse and the supplies and her aching legs and her frozen feet. Then he stood, gently helped her up and said: "We mustn't stop."

"But how can we go on?" she cried. "We've nothing to eat, we can't boil water, we've no sleeping bag, no medicines. . . ."

"We've got each other," he said.

She hugged him tightly when she remembered how near to the edge he had slipped. If we live through this, she thought, and if we escape the Russians and get back to Europe together, I'll never let him out of my sight, I swear.

"You go first," he said, disentangling himself from her embrace. "I want to be able to see you." He gave her a gentle shove, and automatically she began to walk on up the mountain. Slowly her despair crept back. She decided her aim would simply be to carry on walking until she dropped dead. After a while Chantal began to cry. Jane ignored her, and eventually she stopped.

Sometime later—it might have been minutes or hours, for she had lost track of time—as Jane was rounding a corner, Ellis caught up with her and stopped her with a hand on her arm. "Look," he said, pointing ahead.

The track led down into a vast bowl of hills rimmed by white-peaked mountains. At first Jane did not understand why Ellis had said *Look*; then she realized that the track was leading *down*.

"Is this the top?" she asked stupidly.

"This is it," he said. "This is the Kantiwar Pass. We've done the worst part of this leg of the journey. For the next couple of days the route will lie downhill, and the weather will get warmer."

Jane sat down on an icy boulder. I made it, she thought. I made it.

While the two of them looked at the black hills, the sky beyond the mountain peaks turned from pearl gray to dusty pink. Day was breaking. As the light slowly stained the sky, so a little hope crept into Jane's heart again. Downhill, she thought, and warmer. Perhaps we will escape.

Chantal cried again. Well, *her* food supply had not gone with Maggie. Jane fed her, sitting on that icy boulder on the roof of the world, while Ellis melted snow in his hands for Jane to drink.

The descent into the Kantiwar Valley was a relatively gentle slope, but very icy at first. However, it was less nerve-racking without the horse to worry about. Ellis, who had not slipped at all on the way up, carried Chantal.

Ahead of them, the morning sky turned flame red, as if the world beyond the mountains were on fire. Jane's feet were still numb with cold, but her nose unfroze. Suddenly she realized she was terribly hungry. They would simply have to keep walking until they came across people. All they had to trade, now, was the TNT in Ellis's pockets. When that was gone they would have to rely on traditional Afghan hospitality.

They were also without bedding. They would have to sleep in their coats, with their boots on. Somehow Jane felt they would solve all problems. Even finding the path was easy now, for the valley walls on either side were a constant guide and limited the distance they might stray. Soon there was a little stream burbling alongside them: they were below the ice line again. The ground was fairly even, and if they had still had the horse they could have ridden her.

After another two hours they paused to rest at the head of a gorge, and Jane took Chantal from Ellis. Ahead of them, the descent became rough and steep, but because they were below the ice line the rocks were not slippery. The gorge was quite narrow and could quite easily get blocked. "I hope there are no landslides down there," said Jane.

Ellis was looking the other way, back up the valley. Suddenly he gave a start, and said: "Jesus Christ."

"What on earth is the matter?" Jane turned and followed his gaze, and her heart sank. Behind them, about a mile up the valley, were half a dozen men in uniform and a horse: the search party.

After all that, thought Jane, after all we went through, they caught us anyway. She was too miserable even to cry.

Ellis grabbed her arm. "Quick, let's move," he said. He started hurrying down into the gorge, pulling her after him.

"What's the point?" Jane said wearily. "They're sure to catch us."

"We've got one chance left." As they walked, Ellis was surveying the steep, rocky sides of the gorge.

"What?"

"A rockfall."

"They'll find a way over or around it."

"Not if they're all buried underneath it."

He stopped at a place where the floor of the canyon was only a few feet wide and one wall was precipitously steep and high. "This is perfect," he said. He took from the pockets of his coat a block of TNT, a reel of detonating cable marked PRIMACORD, a small metal object about the size of the cap of a fountain pen, and something that looked like a metal syringe except that at its blunt end it had a pull ring instead of a plunger. He laid the objects out on the ground.

Jane watched him in a daze. She did not dare to hope.

He fixed the small metal object to one end of the Primacord by crimping it with his teeth; then he fixed the metal object to the sharp end of the syringe. He handed the whole assembly to Jane.

"This is what you have to do," he began. "Walk down the gorge, paying out the cable. Try to conceal it. It doesn't matter if you lay it in the stream—this stuff burns under water. When you reach the limit of the wire, pull out the safety pins like this." He showed her two split pins which pierced the barrel of the syringe. He pulled them out and put them back in. "Then keep your eye on me. Wait for me to wave my arms above my head like this." He showed her what he meant. "Then pull the ring. If we time this just right, we can kill them all. Go!"

Jane followed orders like a robot, without thinking. She walked down the gorge, paying out the cable. At first she concealed it behind a line of low bushes; then she laid it in the bed of the stream. Chantal slept on in the sling, swaying gently as Jane walked, leaving both of Jane's arms free.

After a minute she looked back. Ellis was wedging the TNT into a fissure in the rock. Jane had always believed that explosives would go off spontaneously if you handled them roughly: obviously that was a misconception.

She walked on until the cable became taut in her hand; then she turned around again. Ellis was now scaling the canyon wall, presumably searching for the best position from which to observe the Russians as they stepped into the trap.

She sat down beside the stream. Chantal's tiny body rested in her lap. The sling went slack, taking the weight off Jane's back. Ellis's words kept repeating in her mind: *If we time this just right, we can kill them all.* Could it work? she wondered. Would they all be killed?

What would the other Russians do then? Jane's head began to clear, and she considered the likely sequence of events. In an hour or two someone would notice that this little party had not called in for a while, and would attempt to raise them on the radio. Finding that impossible, they would assume that the party was in a deep gorge, or that its radio was on the blink. After a couple more hours without contact, they would send a helicopter to look for the party, assuming that the officer in charge would have had the sense to light a fire or do something else to make his location easily visible from the air. When that failed, the people at headquarters would start to worry. At some point they would have to send out a search party to look for the missing search party. The new party would have to cover the same ground as the old one. They certainly would not complete that trip today, and it would be impossible to search properly at night. By the time they found the bodies, Ellis and Jane would be at least a day and a half ahead, possibly more. It might be enough, Jane thought; by then she and Ellis would have gone past so many forks and side valleys and alternative routes that they could be untraceable. I wonder, she thought wearily. I wonder if this could be the end. I wish the soldiers would hurry. I can't bear the waiting, I'm so afraid.

She could see Ellis clearly, crawling along the clifftop on his hands and knees. She could see the search party, too, as they marched down the valley. Even at this distance they appeared dirty, and their slumped shoulders and dragging feet showed them to be tired and dispirited. They had not seen her yet; she blended into the landscape.

Ellis crouched behind a bluff and peered around its edge at the approaching soldiers. He was visible to Jane but hidden from the Russians, and he had a clear view of the place where he had planted the explosives.

The soldiers reached the head of the gorge and began to descend. One

of them was riding, and had a mustache: presumably he was the officer. Another wore a Chitrali cap. That's Halam, Jane thought, the traitor. After
what Jean-Pierre had done, treachery seemed to her an unforgivable crime.
There were five others, and they all had short hair and uniform caps and
youthful, clean-shaven faces. Two men and five boys, she thought.

She watched Ellis. He would give the sign at any minute. Her neck
began to ache from the strain of looking up at him. The soldiers still had
not spotted her: they were concentrating on finding their way along the
rocky ground. At last Ellis turned to her and, slowly and deliberately, waved
both his arms in the air above his head.

Jane looked back at the soldiers. One of them reached out and took the
bridle of the horse, to help it over the uneven ground. Jane had the syringe
device in her left hand and the forefinger of her right hand was crooked inside the pull ring. One jerk would light the fuse and detonate the TNT and
bring the cliff tumbling down on her pursuers. Five boys, she thought.
Joined the army because they were poor or foolish or both, or because they
were conscripted. Posted to a cold, inhospitable country where the people
hate them. Marched through a mountainous, icy wilderness. Buried under
a landslide, heads smashed and lungs choked with earth and backs broken
and chests crushed, screaming and suffocating and bleeding to death in
agony and terror. Five letters to be written to proud fathers and anxious
mothers at home: regret to inform, died in action, historic struggle against
the forces of reaction, act of heroism, posthumous medal, deepest sympathy.
Deepest sympathy. The mother's contempt for these fine words as she recalled how she had given birth in pain and fear, fed the boy in hard times
and easy, taught him to walk straight and wash his hands and spell his
name, sent him to school; how she had watched him grow and grow until
he was almost as tall as she, then even taller, until he was ready to earn a
living and marry a healthy girl and start a family of his own and give her
grandchildren. The mother's grief when she realized that all that, everything she had done, the pain and the work and the worry, had been for
nothing: this miracle, her man-child, had been destroyed by braggardly men
in a stupid, vain war. The sense of loss. The sense of loss.

Jane heard Ellis shout. She looked up. He was on his feet, not caring
now whether he was seen, waving at her and yelling: "Do it now! Do it
now!"

Carefully, she put the pull-ring device down on the ground beside the
rushing stream.

The soldiers had seen both of them now. Two men began climbing up the side of the gorge toward where Ellis stood. The others surrounded Jane, pointing their rifles at her and her baby, looking embarrassed and foolish. She ignored them and watched Ellis. He climbed down the side of the gorge. The men who had been scrambling up toward him stopped and waited to see what he was going to do.

He reached the level ground and walked slowly up to Jane. He stood in front of her. "Why?" he said. "Why didn't you do it?"

Because they are so young, she thought, because they are young, and innocent, and they don't want to kill me. Because it would have been murder. But most of all . . .

"Because they have mothers," she said.

Jean-Pierre opened his eyes. The bulky figure of Anatoly was crouching beside the camp bed. Behind Anatoly, bright sunlight streamed through the open flap of the tent. Jean-Pierre suffered a moment of panic, not knowing why he had slept so late or what he had missed; then, all in a flash, he recalled the events of the night.

He and Anatoly were encamped in the approach to the Kantiwar Pass. They had been awakened at around two thirty a.m. by the captain commanding the search party, who in turn had been roused by the soldier on watch. A young Afghan called Halam had stumbled into the encampment, said the captain. Using a mixture of Pashto, English and Russian, Halam said that he had been guide to the fleeing Americans, but they had insulted him so he had abandoned them. On being asked where the "Americans" were now, he had offered to lead the Russians to the stone hut where, even now, the fugitives lay in unsuspecting sleep.

Jean-Pierre had been all for jumping into the helicopter and rushing off right away.

Anatoly had been more circumspect. "In Mongolia we have a saying: Don't get a hard-on until the whore opens her legs," he said. "Halam may be lying. If he is telling the truth, still he may not be able to find the hut, especially at night, especially from the air. And even if he finds it they may have gone."

"So what do you think we should do?"

"Send an advance party—a captain, five troopers and a horse, with this Halam, of course. They can leave immediately. We can rest until they find the runaways."

His caution had been vindicated. The advance party reported back by radio at three thirty, saying that the hut was empty. However, they added, the fire was still alight, so Halam had probably been telling the truth.

Anatoly and Jean-Pierre concluded that Ellis and Jane had woken up in the night, seen that their guide was gone and decided to flee. Anatoly ordered the advance party to go after them, relying on Halam to indicate the likeliest route.

At that point Jean-Pierre had gone back to bed and fallen into a heavy sleep, which was why he had failed to wake at dawn. Now he looked blearily at Anatoly and said: "What's the time?"

"Eight o'clock. And we've caught them."

Jean-Pierre's heart leaped—then he remembered that he had felt this way before, and had been let down. "For sure?" he asked.

"We can go and check just as soon as you put your trousers on."

It was almost that quick. A refueling helicopter arrived just as they were about to board, and Anatoly judged it wise to wait a few more minutes while their tanks were filled, so Jean-Pierre had to contain his consuming impatience a little longer.

They took off a few minutes later. Jean-Pierre looked at the landscape through the open door. As they flew up into the mountains, Jean-Pierre realized this was the bleakest, harshest territory he had yet seen in Afghanistan. Had Jane really crossed this bare, cruel, icebound moonscape with a baby in her arms? She must really hate me, Jean-Pierre thought, to go through so much to get away from me. Now she will know that it was all in vain. She is mine forever.

But had she really been caught? He was terrified of another disappointment. When he landed, would he find that the advance party had captured another pair of hippies, or two fanatical mountain climbers, or even a couple of nomads who looked vaguely European?

Anatoly pointed out the Kantiwar Pass as they flew over it. "Looks like they lost their horse," he added, shouting into Jean-Pierre's ear over the noise of the engines and the wind. Sure enough, Jean-Pierre saw the outline of a dead horse in the snows below the pass. He wondered if it was Maggie. He rather hoped it was that stubborn beast.

They flew down the Kantiwar Valley, scanning the ground for the advance party. Eventually they saw smoke: someone had lit a fire to guide them in. They descended toward a patch of level ground near the head of a gorge. Jean-Pierre scrutinized the area as they went down: he saw three or four men in Russian uniforms, but he did not spot Jane.

The helicopter touched down. Jean-Pierre's heart was in his mouth. He jumped to the ground, feeling sick with tension. Anatoly jumped out beside him. The captain led them away from the helicopters and down into the gorge.

And there they were.

Jean-Pierre felt like one who has been tortured and now has the torturer in his power. Jane was sitting on the ground beside a little stream with Chantal in her lap. Ellis stood behind her. They both looked exhausted, defeated and demoralized.

Jean-Pierre stopped. "Come here," he said to Jane.

She got to her feet and walked toward him. He saw that she was carrying Chantal in some kind of sling around her neck which left her hands free. Ellis started to follow her. "Not you," said Jean-Pierre. Ellis stopped.

Jane stood in front of Jean-Pierre and looked up at him. He raised his right hand and smacked the side of her face with all his might. It was the most satisfying blow he had ever struck. She reeled backward, staggering, so that he thought she would fall; but she kept her balance and stood staring at him defiantly, with tears of pain running down her face. Over her shoulder Jean-Pierre saw Ellis take a sudden step forward, then restrain himself. Jean-Pierre was mildly disappointed: if Ellis had tried to do something, the soldiers would have jumped him and beaten him up. Never mind: he would get his beating soon enough.

Jean-Pierre raised his hand to slap Jane again. She flinched, and covered Chantal protectively with her arms. Jean-Pierre changed his mind. "There will be plenty of time for that later," he said as he lowered his hand. "Plenty of time."

Jean-Pierre turned away and walked back toward the helicopter. Jane looked down at Chantal. The baby looked back at her, awake but not hungry. Jane hugged her, as if it were the baby who needed comforting. In a way she was glad Jean-Pierre had struck her, although her face was still hot with pain and humiliation. The blow was like the decree absolute in a divorce: it meant that her marriage was finally, officially, definitively over, and she had no further responsibility. If he had wept, or asked her forgiveness, or begged her not to hate him for what he had done, she would have felt guilty. But the blow finished all that. She had no feelings left for him: not an ounce of love or respect or even compassion. It was ironic, she thought, that she should feel completely free of him at the moment when he had finally captured her.

Up to this point a captain had been in charge, the one who had been riding the horse, but now it was Anatoly, Jean-Pierre's Oriental-looking contact, who took control. As he gave orders, Jane realized that she knew what he was saying. It was more than a year since she had heard Russian spoken, and at first it sounded like gibberish, but now that her ear was in tune she could understand every word. At the moment he was telling a trooper to bind Ellis's hands. The soldier, apparently prepared for this, produced a pair of handcuffs. Ellis held his hands out in front of him cooperatively, and the soldier manacled him.

Ellis looked cowed and dejected. Seeing him in chains, defeated, Jane felt a surge of pity and despair, and tears came to her eyes.

The soldier asked if he should handcuff Jane.

"No," said Anatoly. "She has the baby."

They were shepherded to the helicopter. Ellis said: "I'm sorry. About Jean-Pierre. I couldn't get to him. . . ."

She shook her head, to indicate there was no need for apology, but she could not manage to speak. Ellis's utter submissiveness made her angry, not with him but with everyone else for making him like this: Jean-Pierre and Anatoly and Halam and the Russians. She almost wished she had detonated the explosion.

Ellis jumped up into the helicopter, then reached down to help her. She held Chantal with her left arm, to keep the sling steady, and gave him her right hand. He pulled her up. At the moment she was closest to him, he murmured: "As soon as we take off, slap Jean-Pierre."

Jane was too shocked to react, which was probably fortunate. Nobody else seemed to have heard Ellis, but none of them spoke much English anyway. She concentrated on trying to look normal.

The passenger cabin was small and bare, with a ceiling so low that the men had to stoop. There was nothing in it but a small shelf for seating, fixed to the fuselage opposite the door. Jane sat down gratefully. She could see into the cockpit. The pilot's seat was raised two or three feet off the floor with a step beside it for access. The pilot was still there—the crew had not disembarked—and the rotors were still turning. The noise was very loud.

Ellis squatted on the floor beside Jane, between the bench and the pilot's seat.

Anatoly boarded with a trooper beside him. He spoke to the trooper and pointed at Ellis. Jane could not hear what was being said, but it was plain from the trooper's reaction that he had been told to guard Ellis: he unslung his rifle and held it loosely in his hands.

Jean-Pierre boarded last. He stood by the open door, looking out, as the helicopter lifted. Jane felt panicky. It was all very well for Ellis to tell her to slap Jean-Pierre as they were taking off, but how was it to be done? Right now Jean-Pierre was facing away from her and standing by the open door—if she tried to hit him she would probably lose her balance and fall out. She looked at Ellis, hoping for guidance. There was a set, tense expression on his face, but he did not meet her eye.

The helicopter rose eight or ten feet into the air, paused a moment, then did a sort of swoop, gaining speed, and began to climb again.

Jean-Pierre turned away from the door, stepped across the cabin, and saw there was nowhere for him to sit. He hesitated. Jane knew she should stand up and slap him—although she had no idea why—but she was frozen to her seat, paralyzed by panic. Then Jean-Pierre jerked his thumb at her, indicating that she should get up.

That was when she snapped.

She was tired and miserable and aching and hungry and wretched, and he wanted her to stand up, carrying the weight of their baby, so that he could sit. That contemptuous jerk of the thumb seemed to sum up all his cruelty and malice and treachery, and it enraged her. She stood up, with Chantal swinging from her neck, and thrust her face into his, screaming: "You bastard! You bastard!" Her words were lost in the roar of the engines and the rushing wind, but her facial expression apparently shocked him, for he took a startled step back. "I hate you!" Jane shrieked; then she rushed at him with her hands outstretched and violently pushed him backward out through the open door.

The Russians had made one mistake. It was a very small one, but it was all Ellis had, and he was ready to make the most of it. Their mistake had been to fasten his hands in front instead of behind his back.

He had been hoping they would not bind him at all—that was why he had done nothing, by a superhuman effort, when Jean-Pierre started slapping Jane. There had been a chance they might leave him unrestrained: after all, he was unarmed and outnumbered. But Anatoly was a cautious man, it seemed.

Fortunately Anatoly had not been the one to put the handcuffs on: a trooper had. Soldiers knew that it was easier to deal with a prisoner whose arms were bound in front—he was less likely to fall over, and he could get in and out of trucks and helicopters unaided. So, when Ellis had submissively held out his hands in front, the soldier had not given it a second thought.

Unaided, Ellis could not overpower three men, especially as at least one of the three was armed. His chances in a straight fight were zero. His only hope was to crash the helicopter.

There was an instant of frozen time when Jane stood at the open doorway, the baby swinging from her neck, and stared with a horrified expression as Jean-Pierre fell into space; and in that moment Ellis thought: We're only twelve or fifteen feet up, the bastard will probably survive, more's the pity; then Anatoly sprang up and grabbed her arms from behind, restraining her. Now Anatoly and Jane stood between Ellis and the trooper at the other end of the cabin.

Ellis whirled around, sprang up beside the pilot's raised seat, hooked his manacled arms over the pilot's head, drew the chain of the handcuffs into the flesh of the man's throat, and heaved.

The pilot did not panic.

Keeping his feet on the pedals and his left hand on the collective pitch lever, he reached up with his right hand and clawed at Ellis's wrists.

Ellis had a flash of dread. This was his last chance and he had only a second or two. The trooper in the cabin would at first be afraid to use his rifle for fear of hitting the pilot; and Anatoly, if he too was armed, would share the same fear; but in a moment one of them would realize that they had nothing to lose, since if they did not shoot Ellis the aircraft would crash, so they would take the risk.

Ellis's shoulders were grabbed from behind. A glimpse of dark gray sleeve told him it was Anatoly. Down in the nose of the helicopter, the gunner turned around, saw what was happening and started to get out of his seat.

Ellis jerked savagely on the chain. The pain was too much for the pilot, who threw up both hands and rose from his seat.

As soon as the pilot's hands and feet left the controls, the helicopter began to buck and sway in the wind. Ellis was ready for that, and kept his footing by bracing himself against the pilot's seat; but Anatoly, behind him, lost his balance and released his grip.

Ellis hauled the pilot out of the seat and threw him to the floor, then reached over the controls and pushed the collective stick down.

The helicopter dropped like a stone.

Ellis turned around and braced himself for the impact.

The pilot was on the cabin floor at his feet, clutching his throat. Anatoly had fallen full-length in the middle of the cabin. Jane was crouched in a corner with her arms enclosing Chantal protectively. The trooper, too, had fallen, but he had regained his balance and was now on one knee and raising his Kalashnikov toward Ellis.

As he pulled the trigger, the helicopter's wheels hit the ground.

The impact threw Ellis to his knees, but he was ready for it and he kept his balance. The trooper staggered sideways, his shots going through the fuselage a yard from Ellis's head; then he fell forward, dropping the gun and throwing out his hands to break his fall.

Ellis leaned forward, snatched up the rifle and held it awkwardly in his manacled hands.

It was a moment of pure joy.

He was fighting back. He had run away, he had been captured and humiliated, he had suffered cold and hunger and fear, and he had stood helpless while Jane was slapped around; but now, at last, he had a chance to stand and fight.

He got his finger to the trigger. His hands were bound too close together for him to hold the Kalashnikov in the normal position, but he was able to support the barrel unconventionally by using his left hand to hold the curved magazine, which jutted down just in front of the trigger guard.

The helicopter's engine stalled and the rotors began to slow. Ellis glanced onto the flight deck and saw the gunner jumping out through the pilot's side door. He had to gain control of the situation quickly, before the Russians outside gathered their wits.

He moved so that Anatoly, who was stretched out on the floor, was between him and the door; then he rested the muzzle of the rifle on Anatoly's cheek.

The trooper stared at him, looking frightened. "Get out," Ellis said with a jerk of his head. The trooper understood and jumped out through the door.

The pilot was still lying down, apparently having trouble breathing. Ellis kicked him to get his attention, then told him to get out, too. The man struggled to his feet, still clutching his throat, and went out the same way.

Ellis said to Jane: "Tell this guy to get out of the helicopter and stand real close with his back to me. Quick, quick!"

Jane shouted a stream of Russian at Anatoly. The man got to his feet, shot a glance of pure hatred at Ellis and slowly climbed out of the helicopter.

Ellis rested the muzzle of the rifle on the back of Anatoly's neck and said: "Tell him to have the others freeze."

Jane spoke again and Anatoly shouted an order. Ellis looked around. The pilot, the gunner and the trooper who had been in the helicopter were nearby. Just beyond them was Jean-Pierre, sitting on the ground and clutching his ankle: he must have fallen well, thought Ellis; there's nothing much wrong with him. Farther away were three more soldiers, the captain, the horse and Halam.

Ellis said: "Tell Anatoly to unbutton his coat, slowly take out his pistol, and hand it to you."

Jane translated. Ellis pressed the rifle harder into Anatoly's flesh as he drew the pistol from its holster and reached behind him with it in his hand. Jane took it from him.

Ellis said: "Is it a Makarov? Yes. You'll see a safety catch on the left-hand side. Move it until it covers the red dot. To fire the gun, first pull back the slide above the grip, then pull the trigger. Okay?"

"Okay," she said. She was white and trembling, but her mouth was set in a determined line.

Ellis said: "Tell him to have the soldiers bring their weapons here, one by one, and throw them into the helicopter."

Jane translated and Anatoly gave the order.

"Point that pistol at them as they get close," Ellis added.

One by one, the soldiers came up and disarmed.

"Five young men," said Jane.

"What are you talking about?"

"There was a captain, Halam and five young men. I only see four."

"Tell Anatoly he has to find the other one if he wants to live."

Jane shouted to Anatoly, and Ellis was surprised by the vehemence of her voice. Anatoly sounded scared as he shouted his order. A moment later the fifth soldier came around the tail of the helicopter and surrendered his rifle as the others had.

"Well done," Ellis said to Jane. "He might have ruined everything. Now make them all lie down."

A minute later they were all lying facedown on the ground.

"You have to shoot off my handcuffs," he said to Jane.

He put down his rifle and stood with his arms outstretched toward the doorway. Jane pulled back the slide of the pistol, then placed its muzzle against the chain. They positioned themselves so that the spent bullet would go through the doorway.

"I hope this doesn't break my fucking wrist," said Ellis.

Jane closed her eyes and pulled the trigger.

Ellis roared: "Ow, fuck!" At first his wrists hurt like hell. Then, after a moment, he realized they were not broken—the chain was.

He picked up his rifle. "Now I want their radio," he said.

On Anatoly's order, the captain began to unstrap a large box from the horse's back.

Ellis wondered whether the helicopter would fly again. Its undercarriage would be destroyed, of course, and there might be all sorts of other damage underneath; but the engine and the main control lines were on top. He recalled how, during the battle of Darg, he had seen a Hind just like this one crash twenty or thirty feet, then lift off again. This bastard ought to fly if that one did, he thought. If not . . .

He did not know what he would do otherwise.

The captain brought the radio and put it into the helicopter, then walked away again.

Ellis allowed himself a moment of relief. As long as he had the radio, the Russians could not contact their base. That meant they could not get reinforcements, nor could they alert anybody to what had happened. If Ellis could get the helicopter into the air, he would be safe from pursuit.

"Keep your gun aimed at Anatoly," he said to Jane. "I'm going to see whether this thing will fly."

Jane found the gun surprisingly heavy. Aiming at Anatoly, she kept her arm outstretched, for a while, but soon had to lower her arm to rest it. With her left hand she patted Chantal's back. Chantal had cried, off and on, during the last few minutes, but now she had stopped.

The helicopter's engine turned over, kicked and hesitated. Oh, please start, she prayed, please go.

The engine roared into life, and she saw the blades turn.

Jean-Pierre looked up.

Don't you dare, she thought. Don't move!

Jean-Pierre sat upright, looked at her, then got painfully to his feet.

Jane pointed the pistol at him.

He started to walk toward the helicopter.

"Don't make me shoot you!" she screamed, but her voice was drowned by the increasing roar of the engines.

Anatoly must have seen Jean-Pierre, for he rolled over and sat up. Jane pointed the gun at him. He lifted his hands in a gesture of surrender. Jane swung the gun back toward Jean-Pierre. Jean-Pierre kept coming.

Jane felt the helicopter shudder and try to lift.

Jean-Pierre was close now. She could see his face clearly. His hands were spread wide in a gesture of appeal, but there was a mad light in his eyes. He's lost his mind, she thought; but perhaps that happened a long time ago.

"I will do it!" she yelled, although she knew he could not hear. "I will shoot you!"

The helicopter lifted off the ground.

Jean-Pierre broke into a run.

As the aircraft went up he jumped and landed on the deck. Jane hoped he would fall out again, but he steadied himself. He looked at her with hate in his eyes, and gathered himself to spring.

She closed her eyes and pulled the trigger.

The gun crashed and bucked in her hand.

She opened her eyes again. Jean-Pierre was still standing upright, with an expression of astonishment on his face. There was a spreading dark stain on the breast of his coat. Panicking, Jane pulled the trigger again, and again, and a third time. She missed with the first two, but the third seemed to hit his shoulder. He spun around, facing out, and fell forward through the doorway.

Then he was gone.

I killed him, she thought.

At first she felt a kind of wild elation. He had tried to capture her and imprison her and make her a slave. He had hunted her like an animal. He had betrayed her and beaten her. Now she had killed him.

Then she was overcome by grief. She sat on the deck and sobbed. Chantal began to cry too, and Jane rocked her baby as they wept together.

She did not know how long she stayed there. Eventually she got to her feet and went forward to stand beside the pilot's seat.

"Are you all right?" Ellis shouted.

She nodded and tried a weak smile.

Ellis smiled back, pointed to a gauge and yelled: "Look—full tanks!"

She kissed his cheek. One day she would tell him she had shot Jean-Pierre, but not now. "How far to the border?" she asked.

"Less than an hour. And they can't send anybody after us because we have their radio."

Jane looked through the windscreen. Directly ahead, she could see the white-peaked mountains she would have had to climb. I don't think I could have done it, she said to herself. I think I would have lain down in the snow and died.

Ellis had a wistful expression on his face.

"What are you thinking about?" she asked.

"I was thinking how much I'd like a roast beef sandwich with lettuce and tomato and mayonnaise on whole wheat bread," he said, and Jane smiled.

Chantal stirred and cried. Ellis took a hand off the controls and touched her pink cheek. "She's hungry," he said.

"I'll go back and take care of her," said Jane. She returned to the passenger cabin and sat on the bench. She unbuttoned her coat and her shirt, and fed her baby as the helicopter flew on into the rising sun.

PART III

❧

1983

CHAPTER TWENTY

J ane felt pleased as she walked down the suburban driveway and climbed into the passenger seat of Ellis's car. It had been a successful afternoon. The pizzas had been good, and Petal had loved *Flashdance*. Ellis had been very tense about introducing his daughter to his girlfriend, but Petal had been thrilled by eight-month-old Chantal, and everything had been easy. Ellis had felt so good about it that he had suggested, when they dropped Petal off, that Jane walk up the drive with him and say hello to Gill. Gill had invited them in, and had cooed over Chantal, so Jane had got to know his ex-wife as well as his daughter, and all in one afternoon.

Ellis—Jane could not get used to the fact that his name was John, and she had decided always to call him Ellis—put Chantal on the backseat and got into the car beside Jane. "Well, what do you think?" he asked as they pulled away.

"You didn't tell me she was pretty," Jane said.

"Petal is pretty?"

"I meant Gill," said Jane with a laugh.

"Yes, she's pretty."

"They're fine people and they don't deserve to be mixed up with someone like you."

She was joking, but Ellis nodded somberly.

Jane leaned over and touched his thigh. "I didn't mean it," she said.

"It's true, though."

They drove on in silence for a while. It was six months to the day since they had escaped from Afghanistan. Now and again Jane would burst into tears for no apparent reason, but she no longer had nightmares in which she shot Jean-Pierre again and again. Nobody but she and Ellis knew what had happened—Ellis had even lied to his superiors about how Jean-Pierre died—and Jane had decided she would tell Chantal that her daddy died in Afghanistan in the war: no more than that.

Instead of heading back to the city, Ellis took a series of backstreets and eventually parked next to a vacant lot overlooking the water.

"What are we going to do here?" said Jane. "Neck?"

"If you like. But I want to talk."

"Okay."

"It was a good day."

"Yes."

"Petal was more relaxed with me today than she has ever been."

"I wonder why."

"I have a theory," said Ellis. "It's because of you and Chantal. Now that I'm part of a family, I'm no longer a threat to her home and her stability. I think that's it, anyway."

"It makes sense to me. Is that what you wanted to talk about?"

"No." He hesitated. "I'm leaving the Agency."

Jane nodded. "I'm very glad," she said fervently. She had been waiting for something like this. He was settling his accounts and closing the books.

"The Afghan assignment is over, basically," he went on. "Masud's training program is under way and they've taken delivery of their first shipment. Masud is so strong now that he has negotiated a winter truce with the Russians."

"Good!" said Jane. "I'm in favor of anything that leads to a cease-fire."

"While I was in Washington, and you were in London, I was offered another job. It's something I really want to do, plus it pays well."

"What is it?" said Jane, intrigued.

"Working with a new presidential task force on organized crime."

Fear stabbed Jane's heart. "Is it dangerous?"

"Not for me. I'm too old for undercover work now. It'll be my job to direct the undercover men."

Jane could tell he was not being completely honest with her. "Tell me the truth, you bastard," she said.

"Well, it's a lot less dangerous than what I've been doing. But it's not as safe as teaching kindergarten."

She smiled at him. She knew what this was leading to now, and it made her happy.

He said: "Also, I'll be based here in New York."

That took her by surprise. "Really?"

"Why are you so astonished?"

"Because I've applied for a job with the United Nations. Here in New York."

"You didn't tell me you were going to do that!" he said, sounding hurt.

"You didn't tell me about *your* plans," she said indignantly.

"I'm telling you now."

"And I'm telling *you* now."

"But . . . would you have left me?"

"Why should we live where you work? Why shouldn't we live where I work?"

"In the month we've been apart I completely forgot how goddamn touchy you are," he said.

"Right."

There was a silence.

Eventually Ellis said: "Well, anyway, as we're both going to be living in New York . . ."

"We could share housekeeping?"

"Yes," he said hesitantly.

Suddenly she regretted flying off the handle. He wasn't really inconsiderate, just dumb. She had almost lost him, back there in Afghanistan, and now she could never be mad at him for very long because she would always remember how frightened she had been that they would be parted forever, and how inexpressibly glad she had been that they had stayed together and survived. "Okay," she said in a softer voice. "Let's share the housekeeping."

"Actually . . . I was thinking of making it official. If you want."

This was what she had been waiting for. "Official," she said, as if she did not understand.

"Yes," he said awkwardly. "I mean we could get married. If you want."

She laughed with pleasure. "Do it right, Ellis!" she said. "Propose!"

He took her hand. "Jane, my dear, I love you. Will you marry me?"

"Yes! Yes!" she said. "As soon as possible! Tomorrow! Today!"

"Thank you," he said.

She leaned over and kissed him. "I love you, too."

They sat in silence then, holding hands and watching the sun go down. It was funny, Jane thought, but Afghanistan seemed unreal now, like a bad dream, vivid but no longer frightening. She remembered the people well enough—Abdullah the mullah and Rabia the midwife, handsome Mohammed and sensual Zahara and loyal Fara—but the bombs and the helicopters, the fear and the hardship, were fading from her memory. This was the real adventure, she felt: getting married and bringing up Chantal and making the world a better place for her to live in.

"Shall we go?" said Ellis.

"Yes." She gave his hand a final squeeze, then let it go. "We've got a lot to do."

He started the car and they drove back into the city.

BIBLIOGRAPHY

The following are books about Afghanistan by writers who have visited the country since the Soviet invasion of 1979:

Chaliand, Gérard: *Report from Afghanistan* (New York: Penguin, 1982).

Fullerton, John: *The Soviet Occupation of Afghanistan* (London: Methuen, 1984).

Gall, Sandy: *Behind Russian Lines* (London: Sidgwick & Jackson, 1983).

Martin, Mike: *Afghanistan: Inside a Rebel Stronghold* (Poole, England: Blandford Press, 1984).

Ryan, Nigel: *A Hitch or Two in Afghanistan* (London: Weidenfeld & Nicolson, 1983).

Van Dyk, Jere: *In Afghanistan* (New York: Coward-McCann, 1983).

The standard reference book on Afghanistan is:

Dupree, Louis: *Afghanistan* (Princeton: Princeton University Press, 1980).

On women and children I recommend the following:

Bailleau Lajoinie, Simone: *Conditions de Femmes en Afghanistan* (Paris: Éditions Sociales, 1980).

Hunte, Pamela Anne: *The Sociocultural Context of Perinatality in Afghanistan* (Ann Arbor: University Microfilms International, 1984).

Van Oudenhoven, Nico J. A.: *Common Afghan Street Games* (Lisse: Swets & Zeitlinger, 1979).

The classic travel book on the Panisher Valley and Nuristan is:

Newby, Eric: *A Short Walk in the Hindu Kush* (London: Secker & Warburg, 1958).

ALSO AVAILABLE

  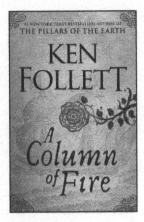

THE MODIGLIANI SCANDAL

PAPER MONEY

EYE OF THE NEEDLE

TRIPLE

THE KEY TO REBECCA

THE MAN FROM ST. PETERSBURG

ON WINGS OF EAGLES

LIE DOWN WITH LIONS

NIGHT OVER WATER

A DANGEROUS FORTUNE

A PLACE CALLED FREEDOM

THE THIRD TWIN

THE HAMMER OF EDEN

CODE TO ZERO

JACKDAWS

HORNET FLIGHT

WHITEOUT

FALL OF GIANTS

WINTER OF THE WORLD

EDGE OF ETERNITY

VIKING

PENGUIN BOOKS